4/76

Dave,

In the hope th~~at~~ you are a consenting adult you will always be a peace-filled person. Thank you for being who you are.

Love,
Tom

Dave ———

The purpose of life is to realize its fullest possible potential. For each person this differs. Few of us come even close for fear of failure, or success, or lack of nerve. Be not one of those, for you have much to offer and there are many who want and merit it. Opportunity presents itself to be seized. Do not falter.

Love,
Fred

Consenting Adult

Novels by Laura Z. Hobson

THE TENTH MONTH
FIRST PAPERS
THE CELEBRITY
THE OTHER FATHER
GENTLEMAN'S AGREEMENT
THE TRESPASSERS

Books for Children

"I'M GOING TO HAVE A BABY"
A DOG OF HIS OWN

Consenting Adult

Laura Z. Hobson

DOUBLEDAY & COMPANY, INC.
GARDEN CITY, NEW YORK
1975

Library of Congress Cataloging in Publication Data

Hobson, Laura Keane Zametkin.
    Consenting adult.

    I. Title.
PZ3.H6544Co   [PS3515.01515]   813'.5'2
ISBN 0-385-03498-9
Library of Congress Catalog Card Number 74-18808

Contents

Part One
1960-1961

CHAPTER ONE

Dear Mama,

I'm sorry about all the rows during vacation, and I have
something to tell you that I guess I better not put off any
longer. You said that if I needed real psychoanalytic help,
not just the visits with Mrs. Culkin, I could have it. Well
now, I think I'm going to ask if you can manage it for me.

You see, I am a homosexual. I have fought it off for
months and maybe years, but it just grows truer. I have never
yet had an actual affair with anybody, I give you my word
on that, not even Pete, whom I suppose you'll think of right
away because we room together and go places together. It's
just that I know it, more and more clearly all the time, and
I finally thought I really ought to ask for help.

I know how much pain this will cause you, and shock too.
But I can't keep it a secret from you any longer if I could get
any help, and maybe if you could arrange some sort of visits
on a regular basis with the right psychoanalyst, the whole
thing would change around. Again, I'm terribly sorry to give
you this shock and pain, but that's the way it is, and I finally
got to the point, after all the rows over the summer, where
I felt I really ought to ask you to help me.

Love,
Jeff

P.S. Show this to Dad if you want to, or not if you think it
might be too much until he's really better again. J.

She came to the end and stood as if tranced, without tears, nothing so easy as tears, stood motionless in the sensation of being smashed through every organ, through every nerve, every reasoning cell. Love for him, pity for his suffering, pride for his courage in telling her, horror at *it*, at the monstrous unendurable *it*—a savagery of feelings crushed her, feelings mutually exclusive yet gripping each other in some hot ferocity or amalgam. She read the letter again. Then only did she begin to cry, but not the ordinary crying, nor she the ordinary weeping woman; it was, rather, a roaring sobbing, of an animal gored. She heard her own sounds, and went to her bedroom door to close it, though there was no one in the apartment.

For the first time she thought of her husband, Ken, seemingly well after last year's stroke, well enough at last to be back at work, but still warned to avoid undue stress, to avoid "overdoing it." Was he now to hear this? Even Jeff in his own crisis had seen the danger of telling his father now.

Or was Jeff taking this way to ask her not to tell him, as if he were afraid of him, Jeff who seemed afraid of nothing? It was impossible to think of Jeff in fear of anything, he a boy of seventeen, tall, strong, beautiful as all young people are beautiful and beautiful to her in his own personal way because he was her youngest child, because, of the three, he was the only one still at home, still at school, still with all the world ahead of him.

Flashing across her mind came a vision of him with some faceless youth, the two close, the two entwined in some intimacy, and she cried aloud, cried out against it, cried in a devastation she had never known before.

She read the letter once more and pride for his courage overcame her. Had he sat there faltering for words? Had he thought twenty times that he ought to tell them, and fled twenty times from the idea? Her body ached as if she were watching him endure physical torment, and again admiration for his young courage filled her.

She reached for the telephone and then paused. Who knew how private were outside calls to students at Placquette School? Not purposeful snooping by anybody in authority, not at a good progressive school like Placquette, but if there was some student earning extra money at the switchboard, listening in whenever he grew bored? She left the phone, went to the living room and began to write. "Dear Jeff, Your letter just came—" She stared at the bland words. Even if they were different words, instantly conveying what he had to know, he would not receive her letter until tomorrow, more likely not until the day after tomorrow. Suppose he were off there wondering what her reaction would be, fearing it, afraid to count on it, afraid that she would turn away in revulsion?

Across the empty space on the second page of his letter, she wrote a telegram, printing each word as if she herself were spinning out the Western Union tape of capital letters:

PROUD OF YOU FOR LETTER WILL ARRANGE SOONEST POSSIBLE WITH BEST SPECIALIST STOP PHONE COLLECT WHEN YOU CAN STOP LOVE YOU AS ALWAYS MAMA.

She reread her phrases slowly, testing each one for possible revelation to some hostile eye, and then, reassured of the innocence upon the face of each careful word, telephoned it in, specifying that the address be followed by the command DO NOT PHONE, and then asking the operator to read all of it back to her. She sat back at last, exhausted.

"You see, I am a homosexual." She could not contain the violence of rejection within her, not of him, not of her son, but of this that he had told her. Apart from his hot temper, he had always been the most lovable and loving of the children, funny as a little boy, irresistible as a little boy, clever in his wisecracks, good at school, the kind of child whose entire future seemed destined to be great, unlimited, happy.

Now in this one moment of opening and reading a letter—the vision leaped back, of Jeff physically close to another boy, and though she sat, spent and motionless, it was as if she were running in some gasping unbearable need to escape. Not Jeff, she thought, never Jeff.

She looked around the room, as if seeking help, an adviser. It was oddly blank, guarded, though it was a room she had enjoyed for years. She returned to her bedroom; there was something private and comforting here. Near her bed, on a chair pulled close to it like an extra end table, were three cardboard boxes, the top one opened to reveal typed manuscript, the first hundred pages removed from the box and turned face down on the chair seat. These she had read the night before in what she called "flash editing," the first overall impression before detailed labor might begin on the novel. Her hand went out to the box and stopped. She could not.

The office. She could not go in today, not possibly. She could not talk to Gail even, the secretary she shared with Tom Smiley, could not talk to anybody in a bright offhand office way. She had not gone back to work until Jeff was seven and Don and Margie independent teen-agers, and in the ten years since then, she had scarcely any absences except during the first days when Ken was in the hospital. She loved her job, loved publishing in general, and in particular loved being the only one of the three women editors at Quales and Park not assigned to mystery stories, children's books or "help" books, cookbooks, gardening books, decorating books. She liked novels that tried to be serious novels, though it was all too rare to work on a manuscript that announced itself almost from page one as a good book, a book she would eagerly read even if another house published it, a book she felt fortunate to work on, doing that amorphous thing called "editing," which was, she supposed, designed to help the author make his or her book even better.

She reached toward the boxes again but once more her hand halted. Not now, not in this brilliance of pain and shock. She called the office and said, "Something's come up, Gail, I can't make it in at all today, I'll work at home. Do I have a lunch date?"

Her voice was calm, steady; she was surprised to hear it so. "Helena Ludwig? I forgot—please say something's come up and set it up for any free day next week, would you? . . . No, not sick, just I can't make the office until I attend to something that's important about a letter—oh, skip it. And thanks."

She actually laughed at the involuted explanation, but the laughing and the calm steadiness were gone when she called her doctor, insisting to his appointment nurse that it was "an emergency of a sort," insisting, "No, I can't give you some idea, I'm sorry. I really do have to talk to Dr. Waldo myself."

A moment later she said, "Mark, it's Tessa Lynn. Please fit me in today. The most horrible thing has happened, and I have to know whether I can tell Ken or whether it would be too dangerous still. . . . Three-fifteen. Oh, thanks."

Five hours, nearly. Should she call Will, her only brother, always so ready to help in a bad time? Not about this, not yet. Perhaps her daughter or her older son? Not yet, not even them. Jeff hadn't even thought of Margie or Don as he wrote his letter, and it would have to be his decision, whether they were to be told, and when. He was on good enough terms with them, but he was six years younger than his sister and eight younger than his brother, and apart from the age differential between them, there was that wider chasm, that Don and Margie were married and out of the immediate family, Don with two children and Margie expecting her first baby before Christmas. To Jeff they were that other world, grown-ups, as his parents were that other world too.

They were both so normal always, she suddenly thought, and both so normal now, so happily married, and they had been brought up in the same way as Jeff, the same father, same mother, same influences and environment. Then how was it possible that Jeff was not equally normal? He must be, he would prove to be, this was an aberration of some sort that he was going through, terrifying to him, terrifying to her, but no more enduring than a nightmare.

You see, I am a homosexual.

Oh, why had he put it that way, why that simple declarative sentence? If he had written, "I think I am" or "I may be" or "I'm afraid I am"—how much easier it would be. Again she put her hand to the telephone. Whatever Mark Waldo said this afternoon, she still would have to tell Ken. You could not keep an enormity like this from your husband; it would be a kind of betrayal, a denying him his right to know about his son. After all, it was a year since his stroke and it had been a mild stroke, with a nearly full recovery. There was no longer that faint drag when he moved his left arm or left leg, there was scarcely any hesitation in his speech, except when he was agitated. Yet he grew depressed so easily and so deeply; how could she think of telling him?

She understood the depression; he was ten years older than she, in his mid-fifties, and even the mild stroke had told him clearly enough that life was drawing down, had told him of death off there, not so far now as it had always been, not so unbelievable now as it had always been, possible for others of course, but never intertwined with one's own existence. Poor Ken, with that semaphore forever raised.

Yet Mark Waldo, who had taken care of them all for over twenty years, had made it specific only a short time ago when Kenneth had returned to a full-time schedule. He was no longer to be treated as an invalid, not to be spared the normal stress and worry of living, he was to be treated like a whole person and not like the remainder of a whole person. To treat him in any other way would be demoralizing.

Demoralizing. Moralizing. Words could suddenly take on teeth and claws. Was she not moralizing now? This horror over Jeff and his letter, what was that? This fear of telling Ken, what was that? Was this not all part of moralizing, and hateful because it was? She had always been sure she was free of prudery, of the vicarious prurience that saw sin and wickedness in anything beyond the primer ABC's of sexual conduct. Particularly when it came to the changing mores of the young, she was not given to moral judgment and disapproval, not even now with the enlarging dreads in this permissive year of 1960. The widening use of marijuana, the widening promiscuity, the reckless speed in cars and on motorcycles, all these new dreads of parenthood she had faced with equanimity. Was it only an assumed equanimity? She had never asked herself that before.

But never once had she contemplated this. Jeff was so normal, so healthy, so stable except for the flaring temper which he alone of all the children seemed to have. He got it from me, she thought instantly, I have to be fair about that. She could hear her own voice as it could be, raw with irritation, and she hated it. Her temper did not get loose often, but when it did it was fiery and shameful.

Jeff had a temper too; last summer their quarrels had at times been unendurable. Had that bursting anger in him anything to do with *this*? If not, what else had she, all unknowing, done to him? What else had she and Ken together done? It must have been something they did; it couldn't simply have "happened" like a spontaneous evil growth.

The sweep of guilt brought new anguish and she turned from it. She had to find out more about homosexuality; she knew nothing definitive about it. She would go seek out whatever experts there were in the field, not only to be in a better position to help Jeff, but also to help herself. This leap of guilt was so fierce an assault—maybe expert opinion denied that fault lay with the parents. With the mother, that was what she really meant. Hadn't she always known that an aggressive mother was the cause for a homosexual son? But she was the same mother she had been to Donald and Margie.

Jeff wasn't the same child as the others—apart from his quick temper, that too was true. He showed no interest whatever in so many things that absorbed Don and Margie; he remained so aloof in family arguments about next month's election, and he put on an air of disbelief that Margie should be working ten hours a day at Kennedy headquarters, pregnant though she was, and that Don grew livid over television commercials for Nixon. Even in college, Don and Margie both had belonged to groups to ban the bomb, to end Jim Crow, and for all the critics of the Silent Generation, she had always had a private satisfaction that in her family, at least, there was no such nastiness as young people who didn't care enough to speak up.

But here was Jeff, silent indeed on any sort of political matter. He belonged to no group, he believed in no cause. He was a star in another galaxy, in two other galaxies. One was sports and one his studies.

She saw him suddenly as they had seen him two Saturdays before when they had driven up for the season's first game, saw the artificial bulk of his shoulders in the football uniform, the long legs racing, and with the memory, hope raced along her nerves that he soon would prove to be as normal and carefree as he looked. He had the lanky build of his father's family, of all the Lynns, the fair hair, the blue eyes, the narrow head. "The Ectomorph Lynns," she had once called them, long ago, when she was still faintly conscious of the difference in their background and their religion. Margie and Don were not so unambiguously Lynns; they did not resemble their Sachs cousins closely, but they both had admixtures of her own family's looks, while Jeff was entirely a Lynn.

She glanced at a picture of him on her dressing table, in his tennis shorts, taken during a match last summer at the shore. There it was again, the special look in his eyes, the total concentration on the ball, on the game itself, oblivious of the people watching, oblivious of himself, all of him intact in the love of the game, the effort, the physical using of his muscles, his skill.

And it was the same with the rest of his daily life, the same zest and intensity about his studies, the same skill and effortlessness, so that he was that seldom-met creature, the athlete-student, like a Greek boy centuries ago.

A Greek boy. A treacherous simile.

Stop this rationalizing, she commanded herself. It is specious and cowardly. He wrote you the truth and you are trying to pretend it is some error, some baseless fear. Perhaps he does have some adolescent attachment to one of his teachers or to one of his teammates, is that so shameful? It happened all the time at boys' boarding schools, English public schools were full of it, and in the end it meant nothing more than experimentation, part of growing up. One of the revelations in the Kinsey report on male sexuality had dealt exactly with this, the frequency of homosexual experience among men, especially among young men. A passing phenomenon, a surface importance, that's what the report had indicated, didn't it? She had never read the book itself, merely reviews and digests of it; now she might get hold of it.

But Jeff was so intense about every aspect of his life. When he was happy it was an intensity of happiness; when he was angry, there was a vitality of anger she had never found before, even with him. Last summer's quarrels had been more savage than any they had ever had, leaving her astonished, enraged, and finally fed up to the point where she was shouting as he was shouting, or perhaps where he was shouting as she was shouting. Now a physical agitation seized her when a row started, perhaps because his angry voice now was a man's angry voice, not a child's but a man's, rough in anger, a voice that could actually yell street words at her—"Don't give me any of that shit."

It was not the phrase she shuddered at but the wildness behind it. With Margie and Don there had also been rows and scenes, but those scenes had always remained within the limits of family squabbles, free of the extremes so often present in upheavals with Jeff. It was as if he were born of different blood, but she had given birth to him, and she had never been the unfaithful wife who might have conceived a child by anybody but Ken. If she had, she might have thought of genes and DNA and have decided, "It's a streak Jeff inherited" from so-and-so, perhaps accepting his differences of temperament with a detachment and secret insight, and be free now of this astonishment, this inability to believe what he was telling her.

Poor Jeff, she suddenly thought, what he has been going through. How early, at seventeen, to be so burdened, to know this horror and guilt. When he wrote of giving her pain and shock, he was thinking too of his own pain and shock. How bitter to know that your child is in agony.

She glanced at the clock. Less than twenty minutes had passed. She again looked about the room as if in search. Again she saw the three boxes of manuscript and once more she thought, It wouldn't be fair now. I couldn't do that, with two or three or four years of work lying there in each of those boxes. Not that she had the final say as to any of them. The firm's staff of readers had already made their first reports and now it was her turn, another step in the sequence and not much more. Yet if she were strongly opposed to any one of the three, and cogent enough about explaining why she thought Q. and P. should not publish it, the chances were pretty good that it would be returned to its author. Thus had her own status gradually become more clearly stated.

It was gratifying. More than that, if one of the manuscripts were to catch at her strongly enough, it was possible that she might be appointed its official editor. That's how it had happened with Helena Ludwig and her other authors, and that was even more gratifying.

"Her" authors. How easy it was to fall into the trap of possession. My author, Helena Ludwig; my author, Virginia Grabig; my author, Mary Jasper—she had said each of these, could hear herself saying each of these, and all at once she felt preposterous. It was the way she felt with some of her friends when they said "my child" about a son or daughter long married and already head of his or her own household, their choice of words revealing an unwillingness to let go, to move back, to yield that "myness" of parenthood to the "ourness" of a mature relationship within a family.

She never thought "my child" about Don or about Margie. Even with Jeff she was more apt by now to think "my son" than "my child." That too was perhaps because he was a head taller than she, departed from childhood in all the visible ways. No, that was too obvious. From the time Don was a baby, she had had her own private struggle to delimit what she thought of as "parentship" and regarded as a principal task of being a parent: to be loving, to be committed but not to try to possess a child, to be happy when things went well but not to feel herself a failure when they did not, as if the child's success were her success and the child's failure her failure. She did not take Don's happy marriage as something she could "take credit for," as some of her friends seemed to do with their married children, nor did she preen herself on Margie's happy marriage. It was Don's doing, and Margie's, not hers and not Kenneth's.

Happy, happily married. Who ever knew the reality behind the words? She and Ken were happily married too.

Well, we are, she thought. We still have so much in common. Even with all our problems about making love—she broke the thought sharply. Their own problems were nothing to think of now, were not what she meant by happy or not happy. Yes, one was happier when sex was uninhibited and full the way it was when you were young, but that did change with time, changed for all people, not just for herself and Ken. They still had so much else to share, so much they could talk about, so much that demanded their energy and interest. In his room there were also boxes of manuscripts waiting for his decision, waiting far more directly, for he was not simply one of a dozen editors, but one of the heads of his firm. Years before she had ever known when she would return to the world of publishing, she had enjoyed being married to a publisher, had in her young days known a stab of snob pride in saying, "Oh, Ken's with Brannick and Lynn," knowing well that the next question would be "Lynn? You mean Ken's a partner?" and that her answer would be a too modest nod.

How innocent she had been then, how little she had guessed that the time would come when she would be half ashamed of Brannick and Lynn for their best-sellerism, which she half envied, half despised. And how little she would have guessed that Ken's boxes of manuscripts, so often holding "made to order" books, would be one of the things they would in time agree not to talk about, for though Ken's temper never flared as hers did, he could go silent instead, be unreachable when he was upset, dipped into a kind of icy plastic she found more forbidding than a bout of hot temper, quickly over.

This about Jeff—how would he take it? He could be so wise and good, but he also could turn into that distant silent man that no troubled youngster could be expected to cope with or understand. When she and Ken had just met, she had been enchanted by the way he would let her talk, listening to her, a college girl, as though her words spoke for him as well as for her. Coming from her voluble family, she had found his reserve, even his silences, one of his most appealing attributes. Other people called him uncommunicative, but it was true that when he did say something, it would be the one thing everybody would later remember.

But now she prayed that he would not be reserved when she told him about Jeff, that instead he would speak out, let go, say everything that came into his heart to say, rather than hold it in, cling inwardly to it as to some dark companion he would share with nobody. Stealthily, a wish stole through her mind that this afternoon the doctor would unequivocally forbid her to say one word to Ken, would forbid her to show him Jeff's letter, would command her with a doctor's final authority. "No matter what I've said in the past," she could imagine him saying, "I never meant anything like this. It is too risky for Ken now to sustain this degree of shock, it is far too soon."

I'm afraid of Ken, she thought, as the fantasy voice ended. If he's remote and inaccessible about it, I couldn't bear it, as well as bearing *it*. "It." Already she ran away by thinking "it," underlining it in her own thoughts. She sank into a chair and began Jeff's letter for the third time. Before she had read more than the first lines, his words blurred and ran together as if a stream washed over them.

* * *

Mark Waldo greeted her with a solemnity that showed he trusted her use of the word "emergency." She was not one to cry crisis over ordinary illness, and now he looked at her with the ready attention that had endeared him to her for all the years she had been his patient.

"Mark, it's about Ken, as I said, but it's also about finding a real analyst for Jeff right away—" She suddenly covered her face with her left hand so that he could not see it go ugly with crying, and offered him Jeff's letter. He read it and remained silent after returning it.

"This must be very hard for you, Tessa," he said at last.

"Did you have any idea?"

"None."

"Nobody would believe it. Looking at him, watching him—"

"Nobody."

"I thought you could always tell, that something always gave it away."

"That's the prevailing idea, but it's untrue. It's not my field, of course, but that much I know."

"You've watched him grow up, and you're as shocked as I am."

He said nothing. He had not been the family pediatrician, but he had seen all three children countless times during the years, and as each had reached the age where they were beyond pediatrics, each had become his patient. Jeff had become a Waldo patient just last year.

"Perhaps Jeff is wrong," he said at last. "Perhaps it is something he misunderstands and fears and magnifies to fact."

"That's what I've been thinking all day. But I'm afraid to sit back and do nothing."

"Of course. Let me find out about the good people up there. Placquette is near New Haven, isn't it?"

"Ten miles this side. Does it—do psychiatrists and analysts think it's curable?"

"Some do, others don't."

"Do *you* think it is?"

"I don't know enough to risk an opinion. I've heard that treatment at the earliest phase is thought to have more of a chance than treatment later, after some years of actual sexual experience."

"Don't," she whispered. "I can't bear the idea yet. If I so much as think of any actual—"

"I know, Tessa." He drew his prescription pad toward him and said, "I want you to take one of these tonight and then another a couple of hours later if you need to. Now about Ken."

"That's mostly why I had to come today. He'll be home in two hours. You did say not to protect him, but *this?*"

He remained silent, writing his prescription. Then slowly he said, "You wanted me to order you not to tell Ken, didn't you?"

"I don't know. Yes, maybe, but I'm not sure of anything. I think one thing, then it changes and I think the opposite. That will level out, I suppose."

"*You* will level out. But about Ken, I can't make up your mind for you on this."

"But can he stand it? You're his doctor, you're the only one who can calculate that."

"He can stand it if he wants to stand it."

"Oh, Mark, you're telling me, a layman, to decide for myself."

"It's not simply a medical question. If you start out now by concealing this from Ken, because you are afraid to shock him, when will it seem right to tell him? Next week? Next month?"

"I thought perhaps after Jeff had started with the analyst, after we had more idea, after we knew if there might be any hope."

"Yes, if that could all happen in a day or two. But suppose it took time, perhaps months—"

"You mean it would only be worse for Ken, knowing then that he'd been kept in the dark."

"Think about it for a day or so, Tessa."

"I didn't mean waiting for months."

"But a week of silence? A few weeks of silence? It gets harder every day to find the right time."

"All right, I'll have to think about it. Thanks, anyway." She left his office quickly, but no sooner was she alone again than she felt a turbulent resentment rising within her. He had left the decision to her. It was a medical decision and he was the medical expert, but he was saddling her, the layman, with the responsibility of making it. "I can't make up your mind for you on this." "Think about it for a day or so, Tessa."

Medical ethics, she thought, like that damn nonsense of letting you be the one to decide whether to call in another doctor for a consultation. How am I supposed to know whether Ken's nervous system can stand this amount of stress this soon, I who haven't had years of medical training? Why couldn't Mark take over on this and say do tell him or don't tell him?

She strode along the street thinking, All right, I'll tell him the minute he gets home, and then we'll all find out whether it's too soon or not too soon. It isn't as if this were the same sort of strain as some problem at the office or something wrong with a contract. She tried to imagine Ken reading Jeff's letter, but memory assailed her, of his pale face above the hospital blanket, his lower lip pulled slightly askew at one corner. Without apparent logic, her resentment at Mark Waldo went quiet and then died away.

* * *

"You look all in," Ken greeted her. "Is anything wrong?"

"Wrong how?"

"You look depressed."

"I'm upset over something. I'd rather not bother you with it right off though."

"Something at the office?"

"Oh no."

"Another row with Jeff?"

"Not a row, just something." He nodded and she saw that he was relieved that she did not want him in on whatever it was. He had aged a good deal in the past year, aged in subtler ways than the new lines in face and forehead, and the further receding and whitening of his hair. Unlike the disappearance of the muscular drag of arm and leg, there was still, somehow, a persisting drag to his mood, a dejection which he could not banish, as if he were always aware that he had been defeated in an irreversible score, with no miracle to be hoped for in the last minutes of play. He was a tall man, thin, handsome still, though his own sadness seemed a skillful robber of the bright good looks he had always been comfortably aware of. Not that he was a conceited man, merely one who knew that others found him attractive. She sometimes looked at pictures of him taken twenty years ago or longer, and marveled that the passage of time could show so sharp a change to the camera when to her own eye it was, in the process of happening, all but imperceptible.

Since his stroke she had sometimes wondered often whether it was not the same with all the sophisticated equipment in Dr. Waldo's office—had not the routine annual electrocardiograms, year after year after year, been as unaware of any deterioration in him, in capillary or vein or artery? That had shaken her, that one fact, that Ken had been pronounced well and fit just a few weeks before the C.V.A. Cardio-Vascular Accident—what a name for that first break in the lovely red thread of life.

Everything came so suddenly.

As she went to the front door for the mail this morning she had been wondering whether to ask the Wisters to dinner the next weekend Jeff would be home, asking them to bring Suzy too, and perhaps treat Jeff and Suzy to seats at some hit show. The theater was becoming so expensive—fifteen dollars for a pair of good seats—that young people couldn't go on their own any longer, the way they did when she was young; balcony seats for a dollar or so were unheard of now, even to shows about to close for lack of paying audiences. Even the producers of shows about to close still treated the going price scale as sacred and kept their prices intact in their empty theaters, except for the occasional issuing of "twofers," which you never heard about in time. How futile, how foolish, their unwillingness to accept reality and offer dollar tickets to students and to people too poor to pay the big inflated prices.

I'm running again, she thought. You'd think my greatest concern was the state of the theater and the fate of producers and playwrights and flop shows. Jeff didn't run, why should I? If ever there was a direct facing up to something, that letter of his was it. No disguise, no fake optimism, no side excursions into other problems, just a flat-out statement, just will-you-help?

A wave of heat seemed to assault her skin. She was ashamed. Ashamed of the evasions, the wrigglings, the pendulum swings of horror and hope. Perhaps she needed to see a psychiatrist or analyst too, to go through this with more maturity, to remember that her pain must be nothing compared to Jeff's pain, her horror puny compared to his.

Again that complex question of parentship, that pulsing lifeline no electrocardiograph could ever trace with its inky squiggles on graph paper. She had to resolve that question more carefully now than ever before; it was vital in a new way, in new ratios, than ever it had been with the other children. Or I will lose him forever, she thought, or I will lose my poor troubled son forever.

"What's bothering you?" Ken asked in sudden sympathy from

the bar table where he was pouring a drink for himself. "You said it was nothing serious, but you're as jumpy as a cat."

"Am I? I'm sorry."

"Let me get you a drink. You've practically drowned that plant anyway."

She looked down at the watering can in her hand. It was always kept on the window, half full, and she had indeed been flourishing it with abandon. "I never knew I had the thing in my hand. I was thinking about other things."

"Sure you don't want to talk about them?"

"Not really. Not for now, Ken." She gave him the flash of a smile, the false smile one manages to give people in hospital beds. "I just want to think this out for a while. Sometimes when you verbalize things, you establish a stance that's hard to shift later on."

"Now you're quoting me back at me," he said. "Or don't you remember where you got that wisdom from, about 'firming up a stance'?"

"You ought to feel flattered. How many wives, after twenty-six years, still really listen?" She was pierced with a longing to blurt it all out, to get Jeff's letter from its hiding place in her purse and hand it over to him, as if sharing this terrible knowledge could somehow decrease it. But she did not move toward her purse, or blurt out a word, not so much out of love for Ken as of fear, as if already she could hear the screaming siren of an ambulance racing to the hospital. "I'm thinking about finding an analyst for Jeff," she finally said. "A real one, not just Mrs. Culkin."

"But why? I thought that was all done with."

"But problems keep arising, new problems—" She turned sharply away, in a new decisiveness. "I meant that, about verbalizing."

"Start him with a professional analyst," he said, half in jest, "and he'll never get loose again."

"That's not so, Ken! You'll be saying 'the shrink' next." She made it sound light, almost merry, and he laughed.

"I guess I'm feeling stingy about any new bills from any new doctors, after being stripped so clean last year."

"We can manage it," she said comfortably. "I asked Mark Waldo to find somebody good in New Haven, and it probably would only be a couple of visits a week, and not cost millions." She moved to the bar table.

"Have you told the school? They'd have to know."

"Not yet, but I will, of course."

"What about talking to Jeff? Have you at least done that?"

"In a way."

"He'll turn you down flat," he predicted. "He's at that age where you don't do things your parents want you to do. Conscientious objectors, all teen-agers."

She laughed a little. "This time I know he will."

"Remembering this past summer, I can just hear you two going at this, the arguments, the yes-buts and no-buts, with Jeff shouting and you finally crying."

"He knows about it already, and he wants it himself. He's being very mature about it, and he'd be grateful—"

"Grateful to parents? A cardinal sin."

"Well, do let's skip it for now. I probably shouldn't have said this much."

He turned back to his drink, clicking on the television set for the evening news. He looked acquiescent enough, ready to stop pressing her, but she saw a jumping pulse at the side of his throat and in the vein at his temple. Veins, she thought. She never used to think, Veins, but now she had an awareness of his veins whenever there was stress for either of them.

Suddenly she felt that she was mishandling this. She was behaving meanly; either you told it or you did not, but half telling and half withholding was paltry and mean-spirited. She had resented Mark Waldo because she had been afraid she would make the wrong decisions and do the wrong things, and sure enough, she was doing them.

But perhaps they were not so wrong. It was better to have Ken perplexed than to shock him to death. The literal meaning of the phrase made her draw back. In crisis, nothing was wrong and nothing right; there was only urgency and the one way to meet urgency was with whatever kindness and tact you could manage. It would all come clearer soon.

The telephone rang and she jumped for it, but it was a wrong number. She had been waiting for it to ring since she came home in the late afternoon. "Phone collect when you can," her wire had said, and after allowing time for Western Union to deliver it in a sealed envelope, she had been waiting for Jeff to call and say whatever it was he would say.

"Gee, Mama, it's swell of you to be this way." She could imagine some such words, faltering, not wanting to thank her openly for her support, yet wanting her to feel it.

"There's nothing swell about it," she would answer, minimizing it, making him feel that this was his due, any child's due.

God, I hate myself, she thought. She shoved the telephone away as if it were mocking her.

CHAPTER TWO

In the wedge of space as the door opened, Jeff saw an inch of Miss Tierney and a yellow envelope in her hand. It was for him. He knew it before Mr. Klingman talked with Miss Tierney, who was from the Headmaster's office, and before Mr. Klingman called his name and said, "You may look at it now, Jeff. A telegram."

He said, "A telegram," not just to put a name to it, but to imply, "This must be important, otherwise it wouldn't be a telegram, so you may read it right away, although the rules are that class cannot be interrupted for messages or telephone calls or letters."

Jeff went up slowly, knowing that everybody was watching him, and took the sealed envelope. An excitement seemed to pump all through him.

"I hope it's not bad news," Klingy said, watching his face for a clue.

Jeff ripped up the flap with his thumb, opened the envelope and drew out the stiff sheet inside, holding it so nobody could get a glimpse of anything in it. The words PROUD OF YOU jumped up at him and he said quickly, "Oh, no, sir, it's not bad news." Then he took one more second to read all of it, stuffed it into his pocket, and with his face burning, went back to his seat.

There was a general stir and buzz about him, but Mr. Klingman said, "Now, class," and the voices stopped and the shuffle and movement fell away. Jeff sat straight as if nothing had happened, but he could almost feel the crispness of the sheet and envelope in his pocket, as if he had his hand around them, touching them. He would have to hide the telegram even though she had written it so it didn't give anything away, or even say anything anybody could start guessing about. Except what kind of specialist and why. But that was nothing much; about six of the guys went into New Haven for their hours with analysts, and everybody knew he had been having sessions with Mrs. Culkin, a kind of child psychologist, though some of her patients were pretty grown-up, the way he was.

But telegrams didn't come about ordinary things like Mrs. Culkin or hours like the ones other guys had. His face burned again; it was hard to believe that not one person in that whole class knew what the telegram was about. Not one person in the whole school. Suddenly he was again hearing the happy roar that had gone up from the whole of Placquette at the game last Saturday when he had intercepted that Hotchkiss pass in midfield and hurled himself free of the tackles, raced left from one blocker, then right, faking another, and gone fifty-two yards for the touchdown. "Lynn, Lynn, Lynn," they had shouted. "Lynn, Lynn, Lynn." If one of them had dreamed the hotshot halfback of their football team was turning queer, if they ever found out that maybe he was, or said he might be, he'd damn well shoot himself.

Maybe it was that horrible fear that finally made him write the letter. It already seemed fifty years since he mailed it, and another fifty since he first thought he would have to write it. He was going crazy over it, really crazy, knowing that he could never tell her face to face and ask for help that way. She would cry and he hated her when she cried. The old man would be worse! Ever since his goddamn stroke, if you said one word he didn't like, you felt like a murderer.

He already knew the telegram by heart, though he had only one flash of it. She was being okay about it. Or maybe she was only putting on an act, for starters. With parents you could never tell. She was all right, mostly, but sometimes she would seem okay and then you would find out after a while that it was all a put-on, and that the real honest thing came out later. He hated hypocrites, and people could be hypocrites while they seemed dead honest. But maybe this was one of the times when she sounded okay and stayed okay later. God, he hoped so.

He could see PROUD OF YOU as if the paper were open before him. She meant she was proud he had told her, not proud of *him*. He felt the writhing begin, the writhing he hated, down deep in his gut somewhere, his viscera, his entrails, he didn't know exactly where, just deep and hidden, at the core. Whenever he thought of it, that writhing and plunging downward began as if he had slipped off a cliff and were going down, down, in a kind of free fall that had no end.

She would get the best specialist. That meant she was pretty sure it was curable, or she wouldn't be willing to spend the money, not after Dad's being so sick for so long. They had plenty of money for important things, he knew that, and this was important if anything was ever important. If only he could talk to somebody up here at Placquette about it, he might never have written her at all. But he didn't dare, not to any master, not even to Pete, his best friend and roomie since sophomore year. Pete was always carrying on about some girl he was in love with, slobbering over what he had done to her and everything he was going to try next time. Jeff hated hearing it, but he half memorized Pete's words, as if he might want to borrow them for his own use. The thing was, he never knew exactly what Pete meant, knew it in his head, sure, but not really *knew*, the way you knew things you actually did know. He listened to all that about kissing and feeling and trying to do this or that, but it was like being locked behind a wall of thick glass where you could see out but not get near anything yourself.

He didn't know exactly when he had first realized that. He only knew that whenever he read a book with a big love scene or saw a movie with passion and breasts and open lips, he had that same dead lost feeling of being locked behind that wall of thick cold glass, watching but not being part of anything.

The first time the glass vanished was that time—God, not last winter at basketball practice, but the winter before that, when Hal Jarvis came off the court with him and slung his arm across his shoulders. Excitement had gone pumping through him then too, a different kind, a new kind, pumping through in big lazy waves, frightening but marvelous, all at the same time. Nothing like it had ever happened to him before, except in dreams. He couldn't believe it and he couldn't get it out of his head. Even hours after, days after, he couldn't. If he so much as thought, Hal, or thought of that arm on his shoulder, it happened all over again, that strange pumping wave, spreading through him like a slow hot river. Even if he thought, Basketball, it would begin and it was always marvelous, but along with the marvelous there was something else.

The something else was being frightened and being ashamed. This kind of marvelous was different from what Pete and the other guys meant. He had an absolute conviction about it. This was all wrong, miserable and wrong.

Yet he didn't want it to end. One night he let himself think about Hal deliberately, as if to see if he could make it happen, and it did happen, just as strong, just as powerful. He knew what it meant. He didn't want to do anything about it, but he did, and it was over in one second flat, wild and pounding.

Afterward he writhed in a shame he had never felt before. He knew that practically all boys did what he had just done, all the crap about going insane was a lot of Bible Belt shit, but he also new that this was different. The other guys thought about a love scene, about a girl. He had felt that arm loose and easy on his shoulder, and that was not okay, not what anybody meant by okay. That was abnormal and it was a disgrace and he lay there in a desperation he had never known.

The bell clanged the end of the period. Jeff leaped from his seat and raced from class. He didn't want any of the guys asking about the telegram, forcing him to make up explanations for it. He wanted to get to his own room, read it again, and then call her as she had said. He would be careful on the phone, the way she was in the telegram, so if anybody heard him, the words wouldn't give him away. Once he started going to whatever analyst she found and started to put out words during the visits, he would have to be on watch for every word he said at school. Not that he hadn't been plenty watchful all along. For a million years he'd watched every syllable, watched every gesture, measured every joke and every action, not even horsing around with Pete the way they used to. Pete didn't have a clue, no doubt of that. If he did, Pete would simply have to tell one other guy, just one, tell even after promising not to say a word, the way people did with secrets, even good people like Pete. And then in five minutes it would be all over school and that would be the end.

Pete never guessed, when he bragged about some girl, that Jeff was listening the way you listened to a teacher in class, taking in the main points, filing them away for some old exam. Nor could Pete ever suspect that the single time the descriptions took on any real meaning was that day Pete was carrying on about touching and feeling and by accident Hal Jarvis called out to somebody outside their open window.

Then for a split second—

Split second was right. It was as if he, Jeff, had grabbed up a great ax, slicing through sharp and sure, the way a lumberman flashed his ax through a sapling tree. Never would he just give in to anything like that, he had thought then, never just let his mind wander along on Pete's slobbery juicy words. Zap-axed. He could do that always. It gave him some comfort: he could zap it off at will. He could take a vow, the way priests and monks did, and put sex out of his life forever. At least until he had been to the analyst long enough to know if he could change around and be like everybody else.

Zap! But suppose sometime I can't lift that ax fast enough? Suppose I can't even find it? Like when I'm asleep?

Maybe this wasn't something you could just zap out or take vows about. Maybe it didn't just pass if you were analyzed. Maybe it didn't disappear as you grew older. It was already over two years since that day coming off the basketball court. Hal had graduated and wasn't even there any more, but nothing had changed for Jeff except it was ten times worse. At the start of this semester, he was the only one in the senior class without a girl. He had begun to make up things about dates he'd had with a girl named Joan during the summer, and that was smooth enough, but then he started calling her Jo, and talking about her a lot, and one of the fellows said, "She sounds like a good Joe," and everybody laughed and he with them. "She's that, all right, wait till you meet her," he said, but he knew he had overdone it, and his gut burned as if he had swallowed a mixture of fire and acid and slime all mixed up.

He finally cooled out but he never called her Jo again. He said Joan or Joanie and then after a while Pete and some of the other guys who also lived in New York started asking him to double-date, expecting him to appear with Joanie. Once Pete asked why she wasn't ever around. Soon Jeff began to drop a few cool remarks about it being all washed up with Joanie. It wasn't her fault, he said, wasn't anybody's fault; they'd just had it and decided to pack it in.

But not too long after that, he'd biked into New Haven and when he got back he talked about picking up a blonde named Gloria. Pete was all ears and it was easy to spill out a lot of pretty smooth stuff. After the first "away" football game, they'd all gone on a tear, with lots of girls around, and later he told Pete all about a girl he called Connie, for Consuela.

"Come off it," Pete finally said. "I don't believe in any of these babes you tell about."

"Okay. So don't."

It was just right, not defensive, not combative, just natural and easy. Pete waited a moment and then said, "You always were the most secretive guy." Jeff liked it, liked the feeling of success. He had put it across. By not trying he had put it across. He must remember that.

There were lots of things he must remember; he was learning them every day. If he slipped he would be found out. That one thing he would never be able to stand. Having everybody know would kill him. He had heard them all laugh and snicker at just about any joke with the word "fag" in it, or "queer" or "fairy" or "queen," and if ever any guy said, "Guess what, Jeff Lynn's a fag," he would kill him.

Or he would kill himself. But it wasn't true, not really true, and it would never be true. He was being slow about girls, sure, being slow about adolescence, about having dreams about girls. The only dreams he ever had, the wet dreams, the wonderful ones, were about vague things mostly that somehow got all glistening or rounding or muscular until it happened—

It didn't mean a thing. Most people were a little of both sexes; they had been told that in sex-education talks. The most masculine of males had a streak of the feminine in him, and the most feminine of females had a streak of the masculine, and it all worked together to produce a deeper, richer humanity in both sexes. He had to remember that too. He wanted to remember it; remembering it was another funny kind of comfort when it got too rotten to think about.

But the main thing to remember was not to lay it on too thick.

"Okay, so don't" had worked. If he had pulled out a couple of snapshots and said this was Gloria and that was Connie, smart old Pete would probably have given him that long look of his that said, "Something's wrong."

Actually he ought to quit laying it on too thick inside himself. He thought about it all too damn much, couldn't keep it out of his head, couldn't give it the old "Okay, so don't" treatment at all. That time Pete dragooned him for his cousin Edey, he got so uptight beforehand he didn't know what to say to her and never even began to like being with her. Then he did all the wrong things to prove he did like her, hurried about dating her again, and then on the second date he had just about crawled inside his own skin. Edey seemed to like him anyway, but all the time that damn glass built up until he felt that he was in a prison looking out at her, talking to her by prison telephone, false and phony as hell.

Also stupid. He was supposed to be a sure thing for *cum laude* or even *summa cum*, straight A's if he even tried, which he didn't, because B's weren't as square as A's, but the minute he got near a girl, the good old stupidity would start. At other times, things came out funny and easy, but with a girl, just stupid sweat.

He turned left, saw that he was already at the dormitory, and hurried to his room. At last he was where he could read the telegram slowly, dig its inner meaning. PROUD OF YOU FOR LETTER, she had said, not just plain PROUD OF YOU, which was how he had caught it on the fly. Natch. How could anybody, especially a mother, be proud of you because you were homosexual? All she meant was that it was better to come clean about it instead of hiding it the way everybody always did. He stared at the phrase and his throat went hot and hard to swallow, as if he were coming down with strep again.

There *were* people who were homosexual that you could be proud of, Leonardo and Michelangelo and Plato and Tchaikovsky and also plenty of living people, famous playwrights and composers and conductors and authors. The string of names came quickly because he had so often gone over them. Telling my beads, he had once thought, a sour smile down inside somewhere. Maybe someday he would do some research, call it "Great Homosexuals down the Ages," like a thesis for a college award or advanced degree. Except you never could do a thesis like that; if you sounded interested in being homosexual, people knew right away about you.

How did he know that? How did he know all the things he already knew about what you had to do and what you could never do? Suddenly he wished he had never given in enough to write his mother. Right there, in writing his letter, he had broken his oath about never letting one human being on earth know about him. Right there in that letter he had done the one unthinkable thing. Admitted it.

But God, if there was any way out after all, didn't he have to take it? He was suddenly hearing the news again about Mick Munson's twin brother, Rex Munson, and his dog's choke collar hanging him to that tree, that awful news flashing around the school like electricity, and feeling again the streak of fear that had raced through him. If there was any way out, of course he had to grab for it, and grab now. And to find out, he had to tell her. Or tell the two of them. Only telling Dad would be one step off the end of the world. Maybe he was yellow to wish his mother wouldn't, but he couldn't help it.

When he first imagined telling them, asking about psychoanalysis, he just iced up all over as if he had a fever. He put the idea out of his head, sliced it off with that ax. But it didn't stay sliced off. It kept coming back at him, sly and cold, working on his nerves until he got that old feeling about going crazy.

"Listen, Dad, listen, Mama, I have something to tell you"—and right away he knew it would have to be done in some other way. At last he began to think, What other way? Instead of pushing the whole thing out of his head in a wild rush, he had begun to make up letters, starting, "Dear Dad and Mama." That didn't get anywhere either.

And then about a month ago, on one of those first days when you suddenly realize that summer's really over and fall is here for sure and winter coming, and in June you graduate—something about all that really got to him, and a panic of hurry seized him like in the last five minutes of an exam, a frenzy springing alive, telling him he'd better speed up and get straightened out and not just wait around hoping everything would just go away by itself like some old aching muscle that gradually lets up.

That was when he got the idea of writing only to her. Even so it was fierce. He didn't know how to say it, he didn't even know how to begin. He couldn't just blast out with "Dear Mama, I guess I'm queer." He must have started ten different letters before he got the one he actually mailed. And the moment it slid into the mailbox, the doubts began again. He had to hand it to her, about the telegram. Now she wanted him to call her, and he couldn't think of anything that would be all right to say; he never would be able to find any words that would sound right. Couldn't she see that for herself, see that was why he had written the letter? She could be infuriating about the things she asked, but she never seemed to think they were infuriating at all.

Maybe anybody would ask you to call. Something seemed to collapse in his mind as he thought it. Maybe this was part of her being okay, and he was glad she was being okay. It made him feel kind of good and sort of sad about having to tell her. He felt in his pocket for a dime; that was all you needed to put in a collect call, and you even got your dime back. Then he went down to the end of the hall to the telephone booth. It was empty and his spirits fell. Doggedly he put in his call. The line was busy and he hung up with alacrity and went back to his room. It was as if God had intervened to give him a breather.

CHAPTER THREE

She slept heavily and then woke suddenly, all at once. Memory whipped at her, of Jeff, of the letter, of *it*. She sat up in the dark room, looking toward the thin oblong of dawn where the shades lifted slightly from the window frames.

The dial of her bedside clock told her it was just past two. She had taken the Nembutal at midnight. Then it was not dawn edging the windows, but moonlight, bright and beautiful. She doubled up her pillows and leaned back against them; upon her lay melancholy, heavy, almost palpable, as if it were rigid. She remembered the plaster cast she had worn through half her freshman year at college, the white inflexibility of it from knuckles to elbow, and inexplicably the white rigidity changed to a vision of two tense white bodies, seeking, entwined, stricken with a horror but seeking.

O Absalom, my son, my son—

Grief for him poured through her, grief at what he was suffering, grief for his need to cry for help, he who until now had known only achievement and pride. He had not telephoned; all evening the silence of the room had been a positive presence, to be endured. Ken had taken her at her word and said nothing further about Jeff or analysis; he had been busy in his room except for a brief appearance at the dinner table, where they had talked publishing and politics and had been rather lackadaisical even about those.

Jeff was probably waiting, she had thought then, for a time to call when his father wouldn't be there to pick up the phone. Ken left half an hour earlier than she did every morning and Jeff knew that very well. Now she thought, It's more than that. Jeff is too wracked himself to want to risk speech at all; that's why he wrote in the first place. Perhaps he needed time. Perhaps some instinct told him she might need time as well.

She reached upward and turned on the light and opened a book, not the manuscript on the bed beside her, but a book already published, which she had been wanting to read whenever she had a few spare hours for what she called "my own reading." She read a page, then another, knew nothing of what the words meant to tell her, what mood they meant to create in her, and finally turned the book face down on the bed. My son, my son—she was not sure where the words came from. A title of a play? A line from a poem? From the Bible? It was part of something familiar and suddenly dear, and she lay there searching her mind, looking toward the thin strips of moonlight. Outside the night was calm and free. Those words too were familiar and dear. Other words could destroy you.

"You see, I am a homosexual." There was such vulnerability in it, it was so young, so bewildered and young. How long had he known it? How long since the first suspicion had risen up in him, to be repulsed in anger, in horror, only to return and strike at him again? It could not be a recent thing. Jeff was not the boy to write such a letter at the first moment of this appalling possibility. "I have fought it off," he had said, "for months and maybe years, but it just grows truer."

My son, my son. She got out of bed, impelled by an obsessed need to know what the full phrase was and whence it came, from what poem, what play, what chapter and verse in the Bible. She went quietly toward the living room in the dark, not turning on any switches to light her way.

She really ought to get to know the Bible better. How often had she thought that across the years, how often had she determined to read all the greatest passages, as a literary experience if nothing else, as an extension of her education and of her preparation for being better equipped as an editor. Her vagueness about the Bible was one of the few bad things about growing up in an agnostic household, with the parents agnostic long before she was born.

Otherwise her agnostic training had always seemed an escape by natural right from all the adolescent soul searchings and all-night arguing about religion that everybody she knew had gone through during their college years.

But her escape was subtly different in any case, since her parents were what was called "Jewish intellectuals" as well as agnostics, and thus had skepticism bred in the bone, as it were, along with their supposedly heightened capacity for emotion. Heightened? How different were her own feelings now from what they would be if she had been born Anglo-Saxon Protestant like Ken?

She never had gone along with the stereotypic clichés about Jewish mothers; she was a mother, not a "Jewish mother" in accord with all the Jewish-mother jokes and the Jewish-mother books and the Jewish-mother plays. She had known other mothers, young mothers and middle-aged mothers and mothers in old age, and the differences between them came not in the framework of their religion or their religious background, but in the framework of inner structure and character, some mothers clutching at their children, others setting them free, some eternally looping them in the hard knots of demanding love, others attached to them only by the easy optional strands of love and returned love. Would this about Jeff seem like a nothing if she were a Protestant mother or a Catholic mother? Could she be any more anxious about what Ken would feel if Ken had been Ken Sachs instead of Ken Lynn?

In the living room, the light switch made a sharp dry click, and she hoped Ken would not hear it, would not come out and ask why she couldn't sleep, what she was doing out there, looking something up in the middle of the night. After a moment she opened her *Oxford Dictionary of Quotations* and looked at the index. There, under "Son," the first reference was "Absalom, My Son," and as she turned back to the proper page she found her heart racing with an expectation.

"Would God I had died for thee, O Absalom, my son, my son."

Grief tore through her with the words, this time not even in small part an admixture of pain for herself as well as for him. This time, solely, solely, she felt knifed through with grief for him, off there alone, wondering, unsure in his cry for help.

She read the words again and again, convulsed with their pain and their love. She reached for the Bible, for the full chapter in

Samuel, but all at once she did not need to read it, could do without the full context of the quoted words. She did not care, except in some distant intellectual way which could wait for another time to be satisfied. The words now had only this meaning of Jeff and this context of Jeff, and she knew that for all the rest of her life, they would for her mean only this first day and night of knowing.

* * *

She awoke to full morning light and silence. It was already past nine; Ken had been gone for a full hour. Before she had finally taken the second Nembutal at five in the morning, she had left him a note. "Had a restless night and took a pill late. Don't worry if I oversleep."

He would worry a little but then the business of the day would take over. She did not take sleeping pills often, and he would pause briefly over the word "late," which would mean to his excellent editorial mind that she had been awake for hours before giving in and taking it. He would wonder even more if he knew that this late sleeping pill was a follow-up one, a repeater, and that she had hesitated about the side effects of a second one, not wanting to risk sluggishness or stupor at a time when she needed all her wits and control. But then she remembered that years ago in the hospital, after her only illness, an appendectomy, there was always the follow-up sedation if the first wore off and the surgical pain returned, and there never had been any side effects but her own gratitude for a few more hours of sleep.

This time she awoke with the same gratitude. She would need help for many another night now, and she would not fight it off; she would take any help she could get until natural sleep was possible again. She knew that one day it would be, but she also knew that it would not be soon. She knew herself too well to have fantasies: a brave stolidity over this was not possible. Intensity was part of her; it was part of living; the bad times were hideous because of the intensity, but then the good times were ten-times-good because of it.

She eyed the telephone. If Jeff had called her in the half hour he knew he could count on finding her alone, no sleeping pill would have muffled the ring enough for her not to hear, which meant that he was again putting off the thing she had asked him to do. He would never call her at the office on this; he knew all about the red light on Gail's desk when the phone was in use. Perhaps he would wait until this evening, and then he doubtless would be put off again for the same reason as last night, that his father might answer or overhear. Should she call Jeff? Phoning sons or daughters at school was one of the taboo things; now it was more taboo than usual. She would sound overanxious; she would sound upset. She might even sound greedy for his praise about the wire.

She had a cup of coffee and tried to absorb the front page of the *Times*. The phone rang and it was Jeff.

"I can't talk much," he started abruptly. "It's just before French. But you said to call you."

"So you did get my wire. I began to worry that maybe Western Union had messed up delivering it."

"I was in Klingy's class yesterday when it came. He let me read it right off."

"I sent it instead of writing because I wanted you to know as fast as possible that I—"

"Does Dad know?"

"No. I decided that for now, until he—no, I didn't show him your letter or say anything, except about analysis."

"That's great. He'd drop dead. I mean, oh God, I didn't mean that."

"That's all right, Jeff. It's just an expression. I saw Mark Waldo yesterday and he's finding out who's best up in New Haven, and the minute he tells me, you'll know."

"Yeah, sure. Well, I have to knock it off for now. Class starts in half a minute. You better write me the doctor's name and not phone it. Okay?"

"Okay." She gazed down at the receiver as he rang off. There was a silence to it, remote, uncommitted, and then the dial tone came on, insistent as a tugged sleeve. Vaguely, a dismay filtered through her mood as she put up the receiver. She had wanted something more than this, wanted something not so laconic. She had wanted him to say one small thing, nothing more than "Gee, thanks for being okay about it." Something.

But she had no business wanting that something, whatever it was. If she began to imagine that he would be grateful for any understanding she gave him, she would launch herself on the long stony road of disappointment. As Ken had said, it was a cardinal sin to be grateful to parents. Jeff would expect her help as his right. And of course it was, as much as being fed and clothed and educated and sheltered until he was grown.

Granted, granted, but still she felt scooped out and empty. Suddenly she was seeing herself again as she stooped yesterday morning to pick up the mail at the front door, just at the instant before she saw the letter in Jeff's young bold handwriting, and longing swept through her, to return to that moment, the moment before she knew.

There she stood, casually picking up the morning's letters, never dreaming that before another ten seconds had ticked off on the clock of her lifetime, that lifetime was to be irremediably altered. So a man might stand on a battlefield in the instant before a bullet exploded within some bone or nerve to cripple him for life; so a woman might stand in a doctor's office in the last seconds before he read from a laboratory report the word "malignant"; so Ken had stood by the telephone a year ago in the instant before receiver and clarity had slipped from him in the first moment of his stroke.

And Jeff? Had there been one specific moment for him just before he discovered this about himself, a moment that he would always look back to longingly as the last moment before he knew?

My son, my son.

She forced herself to stop thinking. She would go to the office and do the office kind of thinking, but no more of this kind. It's like holding one's breath under water, she thought as she dressed, like a kid holding his breath to make his face go blue. But the artifice worked; she was disciplined enough to do this non-thinking for short stretches, during the daytime at least. She had done it in other crises of her life; at times it was the only way to manage.

The telephone rang again and she picked it up, expecting it to be Gail. It was Mark Waldo. "There's an analyst named Dudley, James Dudley, who has been specializing in cases like Jeff's for about twenty years," he said. "He's supposedly very good; two of my colleagues know of him and said so."

"In New Haven?"

"On the outskirts, the more convenient outskirts for Jeff. He won't have to go through the heart of the city. It's in a suburb called Ripley."

"I know Ripley. Jeff could get there by bus or on his bike. Oh, Mark, thank you. Can he take Jeff soon, do you know?"

"He can. I've already called him and asked him. I didn't use Jeff's name. Or yours."

Her face went hot. "How awful. Not to be able to say his name."

"You'll say it yourself. Dr. Dudley expects a call from you. I said you'd introduce yourself as my patient."

"I'll call right away. Will he want to see me first?"

"Jeff is a minor, so perhaps he will. I told him you'd probably call this morning."

"Oh, I will. And thanks again, Mark. Really thanks. If Dr. Dudley can possibly cure Jeff, I'd never stop being grateful—"

"Don't think ahead. Don't jump any guns. Agreed?"

"Agreed."

She put through her call to Dr. Dudley on the heels of her thanks. A minute later she had an appointment with Dr. Dudley for six the next afternoon. She would drive up, she said, and be free of train schedules, and she listened to his road directions as if within the texture of their words and numbers she might detect some omen of the future success or failure of his treatment of Jeff. He sounded young on the telephone and yet Mark Waldo had said he had been in practice for twenty years. That was safer, she thought, and then paused. What had that vagrant thought meant? Was she going to begin looking at every man or boy Jeff knew with eyes that questioned and surmised?

At the office, she went through all the familiar routines, spoke all the familiar sentences of greeting, went to an editorial meeting about the firm's big book on the spring list, and functioned well, as far as she could judge. Yet never once did she feel usual and ordinary, never once did she become absorbed in her work, never could she free herself from the tight skein of memory. As the afternoon began, she thought ahead to the evening with Ken and panic pinked her; if only she need not tell him for a while longer. After she had seen Dr. Dudley, with definite things to report, it surely would be easier for her, easier too for Ken.

He had always taken difficulty well, always been strong and kind when things had gone badly for them. That time her parents had

died, first her mother and two months later her father, he had
been a rock of strength, a rock with warmth, if such a metaphor
could be allowed. He had said little, as he always said little, but
when she had lain there weeping like a child, he had held her as
if she were a child, stroking her hair, saying only, "I know, I know."
And he had been wise about her sudden disorientation, without
parents somewhere off in the background as they had always
been, for when she had thought of staying away from the office
for one more day, he had said, "I'd go in if I were you. You're glad
to be back at a job, don't derail yourself."

Ten years ago that had been, of course, during the first month
of her return to work. All three children were still at home; life
was full indeed, their family intact and Ken still at the peak of his
powers and she at the start of a new chapter, her emergence out
of the home-and-wife-and-mother world she had known since marriage at twenty. She had gone to the office that day and found out
at once how right Ken had been.

But never before had they had this kind of unhappiness. Ken
had never been able to take anything lightly about any of the children and this news about Jeff was coming at him when he was just
back in stride. In her own nerves and veins there was still the tingle of first shock—how then would it be in his? Some instinct, some
unspoken directive told her, Give him as much time as you can.

She called her son Don at his office and to her own embarrassment lied about having "a great roast of beef and wondering if
you and Jenny are free tonight." They weren't, Don said, sounding polite, but with that faint tinge of remoteness that had begun
to characterize his relationship with the family some time before.
She called her daughter Margie and repeated the lie about the
roast of beef. Margie said, "We'd love it, let's make it early so we
can catch up on everything," and her heart rose as she suggested,
"Six-thirty, and I can finally make Nate tell us about his new job."
Daughters stay daughters, she thought, proving the old saw, which
came from the experience of the race. She called the butcher and
then Betty, their three-times-a-week maid who was an excellent
cook.

I'm artistically arranging a delay, she thought, I'm shoving it
aside a while longer. There were already so many subjects in life
that she shoved aside, unwanted intruders she unceremoniously

ordered to depart. Ken's stroke, of course, and the ever-present watchfulness for signs that might threaten another stroke. There was the other also, and that had begun long before the stroke, five years before, maybe seven or eight years. There was a vagueness about time in regard to it, perhaps a saving vagueness, about the first slow realization that he had begun—that they had begun—to have difficulty about, difficulty when, they tried to make love.

She never actually phrased it. It was easier without the hard boundaries language could give. To make love had always been so natural and complete for them both, a varying intensity, of course, the insistence of their first years shifting by infinitely small degrees to the lovely shared closeness that later took its place. But never had there been any constraint or problem between them about their sexuality. Even after some years of marriage, after Donald's birth and Margie's, when flare-ups had become possible between them, they knew the quarrel was not fully over until they could approach each other in bed again to make love. Sex, the great solvent, the great amalgam and uniter—afterward they were always whole again, no longer sealed off in the sacks of their two individualities.

Then it began. Another *it*, she thought now, a something she did not label, a something Ken did not label. It happened so often with men in middle age; analysts' offices were full of men seeking help because they found themselves inadequate, decreasing, wanting as lovers. It had begun so cunningly with Ken, it had crept up so stealthily, first as a lengthened time elapsing, that neither of them had taken particular note of it. She thought it was happening to her as well as to him, felt that here too they were keeping pace with each other, and she had accepted the lessening as one of the great naturals, not to be dreaded or concerned about.

And then had begun the times when they had apparently been in the mood again, equally in the right key, but instead of the easy steady achieving—she hated to remember—then had begun the effort, the experimenting, the new need to "try" this or that, the conscious efforts, the stubborn seeking, rather than giving in and saying that something was wrong.

And then it was that she realized that it was Ken alone who was having the new problems, that she was as she had been all along, but that the changing had been happening to Ken himself. It had saddened her, more than if it had indeed been a mutual and shared new stage of living, of growing older. Would he resent the still-high energy and drive of her sexuality as compared to his? As their tacit agreement became more evident, not to "try" because failure was so punitive for him, he did begin to resent, not her, but her freedom from his deepening burden. Often he made her feel that he resented sex for anybody; he was impatient and fretful over the new frankness in books and on the stage and in movies. She considered telling him of this change creeping into his personality but there was no way she could put it into words without hurting him.

And now this about Jeff would hurt him in a different way. That must be in part why she wanted to delay telling him, why she was so glad Margie and Nate were coming, why Margie's quick assent had given her a sense of escape.

They arrived promptly at six-thirty, Margie still slender and graceful despite the reticent bulging of her body, and Nate, who was the same age, looking more than ever like a college student, nowhere near his twenty-three, nowhere near the fatherhood that was less than three months distant. They at least were happy.

"You should hear them, down at Kennedy headquarters," Margie said, catching at her full attention. "About the first television debate. Everybody says it killed Nixon off for sure. Are you getting that kind of reaction too?"

"Don't answer that," Nate said, "or you'll have Margie talking about the election for the next four hours."

"That's all right with me," Tessa said. She glanced over at Ken, smiling. He looked as pleased to have Margie and Nate there as she did. "What do you think *we* talk about these days? Politics and publishing, and that's it."

It sailed over like a kite, free and high, with no thought of dissembling as she said it. For the moment it became true; suddenly she was tranquil and sure again. Her daughter was going to have her first baby before the year was out, her daughter was discovering the huge gratification of working along with others at an objective that she found more important than anything she had ever attempted before, her daughter was happy with this young husband of hers. It was all so good to see. Calming and good and normal.

"How's the job, Nate?" Ken asked. "Before these women get on to their dear Senator Kennedy, let's hear about the paper."

"*Your* dear Senator Kennedy," Margie retorted. "You don't think we've got you down as a Nixon man?"

"No, no, don't get your hackles up." He laughed and looked approvingly at his daughter. Her brown hair was cut in a new way and it swung in loose dark waves as she moved her head. In her pregnancy her good looks, so much like Tessa's, were clarified and intensified, and it gave him an odd proprietary pleasure, though he knew full well that modern parents were not permitted a single possessive moment. Nobody could call her marriage to Nate a good marriage in the worldly sense, a marriage to a young man without a dime to his name except for his weekly paycheck, but the evidence was pretty clear that it was good in other ways. They enjoyed each other, they thought the same things desirable, so that the eroded old phrase about liking each other as well as loving each other regained some freshness in relation to the pair of them. Once he and Tessa had been like that. It was the summit of life while it lasted and perhaps for Margie and Nate Jacobs it would go on lasting.

Just the same he wished that Nate was more like—was less like —was not quite so . . . He searched for the right word and was surprised that he was in need of one. He was a man without prejudice, and had earned the right to that overworked assertion throughout his life. Yet he wished that Nate were a little more like Margie and Don and Jeff. Not quite so Brooklyn. There, that was the right word. It was not Nate's being Jewish that was faintly bothering; Tessa was Jewish and he had scarcely given it a thought, either when they had been young and getting married, or across all the years since. But Tessa wasn't Brooklyn. She wasn't Bronx. Nate was different from Tessa.

A funny thing, assimilation. He believed in it, Tessa believed in it, Tessa's parents had believed in it, though his own had not. ("I know her parents were born here, and her grandparents, but you'd be happier with a girl of your own background." "She is my own background." "She seems it, but there's always a difference.") They had been polite and cordial with Tessa; they were too well bred to be anything else. They were of course both Vermonters, third-generation Manchester Vermonters, churchgoing and puritan, his mother a bit much on her D.A.R. heritage, his father, a banker, a bit much on rectitude and tradition. Considering all that, they really had been admirable in their acceptance of his college-bred agnosticism and then in their acceptance of Tessa Sachs, yet the reservation had always been there, obvious to him, their only son.

Now here he was feeling a twinge of a related reluctance about Nate, perhaps because Margie was his only daughter, but his reluctance was the opposite number to his parents' reluctance about Tessa. If Nate's family had been like Tessa's, if Nate had grown up among assimilated Jews instead of Jewish Jews, he, Ken, Nate's father-in-law, would now be feeling no twinge of reluctance at all. Yet it was shocking that he did, he supposed, even understanding it as he did. What the devil did intonations and gestures, a hard *g* in "Long Island" or "singing"—what did any of that have to do with the price of beans? Especially to him, whose gut heaved at prejudice in others?

He supposed he should cry *mea culpa* and own up to a buried and vestigial prejudice, but he'd be damned if he'd be that much of a hypocrite. There was something here to be thought about, to be analyzed, maybe to be erased for good. It was nonsense to think that you had no choice about prejudice, that if you had any you were eternally stuck with it. You could, slowly maybe, reprogram yourself, re-educate yourself, rid yourself of it. Especially when you were a man basically free of prejudice, as he so demonstrably was. His own wife was Jewish, his children half Jewish, half the people at his office were Jewish, many of his authors were Jewish. Living in New York, how could it be anything else? So the twinge of reluctance was laced through not with being Jewish but with the concept of assimilation. That was mighty different, easier to accept. When he and Tessa were young, assimilation was highly approved of, but later on the word had been tinged with accusation. It turned into a dirty twelve-letter word (he counted on his fingers). Was that because of Hitler or was it later, when Israel became a state? He rather thought it was later, in the Forties and Fifties, when many Jews felt a heightened awareness of being Jews, of having a Jewish heritage, of a duty to keep their Jewishness unimpaired.

"What did you count that came up to twelve?" Nate asked.

"Up to twelve?"

"You asked me about my job at the paper, then you got thinking about something else, I could see your mind tick over with whatever it was, and then you counted on your fingers, the way Margie did at the start of her pregnancy. Only you didn't stop at nine. You made it all the way up to twelve."

Ken burst out laughing. He looked at Nate, sprawled on the sofa, and thought again that he was glad he and Margie were there for the evening. This afternoon when Tessa called him at the office to say the kids were coming over for an early dinner, he was relieved, about what he didn't know. He didn't like it when Tessa and he disagreed, even about something like analysis for Jeff, but life with Tessa had its built-in tensions and he had given up fretting about whose fault it was when the bad times came, who had started it, who had said what or who ought to say what. Just the same his mood now was higher than it would have been without the young ones there.

"I was thinking large thoughts," he said to Nate. "Large thoughts often come in round dozens."

"In rounded periods, maybe, but not in round dozens."

"The large thought was a twelve-letter word, 'assimilation,' a word I gather we all approve of."

Nate sat up; instantly the lounging boyish sprawl was gone, in a kind of leap to attention. "It's become a hot word," he said. "Like 'integration.' "

"That's what I was thinking, though I didn't put it as neatly."

"A hot word among liberals," Nate went on, emphasizing the point, "not just among Orthodox Jews, where assimilation is as big a crime as intermarriage, but a hot word among liberals and radicals too."

"I wasn't thinking of Orthodox Jews either," Ken said.

"Look at my own family. Reform Jews, right? You've met them, you know they're not Orthodox, but get them going on somebody who's Jewish but sounds goyish, or looks like a goy or acts like a goy, and they decide he's a rat who's trying to pass." He laughed. "They believe in something you could call 'Jewishness Intacta.' "

This time Tessa and Margie joined in the laughter. Tessa looked at Nate with affection. He was a good boy and he would make Margie happy. He seemed to enjoy visiting them, and if he was shy at being with his in-laws, he gave no sign of it. There was a readiness in him, as if he were signaling that he wanted to be "family" in a real sense, not an outsider who had technically become one of them but who privately meant to remain aloof.

Suddenly she felt a surge of kinship with Nate and thought, He's the one I'll tell first when Jeff says it's all right.

She turned toward the bar table, fished for another ice cube, wondering, Why Nate? What made me so sure? Why my son-in-law instead of my son? Why Nate instead of Margie, and as a matter of fact, why Nate instead of Ken? That's what I really mean, that I wish I could talk it out first with Nate, to help me about how to tell Ken.

It startled her. She let the conversation of the others drift off into the space beyond her attention while she pondered that. It's because Don and Margie will each tell me not to take it too hard, and Ken will take it too hard himself, though he'll not really show it, probably not want to talk it out or need to talk it out the way I will.

But Nate will understand the way I take it, he'll know that if you suffer maybe you should show it. Nate and I—we know something. Maybe there's some sort of kinship bred in the mores of one's ancestors that gets handed down through environment if not through genes and DNA and such. Jews at the wailing wall, Irish Catholics moaning and keening at a wake, Russians and their melancholy, there's a world of difference in all of it, compared to the Anglo-Saxon puritan control of Ken and all the other Kenneth Baird Lynns of the earth. Ken never could be really free about showing what he felt. He bottled it up—maybe that's why, in the end, he blew an aneurism and had a stroke.

She drew back from the thought. It was distressing, as if she had blamed Ken for being Ken, separating herself from him, elevating herself above him in this matter of emotion. How complex everything was when you were unhappy. What labyrinths and mazes there were to frustrate and bewilder you before you came anywhere near certainty.

She glanced from Ken to Nate. He was telling of his first assignment as a reporter, down at police headquarters, a routine and lowly assignment, classic for beginners on big-city dailies, but to Nate a marvel of passion and drama.

"When you're right there in Night Court," he was saying, "you can't escape the fact. Out of every ten people arrested, nine are Negroes. All minor offenses, drunks, vagrants, muggers, street pushers of pot, but nine out of every ten are Negroes. It gets to you, unchanging, night after night. You've always known it, but when you see it for yourself—wham."

"I went down one night," Margie put in, "just to see, and I couldn't stop wondering if it isn't partly rigged by the police attitude. You know, more on the lookout up in Harlem than anywhere else."

Tessa nodded at her daughter but she was still preoccupied with Nate and the silent sense of kinship pulsing through her.

* * *

After the evening was over and she was alone, getting ready for bed, it was Nate who stayed in her mind. He had been a catalyst that had brought into being a high longing that she could again feel that strong sureness with Ken, feel it now when it was so essential. Long ago it had been there, just as warm, just as strong, as this new feeling about Nate, but it had slipped away somehow, down the long stream of time, or else she would not be so anxious now. If Ken were still the long-ago Ken, she would not be having fantasies about talking it all out first with Nate.

During the entire evening she had been more and more drawn to a certain simplicity in Nate's warmth, a kind of easy quality in it, arousing a corresponding warmth and ease in her, and along with it a sadness that it was this very ease and simplicity that had once been Ken's and hers, one of the basic elements for their life together.

That time he was taking her for her first weekend with his family—suddenly she was back there on the warm leather seat of his old Buick, a girl of nineteen needing his reassurance about what lay ahead. How funny and dear he was, how direct and simple.

"Ken, will they mind, about me being Jewish?"

"Sure they'll mind, a little, but they'll never be mean or small about it. Let's give them the room they need."

The room they need. It had become one of her own phrases whenever a disturbing situation arose between them, whenever she felt that patience and insight were needed. Always it had worked with Ken, as if the very phrase could touch off some hidden spring in his own personality, loosening him and returning him to the easier ways he had had when they were first starting out.

But people changed, she thought now. Life stiffened the joints and sinews of character as well as of hips and knees and muscles. She too must have changed in the quarter century of their marriage, despite the charge that she didn't change enough. That was the family accusation, jokingly put for the most part, but with plenty of evidence behind it, as she well knew. She dealt with the same grocer she had dealt with for the past twenty years, and the same butcher and the same laundry. She liked the big old-fashioned apartment they had moved into when Margie was born and had never considered changing it while all their friends kept moving from this place to that, moving to the suburbs, moving to cooperatives or more modern buildings.

She was the one to stay put. It was true enough. And when it came to matters larger than grocers and butchers and apartments, it remained true. She grew irked and angry at public things, enraged at injustice, at poverty and prejudice, but within the sphere of her own life with her own family, she rarely had any impulse toward change or upheaval. She marveled at the increasing number of breakups in the marriages of their friends, marveled at the number of divorces as the anniversaries mounted. Here at least Ken and she remained as close as ever they had been, both feeling that there was an immaturity in this search for new beginnings. Not too long ago, when he had told her that his partner Ted Brannick was ending a marriage of thirty years, he was impatient as well as amused.

"The chump," he had said. "What he's really doing is trying to be twenty-five again. A great idea. Except when you're over fifty."

"Do you ever wish you were twenty-five again?"

"Not before last year, never. But that stroke—"

"I didn't mean that way."

A remorse swept through her and she sat down on the edge of her bed, feeling it as a physical sensation. She must not forget the stroke, even though she was ordered not to remember it. It was there now in their lives, in both their lives, sat there with them every time they faced anything difficult. Stress was the enemy; she knew that, as did Ken, and fantasies about talking things out first with Nate proved she could be a chump too. It was Ken she would be telling about Jeff, Ken and whatever went with Ken.

CHAPTER FOUR

Dr. James Dudley was standing as she was shown into his office, and she answered his greeting by saying, "Oh, Doctor, if only you can help my son Jeff, I—" Her voice thickened and darkened, and she halted abruptly.

"Dr. Waldo told me a good deal about him and your family," he said as he indicated the chair she was to take. "Perhaps it will be easier for you now, just talking about him in general, since I know the specific problem."

But she talked as if Dr. Waldo had told him nothing, compelled to begin with Jeff's letter, compelled to tell him of her telegram, compelled to talk of her pride in Jeff's forthrightness and of her own shock and horror about the thing he had told her. "I'm getting this all out of the way now," she ended, "so you won't need to wonder about how I feel toward him."

"That is, of course, a vital element in Jeff's future," he said. His voice was kind, but there was a blandness mixed with the kindness. He's schooled himself, she thought, to sound a little remote with distraught parents, as if we also are patients. Maybe we are. In a way we must be. Instead of making it easier for her to go on, the professionalism of the doctor's voice and manner was an unexpected hurdle. Would he sound this way with Jeff? For a moment she sat mute, staring at the doctor. He was in his early fifties, quite good-looking though he was overweight, even a little stout. That surprised her. Did he have a compulsion to eat? Did he have his own set of problems?

"Does Jeff's father feel this same pride in Jeff's ability to approach you for help?"

"I haven't told my husband, not yet." She spoke briefly about her reasons for delay. "And I won't tell Jeff about my own horror."

"Why, Mrs. Lynn?"

"Why? It would only add to his guilt. And that would make him resent me, wouldn't it?"

"But Jeff's letter shows that he knew this would be a shock to you and that you would suffer about it. He was facing up to that. Actually that is a good sign in itself."

"A good sign? Do you mean that there is a reasonable chance that you might help him?"

"It is impossible to make predictions. I am sure you understand that. You are, of course, anxious to have any kind of promise, but you would recognize the fallibility of it, if I made even the most tentative one at this time."

"How soon might you be able to tell whether he can be helped?"

"Not for a considerable period. Even after I began to see Jeff, it would be some time before I could arrive at any judgment. I might say, however, provided that you will not leap to any conclusions—"

He hesitated and she said quickly, "I won't leap. Please say it."

"Numerous authorities do report a successful outcome in a significant percentage of such cases."

"Significant?"

"Somewhere in the neighborhood of twenty-five percent."

"Oh, if the percentage were only half that big! You mean that they were cured?"

He looked at her almost glacially, as if to emphasize the danger of emotional responses to what he was telling her. "These past twenty years, that same percentage has applied to my own patients as well. About twenty-five percent did turn exclusively to heterosexuality."

"Oh, Dr. Dudley, I—"

"These patients, of course, were highly motivated young people who really wished to surmount their homosexuality and who remained in therapy a sufficient time."

"Jeff will remain as long as it's necessary. I know he will. He never gives up easily on anything, never did even as a little boy."

"This is a most complex problem, as you surely realize, Mrs. Lynn. Suppose you tell me now of your son when he *was* a little boy, his relationship to you and to his father, friends, school, anything you can."

She didn't want to talk about Jeff's childhood; he would be telling that himself. But obediently she began to talk of him as a baby, as a toddler, a first-grader. A difficult time, she said, yet wonderful too. "He was six years younger than his sister, and eight younger than his brother, so it was marvelous to have a baby again—perhaps I enjoyed him too much, spoiled him, though I can't really believe in words like 'spoiling' a child. And he was so bright, so alive to everything, it was always such a joy to come home at night from the office—"

"You are in publishing, I understand."

"Yes, an editor."

"Did you go to the office when the other children were small?"

"No, I didn't. I was thinking about going back to work when Margie was about five and Don seven, but then I got pregnant again, with Jeff, and I didn't actually go back for years. He was seven when I did. Could that explain—?"

"Try not to draw inferences," he said. "My questions have no judgmental load. I am simply interested in whatever you can tell me of Jeff and yourself and the family."

"I was being defensive," she said quickly. "It's true. One of the awful things these past two days is wondering what we did wrong. To be honest, what *I* myself did wrong, because it's always the mother somehow, isn't it?" Her voice did break and she put her hands to her face, sliding the fingers upward swiftly, closing them together to make a shield over each eye. Behind the closed fingers, the tears were hot, and she was embarrassed and helpless before the stranger across the desk.

"I would suggest that we skirt the field of causation for the time being," Dr. Dudley said firmly. "Our interest now is not primarily in developmental history or theory, but in the possibility of heading off a true inversion."

"True? Could this be *not* true?"

"If Jeff actually has had no physical experience as yet—"

"He wouldn't lie. He always told the truth, even when he was a child."

"My point is that patients who have been practicing homosexuals for years, patients much older than Jeff of course, are the ones whom it is very difficult to treat. But even then, one cannot always rule out a successful outcome."

"And at Jeff's age, a seventeen-year-old?" She waited, but there was no answer. He again responded by waiting himself. He had a folder open in front of him, but beyond Jeff's name and address and the telephone number at school, nothing was written there. He was staring down at the nearly empty page now, and once more she felt an obscure wish that he was not quite so controlled. She finally said, "Well, about Jeff at school—" and talked almost uninterruptedly for the rest of the fifty minutes, talked only of Jeff as a boy in kindergarten, in the first grade, starting at Placquette, his prowess at sports, talked without faltering for a word. It all came back with the clarity of safeguarded memory, fresh again, happening again. She looked only occasionally at Dr. Dudley. He continued to look down at his desk, his face blanked of expression, of promise or commiseration. A clock struck and he stood up.

"You have been very helpful, Mrs. Lynn," he said unexpectedly.

"I didn't know what this visit would be for. I hope I have been."

"I won't be seeing you again for the present. It is better for the patient not to feel that he is being 'reported on' to any outsider, even his parents. You do understand that?"

"I think so. Yes, I do understand. But try to help him, Dr. Dudley, will you, please?"

"I'll try."

The drive back to New York was an automatic procedure for her, as if it were done by some force other than herself. Her brain seemed to have stopped functioning; she seemed to have no thoughts, no emotions, no faculty for making a judgment of the hour she had spent with James Dudley. She sat numb behind the wheel, piloting the car through the thin city-bound traffic, hardly aware of where she was.

There were so many things she should have asked him, things she had meant to ask him, and had not got to. Is it a disease? Is it abnormality? Is it a psychic disturbance, like schizophrenia? She did not think in terms of "sin" or "evil," and it would not have occurred to her that any physician would, but already she knew that there were sharp and divergent differences of opinion about the age-old phenomenon of the homosexual in a world predominantly heterosexual.

She thought suddenly, I could stand it if it weren't sex, if it had nothing to do with sex, if the idea of "sexual aberration" didn't even enter into it. If it were any other abnormality or neurosis, I could say, Oh well, and try my best to help Jeff without this inner horror. I'm so afraid for him, so afraid he will suffer terrible things because of something he didn't arrange or seek out. He can't help it, he didn't choose it; if he had, would he be writing this strangled letter for help?

Would Ken see that? If it were about anything besides sex, there would be no doubt. At his office, he had been patience and loyalty itself to Fred Dirkeley and his incessant drunkenness, and Fred had not been a member of his family, only of his firm. Ken had been the bulwark between Fred and the rest of the company, had stood by him through all his periods of drying out, slipping again, of being hospitalized once more, had withstood all the pressures within the firm to get shut of Fred Dirkeley. "It's a disease," Ken had said repeatedly, "sometimes a fatal disease, but don't let us be the ones who kill him off."

Until Fred Dirkeley's death Ken had remained unchanged in his attitude. Surely he would be equally steady if one of their three children had been involved.

Yes, but this was not alcohol. She herself had just wished with all her heart that this crisis had nothing to do with sex—how much more strongly would Ken feel that? That was another reason for all these delays about telling him. That morning she had said she would be home too late for dinner, but she had ascribed that to "going up to see an analyst Mark Waldo recommended." She had made it sound offhand, almost casual. It was an a priori judgment about Ken that she was suddenly appalled by, a sort of superiority she was assuming.

On impulse she stopped at the next highway gasoline station and called home. "I'll be later than I thought, Ken," she said. "I thought I'd better let you know."

"Where are you calling from?"

"Near Norwalk. That analyst is in New Haven, didn't I say that?"

"I suppose you did." His tone changed. "I've been wondering, why this much of a rush. I hadn't thought you'd be going up all this fast."

"It seemed better to get things in motion."

"There must be some sort of crisis I don't know about," he said slowly. "It's been building up in my mind that there must be."

"I'll explain it all when I get home, every bit of it. But if you get hungry before I get there, there's cold roast beef from last night."

She drove the rest of the way in an emotional stupor, unable to devise an opening that might make it easier for him. There could be no putting it off now and there was relief in being committed, but she could not put two sentences together in her attempted rehearsal. Perhaps it was best this way; there was something false in prepared statements within a family. She drove the car harder. Decision itself was a relief.

"Well, what's this all about?" Ken greeted her when she at last got in. "Here, you'll want a drink after all that driving. What'll it be?"

"A light one, vermouth, I think. Thanks."

"Are you hungry?"

"Not really, thanks."

He waited until she had had two or three sips of her drink. She looked tired, in that special way she had of looking tired when fatigue was laced with depression. "Come on, Tessa, let's have it. I knew the other night that something was up, I think I did anyway, when you were so intent about 'not verbalizing.' I suppose I was willing enough to let it slip by, but now, with your rushing about lining up an analyst, why, I realize it must be something pretty serious."

"It is, Ken. But it's something that might be changed around, so don't be too unhappy about it."

"Too unhappy about what?"

"Jeff told me, he wrote me that he—he's terribly disturbed about it himself, but Mark Waldo thinks, and this new analyst, Dr. James Dudley, seems to agree that if it's still in the earliest stages, the formative stages, it can be cured."

"Tessa, what are you getting at?" He was standing still, looking down at her. The color in his face had mounted. "You really are making a mystery of whatever it is. What happened? What did Jeff write you?"

"Two days ago I got a letter from him."

"What did it say?"

She swallowed audibly, trying to rid her throat of the knotting constriction there. If only she could say it matter-of-factly, if only she could stay easy and controlled as she said it. She shook her head as if in negation, opened her purse, drew out the letter and held it folded for a minute. "Darling, try not to feel hopeless about this. It seems there is a large chance—he's so young, so pliable still—" Her tone shifted in intensity. "In fact, Dr. Dudley said that about twenty-five percent of the time, there's a complete cure."

He reached for the letter and took it from her still-tight fingers. She could not watch him as he began to read it, as if she would spy upon him in his first moments. He said nothing as he read. Long after he must have finished it, he said nothing. She still did not look up. He did not return the two pages to her. He did not crumple them. He did not put them down. He simply remained standing there in silence.

At last she raised her eyes. She had never seen his face this way, a yellowish white, like wax and iron fused, the muscles standing out as if wiring his jawbones. Not even at the worst of his stroke had he looked so ill, so done for. Her heart went out to him but she could not speak. This was the first moment of his knowing, this his first step into this new pain. He needed time; give him the room he needs. This was *his* dividing line, separating all of what life was before he knew from all of what life would be from now on.

He said, "Oh, my God. Oh, my God, if it's true."

"It may be true. It may change."

"If it's true now, it will stay true."

"We can't know. He's never *done* anything. You know Jeff never lies."

"I know he doesn't." He put the letter down, quite gently, put it into her lap as if it were a bouquet of flowers he was presenting her. Then, slowly, he left the room. She stared at the white pages.

From down the hall she could hear him softly close the door to his room. Then there was a new sound, convulsive, drawn-out, and she knew he was crying.

* * *

It was the next day that she canceled a luncheon engagement and went to the public library on Fifth Avenue. She had to learn whatever there was for a layman to learn about homosexuality, learn it fast, learn it for Ken's sake, her own sake, perhaps for Jeff's.

Freud, Krafft-Ebing, Havelock Ellis—she could make a start, go through a cram course for a few weeks to give herself some foundation, and then she could narrow down to more modern texts—were there any? She, an editor, did not know. Ten or twelve years ago, of course, there had been the Kinsey report on male sexuality, with its phenomenal success and immediate respect; she had leafed through it, but it had been too technical for her to read carefully. From reviews and discussions she knew that Kinsey's work showed that homosexuality was no infrequent phenomenon, far from it, but that was about the sum of it. How little one did know about it, how vague and cloudy the whole subject was, even for people who held themselves generally well informed.

At the card catalogue, she riffled through the *K*'s, but the memory of Kinsey's pages of scientific charts and data came at her with an unexpected oppressiveness, and she went instead to the drawer where Sigmund Freud was listed. She found that he had written *Three Essays on the Theory of Sexuality* back in 1905, but the card indicated that the essays dealt with homosexuality, and she made out a slip for the volume, and another for his famous *Outline of Psychoanalysis*.

An agitation began to weave through her as she waited for the books to arrive from the stacks. She opened the essays first, and agitation mounted. She began to read but it was as if her eyes could not see accurately; the words stared up at her from the page, little black letters, spaced off in groups, meaning nothing, sentences rippling, gently tossing up and down, like brooks. She persisted, turning pages, seeking, catching an occasional familiarity, oedipal, libido, fixation, castration-anxiety, hypothesis that it is innate . . . or acquired, pregenital objects. But soon she shut her eyes and leaned back against the solid wood of the chair she sat in.

She could not go on. It was too soon; she should have known it. This frantic scrabbling for knowledge, this obsessive need to discover, to make herself an expert—there was something ignoble in it, rising not from the love of knowing but from some desperation spawned by fear and shame.

She shoved back harshly from the table and left.

CHAPTER FIVE

"Hi," Jeff said as he flung open the door. He squeezed her shoulder in his new form of greeting but he did not look directly at her. "Is Dad home?"

"He had a late meeting." She reached up, and he stooped to the gesture, again squeezing her shoulder as she kissed him. "We might go out for dinner, if he's kept too late."

"That would be great." He never carried a suitcase for these once-a-month weekends, truncated during the football season in the fall and the baseball season in the spring to a mere Saturday night and Sunday, only an old B.O.A.C. airplane bag he had salvaged from one of their trips to England. This he called "my Bo-ack," clearly preferring its worn fabric to the handsome tweed and leather carry-all they had given him for his sixteenth birthday. He tossed it down now on a chair in the small entrance hall and made his way to the living room ahead of her, taking over the largest chair.

He looked well, enough of his summer tan lingering to make his gray eyes brilliant, and his light hair was still sun-streaked as it was when he had left on Labor Day for early football practice. He had grown, she was sure of it, but it always displeased him to have her say, "You're taller," so she made no mention of it. Long ago when he was still small enough to be stood up against the kitchen door at birthdays, to have his height recorded, in a different-colored crayon from the ones that had ticked off Don's and Margie's progress upward, he had begun to fidget and finally to protest that he didn't want to be "measured like how many hands high is a horse," and it had become a family anecdote. But when he was ten, he had got hold of a can of enamel, when a neighbor's apartment was being redecorated, and had painted out the whole series of marks, his brother's and sister's along with his own. She had been immoderately angry at him then, but he had never been measured since.

Now she thought, He'll be six-two or six-three before he's through, a smugness of pride touching her, but with it a nip of the old anger at his vandalism in painting out three childhoods from that kitchen door. He would never understand that anger, not until he had children of his own.

Children of his own. There she went again, up to her old trick of imagining the future. It would have to be the future she wanted, the future she needed; it could not be some other future that she could not bear. In her mind she apologized for her folly, apologized to whom, she did not know, for what, she did not say. It was an amorphous wrongness, that was all she could call it, a weaving softness of desire, instead of reality. Jeff had had four sessions with Dr. Dudley, and here she was envisioning him as a father of his own children. She made an impatient sound and was glad he made no response to it. He was leafing through a magazine, examining it with diligence, as if his entire attention were focused and active. It was hard for him to discuss Dr. Dudley with her; he had not mentioned Dudley the one time she called him at school, guardedly saying she "had decided to talk it all out with Dad." He had said, "Well, okay," but asked no questions, offered no comment. She hadn't pressed him.

"Hungry?" she asked now.

"Yeah, some."

"Shall I fix you a sandwich? Dad could be held up quite a while."

"I'll get a Coke."

He went to the kitchen, uncapped a bottle, and took it with him to the telephone. "I said I'd call Pete," he said, dialing.

"Didn't he come down?"

"Sure, but I'm supposed to check in with him."

"But you just left him" would have been the odious thing known as "parent stuff." Ordinarily she took this without a tremor;

the other two had had their own sets of regulations for parents, and she was long accustomed to the strictures, some quite elaborate, others pointless. But now with Jeff home for the first time since the letter that had changed everything?

At the phone Jeff was already laughing in delight, his words unintelligible amid his chortles and guffaws. From the receiver she could hear Pete's voice, foaming with laughter also, carefree, as unaware of passing time as Jeff. A spear of anger pierced her.

"I don't know," Jeff said. "My mother said something about going out for dinner." He turned to face her. "Pete wants me to go to this movie with him, Olivier in *The Entertainer*—we're crazy to see it, and he can't go anytime except tonight."

"But, Jeff, I told you—"

"It could be after dinner. Please, Mama. You know."

She knew indeed. The anger subsided. He was tense under all the jokes and laughter. He didn't want to spend a whole evening with his father, and didn't relish spending it with her either. An immense feeling for his situation filled her, and an immense love. He was so young. She was suddenly aware of that still-forming mouth and jaw, that rawboned stretch of body.

"I guess we can manage," she said. "What time's the movie?"

"I can," he shouted at the phone. "Meet you there for the nine-o'clock show. You better get on line first, in case I'm held up. My father's not here yet."

Another few minutes of talk ensued, to recheck the time and the location of the theater. At last Jeff hung up, set the empty bottle aside, and headed for his room.

"Jeff."

He turned, unwilling, refusing to look at her directly, gazing instead at some vague point in the vicinity of her collarbone. He picked up his airplane bag, swinging it as if it were a bag of laundry he was about to pitch down a chute. He waited.

"Did you like Dr. Dudley?" she said at last.

"He's okay."

"Is he—did you feel—do you think he can help you?"

He stood, rigid as a column, silent. Then suddenly he flung his bag to the chair again, faced her, his eyes hot with injury and his voice raw. "I'm not supposed to talk about my visits," he said. "Dr. Dudley says he told you that. He says you understood that."

"I do. I didn't mean 'talk about your visits,' just whether you thought he was a person you could relate to, somebody you would like."

"Then don't talk about the visits," he said roughly. "I'm not supposed to report back and I won't."

"You needn't. But after all, this means a lot to me too."

"I can't talk about it, that's all."

He tore his bag off the chair and strode down the hall to his room. In a moment she heard the transistor radio, blaring, and resentment gushed up in her. He saw this only as his own, as if it were a possession, his and only his, by title his, his own unhappiness, his own fear, his own life. She stood quiet, in the hall, waiting for the resentment to pass. It would pass, she could count on it passing. But it would leave a residue of something for which there was no label, an ashen and gritty residue of pain, no matter how forbearing and wise she might try to be. Why didn't children ever see that they could damage and harm their parents as much as parents could damage and harm children?

She went back to the living room. Ken was in a late meeting with Joel Massovic, one of their major authors. That had surprised her, for though Massovic always had to be seen after hours, since he refused to interrupt his writing schedule during the day, it was equally true that Ken usually refused any kind of business appointment over the weekend. Poor Ken, he didn't want to be there tonight when Jeff came in. In the two weeks since the night she had told him, he had been like a man stunned and bereaved, silent for the most part, in a kind of strangulated silence as if his vocal cords had been damaged in some surgery, so that he spoke hoarsely and with effort when he did speak. Then it was usually not about Jeff.

"Ken, would you like a Nembutal for tonight?" she had asked him on that first night.

"No, thanks."

"I'll leave one in your room, in case you decide you do want it."

"Thanks, that will be fine."

"Darling, I know how hard—"

"I'm sure you do, but please let's not talk it out for now?"

It was an entreaty, and her own ambivalences pulled at her. She felt for him but she also resented his ability to say nothing. He was doing the same thing Jeff was doing, seeing it as possession too, his possession. And she, was she doing that too?

Each one of us, she thought, is always and forever at the core of our own pain; each one looks outward to others as if they were indeed outside the core. Each wants help, but to offer help is another matter. How do you offer help in any case? Arranging about doctors and analysts and fees and hours—that's the logistics of treatment, but it's not, in any deep sense, help. Nor could you offer real help if every tender of it was thrust aside.

The telephone rang. "I'm held up with Joel," Ken began. "He's upset about the progress he's making, and this may go on quite a bit longer. You better go out to dinner without me."

"Oh, Ken. He'll guess that you don't want to see him. Jeff, I mean."

"I don't think he will. Tell him about Joel."

"But we're just at the beginning of this, and I think we both have to try—"

"Of course we do, but for now anyway, I think this is a lot better way. I'll see you later on. If he wants to go out tonight, that would be better yet."

"He's going to a movie at nine."

"Then I'll get home about nine. Goodbye for now."

She sat, dejected, her hand still on the telephone. That old notion about sharing your sorrows with your husband probably was outworn and threadbare by the time two or three decades had passed. Had his stroke added its own attrition, or would it be the same if he had not been sick? Perhaps he too felt that he had to bear this alone; perhaps he was dejected too. She set aside the telephone and went down the hall.

"Time to go, Jeff."

He came out instantly, looking past her. "Where's Dad? Are we meeting him in the restaurant?"

"He got held up. He won't be home until nine or later."

"So it's just us? Great." The wary look was gone. He began to talk of the movie he and Pete were to see, relief sounding in his big voice, and through their dinner at a small restaurant nearby, he talked of school, of football, of his new set of teachers. She sat listening; he would ignore what she most wanted to hear. It was as if she had no existence for him just now except the tangible biological body he saw. Underneath the fast persistent talking, she could see his hidden life in his tight features, could see his boyhood going away, leaving him troubled and old at seventeen.

"Isn't that right?" Jeff demanded.

"Isn't what right? I'm sorry, I must have lost a sentence."

"You keep looking up at the wall, at the clock."

"I didn't know I was."

"Are you going to meet Dad after I go?"

"I'm going home. He'll be home when he's through with that Joel Massovic." Again she glanced at the prodigiously large clock over the cashier's desk, seeing the jerk which the minute hand gave as it left its position of the preceding sixty seconds and lurched forward to the one it would hold for the next sixty. She had never before longed to get away from any of her three children, but suddenly she could scarcely wait for this meal to be over. Falseness lay embedded in each word by either of them; they talked of trivia while the core went unmentioned. "I must have lost the thread of what you were saying," she said, "so tell me again."

"Skip it. I'd better go meet Pete anyway." He rose, and she said again, "I'm sorry, Jeff. My mind kept wandering."

He sat down again. His color had risen. "Look, if you're going to keep harping on things—"

"I'm not harping."

"I can feel it. I can practically hear the questions and the digging. If it's going to be like that, maybe I'd better ask at school if I can stay up there without any weekends at all. At least to Christmas."

"That's nasty, Jeff, threatening me. I'm not harping and I'm not digging at you."

"I tell you, I can feel it."

"It's perfectly natural for me to think about your first sessions with Dr. Dudley—"

"Think as much as you want. Only let me alone."

"If you turn on me that way, I can't talk to you at all."

"Then don't." He shoved back from the table, muttered good night and left the restaurant.

She sat on, half sick under the assault. Agitation stirred within her, the same agitation that had so often wracked her during their fearful quarrels of summer. Quarrels whose ferocity she could for the first time begin to understand on a new level. In theory new insight brought surcease but this new insight seemed to bring only a heightened apprehension.

She walked home. The city was at its best in October, swept by winds that seemed brisk and clean, and usually she enjoyed these cool tart evenings, but tonight she walked heavily, as if she were plodding along under a stifling heat wave, sapped of energy. She tried to forgive Jeff his attack, but it was too soon. She could not make herself into a fatuous mother who accepted any mistreatment from a child; all the children knew that there were limits beyond which they could not go, and limits beyond which she would not go. If there was soundness in her relationship with them, it was rooted in that double knowing. But what if Jeff's own anguish were to make him oblivious to the anguish he might cause in others who loved him?

When she got home, Ken was still absent. If only they could talk about this as they used to talk. It might come, but that too would take time. The strangulated hoarseness would go and he would be Ken again, but for now she felt as alone as if she were widowed and bringing up Jeff by herself. There was constant constraint in Ken now, as if he were holding himself immobile.

When at last he arrived, it was past ten. He had had something to eat, yes, he wasn't hungry. But he was feeling pretty bushed and he might go straight to bed. She said nothing to dissuade him, watching him go in a sort of defeat she rarely knew. In a few minutes he returned, already in his pajamas.

"Tessa, don't be annoyed, but I've decided to go out early tomorrow."

"Oh, don't do that, dear. You can't keep avoiding him."

"I can't manage it yet. I've been thinking about that, and so far I simply can't manage it."

"But you've got to give the analysis time. You've got to give *him* time."

"I know. I agree with you."

"It might turn out not to be true, or it may be temporary, or curable."

"It's true," he said, his voice inert. "He knows it's true or he never would have written that letter."

"Even if it is, it could change. And even if it didn't change, you can't be out every time he comes home. Oh, Ken, that would be like throwing him out of your life."

"Don't think too far ahead. I'm trying to manage this for now, only for now, and for now I just can't face him."

"You'd face him if it were anything else. You'd want to help him."

"But it isn't anything else."

"Even if it were incurable, if it were leukemia or cancer—"

"There's no disgrace to cancer."

She flinched. "That's a brutal thing to say. You sound as if you'd rather he had cancer."

"I shouldn't have said that," he conceded. "Of course I didn't mean it. But you can't imagine what it's like for a man to think his son might be a queer."

"I can't imagine."

"I shouldn't have said that either." He put his hand out as if he would touch her arm, and then let it fall. He looked exhausted and her heart softened. The old saying about women being able to stand physical pain better than men—perhaps it was true about other kinds of pain. She did not have that beaten look of exhaustion, she was sure. A surface comment only, but sympathy for him surged in her for his white face, for the way he sank back into his chair, closing his eyes.

Behind his lowered lids Ken wondered again why this was so unbearable. He had perhaps loved Jeff with too much of a vested interest in the future he would be sure to have, and now felt too much apprehension that there might be no future at all. He had never believed that anything about the young and their sex life could trouble him; he knew perfectly well that youth had to experiment and would experiment with all sorts of sexual activity. He suddenly remembered that hot summer night long ago in Vermont, when Jimmy Neidham had stayed overnight because Mrs. Neidham was having a baby. They had slept in the same bed and they had embarked on a whole tangled exploration of "dirty things" and it had been fiercely exciting and wicked and he had been sure that all the damnation of hellfire would descend on him, but he had gone ahead anyhow. Of course, he had been only ten or so, and Jimmy about the same. By the time he was Jeff's age that had been long forgotten, with life's concentration transferred to girls, in the mawkish way of the other boys in Manchester, prurient in thought and prim in actuality, as if they were their own puritan ancestors.

They had all changed, and yet here he was so certain that his own son would not change. Why that certainty? Families were different when he was growing up in Vermont—perhaps that was why. Tessa and he never had believed in "being strict," the way his own mother and father had believed in it, strict about what was right, what was wrong, what God frowned on, what was sinful.

No, he thought, don't take that phony line of blaming yourself and Tessa. There is so much of it these days, blaming yourself for anything that goes wrong with children. It's always the broken home or the permissive home or poverty or society. Don't some things simply happen, like an earthquake, a hurricane, any natural catastrophe?

Another kind of phoniness would be his putting on an act with Jeff. It wasn't in him. He could not put on a show of naturalness, not yet in any case, and it was better to recognize that inability than to ignore it and then—God knows what. If he were ever once to let loose to Jeff about how he actually did feel, he would only make things worse. Worse for Jeff, worse for Tessa, and as for him, he would be painting himself into a corner forever, the corner of a man who professed never to judge lest he be judged, but who was in fact shaken by revulsion that anybody of his blood and bone might have sexual connection with somebody of the same sex.

* * *

Tessa awoke early next morning, but Ken had already left. It was noon before Jeff appeared, offering his usual "Hi," but managing to give it an overlay of apology. She never failed to recognize his contrition, however unexpressed, after a bad time between them. It was hard for anybody, even the fully mature, to find words that said, "I am filled with remorse, forgive me," and for anybody of seventeen doubly hard. This time Jeff added, "Olivier was terrific, you've got to go see the movie," and in the private code of his relationship to her, this translated into a rueful acknowledgment that he wished he could undo what had happened, that he asked her not to hold it against him.

"I've heard it's the best film he's done," she said. "Dad and I will get to it the minute we can." She spoke in her ordinary voice, but she knew that he also was reading a coded message in her words, that she did understand, and that she loved him. From the dining room, she could follow every step of his preparations of breakfast, which he was getting for himself in the kitchen. The metallic zing was the toaster as he plunged down the lever, that dry rattle was corn flakes filling a large bowl, the soft susurrus was sugar sifting over it, and the crisp snap was the opening of the milk carton to form a spout. They were comfortable sounds, the sounds of home, of a family, and for a fleeting moment she was content.

Jeff appeared again, all his dishes precariously perched one atop the other on his arm, like a practiced waiter in a beanery. "Boy, am I starved," he said, setting everything on the table. "Oh hey, the orange juice."

Again she could interpret the sounds in the kitchen, the slap of the refrigerator door, the clink of the spoon with which he stirred the juice she had squeezed from fresh oranges hours before. Why did the pulpy thickness rise, leaving a thin golden fluid underneath, if you let juice stand? Why didn't it do the opposite, and have the heavier part sink, according to all the laws of physics?

"You smart fellow," she said, "I have a question in physics to ask you." The code again: we are at peace.

"About the movie," he said almost simultaneously, reappearing with his glass half emptied. "I'm not going to tell you enough to spoil it for you, but it sure is different from anything he's ever done before."

He began with alacrity and she sat back to listen. The physics question could wait; he evidently had not heard it. He was almost at once caught up in his recital, telling far more than he meant to, the way children always told plots of books or movies. Selectivity, she thought, comes only with boredom; in the teens, not even the tritest scene is tedious, and apparently this film of a fading third-rate vaudeville entertainer was anything but trite, with Olivier playing it.

"Dad will want to see it as much as I do," she said when he finally ended. "We haven't seen a good movie in months."

Jeff suddenly looked around, looked through the doors into the living room. "Is he asleep or what?"

"He's out. He left before I was up."

"Is he going to be back this afternoon?"

"He didn't say exactly."

"For dinner tonight?"

"Jeff, I haven't the vaguest. He said he'd have to be out today. That was last night, and I, well, I suppose I thought I'd see him at breakfast, so I didn't pin him down."

For a moment he stared at her, his expression darkening. "He can't look me in the face, is that it?"

Her heart seemed to stumble. It was the Jeff of the night before. His voice roughened, his face went tight, went into hiding, and again she felt that she could see his boyhood going away, draining out of him.

"Jeff, dear," she said. "He's not himself yet, even though he seems to be over the stroke. So maybe he can't handle—maybe it's best if he doesn't get too involved with this now."

"That's not why he's out. That's not why he didn't eat with us last night. He's going to give me the silent treatment, like that time about the boat."

Instantly she saw the small sailboat again, Pete's boat *Finch*, coming in after the storm with Jeff looking so untroubled and Pete equally free of concern. Summer a year ago that had been, in Connecticut, and both boys out on the Sound when the storm struck, the whole coast attacked by the roar of the sudden wind and the crack of thunder through the summer skies. Radio news all at once gave way to small-craft warnings about gale velocities. They were both good sailors, but they had announced their destination as Oyster Bay and had been gone long enough to be halfway across when the storm hit, nowhere near a safe cove or dock or harbor.

She and Ken had full confidence in their skill, but the unspoken worry, sharp enough while the storm was still raging, had grown for some perverse reason after it was over, grown with the reappearance of sun and fair sky, grown with the silence that extended long past the time when they could have reached shore, could have telephoned to say, "We're all right."

Nothing. Quarter hour by quarter hour and still nothing. It was Ken who finally called Pete's parents to ask if they had had any word, Ken who had then phoned the Coast Guard to ask about sailboats in trouble during the storm. And when the response was yes, that two boats had capsized in the open Sound, with a search still going on, it was Ken who had asked the impossible question, "Any deaths reported?"

Three more hours had gone, the question still officially unanswered, and then in the waning afternoon *Finch* had appeared at the little dock, and Jeff and Pete, happy and untroubled, had greeted the crowd gathered at the small marina, the four parents and others in the two families, as well as neighbors and friends.

She had flown to Jeff and hugged him, as Pete's parents had gone to Pete. There were the explanations, so simple that the anxious crowd ashore felt like simpletons: That morning at the marina, they'd been warned of a possible squall, had changed their route and sailed south, along the shore, down to the Norwalk Yacht Club, thinking they'd meet up with two fellows from school there and have a swim and their lunch until the storm situation showed more definitely.

"And when it did hit, you never thought of phoning home?" Ken asked. His voice was unemphatic.

"It just never occurred to me," Jeff said.

"Me either," Pete put in.

Ken had remained silent, perfectly polite, drifting into the background while others took over the questioning. Tessa had seen that Ken was no longer listening to the rest of their recital, how they had sat out the storm in the luxury of the club, their boat safely moored, the huge storm a theatrical scene staged for their amusement. Then Ken had departed alone, had gone home alone, had gone to his room, and remained there. He had appeared for dinner, but at the table he was detached and quiet. "I have a headache," he had soon said, and had gone back to his room.

His silence finally became more punitive than a shouted scolding could have been. She could see that Jeff was not only uncomfortable but furious. In the end, there had been a raging fight, not between Jeff and his father but between Jeff and her, she defending Ken, Jeff attacking.

"It's his way, Jeff," she had cried out. "He does go silent when he is upset. He was brought up that way."

"It's the oldest cheapest trick in the world—'giving somebody the business' is what it's called."

"It's not cheap. And it's better than giving way to temper the way I do and you do."

"My God, I feel like some old criminal."

"It was a pretty bad time you gave us. You might be a little more contrite about how he took it."

"You didn't take it that way."

"Jeff, people are different."

"I'll say they're different."

He had stared at her pugnaciously, and now again he was staring at her as if whatever guilt there was lay with her. "That's why he was out last night," he repeated, "and that's why he's taken a powder today. Give him the business. The silent treatment. Well, just let him."

"He needs a little time, that's all. You ought to see that and give him a little room."

"What the hell for? What business is it of his anyway? It's not *his* life, it's mine. It's not his trouble, it's mine."

"But, Jeff, it's also his. It's also mine."

"Parents think they're just naturally into everything. They think they own your whole life and everything you do is to their credit or not to their credit. It gets me sick."

"That's unfair. Neither Dad or I have ever gone in for that stuff about living through our children, and you know it."

"That's a good one." He laughed, an artificial raucous laugh. "Every damn time one of us got a prize at school, you'd glow like a lamp, as if it was *you* getting the prize. Every time one of us got in a jam, you'd look like it was *you* in trouble, as if we'd stabbed you in the back. All my life I've had both of you on my back every minute, every day. We all did. Ask Don. Ask Margie."

She was astounded. The sudden attack, the injustice, the sense that it was absurd to argue—all this kept her silent. Twenty-five years ago when Don was a baby, she and Ken had pledged to each other that they would never live vicariously through their children, had promised never even to suggest that a child follow in their footsteps, in the smallest thing or the largest. Never would Don feel prodded to go to Dartmouth because his father and grandfather had gone to Dartmouth; never would any daughter feel slated for Radcliffe because her mother had gone to Radcliffe. Consistently through the years, they had each checked up on every impulse of "guidance," in their wariness over "parentship" they had often been too self-conscious about visible control or discipline, also worrying about being too permissive long before the word became the tag for any kind of parental abdication.

"That's not fair," she said again. "We felt pride or worry but we were never on your back. Nor on Don's. Nor on Margie's. You're lashing out with accusations, and that's not fair either."

His voice rose to a shout. "Fuck fair. What's fair anyway?" He shoved all his dishes violently from him, toward the center of the table. The glass toppled; milk poured forth. Instinctively she slapped her napkin down to blot it up, only to have him tear the napkin up from the table.

"Leave it alone," he shouted. "Leave me alone. I'll fix it. I'm not a baby you've got to clean up after."

She stood up waiting for a moment for some change in him. Then she took up the morning paper and left the room. Behind her he yelled, "You running out too, like him? Can't stand it unless I kowtow to you every minute, can you?"

She sat on her bed behind a closed door. She could not stanch her tears, tears she hated. He was lashing out because he was lashed. Soon she heard inexplicable bangings and pullings from his room, as if he were moving furniture there. She considered going in to him, but she did not. Once this stage was reached, there was nothing for it but separateness and waiting. She turned on her bedside radio for music but she could not sustain three notes in sequence. She twirled the dial for news, but the words held no meaning. She picked up the one manuscript still unread of the three that had been there a fortnight ago, but she gazed at it as if in a stupor.

At last silence descended upon the apartment. Tentatively she opened her door an inch. Jeff's door was closed, but from behind it there was no sound. She left her own door open, and sat down in a small swivel chair by the window, where by craning a little

she could see the dusty yellows and golds of the trees in Central
Park. Fall in the city was never the clear flaming of the country;
it was as if the dust of August had lingered on through the turning
of the leaves, to mute their flare of crimson and gold. Muted, the
way she felt now.

The silence remained. A sense of emptiness now came to her
from the entire house; this stillness was too complete to be merely
stillness. Jeff too had gone out. With a rising dread she went back
to the living room. Beyond it she could see the small dining room,
its table cleared and put to order. In the kitchen all was tidy, the
dishes out of sight in the dishwasher. Taped to one of the cup-
board doors was a note.

"I've gone back to school. Sorry. J."

* * *

He couldn't look me in the face, Jeff thought, damn it, I'll show
him. All the way back on the train he felt the hate hammering at
him, pounding at him, hotter and bigger all the time. He'd never
go home at all if the old man was going to give him that. The business. The silent treatment. The cheapest trick in the world.

There was no train direct to Placquette on Sunday afternoon;
he had caught this one to New Haven. In Grand Central, he had
actually gone to a phone booth to call Dr. Dudley and ask for a
special visit, but something had held him back. "Anytime you feel
the need for an extra visit, Jeff," the doctor had told him, "any
evening, any weekend, whenever there's any emergency, just call
me and I'll do my best to make extra time." Now as the train began to slow down at the end of the trip, he considered it again,
but once more there was something repugnant in the idea. "I'm
no baby you've got to clean up after." He could still feel the way
he had yanked the napkin away from his mother at the table.
Rushing to Dr. Dudley for help on a Sunday afternoon would
make him feel the same way.

But he couldn't get out of that train and meekly take the first
bus back to school either. Just before New Haven it began to rain,
and by the time he was walking away from the station, the sky was
nearly black. He felt just like that, a blackness flowing through
him. He wished he had his bike and could ride the ten miles
through the drubbing rain all the way to school. He needed action

or he would explode. He felt choked on the blackness, as if it were not only in his veins but in his throat, clogged and sticky. A dog ran by him and he thought of the choke collar and that poor bastard hanging from that tree.

He reached his bus corner, saw a bus approaching, but suddenly he turned away from it, almost spun around and started to walk rapidly back toward the center of the city. He couldn't face school, not yet. He had to go somewhere, see a movie maybe, anything to climb back up to where things felt ordinary again. Not happy, not cheerful and great, just ordinary and free of this rage and misery.

Tomorrow on his regular visit, Dr. Dudley would probably tell him that all this was valuable material. He was always talking about new material, useful material, as if he, Jeff, were being measured off like yards of cloth from a bolt of goods. The whole analysis so far was like that, a measuring, a ticking off, a prying and digging, and all of it a confessional to the priest seated behind your head. A priest that every once in a while showed you scientific models of male genitalia and female genitalia and talked up the wonders of nature's intention and the instinctive joy and satisfaction waiting ahead for you.

God, those plastic models.

The sleety rain increased further; wet needles pricked at his face and he looked about him for shelter. Ahead of him was a sign blinking feebly in the light. Grymin's Café—he hadn't realized he had walked far enough to have reached it. Gremlin's, the fellows called it, and it was more of an eatery than a café or bar. He might get something to eat, though he was in training. But one of the guys from school might be in there, ready to talk his ear off.

He was really spooked up, thinking there'd be somebody from school. He was spooked up all the time now, about a hundred things, and once the blackness hit him, it was a million things. He flung himself at the door.

There was nobody he knew. The place was empty except for a cop sitting on the first stool at the counter, just inside the entrance, and down at the far end a guy in chinos and a black sweater, thick with cable stitches. He took a stool about halfway between them, ordered a hamburger and a bottle of beer. He'll ask for proof I'm eighteen, he thought, and said, "Make it a Coke instead." At this, the cop looked over at him lazily, noticing him for the first time, and Jeff flushed. He was getting to be so uptight he was doing everything wrong. The cop wouldn't have given him a glance if he had let the beer order stand; he was forever worrying too much, as if he expected to be found out for God knows what.

The hamburger came and he stared down at it; he wasn't hungry after all. He drank the Coke slowly, and sat there.

"Anything wrong with it?" the man behind the counter asked, eying the hamburger.

"Any rush about my eating it?"

"You looking for a fight or something?"

Jeff shook his head and sat on, looking ahead. The mirror opposite him was of blue glass; in it he looked as if he were half sick. Well, he was. He finished his Coke, stood up, and reached for money. Halfway to his pocket his hand stopped; if he left, he'd have to go back to that corner where you got the bus to Placquette, be marooned in it, unable to move. He sat down once more, ordering a cup of coffee. The cop was glancing at him again, and in the mirror he saw that the guy in the cable sweater was watching too. He shrugged at the mirror as if to tell them both they could stuff it.

The coffee smelled good, and he poured sugar in it from the sifter. At his left he heard the guy in the cables say something, but he didn't look up or turn toward him to see if it was to him he was speaking. A moment later the words were repeated.

"You a Yalie?"

It flattered him. "No, are you?" His answer surprised him, it sounded easy and cheerful, and he turned his head toward the speaker as if he were in the mood to talk with people. He saw at once that he was a shade too old to be at Yale, but he had that look or maybe the voice or outfit that said college somewhere.

"I couldn't hack it," the other answered. "I cut out after sophomore year."

"No more student exemption?"

"I'm okay anyway. I've got a trick knee."

He said this with such satisfaction that Jeff grinned, as if he had boasted about having some special talent. The ex-Yalie paid his check, came back to leave a quarter tip, and then nodded at him as he left the café. Jeff nodded back, somehow cheered by the brief exchange. A moment of friendship. Well, companionship then.

He finished his coffee slowly, left a quarter tip himself, paid the check, again told the café owner there was nothing wrong with the hamburger, still untouched on the plate, and went outside.

There on the sidewalk was the guy in chinos and cables. "Well, hi," Jeff said in surprise. The sleety rain had changed to plain rain, the afternoon light had shifted to a flat even gray.

"Where you off to?" the other said. "Need a lift?" He pointed to a station wagon halfway up the block. "I'm through work for the day, and I don't have to check out for a while."

Jeff was staring at the station wagon. "Boy, that's nifty. I've always gone ape over cars." The wagon was obviously new, gleaming in the rain, one of those styles that looked as if they were made of wood. "Through work on a Sunday? What kind of work?" He was still staring at the car. Again his voice surprised him; he sounded like anybody else, sounded the way he did when everything was all right.

"In a medical lab. They run blood tests for doctors, pap smears, VD, that kind of stuff. I'm a trainee for lab assistant, but I also do pickups and deliveries, so alternate weekends is all I get."

"Were you a premed at school?"

"Nothing like. I was straight art and all that bullshit."

They both laughed, and again to Jeff's surprise, they began to move toward the station wagon. An instant longing to ride in it, maybe even to drive it, stirred in him; his spirits rose, this time really rose. With the connivance of his brother Don, he had learned to drive when he was twelve, and being at the wheel always gave him some fantastic sense of being in charge of the whole damn universe.

"That sure is one neat wagon," he said, brushing his fingers over the hood, looking down its whole expanse. Behind the driver's seat was another seat for passengers, but behind that stretched an empty deck with nothing but a few small packages ranged at one side. "Are you going toward Placquette by any chance?"

"That's not much of a lift. We have a couple of medical clients thataway. My name's Hank." He opened the door on the driver's side.

"Mine's Jeff Lynn." He went around to the other door and got in. The smell of the leather was so new he looked at the odometer.

Sure enough, only eight hundred miles. Maybe the smart thing to do next summer was to stay away from the office-boy job he'd had last year and find a job out of town somewhere, this sort of job, driving a good-looking rig like this. He'd be eighteen by then and have a real license instead of a learner's permit.

"Are you in a rush to get to Placquette?" Hank asked. "I'm sort of gone on this wagon too, and we might take off for a spin for a while. I think the weather's clearing."

"No special rush." A sweep of warning went along his nerves as if a thin current of electricity were charging a battery buried deep within him. There was an excitement to it, though, a sense of adventure, maybe even danger.

At the next corner Hank turned off the road that would take them toward Placquette and drove along in a careless zigzag of streets that took them away from the city and yet kept them clear of the highway.

They rode in silence. Soon the rain began with renewed fury and Hank reached out a hand to click on the windshield wipers. Something about the curve of his arm made Jeff remember Hal Jarvis, and there was a leap in his loins and in the same instant he knew why he was there, why Hank wanted him there, knew that he could do nothing but what he was doing. He heard his own breath draw in hard, and in the next second felt Hank's right hand drift along on his thigh, loose, easy.

His breath drew in tighter and his whole body seemed to expand. He said nothing. Hank removed his hand and the car turned gently around a corner. The rain came down in fluted sheets, as if it were a curtain across the window of life itself. They were on a country lane now, at the outskirts of a village. The car was stopping.

"Let's wait this rain out a bit," Hank said, glancing over his shoulder into the rear of the wagon.

Jeff glanced back too, then sharply away. "No. I've got to get back."

"Come on," Hank said.

"I can't."

"It's all right. Who's going to stop you?"

Jeff didn't answer. He didn't move. His mind did not move. He seemed anchored deep so that he could not get adrift, yet he

felt at the same time caught and tossed by wave upon wave of
need, of curiosity, of insistence. A car door thumped; Hank was
no longer at the wheel. Behind him, from the inside of the station
wagon, Hank said in a new urgency, "It's what you want, man.
Come on."

Jeff opened his door. Never was he clear, later, how he went
back there, but never could he forget that driving necessity that
propelled him onward. He had to or he would die. It was all happening in a great swooping free fall, irreversible, free of decision,
in the full pull of gravity toward whatever was to be.

* * *

That night around midnight he tore out of his sleep, hit by a
swoop of depression in an impact so palpable it might have been
the thud of a great heavy body, smashing you to the ground, grinding the breath out of you, leaving you stunned and fighting to
shake the film from your eyes so you could focus again. It was
worse than anything he had ever felt. He'd be better off dead.

He thought again of Mick Munson and his twin brother, Rex.
Rex was a senior too, but he went to Hotchkiss instead of Placquette, because his family believed that twins should find their
own identity. And one day last spring Rex had hanged himself off
a high branch in the woods near Hotchkiss and nobody knew why.
The suicide was written up in detail in all the New Haven papers
and even in *The New York Times* because Mr. Munson was a big
banker type in Hartford with connections in Washington. All the
fellows in Mick's class had met Rex, and they kept talking about
it day after day, falling silent only when Mick got back after the
funeral. Nobody could understand any part of it because the Mun-
sons led a life where everything was desirable, everything any guy
could want, with a second house in Florida—with their own boat,
maybe an actual yacht—with a private tennis court not only in
the South but also up at their house in Hartford. The papers all
said there had been "no known romantic disappointments" in
Rex's life, and the fellows at Placquette said that Mick's brother
was good-looking, got good grades, had never needed a shrink,
nothing like it.

And then he had gone out to those woods near his school and
climbed up that tree, and rigged up a careful contraption of his

own leather belt and his dog's choke collar of steel chain and he had hanged himself. And nobody knew why.

Well, he knew why. He bet he knew why. Even last spring, when it first happened, he was pretty damn sure he knew why, but now tonight, after this with Hank, he was ten times surer he knew why. Maybe Mick Munson didn't know about his own twin brother, maybe the big banker didn't know about his own son, but there had to be a reason that drove him to that tree, and now he'd be willing to lay down his own life that he knew exactly what that reason was.

If only he had never gone near that station wagon. If only he had told Hank to go to hell, if he had got out, walked off in all the rain. Oh, God, if he had only hated it.

He sprang up from bed, and then stopped short. From across the room came Pete's even breathing. He had to be careful. If he went storming around and woke Pete up, Pete might read in his face that something horrible had happened, and worm it all out of him. He always felt he had to tell somebody, not just Dr. Dudley, but somebody real. If you kept everything locked up forever—

A vision of Mick Munson's brother swinging from that tree loomed up and he shuddered. The most awful part was that choke chain he had used, slipping his belt through the handle of it, buckling his belt tight around the limb of the tree, and then slipping the loop around his own neck. Choke collars were what you used to train or control vicious dogs; the more they pulled at the leash, the tighter the noose went around their necks, strangling them into obedience.

But Rex Munson wasn't any vicious dog. He was a smart goodlooking kid of eighteen, with everything going for him, everything right, everything anybody knew about. And nobody was allowed to have their dogs with them in their dormitories at school, so he must have brought the choke collar back to school with him purposely, the last time he had been home in that big place in Hartford.

The poor son of a bitch, he thought. The poor lonely son of a bitch. He couldn't tell anybody either.

CHAPTER SIX

Morning after morning Tessa awoke convinced that today would be the day Jeff would call and say, no matter how elliptically, how discreetly coded, that he wished he had not yelled at her, wished that he had not slammed off back to school. Each time she stooped at the front door for the morning mail, she looked for his writing, young in itself, with its quirky mixture of printed and cursive calligraphy. Nothing. Day by day nothing.

And then suddenly one afternoon in November, in the middle of a session of editing with Helena Ludwig, in the middle of a sentence about managing a flashback in an important part of Helena's new novel, another sentence shaped itself firmly in Tessa's mind. "He won't do anything at all. He won't come home for Thanksgiving or even Christmas."

This stopped all processes of thought about the manuscript before her, and about the young novelist waiting for her to round out the point she had been making. She saw Helena glance at her inquiringly, and she nodded as if to say, "Yes, give me a minute and I will go on with this point of technique." But all she could think was, He won't write, he won't telephone, he won't be home at all, not even for the holidays. Not home for Thanksgiving, for Christmas? Impossible.

Thanksgiving, Christmas, birthdays, all were special days to Jeff and the whole family, perhaps because they had always been so important to her. When she was a child, all holidays were made much of by her own parents, were reasons for reunions with all

Sachs and Neufeldt cousins, for gifts, for visits and celebrating. Even Christmas, which her no-religion parents diminished by terming it a sort of folk festival, a slightly more elaborate Thanksgiving or Fourth of July, was in fact always a prolonged gala, planned and whispered about beforehand, engendering a delicious mounting of excitement and cupidity in her and in her brother Will, originally Wilhelm and never Bill.

Occasionally, when they were grown, Will and she had discussed the peculiar ardor of holidays in the Sachs household, and had agreed that "ardor" was a good word for it, and that the heated fervor might well have been begotten in the agnosticism of their parents and their fear of robbing their children of the securities of conformity. Apparently Will and she had each absorbed that same fervor; certainly they had each heightened all holidays in their own marriages, and though Will and Amy lived in Phoenix, there was still a vast to-do, by long distance, about what everybody wanted and what the children's sizes were, and what were the records and books and toys and hobbies that had to be sought for and transmitted in plenty of time. The only exception had been that first Christmas after Roddy.

Tessa sighed. Christmas was too far ahead to worry about, of course, but Thanksgiving was only two weeks off. Margie and Nate, Don and Jenny, Jenny's parents, the grandchildren, Ken's old mother—all gathered there together, but no Jeff. No little story could be fobbed off about his being in the school infirmary with the flu, no little fib about his visiting friends.

"This flashback," Helena Ludwig finally said. "Are you still trying to figure out some way I can avoid it altogether, or just trying to explain how I could make it work better?"

"Oh, Helena, I'm so sorry." The office suddenly seemed overheated and close. "I wasn't even thinking about the flashback. I was suddenly caught up in a private train of thought, it has nothing to do with your scene at all, and I do apologize to you."

"But the scene must be wrong or you wouldn't have had that private train of thought."

"In general that's right, but not this one time." She looked contrite and felt contrite. Such a lapse of attention would upset any author, especially a young author like Helena Ludwig, who had too much uncertainty about her own work as it was.

"Then how could I rewrite it, do you think?" Helena liked Theresa Lynn, liked working with her on this her second novel, and had never before seen her this tense. It had never occurred to her that Mrs. Lynn might have private tensions, the same kind that she, Helena, so often had, the kind that drove her to the catharsis of writing. Or if not the same kind, then another kind, yet related. All pain was cousin to all other pain, all unhappiness cousin to all other unhappiness. She glanced again at the editor. Tessa Lynn must be in her middle forties, what with her married children, yet she looked years younger. She was pretty but Helena was pretty herself—no envy there. What she did envy was Tessa Lynn's being so small and being so slim. To anybody like herself, five-eleven in height, thirty pounds overweight, Tessa Lynn was a living rebuke, yet from their first meeting they had been drawn to each other like good workmen on a hard project.

"Should we put this off till you feel better, Mrs. Lynn?" she asked. "We could make another date. You mustn't feel forced to go on."

"I'd rather we went on. The point I was raising here, before that detour of mine, was that it's such a central scene that I wondered why you wanted it in flashback, a week after it happens in time. I think it would be even stronger if it happened *for* the reader, you know, if you showed it as it actually happened."

"I don't know why I did it the other way," Helena said. She picked up two or three pages of her manuscript and began to read. Suddenly she squeezed her eyelids shut and turned away, so that she no longer faced Tessa. "Maybe it's easier for me to look back on it, even in the book, than to relive it, as if it were freshly happening."

"Yes, it could be that."

"Not that it's exactly autobiographical. But it always is partly, isn't it? Maybe I just couldn't manage it face to face, even at the typewriter."

"I think that's very perceptive," Tessa said quietly. "I have things like that too, everybody does, not only novelists. Maybe this scene should stay the way it is."

"I'd like to think about it. I want this part to be right."

"Think about it for a few days, or better yet, don't think about it, let it get thought about in your unconscious; that's where you

do your best work, after all. Maybe you'll want to try it another
way, maybe you'll say, 'Stet,' and tell me to go jump."

"You know the way I usually rush to make any change you
suggest."

"Someday you won't rush to, and that will mean progress on
all fronts." Tessa consulted a sheet of notes on her desk. "There's
one more scene, here it is, the opening of Part Two, page 184."

"I'm worried about that too," Helena put in nervously. "It must
be way off if both of us think there's something the matter with
it."

"But I don't. I find it so good that I wondered if you might stay
with it a little longer, expand the way Paul faces the fact that love
can be a tyranny as well as a blessing."

"How marvelous that you like it. I worried about it so much and
rewrote it so often, I've gone dead on it. At the beginning I did
think it was a good scene, but then I, well, you know the way
doubt hits you. Hits *me*."

"Hits me too." She thought of Ken and added, "Most of us, in
fact." Ken still remained largely silent about Jeff, as if he were
filled with doubt about how she would receive any words and feelings he might offer. She made several attempts to talk about Jeff,
but once he had congealed with unwillingness, and on another
occasion had only said, "Please, let's leave it."

Aloud she said to Helena, "If you've already rewritten Paul a
lot, it could be the old diminishing returns to go at it once again."

"I'll think and not think." Helena sounded relieved, even happy,
and the rest of the session was a concentrate of concern for the
manuscript, so that by the time she rose to go, she was confident
again, sure that she could make the changes she meant to make.

Tessa escorted her out to the bank of elevators, something she
had never done before with Helena, and as she returned alone
down the long corridor to her office she thought, That was
penance.

*   *   *

As the days fell away toward Thanksgiving, her anxiety grew, teth-
ered and balked while she was actively at work, but always there,
crouched and waiting for release, ready to pounce on her mind
the moment it idled.

On Friday preceding the holiday week, she turned to Ken as soon as he came in from the office. "We have to talk about next Thursday. There's just no way to ignore it any longer."

He fixed himself a drink and flung himself into a large armchair. The loose sprawl of his long legs reminded her of Jeff; she had never noted before how alike father and son were in this gesture. It touched her. Her voice softened and she said, "I think so often, Ken, of what you've been going through."

He lowered his head, eyes closed, his palm raised to stop her. He was tired, bereft of energy. For all the boyish sprawl, he looked old, as if he could no longer summon up the vigor and strength to combat this assailant, knowledge.

She went to the bar table, poured dry vermouth over ice cubes in a wide squat glass, and made circles with the glass to chill the drink. The sound of the ice against the crystal—how lighthearted it was. This was the sound of friends and laughter, of people at a party, of people in love and privacy. A nameless yearning awoke in her, to be happy again, to be eager for an evening, to be raising a glass in a moment of congratulation or joy. "Let's find our own way to feel more cheerful, darling," she said without looking at him. "Let's both of us try to."

He looked up. "You know I'd like that."

"Maybe we could declare a moratorium for a little while. On everything serious."

"If people could declare respite at will, they'd be lucky."

"Yes, they would." She thought of Jeff stretched out on that couch she had seen in Dr. Dudley's office, saw his fair head on that stuffed bolster at the end of it, saw him talking up at the ceiling, talking of his young misery and fear. Jeff couldn't declare any moratorium, not yet, not for now, not for a long time, perhaps for a terrible stretch of time. If there were to be any respite for him, surely his own father and mother ought to be the ones to offer it. Aloud she said, "Let's try it, Ken? For a few days over the holiday?"

He leaned forward, toward her, his face taut. "Don't you realize I've been thinking about Thanksgiving too? I've been knocking myself out, just thinking. The minute I turn my light out at night, it starts, the damn thinking and thinking and thinking."

"I know."

"It's not only at night. Every time somebody says the word 'fag' I want to hit him."

"I know," she repeated. "I can't bear the word either." She sounded equable, but thought, Imagine what happens to Jeff when he hears it. And someday when Don knows, when Margie knows, imagine how it will hit at them when they hear "fag" and "fairy" and "queer" and "nance," and think of their brother.

"So when I think of Jeff here for four days," Ken went on, "I wonder if I can make a go of it, and that's the long and short of it." He sounded almost gentle and she thought, He is adapting a little even though he doesn't know it. Don't insist, don't crowd him. Talk about him and you, not Jeff. It's easier for him when you don't talk about Jeff. My God, she thought, here I am, editing my own dialogue with my own husband in a scene about our son. She thought of Helena Ludwig and thought, She's not the only one who isn't sure.

"Anyway," Ken said then, "what makes you think he'll let it be a moratorium?"

"Maybe he won't. But I thought I might drive up this Sunday and ask him to try."

Ken said nothing and she wondered how best to put it to Jeff. There was need for care with him also. It's more than editing, she thought; it's all turned into diplomacy. We used to be a family, with the easy give-and-take of a family, but now it's as if each of us were negotiating on the most delicate of treaties, weighing each word.

She went to her own room to call Jeff, admonishing herself, Not a word about his not writing, not calling.

"It's me," she began, "with a good idea."

"What good idea?"

"I'd like to drive up to the Yellow Barn on Sunday, just me, and treat you to one of their big country dinners."

There was a moment when he did not speak. Then he said carefully, "You want to talk about am I coming home for Thursday."

"But not in any you-ought-to way. Nobody's going to get jammed up over this."

"Fat chance."

"A good chance. I mean it."

"Well, sure, I'll meet you at the Barn. What time do you think?"

"Around two, unless traffic is too rotten. And, Jeff, I really was leveling with you about not making any big deal about Thursday."

"If you can help it."

"I'll help it."

"Well, see you."

I'll have to help it, she thought as she hung up. Ken will have to help it too, when the time comes. If he's going to go on banishing Jeff from sight, he will end up by exiling him permanently. The word "exile" pierced her with dread. The one grief she could never absorb was the loss of a child and exile was loss as death was loss. Her brother Will and Amy had lost their son Roddy, a boy of twelve, drowned in a hideous vacation accident on the Colorado River, and though eight years had passed since then, she had never seen Will or Amy since without thinking, They're not over it yet. They would never be over it; all the remaining years of living would not be enough to heal them. So would it be for her, Tessa Lynn, if ever she were to lose one of her children. If Will and Amy, she suddenly thought, were given their choice, of having Roddy back but homosexual, how they would leap at the chance.

Life was all, life was central, everything else was tangential. Pain was tangential, regret, grief, remorse, fear. One's heart might fill with longing that such and such were not so, but if life continued despite it, one was still a victor. She imagined herself trying to confide in her brother about Jeff, heard how her voice would falter and thicken over the syllables of "homosexual," but she knew that Will's face would show only envy. But he's alive.

* * *

Just before she turned off the highway for Placquette, the gray of November skies lifted and the sun came out. She didn't believe in omens but her spirits lightened. The highways leading from the city were no longer ablaze with the brightness that she loved, a precarious brightness, for the first smashing November rain would hurl the gold and red and amber to the earth and strip the larches and maples and oaks to the ashy tones of early winter. But now as the sun came out, a fresh high wind swept the sky clear of cloud, and a piercing blue replaced it, a celebration of swift change and hope.

As she approached the country-house setting of the Yellow

Barn, she saw Jeff striding forward to meet her, and her heart spun with love and longing. This tall beautiful youth, this boy, this young man, was not doomed forever to suffer, he could not be foredoomed to anything. They called out in greeting and he played traffic cop, waving her around the wide front lawn to the vacant property at the side that had been turned into a parking lot.

"Jeff, you look grand."

"That's the way to talk. How was driving?"

"Easy. Almost no traffic." She looked at him and laughed again, wondering again if he could have grown taller. Impossible in five weeks, but he did look bigger. Despite the tweed jacket and proper tie prescribed for restaurant appearances, an athlete's muscularity was there, the fitness of a man in strict training, and a deeper resonance sounded in his voice, almost an authority. "Are you hungry?"

"You better believe it."

As they ordered, she asked about yesterday's game and with alacrity Jeff told her all about it, but it was he who at last nudged them back to the accepted reason for her visit. "About Thanksgiving," he said. "Let's get into that high grass."

He said this cheerfully, as if they were friends again, not problem solvers. He let a pause develop and then, without transition, said, "If I went to Yale next year, I wouldn't have to transfer from old Dudley and start all over someplace else with some other guy."

"Yale." It sounded as if she had never heard of anything called Yale.

"Would it make any difference?"

"Of course not. You sound as if it were already decided that you'll be continuing analysis past June."

"It isn't what you'd call 'decided.' But those things aren't rush jobs."

"I know they're not, but next June would be eight months, and I had half an idea—"

"Better skip the half ideas." He said it as if he were trying to ease it for her, but he wasn't thinking of her. It was Hank and the station wagon that had first told him he was nowhere near ending the analysis. It had been hell telling Dr. Dudley about it, it was still hell to remember it. "It's me who guesses it's going to keep on longer than June. That is, if you'll keep on too."

"I'll keep on, no matter how long it takes."

"It just doesn't go one, two, three, presto, change-o, you're cured."

"I know it doesn't." She thought about her next words. "Look, Jeff, you've helped me out about what to say about Thanksgiving and your coming home. Things don't go presto, change-o, for parents either. If we only could all allow a little leeway, a recess from problems."

"You mean leeway for Dad."

"For me and Dad."

"If he's going to give me that silent treatment."

"I'm asking you, Jeff, to make allowances for us, if we stumble around or—"

"Allowances for him!" He no longer sounded cheerful and her heart sank. "Give him leeway to adjust! I tell you it's not his life, it's my life."

"It's everybody's life, and we could all declare a moratorium on problems."

"You said you weren't going to make a big deal about it. You're putting it to me pretty hard, aren't you?"

"I didn't mean to, but okay, I'll quit. If you don't come down, I'll dream up some damn good fib for the family, you can count on a good one." Her voice was lighter. Beneath it she thought, All this ghastly hypocrisy. Leeway. Allowances. If we stumble. God, I'm as brave as a rabbit.

"Whatever fib you hit on," he said unexpectedly, "it would only set everybody speculating."

"It might." She shrugged. "Anyway, enough! What I drove up for, to say all this, is said, and seeing you is lovely. You really do look marvelous."

"Yeah. This was a great meal."

"Would you like to drive the car a bit before I start home?"

"Would I ever. Let's go." Good humor leaped alive in him and before they were through with the check and the tip, he said, "I might get a ride down Wednesday night sort of late." Again he thought of the station wagon and Hank and again he blocked the thought. He had never seen Hank again, never gone near "Gremlin's" again. The moment Hank let him off, half a mile from school, he realized he didn't know Hank's last name or the name of the firm he worked for. Hank had said nothing after it was over. It was he, Jeff, who had finally asked, "What made you wait outside the restaurant?"

"You looked low. I was low myself."

"Did you have any reason to think I'd go along with it?"

"No way. In fact, the opposite. But you can't win 'em all, so you try it on."

There had been some comfort in that, but for days afterward, every time he saw a station wagon he was stabbed with the fear that it would stop; each time it drove past he gulped with relief. It was days before it began to dawn on him that he might never see Hank again, that Hank might be one of those guys who wanted to be anonymous, wanted one-time shots, wanted never to see anybody a second time. He shuddered. That was even more degrading.

Now his mother said, "Is there any show or musical you want to see? I might get us some tickets for Friday or Saturday. Wait, maybe you'd rather go with Pete or somebody."

"Not Pete," he said quickly. "We've had a spot of—well, never mind, no sweat. Could you get tickets for *Toys in the Attic*, or is it too big a smash?"

"I can try."

"Gee, that would be great. So is this." He turned the key in the ignition, backed expertly, and then grinned at her as they drove off. They stayed away from the parkway, choosing country roads instead, Jeff glorying in the process of driving. He had learned to drive, as a kid, illicitly enough, and by the time he could be licit, he had become an expert, not only at the wheel but at repairing virtually anything that could go wrong with a car. Now he was so absorbed in his own pleasure at driving again that an answering pleasure arose in her.

Had Jeff told Pete? The hunger to talk of your deepest feeling to your best friend was a universal, to talk it out in your own language, on your own level, not to a parent, not to a doctor, but to a friend—it was vital. Often it was compulsive, a drive to share the hidden pressure and thus divide it or diminish it.

Jeff turned the car into a narrow pebbled road and the look of country deepened. "This could be Vermont," she said, "or Maine. What's it called?"

"Just a detour, but it's nice. In the winter we come here to ski."
He pointed ahead and she saw that they were approaching a crest,
beyond it nothing but sky, and a downhill slope that would make
a good ski run. "About those tickets for *Toys in the Attic*," he said
casually. "I wonder if Sue is going to be around. She might want
to see it."

"Sue? Suzy Wister?"

"That's the only Sue I know. Suzy, if you still call her that. She
hates it."

"I didn't know she did. I suppose she's around or will be for the
holiday."

"I thought I might ask her, and if she hasn't seen it, she'd probably want to, wouldn't you think?"

"I'd think yes." Careful, she thought, don't assume anything,
don't sound anything. Matter-of-factly she said, "If it's a dead sell-
out, have you a second choice I might try?"

"Nixville. Unless you know something else that's good."

They talked about plays but she scarcely knew what she was saying. An incredible emotion suffused her, one she dared not acknowledge, one she dared not let him suspect. She talked of a new
theater-ticket broker Tom Quales had mentioned at the last staff
meeting and was glad when they turned back toward Placquette.
They parted at the entrance drive to the school, Jeff saying, "This
was swell, the dinner and all," and she was glad to drive off alone,
uninhibited as to what she might think, free to speculate without
monitoring her expression or voice. She was impatient to be at
home again. There would be no need to tell Ken now that Jeff
might remain in analysis for another full year, nor any point in
bringing up his choice of Yale. But she knew she would mention
the tickets he wanted for *Toys in the Attic*, that Suzy Wister
would come into it, and that without making much of it, she would
somehow manage to let Ken know that taking Suzy was Jeff's own
idea.

* * *

Behind her, watching the car drive off, Jeff thought, Brother, why
didn't I think of that before? A swell way, easy, and perfectly fair
to Sue or anybody, just taking her to a theater, how could that be
anything but okay? A dart of gratitude to Dr. Dudley nicked him,

perhaps for the first time. It was the visit after the one about the station wagon, and Dr. Dudley still said nothing directly about that. But he had asked, a couple of times, whether he was dating any girls or whether he planned to. The doctor so rarely said anything positive that it had sounded almost like an order: Date a Girl. Date a Girl Soon. Remember the Wonders of Nature's Intentions—Jeff had expected the plastic models to appear next, but they didn't, and in his relief, he had been like a kid trying to be teacher's pet. He sure would give it a try, soon, really soon, uptight or not, he would go ahead and date a girl soon.

And now he was about to do just that. If he knew his mother, those tickets would be bought if she had to turn into Mrs. John D. Rockefeller to buy them. That was the sickening part of it, how she sort of lighted up when he asked. Oh, God, Parents.

Back in the dorm, he told Pete about their supposed falling out, so he could have the tickets for Sue instead, and Pete just lapped it up. You always had to say small things like that to parents, Pete said, to swing things the way they should go. And then he asked, "Who's this Sue anyway? She's one you never even mentioned, you old fox, so give."

And for once Jeff didn't have to grab wildly at bits and pieces. No Joanie or Gloria or Connie, just real talk about somebody he actually knew. He tossed it off, keeping it all cool and steady, but it was what she looked like and where she lived, what school she went to—it had a good ring of truth. That was something new, and he liked it. The idea had come in a flash the moment his mother got talking of a show, and now here he was, feeling great about telling Pete. Now Pete would mention it in front of a couple of guys, and the whole school would know. What's more, he couldn't wait for his next hour with Dr. Dudley.

* * *

Waiting on Thanksgiving eve was harder than Ken had imagined it. Jeff was due at about nine, and by eight there was a physical sensation of discomfort to contend with. Within his rib cage, everything seemed to be stiffening and turning, as if there were a great mass of dough there being kneaded, thumped and flipped over and kneaded once more by bony hands. When at last Jeff's key turned in the lock and he heard the inevitable "Hi" to Tessa, he called out "Hi" himself. To his astonishment, no sound came from his lips.

As Jeff came in, he tried it again and this time it was vocal. "Hi, Dad," Jeff answered, and they looked at each other. Ken was careful not to look strained, but inside, the stiffening dough seemed to be rising, crowding out air from his lungs, removing space in which his heart could beat freely. He stood motionless, waiting for air and space to return, and as Jeff turned to his mother and then headed for the kitchen, he began to feel easier.

A small victory arose in him, but with it a rising tide of warmth, not a pleasant warmth but the tight flush that meant a sharp climb of blood pressure. Alarm buzzed its warning at him and he sat down carefully, laying his head slowly against the high cushioned back of his wing chair and adjusting his breathing purposely to a slower rhythm. In, pause. Out, pause. In. Out. You are not going to let this break through somewhere in your brain. This is only about four minutes of time since he opened the front door and there are four whole days ahead. You owe it to Tessa, you owe it to him, to control what you feel. You also owe it to yourself.

For the hundredth time he wondered why he felt so hopeless about Jeff, why he could not share Tessa's optimism or trust or faith or whatever it was she seemed to feel. Clearly she had no inkling of the dangers that could beset any young homosexual, or any young man with a tendency or curiosity about being homosexual. She seemed never to have heard of the hustlers or cruisers who might accost him, in a park, at a movie, in a public toilet, seemed totally ignorant that a Vice Squad cop might seek to entrap him, beat him up, arrest him, even shoot him. It was unthinkable to ask her point-blank whether she knew of any of this; one new reason for his silences was this dread of blurting out any of it to her and enlarging the scope of her fear.

And so she knew nothing of these extra ingredients in his feelings. She did know that he was not one of those Bible-Belters who cried down fire and brimstone on all homosexuals; he could no more take the punch-in-the-jaw male attitude if one of them approached him than he could yell Commie at somebody who thought the Cold War was as much our fault as Russia's. And yet there was this stony lump lodged in his gut ever since the moment he had read the letter. Nothing would act as solvent for it, nothing could dislodge it. It's because I know Jeff, he thought now, I see him more clearly than Tessa does. I'm not blessed with her blindness.

The very thing he admired in his younger son, his will, his stubborn following of his own impulses, his refusal to be stampeded by the family or anybody else into professing interest in their causes—all this gave a strength to Jeff, but an inelasticity as well. He was not flexible, not easy to persuade or shift or detour from his chosen path. There were plenty of kids who might change and be influenced or analyzed out of a neurosis, but not Jeff. If he had come to his eighteenth year thinking he was a homosexual, the chances were all that he was a homosexual by nature, by inclination, by whatever mysterious compulsion made people homosexual. Medicine knew so damn little about it. He himself, of course, knew even less about it, but he knew Jeff.

Tessa had followed Jeff into the kitchen and he was glad to be alone. He needed respite and would continue to need it periodically for the whole four days. That excitement of Tessa's about Suzy Wister and the theater. She had paid a sharper's price for the tickets, as if some magic attached to *Toys in the Attic*, as if no second choice would serve to achieve the miracle that was to be achieved. That's what he envied in Tessa, her capacity to believe what she had to believe, to hope for what she had to hope for. He hadn't had the heart to tell her that homosexuals often took girls out in the hope of that same miracle, or, more cynically, in the hope of setting up an effective disguise for themselves in a heterosexual world.

He thought of Jeff and Suzy and the theater. Some people would think he ought to warn her, or at least her parents, but it was an impossibility. Even to think it was a betrayal of his own son, yet there it was, full-fledged, three-dimensional, not contrived, not put together bit by bit in some dementia of planning, but there in the round and therefore as legitimate as any other thought. To keep quiet, to stay loyal and silent, was to let the Wisters' young daughter get snared up in God knows what tragedy or farce, and it might ensnare Jeff too. He knew of such farces, had heard of them or read or found out about them in the rough commerce of men's talk and men's jokes.

Jeff appeared again, leaning against the kitchen door, looking for all the world like a son you could be proud of. What fearful things could be thrown at a man as life went on. Last year the stroke, this year this. If only it had been another stroke instead. Over that you could triumph.

"Do you want a snack, Ken?" Tessa had a tray of sandwiches and milk.

"How'd the season wind up, Jeff?" he said, taking a sandwich. "I missed out on a couple of scores."

"We're tied with Redfield Acad. The final game is a week from Saturday."

"Is it a home game?" Tessa asked. "I wish we could get up for it."

"Yeah, at home, but it will be December by then and probably freeze your butt off."

"We're not such softies."

Ken shook his head, which she understood to mean, "Better drop it," and she continued, "December! I wonder whether Margie's going to be early with that baby. She just might be closer than the official date."

"First babies are always unpredictable, aren't they?" Ken asked, a note of eagerness sounding, as if nothing mattered except being on hand for Margie's first labor pains.

Tessa thought, He's doing his best, and gratitude warmed her. Some old protective emotion awoke also, and all at once she felt split between the two of them, between the young one her son and the old one her husband. The words ran together as if each phrase made a single noun. The two sides of an equation, she thought, the x and the y. But they're not separate sides, not x and y. No matter what, they add up, we all add up. And what we add up to is a family.

CHAPTER SEVEN

Thanksgiving dinner was nearly over when it happened. Until it did, Tessa was wryly aware that it was easy to glaze over reality with the varnish of cliché, that from the moment they had all settled into their places, all twelve of them, they might have been the living models for another of Norman Rockwell's *Saturday Evening Post* covers of the happy family gathered to give thanks to the Lord for the bounty and delights the year had yielded. There it all was, the loving talk, the smiling faces, very young to very old, all eyes focused on the great glistening turkey, all appreciative as Ken made his first slash with the carving knife.

The two extra leaves in the oblong table had elongated it sufficiently to make room for Don and Jenny and their two youngsters and Jenny's father on one side, and for Nate and Margie and Jeff, as well as Jenny's mother and old Mrs. Lynn on the other side, with Ken at one end and herself at the other. Ken's mother, eighty last month, was the one survivor of the four grandparents who had been there so often for holiday dinners when their own children were small, and for one pensive moment Tessa visualized herself at eighty, sitting at some future festive table, the sole survivor of her own generation, and she found herself suddenly fervent with a new insight into Grandma Lynn's long silences, and with a private wish that she never would need to know them for herself.

Suddenly there seemed to be a fervency of another kind down at Ken's end of the table, with Nate leaning forward, talking past

Mrs. Lynn to Ken, as if to intensify what he had just said, with Margie nodding her agreement, and with Jeff, seated between the two, holding himself erect, stone still, listening. Ken's color had already risen to the hue she found alarming.

"But it was so damn ugly," Nate was saying to Ken, insisting on it as if he had already made the point but needed to press it further. "Like the roundup of so many cattle. And I couldn't even say so in my story. The Objectivity of the Press. God."

"What roundup, Nate?" Tessa asked. "I missed that."

"This police story I covered last night. About the cops raiding a bar in the Village and pulling in six men."

"Arresting them for what?" Tessa asked. But she knew and a knot tightened in her throat.

"For none of their goddamn business. The place is known as a homosexual bar, but the men weren't doing one damn thing except *being* there, having drinks."

"The police," Ken said resignedly. "You can't expect them to behave like the American Civil Liberties Union."

"But I can't say, 'Oh, well,' and think it's okay either. Can I?"

"Of course not, nor I. But when the day comes that the Vice Squad doesn't round up prostitutes on Mondays, Wednesdays and Fridays and homosexuals on Tuesdays, Thursdays and Saturdays, why, it'll be a different world, that's all."

"I know," Nate said, still sounding strenuous. "But to slam in as I gather they did, just bust in and round up half a dozen guys—"

"Do they do it as a routine thing?" Tessa asked, her voice guarded. "I never realized that."

"Sacred routine, the way I get it," Nate said. "I couldn't work that into my story either, not this time. New York's finest have never even heard of the Wolfenden Report or any other point of view."

Old Mrs. Lynn leaned forward. She had said little during the meal except for talking to Don's youngsters, but now with sudden energy she said to Nate, "There can't be too many points of view about abnormal acts, can there?"

Ken looked at his mother as if in reproof for this old-fashioned New Englandism, but to Nate he said, "The Wolfenden Report is that English bill that was voted down by Parliament, isn't it?"

"Vetoed the first time around, yes. I'm checking into its current status as soon as I get a free hour or so."

"What's the Wolfenden Report, Nate?" It was Jeff, speaking for the first time. His voice was deeper than usual, as if he were wrung with feeling too big for him, or too violent to let free. Tessa had not looked at him during the exchange between Ken and Nate, but now she glanced at him as casually as she could.

"It's a big study ordered a few years ago by the British government," Nate answered, "and this Wolfenden is the head of the group making the study."

"About what?" Jeff asked.

"It's complex, but mainly about whether the state or the law should or should not have any power in regard to homosexuals."

"What sort of power?"

"Any right to arrest somebody who is homosexual just for being homosexual or for having sex with another person who is homosexual. Of course the report says no."

"No what?"

"No, the state does not have the right to arrest or interfere with homosexuals. Not when the people involved are two consenting adults and acting in private."

"I did read something about it," Tessa put in. "But I can't remember exactly what it was or when it was."

"I was pretty vague too," Nate said. "But last night I looked up what the paper had in the morgue, in a big hurry, with my deadline hanging on me, and knowing damn well they'd never give me the space for any background fill-in."

"Why wouldn't they?" Margie asked.

"You know why, darling. Because they're shoving things like this under the carpet. But pretty soon I'm going to check it out some more, this Wolfenden Report, and the next time there's this kind of a story, maybe I can talk them into more space."

Ken said nothing. He no longer was looking at Nate. Tessa thought, He's upset and Nate's angry, and there's something awfully decent in Nate's anger. She did not look again at Jeff, but suddenly she felt as if she *were* Jeff, listening to this kind of talk for the first time, presumably for the first time, certainly for the first time in his own house among his own family. She felt a surge of thanks toward Nate, and in the same instant heard again his words about "the next time there's this kind of story," and the prophecy in them seemed to set a steel string vibrating in her mind as if his words were metal and clanging out a warning.

* * *

Through the rest of the dinner and then all evening long, Jeff kept hearing Nate's voice, as if it were on a tape-recorder, being run over and over. It was exciting and wonderful; he felt lifted up and terrific, like the feeling right after a big rushing gain on the field or a solid thwacking tackle at the key moment. "For none of their goddamn business . . . like the roundup of so many cattle . . . weren't doing one damn thing except *being* there . . . look at the Wolfenden Report before the British Parliament."

It was horrible and yet marvelous. It was the first time anybody ever had talked about it as if it was any other big question, like ban-the-bomb or civil rights or Kennedy-and-Nixon, not as if it was something to send you to a doctor or psychoanalyst. It had given him a brand-new feeling about Nate, not just as a brother-in-law, not just as Margie's husband, but as somebody important to *him*, somebody to value in his own life. Nate really was sore about those cops busting in there, not just because it was a police story he was covering, but because something in the idea itself got him damn mad. Nate was married to Margie and they were going to have a baby any minute and he was happy, but he was angry just the same about the roundup, and when you put it all together, you just had to feel that there was something in Nate that was one hell of a lot different from what you always expected in people.

He had heard of bars like the one Nate was telling about; where, he did not know. Read about such bars, rather, for nobody in his whole life had ever just sat at a table with a lot of people and talked out just like that about anything connected with being homosexual. Dr. Dudley of course; he had forgotten him for a minute, but that wasn't what he meant. That was a doctor, being paid big fat fees to talk about it, not just somebody in your own house, having dinner with your own family, just talking right out as if it were any other subject.

The roundup of so many cattle. It was so *big*, sitting there next to Nate, listening to him, hearing him shove all that Civil Liberties crap right back at the old man. Just like Grandma Lynn's "There can't be too many points of view about abnormal acts, can there?" That's what Dad had grown up with, and what he still felt way down deep, in secret, where he didn't have to make like a liberal about things.

There couldn't be two points of view, he supposed, otherwise why would he, Jeff, writhe so about the way he was? Otherwise why would he be going to Dr. Dudley, trying to get over it? That one time with Hank—God, he'd give a million if it had never happened. He'd give a million if he had hated it, that's what he really meant. He supposed other guys felt the same incredible and terrific thing with girls, and being so different from them was what he hated. He would go to Dr. Dudley forever if there was any chance that he could get away from it all. None of that was altered by Nate and Thanksgiving dinner.

But even to know that somebody like Nate and this Wolfenden man and his committee didn't think it was anybody's business if you were a homosexual or not—it was so huge a discovery he couldn't get used to it. It had never even occurred to him that there might be that kind of people. Not once had he ever thought there might be another way you could feel about it.

Nate and Margie had stayed around long after Don and Jenny took their kids home, but he had kept away from Nate because he might reveal how happy he had made him. Now he wondered if he might go out for a walk and drop in on Margie and Nate, sort of casually, not to talk about it, but just in general. They lived on West Eighty-fourth Street near the park in a sort of dump of an old house with bay windows that Nate's parents had unloaded on them for a wedding present, all crummy and run-down, that they were remodeling by themselves. They loved it and were always repairing things and planting the garden behind it, and right now you could count on their being in, what with Margie about as big as the house itself. They'd be surprised to have him pop in but they wouldn't mind, and even if he didn't mention the roundup at the bar or Wolfenden or anything, it would be great just to go over. He simply had to go somewhere; he couldn't just sit around until Grandma Lynn went to bed and he was left alone with Mama and Dad.

If his father ever said anything about what Nate had told them, it would come out in that "liberal" way Jeff couldn't stand, and if his mother did, it would be unbearable in a whole other way. She would never see that he did know how different she was from his father but that he still couldn't have a nice cozy talk with her about any part of it, not about Dr. Dudley, not about Nate, not even about things like the Wolfenden Report.

He jumped up, kissed Grandma Lynn on the cheek and said, "I'll say g'night, Grandma, I have to go out." Then he waved to his parents and said, "I'm catching a flick, okay?" and was on his way out before they could stop him.

Once outside he began to walk down Fifth. There was a picture he could see, at the Paramount, or Rivoli, but he couldn't sit still right now and watch a movie. There was a holiday air on Fifth Avenue, he could feel it. What a day it was, one of the greats. Windows were alight in all the apartment buildings on his left; way ahead, below Fifty-seventh, the Christmas lights were already shining around a lot of the stores, and in his pocket right now were those two theater tickets for tomorrow night.

A first step anyway. The good old journey of a thousand miles and that good old first step. Nate talking that way today—somehow that was a first step too.

* * *

Jeff tapped the brass bell at the Wisters' pinkish brick house and wished he was meeting Sue right at the theater instead. She had suggested "dinner at my house," but the idea of a couple of hours with her mother and father watching how he acted gave him that sliding in the solar plexus, as if it were a 7–6 score with one minute left on the clock. The Wisters owned a big printing plant that specialized in books, so naturally they were business friends of his own parents and they all had dinner once a year or so. That was how he had met Sue a couple of years back, but having dinner alone at her house would be a whole other thing, so he had made up an excuse and said they'd go to Antonio's for pizza afterward.

She opened the door, looking pretty and glad to see him, and a sort of excitement hit him. Here he was on his first real date with a girl, not a kids' birthday party but a real date. She was wearing a dark-red dress and looking like a college girl, and he suddenly felt grown-up and sophisticated himself. He whistled up a cab from

Park Avenue and said, "Now this is what I call all right. Right?" Sue said, "Right," and they both burst out laughing for no good reason. A cab came squeaking to a stop at the curb.

Inside the cab, he remembered the cigarettes in his pocket and drew the pack out. He had bought it that afternoon so he wouldn't look like a fool if she wanted to smoke and he had to say he never did and had none. He had even opened one end of the pack, pulled out two cigarettes and tossed them away, to make it all look more natural. Now he offered her the pack and when she took a cigarette and asked for a light, leaning toward him for it, he felt more man-of-the-world than before. Free and fine and like everybody else. She blew a wisp of smoke at him and he realized that burning tobacco really did have a pleasing aroma.

"No wonder Sir Walter was a great big hero," he said.

"Sir Walter?"

"Raleigh. Didn't he discover tobacco in Virginia, and get knighted by the Virgin Queen after the first puff or something?"

She laughed again. He felt clever, even witty. He knew how to get along with a girl; this wasn't some trumped-up Joanie or Connie or Gloria, this was a real girl and he certainly wasn't behaving like somebody who couldn't like a girl. He did like her, liked being in a cab with her, liked knowing she liked him. Again he was glad he had thought up the whole evening. How could anybody tell what might come out of it? Not right off, but there was no sense in not giving yourself every chance. Dr. Dudley had made that plenty clear, that he should start real dating and see how it went. It couldn't hurt Sue in any way, that was for sure or he wouldn't have tried it. She was too nice as a person, apart from being good-looking and tall, not like Margie or his mother.

"It's crazy," he said, "but it's great that you're tall, not a peewee like my sister." He saw her astonished look and went on, "That sounds queer, but it always gives me a pain to look down and see the top of somebody's head."

"I'll stretch myself and be even taller." She straightened her back, raised her shoulders, tilted her chin. "See how tall?" He joined her laugh but he scarcely had heard her. He kept hearing the word "queer" in his own voice and realized how naturally he had said it. He must remember that when other people said it. They were just using one little old word that was like any other word in the language, not loading it with special meaning. Dr. Dudley had already asked why some words took on such "lethal power" for him, had even made him say some of them out loud, right there on the couch, as if to defuse them. "Queer," he had said obediently, "queen," "swish," "one of the boys," "fairy." The only one he couldn't manage was "faggot."

The cab was stopping in front of the theater.

"Just look at the mob," Sue said. "Oh, Jeff, thanks for asking me."

In the theater he helped settle her into her seat, reaching around to pull her coat off her shoulders as he had seen other men do when they were with girls. It gave him that sophisticated feeling again, almost courtly and protective. He felt good, relieved and good. My God, almost happy.

All through the play, through the intermissions, afterward, walking over to Eighth Avenue to Antonio's, his mind kept racing with that feeling that it was *almost* true. He really was having a good time, like any other guy, wasn't pushing for it, like having a doctor's prescription filled because you had to. He would date Sue every time he came down from school.

At Antonio's, as they ordered, Sue made a face at her watch and said, "I can't be too late. They still think I'm about thirteen."

"What a drag. Parents sure know how to bug you."

"Do yours? I mean, are they a drag?"

"Not my mother so much."

"She's the one you get along with?"

"Not all the way, but so-so." He grinned.

"But better than with your father. It always seems to go that way."

"With you too?"

"I meant, the boys I know."

"I think it's because mothers are—" He paused. He had been about to say that it might be because most mothers were more emotional and therefore more understanding, but Pete's mother was a shrew, and as cold as ice. "I think it's because my mother is—" Again he paused. He had been about to say that his mother might be more emotional because she was Jewish, and it surprised him that he had even thought of tying the two together. He usually got it said about himself, about being half Jewish,

somewhere in the beginning of any new friendship, just to get it
on the record right off and to hell with them if they didn't like it,
but never had he considered it as his own reason for liking his
mother better than his father, and it shook him up that the idea
had hit him now. It had popped up so vividly though, so clear and
bright, the way his sudden feeling that Nate was important had
popped up last night. Nate was Jewish too. He hadn't thought of
that either.

"Because your mother is what?" Sue prompted.

"I just got hit by this idea," he said, sounding pleased, "that
maybe it's easier to get along with my mother because she's Jewish, and harder with my father because he isn't. Maybe being Jewish helps you dig other people's hang-ups more."

"I didn't know she was Jewish."

"And you're wondering if she's one of those Jewish mothers
with the chicken soup."

"I am not. I've met her, remember. She's awfully good-looking."

"I guess she is."

"And my dad says she's awfully good at her job."

"I guess she's that too."

He suddenly looked upset, Sue thought, and wondered if she
had hurt his feelings in some way. She didn't want anything to go
wrong with this wonderful date; it was too important. She had
liked Jeff the first time they had ever met, but he had scarcely
noticed her, she being young for her age then when she was thirteen. Even now at sixteen, she wasn't much of a swinger, the way
you were supposed to be if you wanted to get anywhere with boys,
especially boys like Jeff Lynn, who would make varsity at any college he went to and be a big man on campus all over again, the
way he was at Placquette. Maybe sometime he would ask her up
for some college weekend; she had never been away to a boys'
school for a party or a prom, and it was heaven to think it might
happen someday with somebody like Jeff. If she didn't say things
that suddenly upset him.

"Go on about what you were saying, Jeff," she said anxiously.

It sounded as if she were asking a favor and Jeff liked that.
There was an earnest, searching look in her eyes, as if what he
said mattered a lot, and he liked that too. It was hard to get back
exactly to what he had been saying because he had gone off on a

tangent in his thoughts, suddenly realizing that he had never before compared his father and his mother as if they were two separate things that you could consider one apart from the other and decide, This one is better, that one is worse. Before tonight he had always thought of them together, joined, but now he felt this terrific need to pry them apart, like two halves of a tight shell.

"I was thinking," he answered at last, "about the different ways you can react to people in your family, something like that. My mother has a temper, the way I do, and we have awful rows, but they're fast and furious and 'gee, I'm sorry.' My father sort of gets me teed off—he goes awfully polite and silent and yet you just know he's all Thumbs Down." He looked away as if he were suddenly embarrassed. "That's enough about me. What about you?"

She was slated for Sarah Lawrence next year, and couldn't wait to get there, and live on campus. "I don't have too many hassles at home or anything," she said. "But I can't stand having to say where I'm going, when I'll be back, who else is going along—yech-h-h." She looked at her watch again and said, "Eleven-thirty!"

He stood up. "Let's not have any hassles at your house, not yet awhile." That sounded right, but he thought, I'll have to kiss her good night. He had thought about it beforehand, but now it was suddenly rushing at him, and he felt the nip of panic. Kissing a girl wasn't something you could get set for in advance, like buying a pack of cigarettes. If he messed it up, he would die.

They were both rather silent in the taxi but by the time they got to her door, she began again to thank him for the show and Antonio's and the whole wonderful evening. He watched her open her purse, scrabble around in it for her keys, and somehow the easy feeling came back, controlled and sure, as if nothing could ever go wrong. He leaned over her and kissed her. Not a kiss in the air somewhere or on her cheek, the way you kissed mothers or sisters, but a kiss right on the mouth, kind of slow, and waiting while she kissed him.

Nothing happened to him, but nothing went wrong either. He kissed her once more and then went off a moment later, striding along the street as if he had just won something.

CHAPTER EIGHT

We live in a world of monosyllables, Tessa thought one night. "Yes," Ken had just said. Before that it had been "No," and immediately prior to that, "Please!" with the verbal exclamation point a streak of stress in the air between them.

It was a February night, snowing gently, the world outside their windows hushed and white, the city's traffic muted as it always was under falling snow. In the fireplace a log tumbled; the room was bright and warm. But for her the chill of a growing dismay dimmed the brightness and diluted the warmth. Monosyllables, she thought again, half-finished phrases, unfinished sentences. A fine thing for two people who live by paragraphs and chapters and completed books. Invisibly in the last few months the barriers of their basic characters had raised themselves higher between them, and by now she had all but abandoned further attempts to achieve what had once seemed so unremarkable, a real conversation with Ken, an ordinary free-flowing conversation. If she so much as said, "Jeff," or mentioned his school or Dr. Dudley, the barrier went up and there was no crossing it. They could still talk about politics, or manuscripts, about the spring list or some special bit of publishing gossip; for a few minutes, their talk would grow normal again, flow smoothly, even contain an amusing line or two. But let it turn toward their son, their own son, their one still-dependent child, and everything halted as abruptly as if they had come suddenly to the edge of a cliff below which was only empty air.

Every week made it worse, she admitted to herself, made it less possible to think of it as if they were in this *with* Jeff, and with each other. It was as if Ken unconsciously had to act as if it weren't there any more, like a paragraph deleted from a manuscript. For a while you could feel that paragraph missing from the flow of the narrative, see the chunk of type crossed out by slashing pencil lines, or see the *x*'s going through the separate words of the killed passage. Then you began to forget what had been there, you lost it for good as if it had never been there, as if it had never existed at all.

"It" no longer meant homosexuality exclusively; it included any aspect of Jeff's life or plans, any letter or phone call, any holiday or weekend at home. Christmas had been a dimmer replay of Thanksgiving, but instead of four days there were fourteen. Apart from the excitement and joy they all shared in the birth of Margie's baby girl on the twentieth, it had been their first sad Christmas. She could feel Ken trying to keep it from being that, could feel him trying to seem casual and easy, with Jeff and with her, and she was grateful to him. But there was all the time the underlying sense of trying and that in itself had destroyed any spontaneity. She couldn't, in any fairness, blame him for it. She too was trying; her trying also showed. Again and again she was caught in a passion of yearning that they could be, if not happy as they went through all the dear familiarities of the tree and the gifts and Christmas morning, at least able to achieve the old family closeness again.

But closeness, as an idea, as a possibility of living, was slipping away from all of them. One night before Jeff's vacation, there was a tap on her door and Ken's voice saying, "Are you awake, Tessa?" It was past one but she was still reading, and she called out, "Yes, come in, dear," and found herself astonished at his coming to her room at all. It had been so long, this onetime need of his, of coming to her late at night in an impulse to be close, to make love. He did need closeness, for he got into bed and took her into his arms; she scarcely knew whether he was comforting her or seeking comfort; unexpectedly she was passionate and eager. That too had been so long gone from the current of life, she was surprised, delighted and surprised. But moment followed moment in a kind of passive waiting, and then Ken was sitting up beside her, his head bowed as in some portrait of an old man saying grace at the table, his eyes closed, his lips moving. She said nothing to prompt him to say it aloud, whatever he was thinking. Her readiness died, her throat ached.

"If I so much as think of sex," Ken said at last, his voice hoarse with the effort to speak, "I think of two men and that kills it off for good."

"Why should it, darling, why?" But immediately she added, "Most of the time, that happens to me too."

"Does it?"

"I can't bear it, it seems so compulsive."

"But there it is." This he said with such finality that her heart shook for him. It was true that since Jeff's revelation, they had no heart for their own problems of sex and making love. Instinctively they had avoided any test; instinctively their own needs had ceased as if they had agreed in a dread collusion that they might shatter whatever there was left for them, unless they remained aloof now.

"Maybe if we could talk to each other more freely about it," she said tentatively a few moments later.

"I keep wishing I could," he said, looking at her for corroboration, as if she alone could attest to his wishing. "But I've never been able to—you know it simply was left out of my nature, a nice easy exchange of talk."

She did know, and more than ever she tried to remain content with the knowing. But saintly patience was not her special gift and at times she wanted to cry out in protest, especially while Jeff was there. Saintly patience was not Jeff's special gift either and when, two days before Christmas, she had said, "We all might try for tact at least, as if Christmas were a family enterprise," he had looked at her with a kind of disdain.

"If Dad won't talk to me, I can't talk to him. I'm not a kid any more that thinks Daddy's the best daddy in the world."

"Another moratorium?" Ken had asked wearily when she repeated her suggestion to him. "Tessa, can't we just let it go on as best it can?"

She had let it go on, but as the days inched by, she felt that something was going to happen to them all, something climactic and dire, irreversible. One evening the TV news showed a bomb explosion in a foreign embassy, and she began to think of an explosive planted in their midst, waiting, ticking off the minutes. When it detonated, it would blow their lives into a thousand pieces, never to be sweet and whole again.

On New Year's Eve she and Ken had gone to a party at the Brannicks', an annual affair as insistent as a command performance. All the firm's editors were there, all its executives, many of its authors, and only the rapid early rounds of trays bearing good champagne could unfrost the formality that seemed to seize all these people who were so congenial in office surroundings and so ill at ease in evening clothes on an occasion of enforced merrymaking. As 1961 arrived, and husbands and wives kissed each other, all saying their habitual "Happy New Year, darling," Tessa had whispered to Ken, "Maybe it can be. Let's think it can be."

"I wish it could be."

But he said it with so little conviction that fear streamed through her like pale ribbons. Many times since that night, the flutter of apprehension returned at unpredictable intervals. It's going to break us completely, she thought now, staring at the bright fire, either Ken or I is going to crack in some awful way. Maybe I'm the one—I've got to get some advice from somebody, maybe from Dr. Dudley, maybe from Mark Waldo, but somewhere. Recently I've been acting as if it's only Ken's silence that's making this into a disaster, but if we had heart-to-heart talks every day it still would be disaster. From the first minute it's been disaster.

For no reason she suddenly saw again the happy look on Jeff's face the night he had come in, whistling, from his date with Sue at the theater.

"How was it, Jeff?"

"Great."

"Did Sue like it too?"

"Yeah, loads."

"I'm glad."

That had been it. He had gone to his room then, and that had been it, then and forever. The curtness was nothing new; Don and Margie had been the same; most teen-agers were the same. Once they reached adolescence and their new estate of separation from mothers and fathers, they all regarded that chasm as more inviolable than the separation of Church and State.

What a metaphor! Even as a joke, it's a revelation of that insidious recurring problem tearing at every generation. Who is supreme? Who comes first?

Funny, Margie seemed to have disposed of the problem since her marriage to Nate. There was some quality in Nate, some outgoing quality, a willingness for dimension in a family, and it had brought out an answering warmth in Margie, so that now she seemed more willing than before to have parents again, as Nate was willing to have his parents. Maybe it was Margie and Nate she should talk to now, not Dr. Dudley or even Mark Waldo.

But of course she couldn't. They were so joyous with their little girl, so filled with discovery. Lynn, they had called her, the name chosen well in advance by Nate. "Whether it's a boy or a girl," he had explained, "it will be Lynn Jacobs. What a great name. Equal status of husband and wife, intermarriage, and damn good-looking on a theater marquee or the spine of a book or a by-line in a newspaper."

She would wait, and not intrude her pain into their happiness. But if she did not talk this out soon with somebody, she would go mad. Somebody who would not retreat into monosyllables. Somebody who would not refuse all information as Jeff so stubbornly did. In a way, she thought, they are alike about it. Each with the same need to slam doors in my face, as if it all had nothing to do with me.

The sensation of a door being slammed shook her, as if the air itself vibrated and splintered about her, as if shock waves actually impacted against her skin. Never before had she felt more isolated.

It's half my fault, she thought stormily. I let them both do it. I accept it as if only they had the right to decide what's to be said and what's not to be said. As if I'm either Jeff's mother or Ken's wife, but never *me*.

An uneasy warning told her that this was no time to switch tactics, not when she was angry. In the same instant she heard herself say, "Ken, I've tried a couple of times to tell you, and I've never really made it clear. The principal reason Jeff applied to Yale is that he needs to be near New Haven, for another year."

"Needs to?"

"Because of Dr. Dudley."

"Dr. Dudley?"

"One more year of treatment. I hope only another year."

"Another year. Oh, dear God, that means there's been no change."

"It means he still is young and unformed, he still needs help and still is going to have it."

"If you want to go on."

"Of course I'll go on."

He stretched in his chair, as if he were comfortably sleepy. Then he said, "I think I've always known that was why he picked Yale."

"If he went somewhere else, he'd have to start all over with a new analyst and cover the same ground. It must be hard for him."

"Analysis is always hard, I gather." He stretched once more and then turned to the manuscript he was reading. A few days later he said, without preamble, "I'm not going to make my trip next month. I don't feel up to it. Maybe later."

Every spring he toured the country in March; once it had been a necessary selling and publicity trip to the major book jobbers and bookstores of the nation, but in recent years it had been an elective trip which he made because he enjoyed renewing old contacts in the field. "A kind of stag holiday," he used to say. "Every man deserves one." She had always agreed, was sorry now that he was calling it off.

"Oh, too bad, Ken. It always does you a lot of good."

"I might go later on."

"Like when?"

At first he did not answer. Then, very quietly, he said, "In June. Before it gets too hot."

For a moment there was a total silence. Then she said, "You can't mean the first week in June?"

"Tessa, I do mean it."

"But you'll miss Jeff's commencement."

"I've thought it all out and I'm positive that this is the thing to do just now. I don't think he'll mind one way or the other."

"He will mind. It will be a kind of public insult."

"Tessa, you're dramatizing. You always dramatize so."

"Now you are attacking me." Her eyes filled. "Either we don't talk about Jeff at all any more, or if we do, we end up in some

sort of polite sarcasm or well-mannered attack. You never used to
be this way and it's awful." This time it was she who left the
room. She discovered something: it helped. Physical separation
eased something.

She began to acknowledge the need to stay away from Ken,
from the house, from the uncertainties that waited there. For the
first time, the telephone calls made late in the afternoon about
having to work late began to come from her to Ken instead of
the other way around, calls about having to see Helena Ludwig
at cocktails, or Virginia Grabig or Mary Jasper. A lifetime of habit
prevented her from lying to Ken, so she lied to her authors instead, contriving to set up the late dates with them instead of
seeing them during normal office hours. Each time she did it, she
felt uneasily that she was jarring loose something that had always
been solid. But that was for the first few times only.

*   *   *

On April 12, Jeff turned eighteen, and Tessa telephoned to wish
him Happy Birthday and offer congratulations about being accepted by Yale. He sounded happy and self-confident. Yes, he
had received her present, gee thanks, and he was going to call up
about it, but then he thought he ought to write instead and had
kept putting it off. Gosh, in the last semester of your last year,
they sure kept you hopping up here.

"That's always the way. Any other news?"

"Well, old Pete drove over to New Haven with me, to help
give it the once-over, and I think he wished he wasn't slated for
Cornell."

"College sounds nearer and nearer. When's commencement
exactly?"

"The sixth, Tuesday the sixth of June."

There was a pause. Self-consciousness took her, like a thumb
against her vocal cords. "Dad might not be able to come up for
it. He'll have that big annual sales trip he always makes."

"In June? Boy, that's a good one."

"This year, the spring trip had to be put off. I think it was
because—"

"Well, I don't! And you don't either. You know why he's shifting his goddamn publishing swing to the first week of June and he can just go to hell and shift it. I have to hang up now."

She could not blame him. Her own heart contracted with his desperate rage at this rejection. Several times she had tried to get Ken to change his mind, but these conversations too were truncated. Even more difficult than the monosyllable was the swift exit from the room, the swift walk down the hall, the finality of his closing door.

More and more now she felt not only isolation and sadness about Ken but a lively anger. His decision to stay away in June was a turning point he doubtless had tried to escape, one he might feel guilty for reaching. But reach it he had, and nothing could make her accept it, though she admitted that if he were there, tense and largely silent, it might be worse than having him not there at all.

By the third of May, when Dr. Dudley's monthly bill arrived, she looked at it in a sudden energy of resentment. He too was always silent; he too acted as if she had no need, no right to know about Jeff's progress. Not once since her single trip to his office last fall had she seen or heard from Dr. Dudley. He had not once telephoned; he had not once written a line. The only link between them was the typed bill which arrived on the third day of every month, unvarying except that most of the time it said, "Eight office visits, Jeff . . . $280," while at other times it changed to, "Nine office visits, Jeff . . . $315."

She had taken her cue from him for the full year, writing out the check herself at home from the checkbook she kept there, not from the master checkbook she kept at the office, to which Gail had daily access. And she would herself mail back the check to Dr. Dudley, also without a personal line, also in the same "no comment" manner. Suddenly it seemed false, loathsome.

She twirled a sheet of note paper into her portable typewriter.

Dear Dr. Dudley,

I will be coming up for Jeff's graduation. Might it be possible to see you then for an hour, as a scheduled visit? Recently I told my husband that Jeff will be continuing the analysis next fall, and it disturbed him very much. I am worried about the summer, with Jeff at home, which is why I seek counsel from you that might help make things easier for him and the family as a whole. You will, I am sure, know how deeply I'd like to have whatever word you might find it appropriate to offer, as Jeff's first year with you comes to an end.

Thank you in advance.

Yours sincerely,
Theresa Lynn

With commendable promptness his reply arrived three days later, and as she tore open the envelope, its brevity told her that it contained denial.

My dear Mrs. Lynn,

I am sorry, but for the present any further meeting between us would not be in Jeff's best interests. I hope you will accept my judgment on this point.

Yours,
James H. Dudley

She did accept it. There was nothing to do but accept it. There was never anything to do but accept it, accept what Dr. Dudley handed out, what Ken handed out, what Jeff handed out. Or what each kept to himself.

Had she been so secretive when she was eighteen, as willing to let her mother stew in the hot juice of worry month after month, with never a word from her to ease or cushion her uncertainty? She could not believe it. Doubtless she too had done things that seemed distant and callous to her parents, but she did not believe that if there had been anything of this size or weight, she would have shut out her own mother or father so implacably.

Back then there were no cliché jokes about "Jewish mothers" and it had never occurred to her to ignore or wisecrack about her mother's concern. At college nearly thirty years ago, the darkest secret that might have arisen was that she was pregnant; she could well imagine not wanting to tell that at all, but once she had told her mother, then she would not have followed up by a cool silence month after month.

And if she had discovered that she was lesbian? Even the supposition came as an impossible shock, but in the same instant of shock she knew that if she had discovered such a thing about herself, she could never have told her mother at all. She would have been unable to give her such pain.

Why had Jeff been able to? It was the first time the thought had ever struck her, but now it hit hard. Why? Really why? Most boys would have hidden it forever, or at least as long as they could keep on hiding it. She had reacted so completely to Jeff's telling it, had admired him so for his young courage. Was it courage, just courage, unadorned and bright? Or was it, in fact, in some dark subterranean way, his own need to stun her, to punish her? Homosexuals disliked women, were even repelled by women, sometimes hated them. Did Jeff hate her? Even not recognizing his own feeling, did he unconsciously want to avoid her, to destroy her because she was a woman?

Never before had this possibility occurred to her, but there it was, sudden, vicious, more monstrous than she could have imagined. Yet within this harrowing hypothesis, so much of his behavior these last months took on a new rationale. His bursts of irritation, his willingness to keep her guessing, his purity of silence about the analysis and any progress away from homosexuality back toward the normal—if he did hate her, his behavior suddenly became explicable. Hideous but explicable. Down there in those subsurface levels of his being that he was now exploring for the first time, perhaps this suffering of hers gratified some obscure and unsuspected need in him.

He cannot help it, she thought, not any of it. Whatever the reasons, he's going through such hell himself it's all he can do to get through himself. He can't even consider what it means to a father or mother.

That story about the wicked prince—suddenly she was hearing it again, as if she were again a little girl of six or seven, sitting there in their big living room up in Pelham, listening to her mother telling the story about the cruel princess and the wicked prince. Her brother Will already knew the story by heart, but he listened to it all over again; it was a favorite with him, a kind of horror story that had an irresistible power to enthrall him.

"This handsome wicked prince," her mother's long-ago voice was saying, "was terribly in love with the beautiful cruel princess, who kept taunting him and putting him off. She swore she would never marry him, but nothing would stop him from desiring her for his wedded wife. At last, one day the princess said, 'If you really want my hand in marriage, then cut your mother's heart out and place it on a silver tray, and bring the tray to me. *Then* I will let you wed me.'

"The wicked prince lamented and wept, but at last he did as the princess had bade him do. Then, as he was carrying his mother's heart through the forest on the silver tray, he stumbled over the protruding roots of a great tree. And as he stumbled and fell, his mother's voice spoke to him from the silver tray. 'Did you hurt yourself, my son?'

"That's the kind of mother I will never be," her own mother had ended the story, looking straight at her and then at her brother Will. "I'll love both of you all my life, but if you hurt me and wound me and do cruel things, I won't be the sappy fool who keeps on loving you and forgiving you and treating you as if my love was yours no matter what."

"Of course not, Mommy," she had cried in a fearful tingle of excitement.

"Of course not," Will had echoed her.

Years later, when her own son Don was about six or seven, she had told him the story one day, and he too had echoed that same passionate "Of course not." "Oh no, never," Margie had whispered when her turn came. "Gee, Mama, you never would," Jeff had said seven or eight years later on.

Always she had thought she never would. Love was a round, a giving and taking and giving, a loving and being loved and loving, endlessly progressing, endlessly assured and assuring and assured again. Tiffs and quarrels mattered little, but if ever there came a supine willingness to accept maltreatment, then loving was degraded into a kind of spineless collusion.

And yet here she was.

* * *

Dr. Dudley's refusal to see her tipped some scale, for the next morning she telephoned Mark Waldo for an appointment. She had not been in his office since that day last fall—only last fall, only eight or nine months back, not a dozen years?—and when she faced him across his desk, she said, "You know why I'm here, Mark."

"I imagine I do. Is there any change?"

"I don't know. Ken doesn't know. The deal apparently is that parents get no report, no prognosis, not even a year later, with a second year coming up." She told of Dr. Dudley's refusal to see her and then, rapidly, with a conscious attempt to be fair, summarized their family life for the past months. "And now Ken won't be at Jeff's graduation. It isn't as if he's tough about it inside—he is in hell about that, about all of it. So am I. It's worst of all for Jeff, but he *is* getting help, whatever help is possible. Maybe Ken ought to start with an analyst too. Maybe I ought to."

"Don't say that with such a jeer, Tessa. In many families with continuing problems—alcoholism, for example—the other members of the family are as hard-pressed as the officially afflicted one." He looked at her thoughtfully. "You've lost weight."

"Have I ever. Look." She pushed up a few inches from the chair and looked down at the thin flat line of her body under the slight curve of her breasts, her stomach almost concave, as thin and flat as that of a girl who hadn't quite reached puberty. "I used to think it would be lovely to lose ten pounds."

"But primarily you're here because of Ken, aren't you?"

"He's killing himself, Mark. The incessant tension, bottling everything up, never letting anything out. I almost wish he had a horrible temper, like me or Jeff. How would it help him, or me or Jeff or anybody, if he works himself into another stroke?"

"Perhaps I ought to ask him to come in early for his checkup."

She seemed not to hear. "But what terrifies me even more is the summer, with Jeff right there, all of us right there every day. It will destroy us, I just know it."

"Could Jeff get a job out of town this year?"

"He's already got his old job back, the one he had last year, at Paperbound Books. He loved it and did so well at it. Anyway, wouldn't he feel exiled or banished if I suggested any such thing? There's no fooling Jeff; he's too bright. He instantly saw why Ken had delayed his trip West."

"I wasn't suggesting you fool Jeff."

"Did I sound as if I were jeering again? I'm too tense too. I lose my temper, I cry. I suppose I'm wrong to reject the idea of an analyst for me or Ken, but he would never agree, and me, I just can't think of Jeff stretched out on one couch and Ken on another in another doctor's office and me on still another in a third doctor's office." She reached for her handkerchief and dried her eyes in a furious swipe. "I get weeping at the least thing."

He reached for his prescription pad and began to write. "This is for you, and this is for Ken's Librium, if he runs out. I'll phone him and ask him to come in."

"Mark, don't let him know how much I've told you. Before, I never worried about what you told Ken, but we've been changing so, since all this began." She hesitated. "You know about our other problems, well, they are about over, I imagine. Neither of us ever can think of our own sex life any more."

He nodded, without speaking. Then he opened the door to his examination room and said, "Let's have a look at your pulse rate and blood pressure. That's easier to measure."

*　*　*

When the sixth of June finally arrived, she did not drive up to Placquette alone. About a week before, she had told Margie and Nate that she would be going up by herself because of "Dad's trip West," and Margie had flared into an irritated attention.

"Whatever the hell kind of row Dad has going with Jeff, I do think he might skip it for the kid's Graduation Day."

"Let's us skip it too." She sounded depressed; she could hear it herself.

"It gets me sick and you can tell Dad I said so."

"It's complex, dear. I've been wanting to talk about it to you and Nate, but as yet I can't."

"Complex? What *is* it?" She waited for a moment, and saw the unwillingness in her mother's face. "Okay, then I'll just get hold of our baby-sitter and drive up there with you." She almost flung this offer at Tessa, but she could see her mood lighten.

"Good idea, Margie," Nate said.

"I wonder if Don could take the day off and come too. *That* would really show Dad."

"Don, the true-blue employee?" Nate put in with a grin.

"You lay off Don," Margie said. "So he's as square as a box, like a few other people we know. Right in this family."

"You must mean me," Nate said.

She laughed suddenly. "Nate Jacobs, Esquare!"

They started early, Tessa shifting away from the wheel as Margie appeared from her front door, in the unwritten law that driving was the prerogative of the young. It cheered her to have Margie going up with her, even though Margie's motive was mainly to punish her father. It was a day that told of deep summer, the sun more insistent than it should be in the first week of June, the sky adrift with strands and streamers of thin cloud, the banks of flowering bushes rising alongside the parkway giving off the ingratiating odor of new-mown grass and clover. The drive up went quickly, and Jeff met them with open astonishment at his sister's appearance. "Look who came up to see me get graduated," he shouted, and gave her a hug. "Great, just great." Then he turned to his mother, happy and still noisy. "Hi, Mama, at last the big day, hey? I'm a college man."

"No Placque any more," Margie said, and they both laughed at this ancient joke once made by their dentist. "Any pangs about leaving the dear old place?"

"I can't wait to get out. Hey, maybe I could stow my bags and stuff in the car before we get started." He glanced at his watch. "Nope, I better get you to the auditorium."

It's like the way you feel at weddings, Tessa thought as the ceremonies got under way. There's something so eternally touching about them, when they're starting forth on a new segment of life. They look so confident and yet so tentative. Nobody could look more sure, more certain than these young men. Including Jeff.

She looked at the others, surrounding him on the platform. All kinds of faces were there, handsome, plain, strong, weak, all kinds of bodies, tall, short, muscular, delicate, plump, lean, all kinds of eyes, noses, hair, hands, and all young, all at the beginning.

Suddenly a thread of envy wound itself through her mind, cutting in its sharpness. None of them faced what her son faced; none of them carried the problem he carried; none of the proud parents all around her in the auditorium knew the problem she and Ken knew.

Equally suddenly she thought, Maybe some of them do. Maybe half a dozen of these proud parents share exactly the same problem, maybe more than half a dozen. According to Kinsey they do. She looked around her at the other parents, and then she looked up again at the platform and at the boys there, studying them one by one. But this was a mockery of everything she knew; she stopped herself. There was no special way a homosexual had to look; there need be no distinguishing characteristics. There were none in Jeff. She thought of John Lanner, one of their editors at Q. and P., a bachelor of about forty who lived with a young man in his twenties. Office talk said they were homosexuals. She had never met the young man, but she saw John Lanner every day and until these last months she had never paused to consider whether he was a homosexual or not.

Why couldn't you be as casual about your own son? Ken, if he were to meet Lanner, would be courteous and unconcerned about the homosexual gossip, would be friendly, might even like him. Ken, after all, was a civilized man. Yet with his own son—

Forget Ken, she thought stormily, you can't be casual either. Sure, you can be about John Lanner, because you don't care whether his life is ruined or not, and because your life can't be ruined with it. But with Jeff you do care, so you're a whole other person. It's a paradox, a crazy anomaly of love.

Up on the platform they were beginning the last formality, the handing out of diplomas, and she watched each boy step forward as his name was called. This thin owlish boy would probably be a teacher, the next a customers' man in Wall Street, this one a scientist . . . the game went on in her mind until Jeff strode forward, to a heightened applause from the audience. That was because of football and baseball, of course, but her heart lifted to the amplified sound. He was so fine-looking, so strong, so intelligent, youth at the threshold of life, and she loved him beyond the limits of all problems.

*   *   *

She kept waiting for Ken to finish his trip. Next week he'll be home, she would think, in three days Ken will be here, tomorrow he'll get back, and finally, as she awoke on Saturday the seventeenth, this afternoon they'll face each other.

At five there was Ken's short double tap at the bell, his key in the lock, their greeting. He looked thinner, very tired, and she thought, as she rarely did, of his age. He used to look so much younger than he was; even after the stroke, with full recovery, a good deal younger. In the past months he had again begun to look all of his fifty-five years, and tonight, just after the nonstop flight back from the Coast, he looked more. Next month he would be fifty-six. He looked old.

"Want to fix me a drink?" he said.

"The ice is out. It'll only take a minute." She reached out her hand to his arm. "Sit down, Ken, just take it easy. Those glamorous airline commercials never mention the drag of waiting around airports, getting your luggage, finding a taxi and getting just plain bushed."

"I do feel bushed. It was a tough trip this time, everybody kicking about high costs and bloody hot everywhere." He glanced at the air conditioner behind him. "I'm glad we got the biggest one. That feels good."

"I'm glad you're home, Ken. I got edgy about you." This was true enough. Once the exceptional hours of Jeff's commencement were over, the sense of occasion disappeared under the onrush of routine living. On the past Monday, Jeff had started in again as mailboy–office boy at Paperbound and she turned to her own work with renewed energy, trying to ignore that imaginary ticking off of time, that shortening fuse burning backward to her hidden and waiting bomb.

There had been only one ugliness with Jeff, and technically, she herself had brought it on, for she had told him of her note to Dr. Dudley and of his curt reply, "Better not."

"My God, you ought to know by now he'd say that."

She could see muscles of his jaw go rigid, saw his fists clench.

"I'm telling you only because I wouldn't want you thinking I wrote him behind your back and—"

"He doesn't *believe* in reporting on patients," Jeff interrupted. "No decent analyst does. His patient has to know for sure that he won't go tattling to his Mama and Papa."

"Not the scornful tone, please. I wasn't asking him to tattle. Dr. Dudley knew that, if you don't."

"You keep digging and digging just the same."

"Now, look here—"

"Christ, damn it, I won't look here." He had started for the door, stopped, and shouted, "If you don't want me with Dr. Dudley, just stop the whole damn thing. I told you, I'm not going to get down on my knees and beg you to keep on."

"Oh, Jeff, can't you see *any* of this from my point of view as well as your own?"

"Your point of view! You'll be talking about your unhappiness next."

This time he left the room; a moment later, the apartment. She stared at the closing door. He was dividing into two people, one the old Jeff, the other solely involved with being a homosexual or not being a homosexual, hostile, attacking, especially his parents.

There are so many by-products, she had thought in a new despondency. It's not just the homosexuality, it's what it does to him and to all of us in fifty different ways, as if one poison engendered fifty other poisons, fifty side effects that are more lethal than the poison itself.

Now with Ken sipping his drink, abstaining from what would have been the simple, obvious question, she said, "He's out. He'll be back for dinner." Ken nodded. "They're giving him sixty-eight dollars at Paperbound this time."

"Good."

"Nate's just had a raise too. He's doing awfully well."

"He's a bright boy, Nate, and a good writer."

"He and Margie are going on that Peace March to Washington, and the baby is going too."

He actually smiled. Just then Jeff arrived, a little early. They heard him in the hall and looked at each other. Ken seemed to sit up straighter, pressing against the back of his chair. Tessa asked something with her eyes, asked a favor, help, a kindness.

"Hi," Jeff addressed the room.

"Hello, dear."

"I hear you're back at Paperbound," Ken said. "They're having the biggest year ever, the biggest list."

"So I gather," Jeff said. "Hardcovers have priced themselves right out of the market."

"Considering the skyrocketing costs of paper, shipping, labor, you'd have to charge the same amount."

They sound like two publishers talking shop, Tessa thought in relief. Maybe they'll keep it this impersonal and we'll all get by.

The impersonal fled during dinner. It was Jeff who first mentioned Yale, almost as if he were driven to that association of thoughts which a moment later had him saying, "I suppose I'd have gone to Cornell with Pete if it hadn't been a question of one more year with Dr. Dudley."

"Isn't there always a question of 'one more year' once you start with analysis?" Ken said.

"What does that mean?"

"Nothing in particular."

"You're sure Dr. Dudley is a big waste of time. Well, he isn't."

"That must mean he is helping you, that you feel better, that something's changing." He put his fork down. "We have the right to know it if that's true."

"The only thing it *must* mean is what it means to the patient," Jeff said stiffly. "It does not have to mean what his parents want it to mean." He also put his fork down.

"Stop talking riddles."

"It's no riddle. Analysis has one job, to help the patient, not his father or his mother or the rest of the family." His voice roughened. "Nor the neighbors nor the executives at the office."

"Jeff, dear," Tessa said. He ignored her and so did his father.

"Very well," Ken said. "The patient is all there is and to hell with his parents, to hell with the worry they live with, to hell with what they feel—"

"Ken, please," Tessa said. "Please, both of you, drop this for now. There's just no point—"

"I can tell you one thing though," Ken said to Jeff, waving off Tessa without looking at her. "I give you exactly one more year to straighten yourself out through this analysis your mother is paying for, just one more year, and that's it. The end. Finis. She's not to go on indefinitely forking up—"

"And if I don't 'straighten out'?" Almost, Jeff laughed. "Boy, what a phrase."

"And if you don't, if you then want still one more year beyond that, and then maybe one more year after that—"

"Then what?" Jeff asked belligerently. "What are you getting at?"

"Don't lay down any ultimatums, Ken," Tessa said, her own temper rising. "If you have to remain apart and silent, I suppose you have to, but don't start laying down the law about what I'm going to do or how long I'm going to keep on doing it."

"And if I don't 'straighten out,'" Jeff insisted, half rising from his chair and leaning toward his father. "Then what?"

"If you keep on feeling the hell with parents, the hell with their right to know how things are going—"

"Stop that, Ken. Stop it. Stop it."

"I will not stop it. If he wants to cut all communication with his father and his mother, why then perhaps a year from now he'll also want to cut loose entirely, in a place of his own somewhere where neither you nor I will dare ask him how things are going."

"I won't wait till a year from now. I'll cut loose right now." Jeff slammed back from the table and slammed out of the house.

* * *

It was more than an hour later when he rang the bell at Nate and Margie's. Saturday was one of Nate's days off, and they were both there. As Margie opened the door, she cried out, "Jeffie, what's happened to you?"

She had not used his little-boy name for years, but his face was so distorted, his eyes so wild, her first thought was that he had been in a fight, an accident, had been mugged in the street. His shirt gaped open over his chest, his face was smudged, perhaps even swollen, his "Can I come in?" was hoarse.

"What is it? What's the matter?"

She stood aside and he came into the small front hall. He stood there just inside the door, shaking his head, his eyes closed, his left hand covering his mouth, the long fingers splayed out over his jaw. Nate was there now, as shocked as Margie, and after a moment he took Jeff by the arm, leading him as if he were blinded, through the hall, up the flight of stairs to the living room.

"You need a drink," he said. "What'll it be?"

Jeff shook his head for no and sank into an armchair. It was good to sit down; he had been charging around the streets like a madman, and the heat and the sweat and the fury all mangled him.

"What, Jeff?" Margie said.

"You know about my letter to Mama last fall." It was a statement, made equally to both of them, a preamble to what was to come, and he drew back as they both said, "What letter?"

"My letter. Where I told her."

"Told her what? She never said anything about a letter. Just that you were going into analysis, is that what you mean?"

"But nothing about the letter I wrote her?"

"Nothing about any letter, no."

He looked from one to the other, disbelieving. "Well, Don? Did Don say anything about the letter?"

"Don never said a word about any letter."

"Oh, my God. I thought she'd spill her guts over it, she always spills everything about any of us."

"Your letter about what, Jeff?" This was Nate, and he put his hand on Jeff's shoulder, pushing him backward against the frame of the chair so that his face tilted upward and his gaze rose to meet his own. "Better let us have it, kid. Whatever."

"It was when I wrote about getting to a real psychiatrist, not just Mrs. Culkin, and I said I thought I had to because I was—"

"Because you," Nate prompted.

"Because I felt surer and surer that I—" He broke off. His fingers interlaced and twisted at each other, knuckle by knuckle.

"That you what, Jeff?" Margie asked. "No matter what, it'll be better to say."

"Felt surer and surer I was queer."

"Queer."

"A fag, a fairy, a homo. That was last October. But now tonight, Dad just said, he warned me I could have one more year of analysis to straighten out, or—" He lowered his head and raised his big shoulders; they could see only part of his face, see the strained torso.

"Or what, Jeff?" Margie asked.

"When I wrote the letter, I said I wasn't sure. But since then a couple of things have happened that—"

"Don't be so wild, man," Nate said. "I'll get you a drink."

"No, I can't, honestly. Anyway, now Dad said if this second year didn't help—he said unless I did get straight for sure by next year, and unless I was willing to spill my guts to them about whether I was or not, why then I could go live in a place of my own."

"That's a good rotten thing to tell a guy," Nate said.

"So I told him I'd get out right now. And I did. I've got some money. I'll go to the Y."

"How the hell much chance does he think he's giving you or

your analysis," Nate went on, "with that kind of threat hanging over you? Christ."

Margie knelt down on one knee so that her face was on a level with Jeff's. "Jeffie, you've got us, whatever happens. And Mama too, I bet."

His hand went out toward her shoulder, but he didn't touch it and he didn't look at her.

"You can live with us," she said. "You just move in here."

"I can't. I'm going to cut loose from Yale and get a job and not take one cent off that bastard for the rest of my life."

"You can still live with us to start with. In that room next to Lynnie's room. We'll stack the junk up at one side and put in an army cot."

Jeff looked at her as if he had never seen her before. Maybe he never had, he thought, you never look at your sister. Her bright dark eyes surprised him, her hair, thick and springing in a way he had never noticed before, her mouth too, strong and full. He had never noticed any of it, her own special face; though he would have recognized her instantly in any street, in any city anywhere in the world, he had never really seen her as a person before, only as part of his family.

Was the same thing true of the way he saw his brother Don? His mother? His goddamn father?

Suddenly his throat knotted and he began to cry, a convulsive sobbing, his body twisting away so that his face burrowed into the back of the armchair. They both stood back in silence. In a gesture to Margie, Nate put his index finger to his lips and went to the bookcase, whose lower shelf acted as their only bar. He poured two inches of Bourbon into a short wide glass and took it back to Jeff. "Here, boarder," he said. "Grab one on the house."

Jeff looked up and suddenly laughed, a burst of laughter. His fingers massaged his face into smooth lines again, as if he had just taken off his football helmet. "I could just use that." He knocked back half of it, then gulped and coughed. "Beer's my speed, but I'm sure glad to get this."

"I'd be glad too," Margie said to Nate.

"And me." He went back to the bookshelf. Their voices were all artificial, too bright, temporary voices for use in crisis. Jeff drank the rest of his Bourbon, coughed again, laughed once more and fell silent. They were being terrific, both of them. He didn't know what he had expected, but they were terrific. Walking the streets, half running, he hadn't even planned to come here to their house, and yet the minute the idea sprang into his mind he had fallen in with it, like getting signals at a hot point in a game. All he had known up to then was that he wasn't going home that night, or any night, that was all that was for sure. He had thought of phoning Pete to ask if he could stay there for the night, but he'd have to explain or make something up, and both things were impossible. He had thought of a hotel, then of the Y. Then "Margie and Nate" ran across his mind, like the news bulletins flashing around the old building on Times Square. Not Don and Jenny, never Don and Jenny, only Margie and Nate. Don would be nothing like Margie at something like this, even if he was his only brother. He would be nothing like Nate either. He wouldn't be like the old man of course, but there would be something controlled and way off there about every word Don said and every word he did not say.

He had never thought that of Don before, but now he was positive. There was something so collected about Don, so regular, so orthodox—God, he was beginning to get measurements of people whom he had never once tried to measure before. Out of your own awful try at measuring yourself, holding that goddamn yardstick up to your own life, figuring, sizing yourself up, you started to get a whole new yield of data on other people too.

Nate had come back with a drink for Margie and one for himself. He had put ice cubes in both of them, Jeff noticed, and water too, neither of which he had bothered with for him. They both sat down, Margie on the floor near the big old sofa, Nate in the sofa, his right arm over the back of it, relaxed and easy. They were waiting for him to go on, Jeff knew, but all at once he felt queasy, just a touch, but enough to make the sweat start inside his shirt.

"Can I say one thing, Jeff?" Nate asked.

"Anything."

"Just this one thing. It's nobody's goddamn business what you are, now or a year from now or ten years from now. Not your father's, not your mother's, not mine or Margie's, not even what's-his-name's, your doctor's. If you believe that, you'll have at least one guy who agrees with you. Me."

Jeff squinted a little, concentrating. He looked down at his sister, then back to Nate. "You don't think it matters, one way or another?"

"Sure it matters. It's a lousy life if you're homosexual these days. It wasn't always, it wasn't in ancient Greece, but it sure is today. But that's your business, or it would be once you get to be twenty-one years old and an official 'adult,' and it's nobody else's business, not your father's or mother's or the cops that go around bars, rounding up guys like cattle."

" 'Rounding them up like cattle.' " Jeff said it with emphasizing quotes around it. "You nearly killed me with that, at our house for Thanksgiving. That was the first time I ever heard of the Wolfenden Report, the first time I ever knew anybody felt it might be just nobody else's business."

"I haven't changed my mind. Neither has Wolfenden. Neither have a whole lot of other people. It's a kind of growing thing. You'll see."

"You don't mean I shouldn't try another year with Dr. Dudley?"

"Of course you should try another year or five more years. I said that the way things are now, it's a rotten deal, and who wouldn't try to get away from a rotten setup if there's any goddamn way he can steer clear of it? But that's *all* I meant and all I'll ever mean."

There was a pause. Jeff said nothing, and Nate felt his own words alive about them. At last Margie said, "Jeff, I'll call Mama and say you're staying here. She must be scared stiff by now." Jeff started to answer, but instead set his empty glass down hard on the table and said, "I'll be back in a minute." He raced to the bathroom and they could hear the spasms of his vomiting. They looked at each other, and Margie put her hand out to cover Nate's.

Part Two
1965-1966

CHAPTER NINE

Just as the year 1960 would forever be for Tessa not the year when
Kennedy defeated Nixon and became President, but the year
when Jeff wrote his letter, just as 1961 would be not the year when
man first orbited the earth, but the year when Jeff left home, so
each segment of the next long period of living, 1962, '63, '64, became for her a twofold experience, one the world's, the other her
own within it, the private memory encapsulated into the public
one as the hidden pulsing heart is encapsulated into the visible
outer flesh.

She had always had a good memory, one that often astonished
—or vexed—other people whose own memory was faulty, and
sometimes she was vain about her ability to recall dates, names,
exact phrases of speech. But in these years of the early Sixties she
came to hate her memory, hate its tenacity, the accuracy with
which it gave her again and again the sight and sound of scenes
she had already lived through and would not elect to endure again.

She tried to blur some of these memories, consciously attempted to erase or at least dull them, tried like some perverse
photographer to get them out of focus, haze them over. With some
she succeeded, but there were others that defied her, that remained clear, sharp, and with them an undimmed tape bearing
voices, also clear, the words distinct, the inflections unchanged.

One such ineradicable memory was that last scene between Ken
and Jeff. A thousand times over, the rising voices came back to
her, the anger as they faced each other across the table, the awful

finality as Jeff hurled shut the door behind him, that furious young voice saying, "I'll cut loose right now."

Until Margie had telephoned late that evening, she had been so distracted by fear of what Jeff might do in his first wild rage that she could think of nothing else. Bizarre notions had crowded in upon her: he would barge crazily into traffic and be hit by a car, he would leap from the highest span of the George Washington Bridge, he would hurl himself from some friend's penthouse window.

"I didn't mean it the way he took it," Ken had finally said, addressing the blind silence of the room. "All I meant was that if he were going to go on acting as if his analysis was none of our business, for another year and maybe another year after that, why then, maybe he'd want to cut loose from the family in other ways too."

She had nodded, as if she accepted his contrition, but afterward, that same evening, when Margie had said Jeff would be living with them for a while, she had behaved outrageously.

"Whatever way you 'meant it,' " she had stormed at Ken, "the result is the same. You, a great big liberal civilized man, you threw him out because you can't stand the idea of your son being homosexual." Her own voice had risen, shrewish. "*Your* son, yours. Anybody else's son or daughter, okay, that's nothing, let us understand life and nature and remain decent. But *your* son?"

They had quarreled bitterly, about that, about everything, about nonsensical long-buried nothings that now became the surrogates for their pain and grief, and at last they had slept together, not even touching, but in the need of each to feel less abandoned. For her that need had kept on long past those first days. She had in part lost her anger at Ken, knowing too well what tangle of emotion lay behind his behavior, and she found that she needed him in a new degree, needed his actual presence if he were delayed or absent, feeling the biting impact of stillness in the house, as if it were now a hostile occupant with her. Unexpectedly she had found a continuing comfort in Ken's continuing remorse. Not that he harped on it, but telltale phrases revealed every so often that it remained an operating factor in his thoughts. "When you get trapped by thinking too far ahead," he had said one evening, talking of some situation at the office, "it can be a tighter trap than not thinking ahead at all." She had heard the double meaning and an ache arose dully within her, for him, for herself, for their shared deprivation of the son they both loved and missed.

When the others had left home, Don and Margie, it was to marry and have homes of their own, families of their own, in the sweet natural sequence of the generations, but this departure of their last child was a knifing asunder, sudden, raw and somehow ruthless in its essence—perhaps as ruthless to Jeff as to them. But this they would never know, for no one would ever tell them.

At the beginning there had been some comfort in knowing that Jeff was living with Margie and Nate, remaining "part of the family," almost like his being off at school and to be home again in the not too distant future. Tactfully Margie had suggested in the first days that it might be "better if you don't phone too often at the start," and Tessa had not called at all, except during the day when he was at work and she could ask for news of him. There was little news, except that he had meant it about not going to Yale. He was going to college right in the city, was indeed already enrolled at C.C.N.Y. and would not need a cent from his parents for the rest of his education.

An unexpected unwillingness had mounted hotly in Tessa at the news, a snob unwillingness she was ashamed of. City College was fine, Hunter College was fine, free education and public schools were of the essence—she had never questioned that. But she had never questioned, either, the other values, the social values, the later-in-life values of schools of a different sort, the private schools with the better facilities and equipment, with the quiet campuses and quads, the better-known faculties and better-known names. It was distasteful to her to feel that dismay within her own thoughts, but she was caught with it. Caught red-handed, she thought ruefully, thinking ahead to his interviews or résumés when he applied for some job at some snob office where Yale '65 would get him the job that C.C.N.Y. '65 might not.

The rueful thought, however, had proved the beginning of a cure, and before too long she had begun a turnabout in attitude which she also could not help mistrusting a little. Soon she had begun to feel proud of Jeff for his independence, for his own lack of the snob quotient, and finally for his determination to do it on his own. She wished she could tell him so directly, instead of through Margie or Nate, and finally she had telephoned him one evening. It had inevitably been a stilted call, with most of his replies the usual Jeff replies of "Okay" or "Great," and most of her own contributions equally pallid, but after she had asked how his job was going and what movies he had seen, she did manage a word or two about finding herself rather impressed at his "gutsy decision" to go to college on his own. "Yeah, well, it's the one way," he had said, his voice putting period, paragraph to that discussion.

Toward the end of that first summer—she still had not seen him—there had come a letter from him; she remembered the twinge of fear when she stooped down to its familiar handwriting on the envelope outside the hall door. But it had merely told her that he had been referred by Dr. Dudley to a Dr. David Isaacs in New York, and before he even paid his preliminary visit to this New York analyst, he thought it best to check in with her about whether she still was willing to have him continue, "despite the big hassle with Dad." The schedule would be the same, the cost the same.

She had written her answer in three sentences and mailed it within minutes. "Of course, Jeff, for as long as it's any good to you. Or as long as you think it might be. And whatever else, don't forget I love you. Mama."

She had been relieved that he was persisting with it. The Greeks had said, "Know thyself." The moderns said, "Get analyzed." The purpose was the same, and for a while she could again think of him in analysis with relief and an unseen comfort. Yet as time had brought another series of "no comment" bills from the new Dr. Isaacs, each as blanked of any awareness of the recipient's anxiety as Dr. Dudley's monthly bills had been, vouchsafing no information except that numerical precision, Jeff . . . eight visits, Jeff . . . nine visits, her own interior rage had again mounted at the resumption of The Silence. This time she could not even visualize the doctor who sat at the head of Jeff's unhappy couch, could not guess whether he was young or old, thin or stout, bearded or clean-shaven. Dr. Isaacs had not even felt the necessity of asking her in for a preliminary visit. Apparently when a patient was in the second year of analysis, all that was regarded as pertinent was the previous analyst's data or set of opinions.

There was something so lofty in all this, she had decided, that it had to be resented by any but the most ignorant and docile of parents. The analytic profession made the assumption, it was clear, that the patient was all, that the patient alone had value or importance. To demur at this was to put oneself into the obnoxious position of saying, "But I am important too." Yet she could not help thinking that somewhere in the ancient Hippocratic Oath there might have been some phrase, some small dangling modifying phrase that said, "And I also affirm that I will never be sadistic to those who love the patient and wait to hear how he fares, well or ill." In other medical situations, the surgeon who did not send out word from the operating room as soon as possible, or the doctor from the sickroom, was regarded as a brutish type; why, then, should there be so gross an exception made so routinely toward parents when the illness consisted of neurosis or psychosis? Had Freud or Adler or Jung all remained so distant from those who longed for a word, a clue, if not anything as definite as a prognosis?

Somewhere she had come across a reference to a letter Freud had written to the unhappy mother of a homosexual, but she had been unable to find the letter itself; no library catalogue listed it, and neither Mark Waldo nor Nate had ever heard of it. But she was somehow sure that Freud hadn't written that letter to be aloof, to be cool and correct, that something of insight and caring had gone into it. If she ever found it she might send a copy, also without comment, to the new Dr. Isaacs, neatly tucked in along with a monthly check. She might even send a copy to Dr. Dudley, for old times' sake.

Ah well, let it go; if Dr. Isaacs could help Jeff, what else would matter? Even if he could not help him change over, any more than Dr. Dudley was able to—

She never knew when it was that she had first given in, as it were, to a theorem she had been harboring for some indefinable time but which she had been steadily shoving out of consideration. Without articulating it, she had somehow begun to know that Dr. Isaacs' "help" would have to come in some subtler form than the simplistic happy-ending twenty-five percent which she had for so long had fantasies about, that miracle transformation into an uncomplex heterosexuality.

There was something cruel, she thought at times, in any psychiatrist even speaking of that twenty-five percent, except to people who had already entered the magic percentile, and to their parents. What of the other seventy-five percent? Did they, who did not achieve "the cure"—did they not find in their analysis an added loss of self-worth, an added burden of failure and exclusion? And if so, was not psychiatry itself adding, to three out of four of its young patients, an extra and overwhelming pain and trauma?

She had kept all this to herself, not wanting to share its sharpness with Ken, but he must have sensed that she was going through some new phase of discouragement, for suddenly one evening in that first fall Ken had looked across the room at her and said, "Tessa, let's clear out for a few days over Thanksgiving. It'll be rough for you this year, so let's take a powder instead, go somewhere way off. What do you think?"

"It's nice, you thinking about it."

"Sometimes it's okay to think ahead, I suppose."

"Oh, Ken, it's a good idea. Let's not think too much, let's just go. Let's decide where and we'll go."

And they had, to London for a week, and it had been strange to spend Thanksgiving far from the family, strange and in its way healing. They had seen plays, they had seen British publishers and agents, they had seen authors, they had forgotten the great American celebration of organized thankfulness, or nearly forgotten. Don and Jenny were managing the whole holiday, and Don was for a while the Don of yore, saying, "We'll take on the whole damn thing for everybody. Go ahead and don't worry about a thing."

Don had been anything but the Don of yore as far as Jeff was concerned. When he first heard of his leaving home and why, he had asked him out for lunch, and later said to her, "It's a damn shame, a kid like Jeff."

"He's still Jeff," she had retorted.

She had been hurt, hurt on Jeff's behalf, hurt on her own, in a solidarity she couldn't quite explain. Siding with one son against the other was a bad business, but there it was. In the ensuing months, Don seemed to stay away from Jeff or any mention of Jeff, as if to protect something of his own that might now be threatened. Don was an architect in a large, rather conservative firm, specializing in public buildings, schools, libraries, museums; he and Jenny had their own children and their own problems. It was natural for him to find little time for a younger brother. Jeff and Don had been drifting apart for some time, but after that one lunch, they drifted further, apparently without so much as a phone call between them. By her own code, she could not chide Don for his neglect, or suggest that this might be a period when an older brother's support could be especially valuable. Only once did she show open irritation at Don; it was at Don's own house and he had been talking about another young architect at the office.

"The word is that he's a homo and—"

"The real word," she said sharply, "is homosexual."

"What? Why—oh, I see. I'm sorry."

That may have been, she was to think much later, the first time one of those words hit me like a rock in the face. More and more, as time passed, did words like "homo" or "fag" or "fairy" send the same knife of loathing through her, at the person who used them, as did words like "kike" or "nigger." But when they were used in a joke that brought loud laughter, the loathing was for herself too, because at the end of the joke she laughed with the others, despising herself for the laughter as for a corrupted cowardice. She noticed that men always laughed at these jokes with a special ring, a salacious ring, and she wondered why this should be so. Ken had once said he wanted to hit anybody who said "fag," yet when he was present, he would laugh too, along with everybody else.

One evening she had asked him about this and in a burst of words, for him a burst of words, he had said, "It's instinctive, not to give anything away."

"I wonder what Jeff does, when he hears the jokes."

"He laughs too." He sounded weary. "The whole business is so nasty and complex."

* * *

Another memory . . . Ken's writing to Jeff. What it had cost him she could only surmise. It was during that trip to London and he did not talk about it in advance, nor did he seem inclined to discuss it afterward. He had gone to the desk in their hotel room

late one afternoon, sat there for a while, pen in hand, eyes raised
to a hunting print on the wall above him, and then wrote rapidly
for several minutes. When he had finished, he handed her a single
sheet of paper.

Dear Jeff,

This isn't an easy letter to write, but I have been thinking
of writing it for quite a while. I think you mistook my resentment to some degree, but I can see why you did. I was
angry at your apparent willingness to go on for an unlimited
time with analysis, without giving us the benefit of any
interim report of progress—or even of lack of progress. I think
you showed that you didn't really believe that we care very
much about your well-being and your happiness and your future. Now, a few months later, and especially with the absence you've elected, it seemed important to me to try to put
some of this into words to you. I hope you'll read between
the lines, since I don't think I've got it down clearly enough
even now. I hope we're to see you before too long.

Always,
Dad

She had read it twice, her throat tight, and she had said only,
"Send it now, Ken, don't change anything." They had looked at
each other and a spurt of sympathy rose in her, a small hot geyser
of feeling, almost pity. It must have been harder for him than
he had been able to say, all these months of knowing that it was
he who had set into motion the roiling turbulences of distance
and separation between them and their own son. She suddenly
wondered whether her own willingness to forgive had been deep
enough. Poor Ken, he had his own freight to carry, piled upon
him from his own childhood and his own upbringing, as every
other human being had his own inherited or environmental burden to carry, through all his ensuing life. As she had. As Jeff had.

Jeff had answered the letter by a phone call on their return
from England, a short call but the first call originated by him.
"It's me, Mama," he had begun soberly. "I got Dad's letter, could
I talk to him?"

"He's right here. It's nice to hear you. Wait a sec."

"Hello, Jeff," Ken had said. "Good to talk to you." There had
followed a few sentences and then she had heard Ken say, "Maybe

we can get together for part of Christmas. I'd like that and so would your mother."

She had nodded to Ken, and then nodded once more, as if she were signaling, yes, yes, get it set, make it firm, a commitment. And she thought, Maybe everything will come back together again after all. Jeff is not vindictive, neither is Ken. Maybe—

Christmas had been merry enough, she remembered, and all the other Christmases since then. It was at Margie and Nate's that the tree and the presents and the gathering of all the family had taken place, and Jeff had managed their first meeting since the break with an odd and mature dignity. The "Hi" and "Great" never sounded; he had greeted her solemnly; she could still hear his "Merry Christmas, Mama," and feel his kiss on her cheek, he stooping in his old way to plant it there. Then he had straightened and looked at his father. For an instant neither of them spoke, then it was Jeff who said, "Dad, Merry, merry," and they had shaken hands. Ken had put both his hands around Jeff's and something in Tessa was moved by that simple fact. The extra hand, the reaching gesture, the small offering beyond the orthodox greeting. If Jeff noticed he had given no sign, and the general bedlam of other greetings, from Don and Jenny and their children, from an excited and bewildered Lynnie, all mixed in with admiration of the handsome towering tree and the lavish spread of bright and shining packages beneath it—it all made a combination potent enough to sweep them all along in what seemed like happiness.

* * *

Her memory again . . . that summer afternoon a year after Jeff had left them, and Margie calling her to suggest she stop by on the way home from the office.

"Just you and me, Mother. Nate won't be here, and neither will Jeff."

"Is anything wrong?"

"Not from my point of view, or Nate's."

"Then it's about Jeff."

"Ring the bell hard, in case I'm in the garden with Lynnie."

It was going to hurt. This was something Margie felt she ought to know, some line crossed, some definition arrived at. As she remembered back to that August heat smashing at her skin, she could again hear Margie's voice beyond the closed front door of their house saying, "It's your grandma, Lynnie, should we let her in?" and again the door was opening on them, Lynnie chittering away, pressing against Grandma's knees in greeting. All young animals were enchanting, she remembered thinking then, puppies, kittens, lion cubs, but a baby human was appealing beyond all the others, and one's own beautiful little grandchild was traditionally irresistible. Her heart had lifted. Maybe it wouldn't hurt.

"You both look grand," she had said. "What a tan." They had taken their vacation in Bermuda, as she and Ken had often done when they were young sun worshippers, but in their own Bermuda days, nobody took year-old babies along on vacations; now all young couples seemed to, their babies slung across their backs in papoose-like harnesses. It was a delight to see them.

Margie led the way to the back of the house to the small oblong of garden that was beginning to show signs of their planting and care. A round table, painted white, shielded by a chintz-lined umbrella rising from its center, had three chairs placed around it, and a sharp visual image struck Tessa, of Jeff and Margie and Nate all seated there together, laughing and talking together, comfortable and free of strain, contemporaries, removed a thousand miles from the continuing crises of Jeff's last year at home. Envy pierced her, almost jealousy. They were the young. Apart from any other tie, apart from any other relationship, they had, all three, that singular relationship: they were the young. They saw the world the way the young saw it, right or wrong; it was their world and their view of it, theirs, as if the older generation were slipping off its very surface, were already loosening its grasp on today's life in today's world, its hold still tight on the past, on memories of the Depression, of Roosevelt and World War II, of Truman and Korea, but yielding to the young as far as the present and the future were concerned.

"All right, dear," she said after Margie had brought out a cool drink for her and one for herself. "What's this about?"

"About Jeff, as you guessed."

"You said nothing was wrong." She heard her own tension and it annoyed her. "Is there something, after all?"

"Nothing he's told us about," Margie said. "Look, Mother,

we've been through this before—Jeff doesn't tell us what he does, whom he sees, whom he likes. Except for that first night he came here, he's never 'confided' one thing."

Then it isn't just me he excludes, Tessa thought swiftly. I'm glad. She said nothing.

"The thing is," Margie continued, "we don't expect him to and he knows we don't." Faintly she stressed the *we* and waited for her mother to make some comment, but in turn Tessa simply waited for her to go on. "The first thing you thought of when I phoned today," Margie continued, "was 'Is anything wrong?' But Nate and I don't even think of 'trouble' about Jeff, and that makes him feel easier with us."

Tessa flushed. "Did you get me over here to tell me how much wiser you two are?"

"Now, Mother. We don't feel wiser or feel anything. I asked you over because I didn't want to blast this at you over any phone. Jeff is moving out."

"Moving out where?"

"Up near college, to 'a dump,' to quote him, that he can afford."

"When, Margie?"

"Next week. He's been searching for it for a long time, and he's been driving a cab nights, to stack up some extra money."

"I didn't know—well, I never do know any more, do I?"

"We didn't know about the one-room flat until he located it, and that was yesterday."

"Driving a cab every night? Can he manage college if he does?"

"You know Jeff. Top-of-the-heap no matter what he does on the side."

"Yes." There was a silence while they looked away from each other. Then Tessa said, "Is he going to live alone?"

"If he's going to have a roomie, he hasn't said."

"I don't suppose he would. Would say, I mean."

Margie made no reply to this and Tessa regretted having said it. The garden seemed suddenly hotter, the air more humid.

"He also said," Margie went on, "he was going to keep on with Dr. Isaacs one more year. Even if there weren't any miracles available. Just as insurance, he said, or maybe a little peace of mind about the way you are."

Tessa stared at the ground. Reason enough, yes. If analysis

could free you of the clawing and clutch of self-hate, then thank
God for that. So all those long-ago daydreams of a "cure" were
dimming for Jeff too, or possibly were already over. Almost it was
as if she too, in this single moment, were feeling a greater peace
of mind. But then there came the wrenching longing that she
could still be back there seeking out Mark Waldo and Dr. Dudley,
still fierce with supplication and hope.

Aloud she said, "Tell Jeff, of course I'll back him for more
analysis. He knows it already, but tell him again."

Suddenly Margie leaned toward her and kissed her. "I wish it
didn't hurt you so."

"If only it didn't. You're a nice girl."

"Some of the world's greatest people—"

"I know, dear. I really do know. I've been giving myself an entire education—"

"Nate told me you were."

"It's none too easy to get any answers, though. There are always supposed to be the right answers in the back of the book, but
not about this."

"So Nate tells me. He says it keeps shifting all the time. And
growing. It's become a sort of special field for him."

"Is he still hoping to get enough space in the paper someday?"

"You know Nate." Unexpectedly she picked Lynnie up and
hugged her, so hard that Lynnie yelped in protest. "He's not the
fellow to lay off a subject just because the managing ed thinks he
should."

"He's a one, that Nate."

Margie hugged the baby again. "We're pretty lucky," she said
to the top of Lynnie's head.

"She has a great daddy," Tessa said in a swoop of resentment.
"You've heard a hundred times over that Dad never meant it for
that day, or even for that year."

"I didn't mean to compare Nate with Dad."

"Unconsciously you did. Dad is what he is, just as Jeff is what
he is. Why can you young people find it so easy to stay loose and
easy about the way Jeff is, and so tough to stay loose and easy
about the way Jeff's father is? Or Jeff's mother, for that matter."

"Oh, Mother, please." She rose, put the baby down and began
to pace up and down on the thin strip of grass beyond the grav-

eled circle. She looked angry and Tessa thought desolately, All I
have to do is antagonize her and Nate. Then my life would be
complete.

*   *   *

There had been no antagonism, and when she had told Ken that
Jeff was moving to a place of his own, he had only said, "He's
never going to come back here, Tessa. I've known that for a long
time, and you must have too."

"You seem acquiescent about it."

"I think I've been preparing for it."

"In general, you seem calmer about him. I'm glad."

"It's easier in the abstract."

"You mean, not seeing him."

"I think it makes it easier." He paused and then slowly added,
"For him too."

It was still vivid, the sound of those slow words. Ken still preferred not to talk in any depth about any aspect of Jeff's life, and
the drift of months and years had not perceptibly changed him in
that regard. Now, in this year of 1965, he would be sixty and there
was no doubting the sixty. He had remained reasonably well; he
had long since lost any look of the invalid. He disliked remembering that he had ever had a stroke and was remarkably free of the
hypochondriac need to talk of symptoms or medicines, but there
was visible in his eyes now a fatigue that eight hours of sleep did
not clear away, and visible in the hold of his muscles and sinews
an inability to give full support to the skeleton and organs within
them.

She was grateful that he had rejected the role of the chronic invalid so stoutly and admired him for it. And somewhere along the
road she herself had managed to reject at least part of her resentment that he did not want even to hear about what she had
once called "my entire new education." It was her own search, of
course, a search that might slake her own thirst to know whatever
there was to know about homosexuality, and Ken could scarcely
be held accountable if he did not share that parched need.

But she had kept on searching. God knew, she had never
stopped searching. It had become an interior part of her life, that
searching. She had never returned to that first obsessed need to

cram herself with scientific works by Krafft-Ebing and Havelock Ellis and Freud; she had realized soon enough that she could not extract true meaning so cheaply from what was to her an alien terminology in an extended foreign field.

But she had begun a different kind of reading, her own kind of reading, layman's reading, fiction and non-fiction, every kind of book about the homosexual and homosexuality, good books, bad books, older works by André Gide and Marcel Proust, newer ones by James Baldwin and Jean Genet and Gore Vidal and Mary Renault, as well as an increasing crop of recent "sensations," these latter mostly novels, and for the most part so explicit in their sexual descriptions that she found them repugnant.

Yet in the moment of feeling bruised and revolted, she would remind herself that she also found many recent heterosexual novels equally repugnant because of their explicitness. Totally opposed to any form of censorship, she had always drawn back in her own tastes from specificity in writing about sex, and now she was growing sick of the vulgar dynamics in so much current writing, the descriptives, the directions, the juices and smells and pulses and stroking and groaning and all the rest of the clinical minutiae which a certain kind of author apparently held essential to evoking in the reader an understanding of passion or love.

One of the greatest love stories ever written, she thought one evening, was *Anna Karenina*, and if she remembered—it was years since she had read it—Tolstoy had given no physical detail at all about their making love. She wondered if she did remember, and with her predilection for looking things up, went to the bookshelves and took down the novel. The gold lettering on its spine was barely legible; she looked inside to the title page to see the date of this particular edition and was not surprised to find it nearly thirty years old, pleased also, for its age seemed to speak of its universality. She began to read, skimming the early chapters until she came to the first meeting between Anna and Count Vronsky, then she began to read the subtle course of their early attraction to each other. Soon she was no longer skimming but reading again the words and sentences she had first read when she was young, read them now with a responsiveness she could never have felt in her youth. And then at last, nearly two hundred pages into the long novel, there came the beginning of a new chapter, and with an admiration that was an admixture of a reader's feelings and an editor's, she read the words Tolstoy had chosen for his grand scene of culmination and passion. She read the brief paragraph and then read it once more; the editor in her made her copy it, to take to the office for future use with some young modern author who felt that the one and only way, the obligatory way, to write about the act of making love was with "honesty" and the inclusion of every detail.

"That which for Vronsky had been almost a whole year the one absorbing desire of his life, replacing all his old desires; that which for Anna had been an impossible, terrible, and even for that reason more entrancing dream of bliss, that desire had been fulfilled. He stood before her, pale, his lower jaw quivering, and besought her to be calm, not knowing how or why."

Tessa read it again in her own typing and visualized it as a few lines in the manuscript of one of her own authors. It was of course out of the question today. There was an other-century flavor to it, a formality, a strangeness which came not only from the fact that it had been written in another language, in another time, but written in another set of values. A gem of a paragraph, a small masterpiece within the larger masterpiece, its delicacy lay not in the retailing of what the lovers had done, what the lovers had touched, fondled, caressed, spoken, but in the consummate art of suggestion.

For still another time she read the few lines. She was a modern reader, a modern editor, a modern woman, and yet the brief passage spoke to her with an import she could not quite measure or describe. For one thing, the lines told her, by the satisfaction they aroused in her, that she herself was not a Peeping Tom while reading about love. They told her that she was one who found authors who do choose to make Peeping Toms of their readers, and those readers who so obligingly become the Peeping Toms—that she found all of them repellent and offensive.

She had never articulated this for herself so clearly before, and there was a thump of recognition now that she actually enjoyed. And it is the same, she thought, when it comes to reading about heterosexuals in bed or about homosexuals in bed. Some things need to remain private.

The Wolfenden Committee had specified "in private." More

and more the decisions of the Wolfenden Committee were becoming her decisions, their attitudes her attitudes. It was a new
experience, on an odd stratum of living; she had become the pupil
again, pupil though adult, pupil though parent, in this vast unknown area of sexual behavior.

.It had been Nate who had at first guided her when she told
him she wanted to know everything there was to know about "Mr.
Wolfenden and his committee."

"It's Sir John, not Mister," he had corrected her, with a small
conspiratorial wink. "He's not a doctor either, but an educator
and sociologist, chancellor of Reading University, C.B.E., and
then knighted, that sort of thing, quite a chap. You won't find
much on him in a library, but you could go to the British Information Service, on Park Avenue, I think, at Fortieth, but you better
check—they're moving to one of the glassy new buildings any day."

"Do I just ask for the Wolfenden Report?"

"Ask for whatever *Hansards* cover the debate on it, in the House
of Commons. It hasn't got to the Lords yet, I gather."

"*Hansard*, oh yes. It's like our *Congressional Record*, isn't it?"

"And just about as exciting reading."

But it had been exciting in strange ways. She went back to the
bound blue volumes several times, following the debates as they
were recorded from the late Fifties up to now, nearly a decade
later, and it reassured her that the committee was no little group
of psychiatrists but a large and complex gathering of illustrious
people from many walks of life, two members of Parliament, two
judges of the High Court, two doctors, three women, several lawyers and ministers. It took on an immense importance that the
famous first report was no off-the-top-of-the-head affair, but that
it had been based on no less than sixty-two sessions over a two- or
three-year period, a report which had been publicly dubbed by
some British authority "the major social statement of the twentieth
century."

All this she made notes on, and from time to time reported her
findings to Nate. Sometimes he himself made notes of what she
told him, saying, "You're my Official Researcher, remember." He
was still building his own file against that "big article" he was
someday going to write, "either for the paper or some magazine
or whoever." From the beginning he had let her see whatever data

he had found for himself, news items he had come across, special pieces he had found in medical journals.

Always she had urged him to keep on with his project and to keep on "educating me." And as her education proceeded, through Nate's material or her own efforts, she would marvel at the fluctuating opinions of the highest authorities. As surely as one psychiatrist wrote a paper pronouncing homosexuality an illness or disease, another would declare that there was nothing ill or diseased about it; as soon as one body of new research offered proof that homosexuals were neurotic or even psychotic, a counter body of new research would offer proof that tests of two scientifically controlled groups of men, one group heterosexual, the other homosexual, both groups matched for I.Q., environment, age, economic factors, parental influences—that these most scientific of tests revealed no differences between the two groups on any level of human behavior or character or potential or achievement, apart from the single level of sex.

Her overriding reaction to such manifold disparities of theory or opinion within the world of psychiatry or analysis had at first been a heightened confusion and a nearly plaintive impatience with all the warring points of view. Later, a good deal later, this gave way to a kind of thin hope. It was a new kind of hope for her, unrelated to that long-ago hope for miracles that would turn homosexuals into heterosexuals. This was not only alien to that frantic earlier hope; it was on another plateau of thinking and of feeling.

So little was yet sure. So little yet known. So many fine minds were out there in the world, in England, in this country, in Denmark and Sweden and France and everywhere else, thinking and theorizing and testing and formulating new approaches to the problem of homosexuality. From this sort of inquiry in other fields, this manifold, warring, contradictory inquiry, all knowledge had finally emerged; could it not be that man was now at some new threshold about the age-old subject of the homosexual?

She had begun to wonder about that, and with the first tentative thought of such a possibility, her life seemed to move a notch from where it had always been. She hoped for nothing less than that threshold; she could feel it off there somewhere, waiting to be crossed, perhaps already crossed, though she did not yet know

that it had been. She whose inner life had so unexpectedly become meshed with the thousand variables embraced by that
single word, "homosexual," with all the thousand questions of
potential, stigma, acceptance, disability, persecution, she who
cared so intensely within herself about the world's history of rejection, now could find in this very disparity of opinion among
the various "experts" the first seeds of change for the future,
change that might carry with it change for her son, change for
all the other sons and daughters of all the parents who had been
unable as yet to move that single notch.

Thinking of them all, her heart filled.

* * *

There would come, every once in a while, a happy stretch of time,
an unexpected respite, unrelated to the great central core of what
life had become, and doubly welcome because of it, welcome to
Tessa and to Ken, welcome to all of them.

One such happy period came with the birth of Margie and
Nate's second baby, born when Lynnie was nearly three, a boy
whom they had named, in some flinging gesture, Jeff. Not Jeffrey,
not Geoffrey, not Jefferson, just Jeff Jacobs, that was it, just by
itself, neat.

"Another great by-line," Nate had said in half a shout when
they had told Tessa, and Margie had added, "When we told big
Jeff, he went bright red and sort of got all husky."

It had touched Tessa too, this sign of a continuing loyalty, part
of the singular relationship that had developed among the three
of them. Long after Jeff had moved out of their house into the
dump near the campus, the center of his family life continued to
be with Margie and Nate; birthdays were spent there, Thanksgiving and Christmas were always there, with Ken and her the "vis-
itors" for part of the day or evening. She remembered Ken's
eighty-year-old mother, sitting so silent and remote at one end
of the table, and her heart quaked briefly that the same role
seemed prematurely to be approaching for them. But it was gone
a moment later, that passing apprehension; neither Ken nor she
was out of it; far from it, with decreasing intimacy among them
all as a family, there was always some big nugget of news to tell,
some coup to reveal and be congratulated about.

One of these was Tessa's—another happy stretch in her life, in her professional life, a new excitement, a time of triumph. In reality it was Helena Ludwig's triumph, and only tangentially hers, yet at the office Tessa had found that it became, in the eyes of practically everybody, her own triumph. Helena was "your author," and the runaway bestseller *Hurricane* was "your book." Again and again she heard "Congratulations, Tessa" and "Great book, Tessa."

Her first disclaimers had sounded so mock-modest, so false ("I only edited it; it's Helena Ludwig who wrote it"), that she soon desisted and began to accept the office tributes as they were tendered, a tribute from her own colleagues for what they regarded as an accomplishment for her own work. Perhaps it wasn't as meretricious as it had seemed on the face of it; editors were part of the process or there wouldn't be any editors.

Helena Ludwig herself insisted on handing over a large share of credit for the unexpected good fortune she and her novel were experiencing. "Without your editing," she said to Tessa, "the book would never have come out right. Never. You will never know what support it was for me just to know you *cared* so about it."

It's like believing your own press agent, Tessa thought, but it's nice. She had never before had an author with a book like *Hurricane*, a major book club selection, an overnight smash in the stores, a movie sale, a big paperback deal, all within eight weeks of publication.

"You sure brought in a big one, Tessa," Tom Smiley said one morning, and Gail, who still acted as secretary to each of them, looked agitated until he had left Tessa's office.

"He's green," she then announced. "Green with envy and miffed as hell."

"Come on, Gail."

"Miffed because he dumped Helena Ludwig onto you after her first book, the one that bombed."

"I wouldn't say that."

"It's true. They're all the same anyway. If a woman makes it big, they hate it."

Loyalty, Tessa thought. Woman to woman. The same side of the fence. Maybe of the barricades. She smiled. A new feeling about women with jobs had been building everywhere in the last years, perhaps the old question of women's rights rising anew in the great new sweep of battle for black people's rights. There was constantly a new and stronger rejection of all the old myths about woman's place, with new emphasis about such practical little matters as women's pay compared to men's pay for comparable work, and about a woman's options about how to live her life.

There had been a burst of new books about this too which she had read, some quarrelsome and strident, others thoughtful and persuasive. On radio and television programs there arose entire new vocabularies about women's liberation and women's refusal to be sex objects, about male chauvinists and even sexist pigs. Magazine articles and feature pieces in the papers were beginning to be peppered by words and phrases that had once been confined to analysts' offices: post-menopausal intercourse, orgasm, male frustration and the ubiquitous penis envy, leitmotif of every mention of feminine stress or neurosis.

Again she had the feeling of a spinning world, of shifting mores and opinions, changing values. Again it was a heady feeling, with a thin new hope threading its way through all of it like a living scarlet thread.

That Christmas she received a three-thousand-dollar raise as well as a three-thousand-dollar Special Bonus. There was no mention of *Hurricane* or of Helena Ludwig, but she knew that by all the standards in the world of publishing, indeed of all business, she had just taken a quantum leap in her own professional status. It was a good feeling, at a time when she needed good feelings.

* * *

Tessa's sudden success was a powerful tonic for Ken. At his own office he was delighted with comments about the "emergency," the need for "getting her into Brannick and Lynn before she does any more damage," and with rebukes that "your wife is like a foreign agent out there." He would telephone Tessa in the middle of the day to pass along these tributes, and in so doing, he realized that it had been years since he had called her in business hours just to talk. Not to say he would be late for dinner, not to announce some change in plans, but just to talk.

It was pleasant. It was a pleasant time, and it was good to have something pleasant that lasted, that wasn't over after an hour or two, like a Christmas afternoon where everybody knew that there was a coating of sham over the "Merry Christmas" flung about so gaily. He had come to dislike these family gatherings, but they meant so much to Tessa that he could never bring himself to say, as he had that first time, "Let's go to London or someplace and skip the whole thing."

And so they had gone on, year by year, with the Happy Birthdays, and the Happy Thanksgivings, and the Happy New Years. That word, "happy." How many daydreams were connected with it. Happiness, perhaps the most elusive of all attainments in the course of life, and yet the pursuit of it was so much a part of the human need and yearning that it had even worked its way into the Declaration of Independence.

A pleasant time, that was attainment enough, he thought ruefully, and we might as well enjoy it to the fullest extent. He wondered how he could prolong it, for himself as well as for Tessa, when the first acute celebrating was ended. Perhaps it would be a mistake, though, to undertake prolonging it, as if by artifice and guile. Moods had a way of turning on you if you kept prodding at them; better to lie back and wait.

His own mood had been slowly changing, hadn't it? That supposedly infallible healer, Time, seemed to have failed him during the passing months and years since Jeff had told them, but though he was not healed, and never could be completely healed, he had surely the right to feel that he had conquered his first reflexes of pure horror. Tessa had helped him across the years; he could admit it freely without being able to say how she had managed to do it. She would never be free of her first feelings either, but after a year or two, it was clear to him that she had at last achieved a kind of weary capitulation to the fact itself, as if she had finally thought, It won't change, so the only thing left is to absorb it more thoroughly.

He too had absorbed it more thoroughly across the wide span of time, but even now, at sixty, it still mattered more than his intelligence told him it should. At times he caught himself thinking, If only it had been Margie. He recoiled from the notion, embarrassed that it should have occurred to him, wishing it had not, almost denying that it actually had. It was an absurdity, a male absurdity he could not account for, but it had always been easier for him to accept the visual image of two girls together than of two men together. Once he had told this to Tessa.

"Why, Ken, you'd better not say that out loud to anybody."

"I suppose it's another subtle sign of male chauvinism."

"Not so subtle."

"I didn't mean it seriously."

But he had felt it and that was serious enough. Some atavism, doubtless, some insistence that more was expected of a man, that nobler creature. This idiot doctrine he rejected out of hand, but as with the other, there was a residue, intact. Like that time long ago when Nate had been new to them and had said, "You were counting on your fingers and you went up to twelve—what's twelve letters long?" "Assimilation," he had answered, and they had laughed, but he still remembered his own struggling not to admit, if only to himself, that he wished Nate were not quite so Jewish a Jew. Now Nate was very nearly the core of the family, and even to remember that old secret wish made him feel iced over with apology or remorse. It had been an unsuspected shred of bigotry, a something he had held abandoned forever. Only when he had finally looked at it square and full had the remnants of it disappeared. As he had said then, you were not doomed to live out your life with every attitude unaltered; you could reprogram yourself if you wanted to enough.

Yet it still seemed impossible to do the same thing about Jeff. He had tried; God knew, he had tried. He certainly was much calmer, much less horrified, much more civilized. But he was always dubious about people who proclaimed how civilized they were, and if he were an outsider looking at the so-called civilized man, Kenneth Baird Lynn, he would be equally dubious now.

But if a total reprogramming were to come about for him, he would welcome it with hosannas. At sixty, though, you knew about possibles and impossibles. He could not emulate Tessa, for example, and make a study of it; he still resisted her when she began to tell him of some book she had read that dealt with homosexuality, nor could he help showing his discomfort, usually in the way she disliked most, by saying nothing at all. Even when there was something in the paper about it, they each reacted so differently. That front page of the *Times*—

GROWTH OF OVERT HOMOSEXUALITY

His eyes could still feel the impact of those large letters. Never before had that word been printed in large black type on the front page of so august a newspaper, never in his memory. Even now, some two or three years later, in 1965, he could feel again his sharp unwillingness to read phrases about New York having the largest population of homosexuals of any city, his rejection of the idea that family patterns and ill-adjusted parents might have played a part in the causation— Again he felt his insides grinding.

And Tessa! You could have sworn that Tessa had read another story from the one he had read. Tessa was excited by it, exhilarated, she saw a new era in it.

"It's coming out in the open, Ken," she had cried in excitement. "It's not just a ghastly thing or a dirty word. Look what it says here about medical opinion and all the difference of opinion . . . some of the leading psychiatrists in the country say there should be no laws whatever to punish homosexual conduct between consenting adults, just like that Englishman, Wolfenden."

Her elation had mystified him. It mystified him still, though he wanted so much to share the swing upward of her mood when this or that story appeared in the press. It was in that same *Times* story that he had first read the new word that was becoming the accepted word for homosexual. "Gay." It was the word preferred by the homosexual world, it appeared, but it seemed false to his ear, a pretend word. Gay? "Gay" meant lighthearted, happy, blithe, carefree. As so often with a new word, suddenly this "gay" was everywhere; one day you had never heard it and the next day you read it in every paper or magazine, heard it on every celebrity talk show. He tried to accept it for his own.

It came hard. It reminded him of the time he first began to hear the word "black," also the preferred word, preferred by Negroes themselves. By blacks themselves, rather. It had been hard to switch his vocabulary to accommodate the new demand but he did it. It was the prerogative of the black, surely, to call himself a black, if it pleased him, and there was none who could say him nay. There were so many new trends in the whole surge toward change in race relations, new trends to be adopted by those who were not black because it would have been an impertinence and a callousness to resist, an outsider's resistance at best, a hostile resistance at worst. In a surprisingly short time, he had come to feel the word "black" easy on his tongue, had come to feel the word "Negro" awkward, old-fashioned, degrading in some vague indescribable way.

Perhaps in time the word "gay" would seem equally the easy word, the right word, the word without criticism in it. He wanted that time to come, if that was what Jeff wanted, and people like Jeff. But he had wondered whether he would ever be able to speak it without feeling a falsity in its single small syllable. Gay, when there was so much pain and shame and fear and secrecy connected with it?

I will never believe it, he had thought then. I'll say it, I'll want to believe it, maybe I'll come to think other words are hate words and want to give them up forever, just as I already want to give up phrases like "Jeff and people like Jeff," lumping them all together, the way bigots lump all Jews together or all blacks together or all cops together or all anybody together. You think you're through with such loaded nonsense and then you get trapped.

That small word "gay" might be a trap. He would watch out for it, would never resist it. In his mind, the next few times he had seen it in print, he had made himself practice the sound of it. Gay, he thought. Gay. Gay.

CHAPTER TEN

In the end it had come down to loneliness, Jeff often thought, had come to the primitive need for another of his own kind. Proximity, closeness, a danger shared and thus halved, a danger shared and thus doubled if the sharer were not to be trusted, an extra risk for those who sought risk, an extra piquancy for those who sought piquancy. He himself sought neither risk nor piquancy, and never had, he saw now as he looked back at the terrible years. What he had sought was completion he could have in no other way, an extra dimension, the sense of his own being, fully his own, not the moralist's, just his own.

None of it was his because he had chosen it out of a field of possibilities; it was simply his despite his choice. He could see that, now that he was twenty-two and an adult, could see it with the clarity that defied four years or more of analysis. He was not the seeker of this state in which his life was being lived; he would yield all of it for the blessed ordinariness of being usual. But he was not usual. For whatever reasons, and his life seemed awhirl with hypotheses, analytic postulates, causal factors, for whatever reasons, from whatever necessities of character, he sought none of the traditional goals, not even sexual release itself, brilliant and crystal-ringing though that might be. Apart from that first capitulation with Hank in the station wagon, furtive, fearful, driven as he had been then by adolescent ignorance and adolescent necessity, apart from that first starved wildness four years ago, he had almost never sought sex as sex, isolated in the single boiling concentration on orgasm. Rather he had sought what he supposed every young creature of any species always seeks, the warm sense of being wanted, of being liked and approved of, the exchange of love, love in the emotive sense far more than the erotic at certain times, and at others far more in the erotic, an imperative driving thirst that demanded slaking.

For him it had never been easy. It would never be easy. He was not a quick-to-be-captivated person, he never had been, not as a child, not as a boy, not now as a man. The word "love" was rarely spoken by him. The concept "love" was rarely freed by him from his locked store of hidden feelings, held together in some secure and deeply vaulted chamber of his being, guarded there, to be contemplated only rarely in his own awareness of their existence and almost never withdrawn from the vault to be put on display for another's inspection.

It was, of course, part of the technique one slowly learned, in this world he found himself inhabiting, the technique of self-protection. He could never reckon the weight of that station wagon and Hank in the ultimate balance of his decisions to leave home, to give up Yale, to give up the football hero worship that was the first form of love he had ever known from his peers. Many times he had tried to evaluate that fear-filled and mesmerizing first episode, in relation to his leaving home, to his refusal of tuition for Yale, to all the external and internal changes he had made in the patterns of his life so soon afterward. But all he could be sure of was that the remainder of his time at Placquette, while his eye still scanned every crossroad for that station wagon, he had lived with nightmares of a new intensity, of himself in the Yale Bowl on some future Saturday afternoon, racing down the field in some unexpected winning play, his knees pumping high, his ears filled with his own name from the heaving crowds in the stands, Lynn, Lynn, Lynn . . . knowing that one of the faces in that crowd was Hank's face, Hank watching him, Hank planning to come forth from the past, planning God knows what horror of revelation.

Those had remained his nightmares, faithfully reported on the couch, recurring and recurring week after week, month after month, bringing the sweat springing under the collar of his pajamas, wetting the hair on his scalp, running down his chest. They had come at him not only in sleep but also in spasms of daytime imaginings until he had wanted to carve away a section of his brain that held them. He saw now as he looked back, how the knots of that nightmare had twisted into a need to escape all ties, the ties of home as well as all others. The crucial fight with his father might otherwise have been no worse than other rows, to be patched up, to be forgotten as a bad job and dumped in the trash of family messes.

He had chosen solitude instead. Even now he lived the life of a recluse. If it weren't so heavy a thing, he would have laughed himself sick over his mother's certainties that he had moved away from Margie and Nate because he was living with a lover. The farce of it. And Dr. Isaacs forever probing into his preference for the life of a loner. Or his rejection of the demands of a shared life. "Perhaps, Jeff, you find it an intolerable thought, that you might enjoy companionship more than solitude?"

That question mark in the voice, that rising inflection, so mild, so unwilling to foist any idea upon an unreceptive mind—it was a trait of both Dr. Dudley and Dr. Isaacs, perhaps of all analysts. He had said so once or twice; the reply, predictably, had been thoughtful, unresentful. "Hostility is part of the process in every analysis."

He did enjoy companionship, on all levels except that of a shared life. That might come in time. He had friends, lots of friends, but all on a specified level. He knew where the limits were, that was all. Campus friendships, drinking friendships, flicks, that sort of thing—nothing deeper than that, and not even that, once sex was included. The inclusion of sex, for him, was almost at once the exclusion of other possibilities, a sort of reverse process of natural selection. Not that he was driven to any furtive encounters with his sexual partners; one-night stands that started in a bar were not his style. And it had surprised him, once he had begun college in the city, how simple, how uncomplex it was to find partners in the hidden world he inhabited, now known more and more widely as the gay world. Once he had quit the struggle—he had almost thought, the Death Throes—against what he knew his nature to be, once he had in some measure accepted himself as a homosexual, he had been astonished to discover how far from being alone he was. Men just like him, good grades, earnest about their work, responsible fellows who were going to be engineers or lawyers or doctors or professors, and all equally set apart from the great big heterosexual world by whatever mysterious force it was that made you seek not the other sex but the same sex.

That much he would grant analysis. Little else, but that much. In four grueling years and more, he had achieved an intermittent escape from some small part of the self-loathing. In four years he had climbed one inch out of the hell of self-hate. He had stopped blaming some inner rottenness, had stopped blaming mother, father, environment, anything. And he had stopped believing that any happy little therapy existed that could ever transform him into that unattainable golden fellow, the average girl-crazy man.

This is it, he had thought one day. This is it for life.

*   *   *

And now he was about to have another Commencement Day, and be through with classrooms and assignments and professors forever. It wasn't the studying he was glad to escape but the regimentation, the strictures of routine. Actually the four years at C.C.N.Y. had meant one thing: work. Science had become his one abiding interest, all of it, any of it. He wished he could become a physicist and a chemist and a biologist and just about everything going, and had said as much to his Faculty Adviser, expecting to be laughed at, but getting a pretty astute nod of the head instead. The guy knew. Way back there in freshman year he had begun taking physics and the rest partly because it was the big thing to do, what with Gagarin and Shepard and Glenn and the whole new thing of blast-off and telemetry and possible moon shots, but for him there had been hot discovery in it from the start, a new world opening, a necessary world of the positive and the demonstrable. He kept adding and expanding each semester, not alone in physics and math but in chemistry and biology and damn near everything he could jam into a schedule without the faculty putting him down for a madman.

The provable, by God, not just theory, not just hypothesis, not dear Dr. Freud or Dr. Isaacs and their probing and positing, but the blessed realm of the positive, of computation and formulae and fact.

What it was all for, where it would lead, he did not know, not even now at the end of his senior year. When the usual bore put the usual query, "What are you going to be when you graduate?" he'd shrug it off and say he hadn't a clue. For reasons unfathomable this didn't raise the hackles of anxiety as so much else in his life did. It would come clear in plenty of time. He could always teach, though the idea sure didn't send him. He had long ago given up any notion of newspaper work—it just wasn't there. He could, of course, qualify for some damn good work in one of the big electronic or aerodynamic plants, but they all had government contracts, which meant F.B.I. clearances and C.I.A. profiles. Not in a million years.

So he had no bright little ideas for the future, but that was all right with him. He could always support himself hacking until it did come clear, and without the college load, he could make a real bundle. Even if he weren't going to say finis to analysis this coming June, he could take over the bills himself.

He had to hand it to his mother on those bills, for the way she had kept on, even giving up at last on the try for interim reports. Whenever they did see each other she stayed off the whole goddamn subject. And if he did feel next fall that he still needed treatment, she would say the same old "Go ahead."

One of the guys he knew was bitter about not being able to afford analysis. He had tried out some group-therapy clinic, and had left in disgust after a couple of sessions. Listening to him, Jeff felt uncomfortable, about being staked to the thousands of dollars that analysis costs. Not since Placquette and Rex Munson had he known personally of anybody who went that route, but he certainly had heard of some poor devil going into the drug scene in a big way, or becoming an alcoholic, or a drop-out, ending up at some puking job where he prayed to heaven they'd never find out about him.

Well, he thought, don't we all? Maybe it was that, above all, that was so hateful. The damn secrecy. The closet. Some new idealistic groups at various colleges were advocating open meetings and open membership for gay people; even up here on campus, there were some noble fellows plugging for the idea, and recently there had been enough action to make a story for the papers. Likewise at Columbia and up at Cornell. Out at the University of Colorado there had been another big to-do, close to a riot. None of this was the old Mattachine line of counsel and help; it was more like the civil rights movement out in the open. It did stir a crazy sort of approval in him, but that was like one's approval of Utopia. A down payment on something a million years off.

For no logical reason he thought again of the bad night he had had at Sarah Lawrence with Sue. The bad night with Sue—what a way to put it. It was in the spring of her freshman year, at that house party she had cared so much about, and he had felt in his bones that he should turn it down. It was his freshman year too, when he was just starting in with Dr. Isaacs and getting from him the same subtle directives about going the hetero route, testing it, giving it a chance—all that and his not wanting to hurt Sue anyway—he had finally accepted. It was still damn near unbearable to remember.

On his next visit to Dr. Isaacs, the words had shot out of him like a hemorrhage: "And then we went out in a car . . . you know how I love to drive a car . . . and then she wanted to stop off at this place off the road, and when I said no she got so uptight, sort of insulted as if there was something wrong with *her* and that's why I said no . . . anyway we did stop and then—oh God, nothing. Just goddamn to Christ nothing. Anyway, she finally knew. I guess she knew."

For a year or more they hadn't seen each other, and then somehow they had met and gone to a flick again. Even now, they still took in a show or a movie once in a while. Among the few straight friends he had, he felt easiest with Sue. In a few weeks she too was getting out of college, Phi Bete and everything, with a job already lined up in, of all things, Peabody Chalmers, the big Wall Street investment house. He really liked Sue, something akin to the way he felt about Margie, and she kept on liking him. Not once had she ever mentioned that house-party disaster, never had made a move toward another attempt, never even asked him to explain anything. He had never tried to explain either. The old rule. You don't admit it. Not for any reason. Not to one soul in the straight world.

Unbelievably enough, apart from whatever it was he had blurted out that first night he had gone over to Margie and Nate's, he had never yet come out with it even with them. When there was something in the paper about gay people, if they talked about it, neither he nor they ever took that step of connecting it up to him. It wasn't a business of telling lies, just that the words were never uttered. Even when he had lived with them, they had never said, "Well, are you?" He had never said, "You know I am." After he had moved out to his own place uptown, it was the same. When analysis was off for the summer, they never said, "Are you changing?" or anything like it. They never seemed to remember why he was in analysis. Not to remember. Brother, that was the real measure.

One night a couple of months ago he had been over there late and they were watching some talk show on the tube where the host was making wisecracks about a famous playwright who couldn't turn out any more plays "because his wrists are too limp." Nate snorted in derision. More and more programs these days bandied about a lot of slippery humor on fruit and queens and hairdressers.

"That guy he's interviewing," Nate said. "He's a famous writer too—why the hell doesn't he nail that smart aleck right on camera?"

"Being a fag himself?" Jeff asked. "Because he can't ever nail anybody, that's why. Call him a coward if you want to."

"I don't want to." Nate sank back in his chair. "That was pure rhetoric. I know damn well he can't."

"It's like a red hunt that goes on forever," Jeff said. "Only this time McCarthy won't ever die."

"Don't be too sure." Then he added, "God damn it."

That was Nate for you. And Margie too. They had talked then of McCarthyism in modern dress, the cops and the peaceniks, the cops and the blacks, the civil rights march in Selma last month, the upswing in the draft for Vietnam . . . It all wove itself together into a good solid evening, the way it always did when he was with them. They had become his real family. Now, when he thought, Home, he thought of Margie and Nate's. His one-room dump was home, sure, where he lived, but that other place, the one that used to be where his mother and father lived, that had shifted for him forever.

CHAPTER ELEVEN

The wedding invitation lay in her lap and Tessa thought, This is only the first, there will be so many more. She ran her fingers lightly over the raised lettering of the vellum paper, as if she were suddenly blind and the message in Braille, this engraved invitation to the approaching wedding of Martha Leggett Wohlmann and Peter Gerville Hill on the eighteenth day of January, One Thousand Nine Hundred and Sixty-six in the chapel at St. Bartholomew's Church.

Pete Hill married. Jeff's roomie at Placquette, Jeff's best friend all those years ago, the endless telephone calls, the flicks, the thousand unknowns of adolescent friendship, and still a friend, she knew, through the four years that had separated them, with Pete up at Cornell. Now Pete was to be married, start a family, have children . . .

A convulsion of the old pain seized her; it had been a long time that she had been free of such sharpness, yet here it was again, a stricture of anguish. This, Jeff would never have, the beginning of that greatest part of life, love and marriage and the unbelievable joy of children growing. This vast human experience he would never know. Just last night, during a visit to Margie, the doorbell had rung, and Lynnie had gone flying to greet Nate, "Daddy, Daddy." This, Jeff would never know, the beloved child rushing toward him, face alight.

She deleted, as it were, the whole picture of Jeff at an opening door. It was a sentimentality; it was her idea of joy, not necessarily a universal, not necessarily one he would ever miss. In the same moment she thought, But he will never know the other part of it, what it is to fall in love, to be in love, to go to bed with a girl he loves, to seek and make love to her, to be loved by her in return, to have her love him.

And suddenly she saw Jeff sitting alone in a chair in some room in some apartment, alone, with nobody there to talk to, to share life with, no one he knew and loved, alone, alone, and her heart convulsed once more.

Let it not be that for him, she thought. Oh, God, let him know what it is to love and be loved, on his terms, but let him know it. No matter how, no matter in which way, it is love that counts, the ability to love, the ability to give love and to receive love that makes life full and beautiful, with meaning, with renewal. Let him not be denied that forever. Whatever he is, it is not his doing; he did not ask it, he did not arrange it; it happened. It is one of the mysteries of life that some people are drawn to their own sex; all the opinions of all the doctors and theorists seem to point to that. Then let him not be punished in the most fearful way of all, that he should never know the good sweetness of being able to love somebody dear and be loved by that dear one in return.

There is no life without that current running from one to the other and then back to one, the completed circuit, the fullness of giving and receiving and giving. Life is a round. Without that round, life itself is disconnected, a broken thing, a torn zero.

Oh, let it never be that for my son. Not once before had she visualized Jeff sitting so in an empty silent room, and now the longing to spare him that void, that present or future void, was so acute it was nearly insupportable.

She turned back to the wedding invitation and mechanically read it through once more. Pete had graduated from Cornell last June, as Jeff had graduated from C.C.N.Y., except that Jeff had done it with high honors and Pete had barely made it. Pete was already a junior member of the Establishment à la Madison Avenue; he had become a space salesman in his father's advertising agency. Jeff was, in his words, still "sizing it up," still on the same self-supporting basis, driving a cab and living in his one-room flat uptown.

Sizing it up. She remembered Jeff saying the words for the first time. It was at one of their rare lunches, arranged by her, "to ask you what you want for a graduation present."

"Dad and I thought—guess what?" she had said, after he had assured her he had no good ideas at all.

"Dad and you?"

"Of course, Dad and me. Would you believe a car of your own?"

"You don't really mean that."

She saw his eyes light up, and she laughed. "I do mean it. It's practically an American tradition, if the parents can afford it, isn't it?"

"Well, thanks, it would be terrific," he said slowly. "But I, but you better not. It's a terrific idea, though."

"Why not, Jeff? We *can* afford it, and we both want to."

"But I couldn't support a car. Garage and gas and insurance and all that."

"But you'll be getting a job."

"I don't know about the job yet." He smiled at her, half regretful, half pugnacious. "I'm sort of sizing things up, measuring all the professions. Don't think I'm not bowled over at the idea of a car, though."

"If you change your mind, you can say. There's no rush."

"Getting through school is graduation gift enough."

"Don felt that way, and Margie. I guess everybody does."

"Sixteen years of books and labs and exams—is that ever enough." He laughed. "And five years on the couch—that's enough too."

"Jeff, really? Have you decided?"

"I thought you knew. Oh yes, *finito*. I announced it to Dr. Isaacs about six months back. I should have told you. I guess I took it for granted Margie or Nate would have passed it on."

"Never mind. Is it really what you want now?"

"Just what."

"Then I'm glad."

Silence had fallen between them then. The old stiff antagonisms had softened in the last years, but in their infrequent encounters, if the subject of therapy arose at all, he still made it all too clear that any mention of it was his to make, his to terminate.

"I'll come up with an idea sooner or later," Jeff had said then. "We can just skip it for a while."

"Of course, there's one other graduation present that's even more traditional. Nineteenth-Century Traditional."

"You're reaching." Again he looked at her with a special interest. He was liking the entire conversation, his expression said, and for a moment she felt as if it were old times, he the young Jeff greedy for a birthday gift, greedy to open the Christmas packages.

"The airlines are putting on all sorts of tourist trips to Paris, London, Rome—nothing too plushy, but that was our other idea."

He had whistled. "The Grand Tour."

"Nineteenth Century, no? You think about it." He hadn't been abroad since he was fourteen, and then he was a boy going along with his family. Now he was a man and would be on his own, the world before him, the time his own, the itinerary his own, his companions and evenings his own. For a moment an envy nipped at her, of the middle-aged watching the young, of a woman nearly fifty saying "Bon Voyage" to a young man setting forth to see the world.

"This is tougher than the car," he said after a moment. "It's just wrong timing for me, though, but thanks anyhow. I mean it, but right now I just can't make it."

He looked wretched. He seemed to be puzzling something out for himself.

"It's sort of like me being in the lab," he finally said, "with a half-finished experiment going on and I can't leave the lab until I know whether it blows the place up or whether it will work out. Does that make any sense?"

"The syntax is terrible, but it makes lots of sense. All right, we'll wait on the graduation gift till you give us a signal."

Graduation gifts, wedding gifts, she thought now. He still had given no signal. He still was driving that cab, "hacking it," "sizing it up." He still seemed directionless but Ken comforted her on that, setting up an unexpected defense. "He's always been pretty solid when it comes to work," Ken said. "School, college, even those summer jobs at Paperbound. Taking his time now is a lot sounder than grabbing at some bore of a job and quitting it in a year."

True enough. And they had seen him on Christmas Day, again

at Margie and Nate's, and though she might have imagined it, he did not seem as lost or directionless as he had on other Christmases in the past. There was indeed something pretty solid about him, as Ken had put it, and not only where work was concerned. Maturity had a hundred ways of showing itself, and with Jeff it had come unevenly, an inevitable corollary to the complexity of his problems. His very rejection of such delectables as a car of his own or a trip to Europe, the discipline that led him to say no to both, could come only from a strength that went deeper than chronological age.

She hoped the announcement of Pete's marriage would not disturb him, as it had her. He would be going to the wedding, though not with her and Ken, and in any case, they would be skipping the reception afterward. She visualized Jeff there, congratulating Pete, kissing the bride, joking with the other guests, perhaps hearing of other weddings soon to take place.

"And what about you, Jeff? Any wedding bells on tap for you, old buddy?"

Outside her window, from the church on Madison Avenue, bells rang out in the gray light of the January morning and she flinched. Again she tried to "delete" the sound of the chimes, irked at herself. A sentimentality again. Doubtless the talk of wedding bells would arouse no pang of denial in Jeff, the happy aura around bride and groom cause no laceration. She had thought she had given up forever the old trick of transposing her feelings onto Jeff's emotive state, yet here it was again.

Guilt threaded its way along her nerves. He senses it, she thought. He still can't feel easy with us because his instinct tells him. Just as my instinct tells me I'm further ahead than Ken is, no matter how Ken has been trying, and succeeding too. But even so, down underneath, those hidden fragments and roots, how deep they are, what tenacity they have.

And in me? The same probably, but not in just the same sense. Something keeps shifting. Unevenly, in lurches, at unexpected times, over unexpected things. It's as if I were in a lab too, with a half-finished experiment, waiting to find out whether it will blow the place up or, in the end, finally work out.

* * *

Nate said, "I've got a copy of Freud's famous letter for you," and handed her a sheet of yellow copy paper. "I copied it myself, and then I made this copy for you."

"Where did you locate it?" Tessa asked. "Whenever I've tried, the librarian didn't even know what letter I meant, and none of the catalogue cards listed it." She began to read the page, but Nate said, "Don't read it now. Better wait till we get started." She accepted his direction and folded the page over.

She was staying with the children for the afternoon while Nate and Margie went off on some project involving major repairs on the ancient electrical wiring in their house. At one end of the large living room Lynnie, now nearly five, was lording it over the baby, Jeffie, but their sounds were still good-natured and peaceful. Usually Nate's days off were given over to plans that included the children, but this time the call had come for her to baby-sit, and as always, she had responded as if she had been offered a treat.

"Where *did* you uncover it?" she repeated, nodding down at the page in her hand. "Even Mark Waldo flopped on getting it; I asked him a couple of times."

"Up at the Academy of Medicine," Nate said. "I was up there on another story and I thought, It's bound to be here, and dug around and finally got it. It was in the *American Journal of Psychiatry*, about fifteen years ago. That's why Dr. Waldo never found it, probably."

"I should have thought of the Academy."

"Freud wrote it," Nate went on, "to an American woman, a stranger, who wrote him about her son. That was back thirty years ago, before the Nazis made him leave Vienna."

"It's so touching," Margie said. "This woman kept his answer for about fifteen years, and then, after the Kinsey Report, she sent it to Kinsey, saying, 'Here's a letter from a great and good man,' and then Kinsey published it in the *Journal*."

Tessa fingered the folded page. "Do you suppose Jeff has read it?"

"I made him a copy too. But you know Jeff. Mr. 'No Comment' on things like this."

"Even with us," Margie said. "So it's not just you and Dad. At least Dr. Isaacs told him, a while back, he could take off the blindfolds on reading whatever he wants, Freud or anybody else."

"I never could see that about not reading," Tessa said. "Like an Index Expurgatorius."

"Most analysts," Nate said, "won't let patients bone up on their own cases. Sort of convenient, maybe."

"Come off," Margie protested. "Regular M.D.s don't want their patients to diagnose their own cases either, looking up symptoms and treatment."

"Well, run along, you two," Tessa said, half opening the sheet in her hand.

Nate rose but Margie said, "I wonder why the *Times* doesn't print this old letter of Freud's sometime. Millions of people must never have seen it."

Before Nate could reply, Tessa said, "Isn't it funny, the way we can talk about this and talk about the woman who wrote about her son, and not one of us says the word 'homosexual' right out? Have you noticed? Even us."

"As if the word itself were an embarrassment," Margie agreed. "Aren't you the bright one, to catch that?"

"It's partly the word that's at fault," Nate said. "The fancy Latinizing of it, or is it as if to make it more genteel. Heterosexual sounds just as phony-genteel to my ear."

"I don't think I ever once thought of myself as a heterosexual," Margie said, "before people began writing and talking so much about homosexuals."

Nate laughed. "Gay sounds more natural to me now," he said. "And straight."

"I never think of myself as 'straight' either, and there's something all wrong with the idea of it. Like when they used to say non-white for blacks. What's the opposite of straight—crooked?"

"Come on, Miss Semantics," Nate said, "or we'll never get there."

As the door closed on them, Tessa opened Freud's letter. It started so simply:

"Dear Mrs. ——,
   I gather from your letter that your son is a homosexual. I am impressed by the fact that you do not mention this term yourself in your information about him. May I question you, why do you avoid it? Homosexuality is assuredly no advantage but it is nothing to be ashamed of, no vice, no degrada-

tion, it cannot be classified as an illness; we consider it to be a variation of the sexual function produced by a certain arrest of the sexual development. Many highly respectable individuals. . . ."

There followed the familiar litany of the immortal names, Plato, Michelangelo, Leonardo, but she paused over it, as if she needed a moment to recover herself. This was indeed a great and good man writing to an unknown mother in despair; the kindness in the words sent her back to the time, six long years before, when she had been in such a stupor of despair. Might it have been easier for her then if she had received some such letter? She returned to her reading, noticing that at the end Nate had written, "Freud wrote it longhand, in English." She paused once more over that small personal addition, of Freud writing in an unfamiliar language in simple terms that a layman could be expected to understand.

"By asking me if I can help you," Freud went on, a few lines later, "you mean, I suppose, if I can abolish homosexuality and make normal heterosexuality take its place. The answer is, in a general way, we cannot promise to achieve it. In a certain number of cases we succeed in developing the blighted germs of heterosexual tendencies which are present in every homosexual, in the majority of cases it is no more possible. It is a question of the quality and of the age of the individual. The result of treatment cannot be predicted.

"What analysis can do for your son runs in a different line. If he is unhappy, neurotic, torn by conflicts, inhibited in his social life, analysis may bring him harmony, peace of mind, full efficiency, whether he remains a homosexual or gets changed. . . ."

She read to the end, but like a persistent counterpoint, the phrase repeated itself: We cannot promise to achieve it, and she kept visualizing that unknown mother who had written that letter to the illustrious doctor in Vienna, wanting an answer she could never have, an answer free of hesitation, an answer with a resounding promise: Of course we can make your beloved son what you want him to be.

Once she too had wanted such promises, had given them to herself in her own fantasies of golden, grasping hope. Looking back, it seemed so forlorn, so childlike, and in some new way, so immoderate. How could any mature person demand of the future so large a promise on behalf of another human being, who alone had the right to make the demand or refuse to make it?

She wondered what Jeff felt about Freud's letter, but this was another one of the things she would never know. Even after all this time, when there was anything about homosexuals in the paper or in a magazine, she could not ask what he thought of it, not even whether he had seen it. That first big story on the front page of the *Times* about three years ago—then she had asked him, in all eagerness if he, too, had read it. One of their ugly flare-ups had been the instant result.

"I saw it. I don't want to get into a big thing about it."

"I didn't mean any big thing."

"You never mean it. It gets to be a big thing just the same."

There was a sudden howl from the far side of the room. The baby must have stepped firmly on a large tufted cotton ball, which was still rolling away from him, and he was asprawl on the floor. Lynnie was bending over him. "Don't be mad, Jeffie," she said. "The ball didn't mean it."

"No, darling," Tessa said, scooping him up in a hug. "Nobody ever means it."

* * *

The telephone rang and Gail called from the outer office, "Your son Jeff, Mrs. Lynn."

Tessa picked up the receiver and said, "Hello there." A leap in her pulse meant only that it was rare indeed for him to call the office. She heard the click that said Gail had hung up at her extension. Jeff heard it too.

"What do you know," he started. "You're talking to a member of the Employed. Not the *un* but the *em*ployed."

"Congratulations. Good for you."

"Three guesses, employed at what?"

"I give up. I can't guess."

"Three million guesses."

"I can't imagine. Tell me."

He laughed. He sounded happy, excited, pleased with himself, and it was immense to hear him this way. "Go on, Jeff, whatever it is, I'm delighted. Tell me."

"A job at St. Luke's Hospital."

"St. Luke's! Doing what?"

"As an orderly."

"An orderly at St. Luke's—how in the world?"

"There's this friend of mine told me about it. His brother works there and they're short on help, nurses' aides and orderlies, and I was interviewed this morning and wham, I'm an orderly."

"Congratulations again. I'm not positive what an orderly does, but it's grand. You sound so happy and I am too."

"I'm not positive either—it's so miscellaneous. I gather he helps prep people for surgery, he gets assigned to the emergency room, he helps monitor equipment in a heart case, he gives a hand transferring a patient from bed to that rolling table for surgery. And he makes sixty-seven bucks a week to start with, and a raise every three months so it's seventy-eight by the end of a year."

"It's wonderful."

"It's another temporary gig, like the cab, but the sizing-things-up can keep on unabated. This sort of appeals to me."

"I can see why."

"My shift is midnight to eight A.M. How does that grab you?"

"It kills me. You sound so good, Jeff."

"I have to beat it now to go—guess where?"

"To start your night shift at eleven in the morning."

"Nope. This pal who clued me in on the job—he teaches Spanish at Columbia. About a third of the orderlies and nurses' aides *habla español,* so I'm in for a cram course on a kind of hospital-Berlitz basis."

"Oh, Jeff, that sounds good too. It's all lovely news."

She hung up, excited in a strange way. To have him turn to her with news was something she had almost forgotten, to have him pick up a phone just to impart something that would please her was a new sensation, a rebirth of long-dead sensations. How long it had been since he had walked into a phone booth somewhere, impelled to reach her, to talk to her, to share some unexpected good news with her.

She called Ken at his office and told him. "Well, that's right out of left field, isn't it?" Ken said. "I've always been a fan of left field."

"You sound happy too."

"Happy and surprised and a lot of things."

"We'll talk tonight—oh, wait, we're having dinner with the Wisters tonight. I kind of wish we weren't."

"Nonsense. You like them and so do I."

"I like everybody right now. It's nice when one of the kids gets a new job."

"The next one, I gather, will be Margie. This whole woman's movement is picking up steam, and about time."

"That's lovely too. Don't be late tonight. We're due there at seven."

* * *

Within minutes of arriving at the Wisters', Tessa's high mood of the day began to fail her. She should have known that Sue might be there, should have known too that seeing her again might set off a train of associations with other times. Indeed she had known; what she had not known was that her mood would shift so unpredictably and that the sight of Sue, a more mature Sue, no longer a schoolgirl but a self-possessed young woman, even prettier than she had been before—that the sight of this Sue could be so troubling to her.

The other guests were three couples, all book people, one pair young enough to be just starting out in publishing, the others her own contemporaries and already known to herself and Ken. Conversation was lively, the easy exchanges of shop talk, except when it turned to Sue and her job at the brokerage house in Wall Street. There was an underlying incredulity, Tessa noticed, in the comments made by the two older couples; only the young pair, still in their twenties, took it for granted that a girl who had majored in economics at college should now have a promising position as an economist with one of the big houses on the Street. Sue herself chided one of the older women, who thought it "so extraordinary, a girl down there with all those Wall Streeters."

"Girls aren't extraordinary anywhere any more," Sue said mildly. "Women, rather. You'll find them in every job or profession there is."

"I didn't mean it that way. They should be, of course."

"And they are—mostly for lower pay than the men," Sue answered, maintaining her good humor, "but they're making their move on equal pay too."

"What's this I hear about the research girls on *Time* magazine, or maybe *Newsweek*," Ken asked. "Aren't they about to strike for the right to be editors, not just researchers, and for equal pay as well?"

"They're still at the organizing stage," Sue said. "Women on all magazines are too, and newspapers and in TV, *everywhere*."

"Certainly in publishing," Ken said, smiling at Tessa. "My wife's just been pushed up the ladder another rung at Q. and P., and one day she might wind up as its president, or commander-in-chief of all the armed forces, or something."

"Then maybe we'd get out of Vietnam," Sue retorted.

Everybody laughed, and the talk branched off to the war and politics. It was not until after dinner, over coffee in the living room, that Tessa and Sue could talk to each other. It was no accident; Sue arranged it, bringing Tessa coffee, saying, "May I?" as she motioned to the seat next to her.

"I'd love it. We haven't had a minute." She wondered if she might volunteer news of Jeff's job, but Sue decided that for her.

"What's the latest about Jeff?" she began. "Is he still driving that cab?"

"As of this morning, no more cab." She told Sue about Jeff's call, her own pleasure reborn in the telling. A new quality appeared in Sue's manner, an almost imperceptible toning down, a quieting. Suddenly Tessa thought, She is hiding something, maybe I have unwittingly shifted her mood the way she unwittingly shifted mine. Do they still see each other every once in a while?

"Jeff's so bright," Sue said. "He won't be an orderly long. He'll end up doing something a million miles removed from orderlies and cab drivers both, is my guess."

"Mine too." She felt the effort at lightness in Sue's words and wished she could think of another subject. Whatever she said would hold risk. Under Sue's composure, it seemed to her now, lay a fine melancholy, touching and unexpected. Never had she, Tessa, even considered that Jeff might have hurt Sue, never had she given any thought to what some other woman might endure one day because of Jeff, might already have endured.

"He is bright," she finally said, a soberness sounding. "But, Sue, he also is troubled and he can be difficult."

"Can't we all?"

"I guess we can."

"Somebody told me he's out of analysis," Sue added. "Oh yes, I know who it was. Jo-Anne Tomson—her brother, Deck Tomson, ran into Jeff at Pete Hill's wedding reception."

"He had been in it a long time."

"My father told me once that if anybody had something chronic like diabetes, he'd stay in a doctor's care a long time—" She broke off, flushing a little. "Listen to me defending Jeff."

"It's nice of you. People don't understand always about things like analysis."

"Nor about lots of other things."

They sat in silence then, the two together, sipping their coffee, neither one willing to break the small contact between them. In repose, Sue again looked young and vulnerable, and Tessa thought, She is in love with him, maybe she has been in love with him for a long time. If she knows about him, she knows already how impossible that love is, and if she still does not know, then she feels only what it is to love someone who does not love you. Maybe she thinks it is another girl he loves instead. A protective instinct arose in her, to assuage Sue's hurt, but an even deeper instinct arose with it, primitive and hot, to protect her own young. She said nothing.

Sue was looking fixedly at the carpet, searching its intricate pattern for some clue about how to go on. Just then her mother came over, and she sprang up to yield her seat, moving off and out of the room. "Now, Tessa," Mrs. Wister began, "what rung did Ken mean? You never did blow your own horn, but don't bury yourself behind a bushel. Oh dear, that's too many metaphors."

Tessa laughed. She liked Marcia Wister and told her, simply and without an assumed modesty, of the pleasing fact that she had just been selected at Quales and Park as the editor of her first non-fiction author, a major writer by anybody's standard, winner of the Pulitzer price for biography, author of some fourteen previous books, and thus a great departure from the young and not yet established writers with whom she usually worked.

"Is it a secret, who it is?" Marcia Wister asked.

"Heavens, no, it's been announced in all the book columns. It's Scott Prentice, who wrote—"

"Scott—a man's name, isn't it? Like Scott Fitzgerald."

"He's a man," Tessa said, amused.

"I didn't think—" She hesitated, confusion sounding.

"That men would work with women editors," Tessa finished for her. "Men like Scott Prentice would. It's less a matter of gender these days, don't you think? Ask your daughter Sue." That sounded like a rebuke but she would make it worse if she tried again.

"Of course, it's different in publishing. It must be a thrill for you, though, being editor for anybody as famous as Scott Prentice."

"I am thrilled," she said matter-of-factly. "What counts is *how* we work together when we get down to actual editing. We've only just met."

Other people joined them and the talk shifted and swung for the remainder of the evening. It was an early evening and when they reached home it was Ken who glanced at his watch and said, "In one hour Jeff appears on the world scene as an orderly in a great hospital. I don't know why that tickles me, but it does."

They talked of Jeff's job, of Margie's plans to get a job herself when Lynnie was six and the baby three, and over them both there was a comradely ease that had for so long been achievable only by an effort which in itself destroyed ease. Toward intimacy neither made a move; by now it was tacitly understood that that once vital beat of life was quiet, if not at a final end, then certainly for an unstated intermission. At times Tessa was acutely aware of this cessation, wondering whether another woman might perhaps be now seeking an outside affair, discreet, uncomplex, never any risk to Ken's ego. But tonight as she undressed for bed she thought instead of Sue, and that fleeting melancholy she had seen. It was so easy to forget how the young suffer.

The old guilt thundered down upon her. She had thought she was through with it forever, but change the circumstances by one small thing, like tonight's talk with Sue, and here it was again.

The accuser again. Sue's pain, Jeff's—it all lay there with her, the basic guilt, the causation.

No matter how often she was given a reprieve by something she read, it never remained in force for long. The next expert she came upon would rescind the reprieve and doom her once again.

Since Nate had talked of going to the Academy of Medicine, she had abandoned public libraries in her quest and had begun to go to the Academy library herself. Now there was a rapid proliferation of new articles and books on homosexuality, and each time she came across another rejection of mother-fixation as too simplistic, she would again feel that blessed exoneration, a gift, a benison.

But never did this freedom from blame become a fixed star in her emotional cosmos. On dark nights that star would no longer be in the heavens to guide her. If she asked herself why it should matter so much, this exoneration, she would think, I do not know why it matters so much but it matters. I could not bear it if it was I who did this to him. And then she would grow ashamed, that she should be so avid to establish her own "innocence."

She felt the slow rise of shame now and thought, It's nobody's guilt, it's nobody's innocence, it happened, it is life. And for the first time she was thinking not only of Jeff but also of Sue.

CHAPTER TWELVE

On the way uptown from the office, Tessa gazed out at the sunny streets, already baking in summer heat although it was still June, but she saw only vaguely the stream of traffic and heard only vaguely the usually insistent clash and roar of the midafternoon traffic. Since Mark Waldo's puzzling invitation that morning, she had tried to guess what could have made him do so unlikely a thing as to telephone her and ask that she visit him at three, at the end of his office hours, before he went off on his hospital rounds. In twenty-five years he had never done that, calling to suggest a call on him.

"It's not about anybody's health," he had said. "Not yours and not Ken's, but I think it will interest you the way it did me and maybe you'll like it in the same way too."

"You know how to arouse my curiosity. Three sharp."

It must be something about Jeff, she had decided at once. Except for his twenty-third birthday in April, they had scarcely talked to him or heard from him since he had begun his new work, and even Margie and Nate had had little to report, except that he was still on the midnight shift, that he dropped by for a meal once in a while and talked about life in hospitals from "a worm's-eye view" and that he gave no sign of being bored with his job or regretting the freer schedule of his cab driving. He looked well, Margie said, he was thinner, he had apparently found a couple of new friends. One always did in new jobs.

And now Mark Waldo had asked her to his office. An anomaly,

the doctor calling the patient. He didn't practice at St. Luke's but he must know doctors who did. Still, if it were simply some praise for Jeff's work, he would have told her on the phone or written one of his two-line notes.

He had sounded urgent, as well as rather worked up, pleasantly so. High, Tessa thought as the taxi came to a stop at his office. That's what it was: he sounded high.

She had to wait. As usual, even at the end of his office hours there were people ahead of her, only two this time, but there they sat, rivals for his attention, already winners as far as seeing him first. She settled back in her chair, ignoring the year-old magazines on the elongated chest that served as a table, telling herself that she must remember to bring with her an armload of recent ones the next time she had an appointment. The Mark Waldos of medicine were too concerned with people and their illnesses to worry about waiting-room niceties. During her annual examination each July, during all the routines of cardiogram and chest X rays and the rest, she always read again the framed medical diplomas on the walls of his examining room and office, certificates or citations from this hospital or that about his superior performance or rating, some going back to the young Mark Waldo as intern or resident, others spaced out during the years, denoting some special honor or award. She actually liked to reread them; her own regard for Mark made each of them a surrogate for her own opinion.

Now she thought, Whatever it is, it's so kind of him to work it in, probably the first minute he could. It must be something that happened yesterday, last night, maybe this morning, and here he is, despite the mad hours he keeps, fitting me in right away. Like every other physician, he left a colleague on call during three weekends out of four, and resisted house calls, but if you were really ill, not merely down with a cold or hypochondria but actually sick, there he was at your bedside, summoned by his wife or nurse or service in the shortest possible time. Like that night of Ken's stroke—

The door to Mark's office opened, discharging one patient and admitting another. Now there was only one other person in the waiting room with her, and she leaned back, consciously trying to empty her mind and wait in readiness for whatever was to come. Perhaps he had sounded pleased by choice, a disguise in his tone so as not to alarm her for the hours she had to wait. No, not Mark. There were no disguises when you dealt with him, no false cheer. What he said was what there was to say, never any less. He never edits, she thought now; that's not his job but mine.

It was after four when her turn came, and as she seated herself across the desk from him, he wasted little time on preliminaries.

"Listen to this, Tessa," he said, and the note she had dubbed high again sounded in his tone. "Last night I was in consultation with a neurosurgeon and an analyst named Halston Richards. This was on a case that concerns surgery on a girl who is my patient and also Richards', because she goes to Vassar and Richards practices in Poughkeepsie. It took us two minutes to discover we had been premeds together thirty years ago, and after the consultation, I took him home with me for some food and we talked the thing all through again. Then we went off on our work in general."

He looked at her expectantly, as if she should already be aware of the importance of what he was leading up to, and she nodded in a silent prodding.

"Richards may be called a maverick by some analysts," he went on, "but he clearly has the professional standing that can't be attacked by a word like 'maverick.'"

"In what way, 'maverick'?"

"He believes that psychiatry needs to revise the whole approach to the homosexual. He as good as calls standard treatment harmful to many patients, even inhumane."

"How? Why?"

"Also he says a growing number of psychiatrists and analysts now have the same conviction, or are coming around to it. He named half a dozen for me, Dr. Judd Marmor in California, for instance, one of the leaders, and several more in New York, in Chicago, in London, in Zurich."

"Harmful in what way, Mark? Revise in what way?"

"Richards has come to the conclusion, this whole group have, that there's been a kind of fixation in the general approach, what he called 'the establishment approach.' For one thing, the assumption that therapy is a *must* in each case. For another, that the one great goal for the patient is to, quote, achieve heterosexuality, close quote." He glanced at her and went on more slowly. "He would say, I gather, that even good men like Dudley and Isaacs have this fixation—I'm putting it into lay terms, but that's the way he put it to me."

He saw the leap of her attention, saw her lean toward him as she said, "Go on, tell."

"According to Richards and these others, there is a potential damage to the patient's whole psyche, or a possible damage, implicit in such an attitude on the part of the therapist. The implication is, If you are not sick, not ill, not diseased, not degenerate —and Sigmund Freud said you are not—then you are certainly something undesirable, unworthy, and we will use every conceivable means to change you around. The one desideratum is being a heterosexual, like me."

"Oh, Mark."

"I'm oversimplifying. One New York analyst coined the word 'homophobia' and says many analysts are homophobic themselves and simply cannot accept the concept that it's possible to be a healthy, well-adjusted homosexual, as happy or as unhappy as any healthy, well-adjusted heterosexual, no more, no less."

"I can't take all this in. I've never come across anything like this, not in all my reading. Nothing by Dr. Richards, nothing by Dr. Marmor."

"What you've seen is mostly by the establishment. The traditionalists, let's say, like Dudley and Isaacs."

"I took them for gospel. Except for that talk of twenty-five percent—you've heard me on that. Is Dr. Richards writing anything? Or Dr. Marmor? And the others who think the way they do?"

"Of course, and it's already getting a major hearing in the profession. In the next year or two you'll be reading their papers for yourself, and maybe their books."

"Mark, do they mean that a boy or girl who's homosexual should stay out of analysis?"

"In some cases no, in some yes. If they're miserable, if *they* feel something is wrong with them, treatment may free them of guilt, depression, let them function more fully in life. But remember, most analysts are heterosexuals, after all, and many of them, despite their own analyses while they were students, still carry a pretty hefty bias about homosexuals. 'Homophobic'—and still that way right through student days into practice."

"It flabbergasts me, all this. It's like a sudden turn in the road."

"You'll need time to explore it, and so will I. It's actually astonishing to me, with a life spent in medicine, to be told that this form of sex choice not only isn't a mental illness—we knew that all along—but that it needn't be tragic or terrible either, unless the world we live in makes it seem tragic and terrible. Richards says it's a variation of the sexual impulse, that it's found in all societies, averaging out at about ten percent, as we found out from Kinsey long ago. 'Variation of the sexual impulse.'"

She heard his slight stressing of the phrase. "Does he call it a neurosis?"

"Many homosexuals are neurotic, he says, and many are not. So are many heterosexuals, neurotic or not. Most patients on the couches this very hour—they're heterosexuals, aren't they?"

"Of course they are. I never thought of that either."

"Screaming heterosexuals, with psychosexual problems, with guilt, with insecurity, and lots of them people who had aggressive mothers and weak or drunken fathers in their babyhood."

A shout of laughter burst from Tessa, and she slapped his desk with the palm of her hand. Mark Waldo laughed with her.

"So that's your own little guilt," he said sternly.

"This is all so tremendous, Mark. Could you possibly get me anything to read, by Dr. Richards or Dr. Marmor?"

"Dr. Richards is sending me one or two of his papers. I'll send them along, of course."

"I wish Ken had been here with me today."

"I thought you'd rather tell him yourself."

"If he will let me." She looked suddenly tentative. "He really has made himself over, year by year he has, but he still seems to go half mute in any talk or discussion about Jeff."

"He was never a voluble man."

"And Jeff—is there any way you could tell him? He really ought to know about this, and he'd never let me. It took me years to learn that, but I finally did."

He shook his head. "I have to accept the reality Jeff presents, just the way you do. I've seen him—what?—twice in the past four years. Once for that mono scare and the other time the strep throat. Both times he volunteered exactly zero about his private self. Silence is a symptom, Tessa, as much as an outburst is."

"But you— But nothing. I know you can't."

"Jeff will find it out for himself. Sooner or later. And so will a great many other people. Richards predicts a major split down the middle of psychiatry and analysis about homosexuals before the decade's out."

"If it could be soon."

"Look how much medicine has learned in the last ten years. The last five. In every branch of it."

"Oh, Mark, thanks for calling me today."

When she began to tell Ken that evening, he did not stop her, but three hours had elapsed between her departure from Mark's office and in that time the impact of Mark's news seemed to have eroded, and as she tried to put it into words for Ken, it seemed to slip through her fingers, seemed diaphanous and misty. What had Mark said that had made it seem so important in the moment of his saying it? How had he put it? That there were a few psychiatrists who believed that treatment itself could be wrong, damaging, that the run-of-the-mill psychiatrist might well be unconsciously biased toward homosexuals, or ambivalent in his judgments, a prisoner of his own heterosexual view of sex. She put it as well as she could, but the feeling persisted, that it was sounding unconvincing and hollow.

"Then does Mark imply," Ken asked, "that all Jeff's years in treatment were wasted? Or damaging?"

"That wasn't the primary point. He made it clear he was thinking ahead."

"He did name Dr. Dudley and Dr. Isaacs."

"Because we knew them. He didn't single them out as any worse than the rest of the analysts, far from it. Just as examples of the state of analysis now, the 'establishment,' as he put it."

"Well, if he sends you anything by this Dr. Richards or by Dr. Marmor, let me have a look at it too."

* * *

The full impact of Mark's revelations returned later when she was alone, and with it a burst of anger, a sudden fury at Dr. James Dudley and Dr. David Isaacs, who must have had some inkling all through these last years of the Judd Marmors and the Halston

Richardses and their work, and yet had never said a word about it to their patients or to the parents of those patients.

How was it possible for any reputable psychiatrist or analyst to withhold the news that some of their colleagues felt that the usual approach might be wrong, even harmful? She thought of a pediatrician withholding from an infant's mother all news of the Salk or Sabin vaccines against polio. She distrusted analogies, but this one aroused an anguish in her that seemed to fit the lunatic rage she was just now feeling at the Dudleys and Isaacses of the world. They *must* know. Whether they agreed or disagreed, they certainly ought to tell the wildly seeking parents on the very first visit that there were other hypotheses they might consider before launching their beloved sons or daughters into four or five years of typical treatment.

Averaging out at ten percent, Mark had said. Eighteen years had passed since the Kinsey report had astounded the world, yet that figure remained a constant in study after study. One out of every ten people, in every society, ten out of every hundred. How often had she read that figure herself, how often had she thought of those tens, those hundreds. At Jeff's graduation last summer . . .

This time Ken had not stayed away. This time they were there together, like all the parents. This time it was a different universe they were inhabiting—the commencement exercises had been held outdoors, and in the evening, so that working people could come to see their children at last in that cap and gown that for so many years had been the secret aim, the private vision. It was at Lewisohn Stadium, uptown there in that overlapping of the Bronx and Harlem, nothing like the propertied domain of Placquette Preparatory School for Boys, yet in its own way beautiful and moving.

Ken too seemed aware of the thronging crowds, the parents of some four thousand graduates, mostly men, mostly white; he kept looking out into the lighted arena, open to the sky, where they had so often gone to hear symphonies when they were young, and once he said to her, "He's the only one of us to do it, Tessa, and yet we all believe in public education."

She knew what he meant but she only nodded and said nothing. She had just remembered that earlier June when she had watched the young faces and thought of Jeff as isolated from all his classmates. Tonight she knew he was not isolated, that among those four thousand young people, there would be some four hundred who were homosexual like Jeff, who had faced and would face the same hazards and the same prejudice Jeff had faced and still would face as he and they went forth to begin life out there beyond the university.

And if there were four hundred, then there were eight hundred mothers and fathers in this surging crowd tonight, and if there were 15 or 20 million homosexuals throughout the nation, then there were 30 or 40 million mothers and fathers out there too, many of whom already knew, many of whom did not know, many who would go frantic with the attempt to help, many who would yell and shout the classic Never Darken My Door Again.

It has to change, she had thought then, it is already changing. We are learning. So slowly, but we are learning.

And now Mark had told her that psychiatry was changing in more ways than were yet known. Analysis would change; society itself would change, would begin to lose its own phobias about people whose sexual needs were different from the majority's. Would begin to lose the cruelties that go with fear.

That was what Mark had told her, that was what had made her heart race. She had lost it for a moment when she tried to put it into calm words for Ken, but now she had it back again, the full meaning, the full projection.

* * *

There was another telephone call within the week that set her guessing, this one from Jeff. Her first thought was that he had seen Mark Waldo.

"Is this a busy week for you?" he began. "I thought I might come and have a talk."

"Not particularly busy. Come on."

"Or busy for Dad? I thought it might be with you and Dad."

"Why sure, Jeff. Lunch, is that what you mean?"

"No, as a matter of fact. What I meant was, in the evening, right there at home."

"Why, that would be fine, and a nice surprise."

"It's pretty important."

"Whenever you say, we'll make it any time."

"How about tomorrow night?"

"Fine. Want to come for dinner?"

"About eight, I thought, afterwards. It's—" He hesitated. "Do you still want to give me that old graduation gift?"

"Of course."

"Dad too?"

"We've just been waiting for a signal from you, remember?"

"This is going to be some kind of signal." He laughed, a mysterious undertone in his voice. "Then eight, tomorrow. Get set for a surprise." Again he laughed a little.

"I'm set."

She was filled with a presentiment that this was to be a turning point in his life, perhaps in theirs, but she was aware that this time it was a pleasant feeling, not the old apprehension that used to be so ready to strike. She sat holding the telephone close to her, as if she liked it, feeling expectant, with a small certainty that was new. Nothing had changed, except in herself, and she was unclear about what that change was, or how to rate its importance or predict its tenure. But here was an event that had not happened for five years, a call from Jeff, proposing that he see them at home.

Not a call from her asking him to a neutral place for lunch, a neutral corner as it were, not a general family arrangement over at Margie and Nate's or, much more rarely, at Don and Jenny's, not a ritualistic gathering like Thanksgiving or Christmas or somebody's birthday. The motivation this time came from Jeff. The place for it was chosen by Jeff, and the place he had chosen was that same old-fashioned big apartment that he used to call home.

Her throat tightened a little, not with the ache of pain, but with an excited sense that this was going to be a major step into the future for Jeff. Let it be a good one, she thought. A reminiscence of days lived through brushed her memory but she banished it. Enough, she thought, it has been enough.

The next evening when Jeff arrived, he looked around the living room with astonishment. "It looks bigger," he said. "Just the same except lots larger."

"The old story," Ken said. "Every summer, while you kids were growing up, when we'd come home from a summer in the country, you all used to insist it was either larger or smaller, but always different. It's nice you're here."

"Yes, it is," Tessa said. "You used to hate me for saying this, but you look taller."

Jeff guffawed. "Come on. Eventually people do stop growing, even me."

"But that Bermuda tan—I'm not imagining that."

"You forget the night shift, and it's a Central Park tennis tan, just as brown as Bermuda tans."

"Want a drink?" Ken asked.

"I'll have a beer if there is any."

"Or scotch, rather?"

"Beer's my speed."

"Tessa?"

"Just soda, thanks." She was looking at Jeff with unconcealed approval. He was in the usual white shirt open at the throat, no tie, no jacket, and the usual chinos. He might have lost some weight, but the general look of him was of perfect fitness, the kind he used to have, the athlete's trained fitness, hard-muscled, co-ordinated and free-moving. The look of the college man was gone; a stranger might have guessed him twenty-five or -six instead of twenty-three, but that deepening maturity sat well on him; he had never looked better.

"Do you still like your night life?" she asked as Ken brought the drinks. "I take it, you're still sold on the job."

" 'Sold' isn't quite the word." He leaned forward in the deep chair, looking from one to the other. "There's something about this job that gets *to* you in the damnedest way. To me anyhow." He took a long gulp of his beer. "After the first few days, when I got the hang of it, it began working me over. It's hard to explain."

"I think I know what you mean," Ken said.

"There's something about working in a hospital," Jeff continued. "I'd never even been in a hospital before, except that one time when you were sick." He turned briefly to his father. "I was so scared, I guess I got fixed in the idea that hospitals were horrible places that smelled of disinfectants and drugs."

"You were fourteen then," Tessa said. "No, fifteen."

"And I didn't even think of it from the other side, the doctors there, and the nurses and surgeons. *And* the nurses' aides and orderlies."

"Why would you?"

"But working there—it's been half a year by now—going in at midnight, staying through those first operations in the morning, you sure get inside of things you never gave a thought to in your whole life."

"You must," Ken said.

"Talk about the last mile. That trip to surgery, down this long corridor, up in the elevator, down that corridor—for some scared kid or some old man or woman who thinks it's probably cancer—" He shook his head and set his beer down. He was looking at the carpet, as if he were embarrassed at his speech.

"It must be harrowing," Ken said. "I must compliment you on strong nerves. I know I never could work in that kind of tension."

"Tension, yes, but there's something else, I can't put my finger on it. There's a resident there I've been talking to, and he got the drift, all right. Dr. Rugov, that's his name, Fred Rugov, and he said, 'This place is a great narcotic for your own *oy veys*.'"

Tessa joined in the general laugh, but she knew there was nothing jocular for Jeff in what he had said. Even about comparatively "talkable" things, he still needed to pave over with the concrete of silence the malleable earth where emotion took root and from which it drew sustenance. This night job of his had reached him at an unexpected level, and was leading him toward whatever revelation this was to be.

"And the hospital work," she prompted after a moment. "In some way it gave you an idea about the graduation gift we still owe you. Is that it?"

"Just so. This has been building up for quite a while, really. I haven't even talked it over with Margie or Nate. I wanted to be sure on my own."

"Let's hear it," Ken said.

"It's nothing like a new car or a trip abroad."

"It doesn't have to be."

"Well, after all the sizing up and mulling around, it started to hit me, what I want to be. Or what I want to do. I want to study medicine. And then practice medicine."

"Why, that's fine, Jeff," his father said. A leap of feeling within him was pride, he knew its contours, and along with it, fractionally lagging behind like a hurdler taking the jump half a second behind the runner ahead, there was another leap, his old disbelief that this splendid young man could be in any way tarnished.

"You want to go back to college," Tessa said slowly. "To be a doctor. How wonderful, Jeff."

"I thought if you would stake me to the first year," Jeff said, rising from his chair in one smooth arc of motion, facing them both, looking down into their upturned faces. "It's a big thing, expensive, I've been looking into what it costs, and it's no go for me to try to swing it on my own, in between driving a hack."

"But it is marvelous," Tessa said. She glanced at Ken, caught his nod, saw the meaning of his rising color, so different accompanied by the pleasure in his eyes, so unrelated to the rising color that went with anger. "Why do you say 'the first year'? There would be four years."

"But the first year would be the graduation present. That would give me all the leeway I'd need to find out how to swing the rest of it—student loans, government loans, guaranteed bank loans for college, all that jazz."

"Hang up your shingle draped in promissory notes!" Ken said.

"Just my style. No kidding, these low-interest loans—you don't start to pay them back until you get your degree, and there are a billion angles I'd be investigating while I was out there, packing in my first year. But that one year alone comes to about two thousand."

Ken looked not at Jeff but at Tessa. "I think we could make that first year our gift, Jeff. It's good news, this."

"And now that you say it," Tessa said, "it seems inevitable, as if it were there all the time, hidden away."

"That's what's so weird," Jeff agreed. "When you think back to all my chem courses at college, and biochem and biology and math and all the science credits, you'd think I had a premed course going the whole time. I'll have some credits to make up, comparative anatomy and stuff, but even so."

"Is there any particular field of medicine you have in mind?" Ken asked. His tone had turned neutral, his eyes were guarded. "Or is that off in the future?"

"No psychiatry, no analysis," Jeff said vehemently. "What I want is something you can see in a microscope, test in a lab, something you can make a culture of and know the antibiotic to kill it, or the injection or drugs to cure it. Something you can X-ray on a big glass plate and study in front of a frosted pane of light and say, 'See, there it is.'"

He was half shouting the words, his voice strident, the syllables pounding; he stopped abruptly. In a moment he added quietly, "I'm not running down all psychiatry or analysis." He looked at his mother. "It sure has its place in medicine, but as a profession for me, never. Not that I've even thought of a specialty. I guess that chooses itself later. Sort of gradual selection."

"There's no rush anyway," Tessa said. To be able to just sit here, she thought, with no need for wisdom, for control. How remarkable that for the first time in years the world of sex is diminished to auxiliary status in the hierarchy of life, his life and ours.

"You said 'while I was out there,'" she said then. "Out where, Jeff? Have you decided where you want to go?"

"You bet I have." For the first time constraint tinged his words. He took up his neglected beer and drank thirstily. "This is going to surprise you too, but I've been looking into it, and it really is the one answer for me. It's U.C.L.A."

"California?"

"That is a surprise," Ken said.

"Their medical school rates as one of the best in the whole country," Jeff said flatly. He began to list his reasons for choosing U.C.L.A.

But California, Tessa was thinking. Again separation. Only this time more so. He wants distance, he wants to give up even the snatches of attachment we still have as a family. He wants to go to the other edge of the continent, three thousand miles the other edge, to assert his separate life, to live where none of us can know what he is doing, not even the little we know now. It's the next step for him, of course. He still feels driven; he drives himself but he still feels driven.

"California doesn't seem as far as it used to," she said aloud. "I remember my first flight there—it took seventeen hours. Right after the war that was."

"And now with the big jets, it's nothing," Ken said, too cheerily. He glanced at Tessa, as if to check her reception of this phase of Jeff's plan. "A doctor has a good busy life," he went on hastily, "a satisfying one. 'My son the doctor.' It sounds good." He laughed. "I sound like the proverbial Jewish mother, don't I?"

They laughed with him, but in a swift aside he thought, My son the homosexual doctor, the gay doctor. Well, it was safer than My son the gay senator, living under the endless threat of political ruin, safer than My son the gay spy, blackmailed into spying, safer than My son the thousand other careers where discovery could mean the crash of a lifetime's work and reputation.

"We'll stake you to that first year at U.C.L.A.," he said to Jeff. "And to some airplane fares home for holidays, won't we, Tessa?"

"Of course we will."

It would be a long time, she thought, before he asks for airplane fare. Certainly not this year; at Christmas he would be just three months into his new world, and too swamped with his schedule for time off. Of that she was already certain. Think of it as if he were drafted, but without the danger of Vietnam. During the years of his student deferment, she had ignored the draft, but since he had finished at C.C.N.Y. she had often felt the absence of that automatic exemption, and each lurching escalation of the war had made her aware of it at a higher pitch. A note from Dr. Isaacs to the draft board would create exemption of another kind, but Jeff would be the last person on earth to ask for such a note or use it if it were thrust upon him. That news story recently about a "Gay Motorcade" in Los Angeles to protest the Army and Navy's outright exclusion or dismissal of homosexuals—she remembered again the primary fear it had aroused in her, and the revulsion. In the old days the armed services assigned men to separate quarters if they were black, even to separate regiments; this was the same official behavior, the same stigma by those in power, without regard to an individual's general worth, his character, his bravery under fire, an assault on his dignity forever. But in the world of medicine, a man earned his dignity and showed his worth and they were his for the rest of his days.

"It's a great commencement gift," she said at last to Jeff, who had been watching her without impatience. "You're going to be first-rate as a doctor, I could bet on it. You're going to have a wonderful life, Jeff."

He looked at her, then at his father. "Thanks," he said. "I—well, thanks."

Part Three
1968-1973

CHAPTER THIRTEEN

You're going to have a wonderful life, Jeff. As time passed, Tessa began to flinch every time she remembered what she had said. It had been a fatuous optimism, blind to the truth. No hospital in the country would ever admit him as an intern if they knew he was a homosexual—she had asked Mark Waldo, and he had hesitated. She had pressed him and he had told her. Not one. No internship, no residency, no official hospital connection later on. Not if they knew. Jeff would have to keep his secret forever.

At Mark's words, an insensate fury had choked her, at all hospitals everywhere. No hospital could risk a homosexual doctor on the staff. He was not to be trusted with young male patients. He was not fit to practice medicine. He was not of the high moral character the hospital required.

Did any hospital waste one minute worrying whether a heterosexual intern could be trusted with a young female patient? There the high moral character was taken for granted, the fitness for the practice of medicine. But if you were gay you were automatically stripped of worthiness, denied your right to follow the practice you had spent years preparing for.

How sexist, how blindly unjust. That any young man or woman who had spent four years in college and then another four in medical school, that he or she had already demonstrated character, responsibility, high standards—this seemed still to elude the authorities of the hospital world.

It was monstrous, an injustice so obvious that its true name should be persecution, oppression. Sexist oppression. There was a good deal of discussion these days, particularly in the strengthening feminist movement, about sexism and sexist oppression, but all too few people saw that the world's treatment of gay people was also a sexist oppression.

Then how could there be a wonderful life for Jeff in medicine? You will have a wonderful profession, Jeff—that much she might have said, without this ensuing feeling that she had been asinine. You have chosen a fascinating field to work in. That much would have been true, clearly was true for him already. Every letter showed it, from his first day out there. He wrote infrequently, but when he did his letters were all about his courses, about lab projects, about the load he was carrying and how he wished he could speed it along and go even faster.

They longed for his letters, Ken as well as she, and for a good long time his letters and theirs had been bright and sustaining contacts with him. It was a long time before she first began to feel some vague sense that something was missing in their letters, and she fumbled about with it by herself, unable to pin it down. Then one day, perhaps in Jeff's second year in California, she was reading one of his letters and at its close she handed it across the table to Ken, saying, "It's like a college thesis."

"What is?" Ken asked.

"I was just thinking . . ."

Ken had already begun reading it, and she dropped into silence. But she had realized why she had been plagued by the feeling that something was missing. Something was. Each of Jeff's letters, now that he had finished his first news of where he lived, what his schedule was to be, each letter now was nearly as impersonal as a term paper. Each was a discourse on some aspect of his work, and a good discourse, clever, sometimes witty and amusing, sometimes perceptive and even touching. This one, in great part, was about the astonishing contrasts he was finding between this second year's lab work and last year's.

"Gone are the comfortable days," he wrote, "of doing a tracheotomy on a carefully anesthetized cat, where you smell only healthy animal tissue and ether. This week, for instance, we're working with fresh human organs, just out of autopsy, and our path. prof. has been holding forth on a cancerous liver, sections of which are right there in a sort of flat well atop the lab table. Mighty different, nasally as well as in other ways. You get this intensely personal sense of warm human tissue, newly dead, there are human smells and it's nothing like the remoteness you got last year from dissecting tissue out of some embalmed cadaver."

She watched Ken reading the letter and saw that it absorbed him too. It did reveal some of Jeff's feelings about his work, but not one line of it told anything of friends, of acquaintances, of his life in general outside the classroom or lab.

Don's college letters, and Margie's, had been filled with young chatter and gossip; they had both known that there was lots you could put into a letter home without yielding what you wanted to keep to yourself. Neither one had ever gone in for intimate revelations—they would have hated it, and they knew that their parents would have hated it too. But they had each found some happy medium, and so far Jeff had not.

As for visits home, her prophecy had proved all too accurate, and it was indeed a long time before they had to send airplane fare for a trip East. She had discovered an equanimity about his absence at Christmas, his first winter at U.C.L.A., that she had never guessed she would have. Maybe, she had thought, that analogy of his being off in the Army but not in Vietnam had more comfort in it than I suspected. She had telephoned him in the middle of Christmas Day, remembering to allow for the three-hours-earlier of California, and she and Ken had taken turns talking to him. He had seemed in good spirits, glad to have their call, had thanked them for their gifts and asked them to deliver his thanks to Margie and Nate, to Don and Jenny, promising follow-up thank-yous of his own as soon as he "wasn't working like a yak."

He had sounded different, not in accent or manner, but in the content of what he said. He talked of "surfing yesterday," dismissed Hollywood and Beverly Hills as "that old-line glam-oor," paying out phrases that seemed to please him, "this lemon tree in my back yard," "a date ranch," "the desert on an August afternoon." He took evident delight in the sound of new place names and street names, "off Sepulveda," "down to La Jolla," "out at San Berdoo," which he later translated into San Bernardino.

He sounded mature, very much grown-up. A stranger from an

unfamiliar region, friendly enough, and yet somehow self-contained, far away. A remoteness grew within her, an echo of the vague sense she got while reading his letters. It might have been a longing for a note of, well, not of love, one could not use words like "love" even to oneself without seeming like a demanding parent, anathema of anathemas. But a note of warmth, affection.

The warmth came when Jeff called them for the first time. They had given him carte blanche to call collect any time he wanted to, but he had never done so until the end of his first set of exams. Then he called one evening to tell them his first official grades: he was in the top five in three of his courses and in the top ten in the others. This time there was excitement and pleasure in his voice, he sounded close again, a member of the family bearing good news. She remembered his call about getting his job at St. Luke's; her voice must have sounded the same to Jeff, proud of him, delighted with his news, even happy. Ken took the phone and he sounded happy and proud too.

"Maybe he can handle it all more easily out there," she said to Ken as they finally hung up.

"When he has the room he needs. Yes."

The familiar phrase touched her. God knows, three thousand miles of continent between them had at last given him enough room. Perhaps Jeff should have made that discovery years ago, when he had gone across the park to live with Margie and Nate—perhaps if he had chosen U.C.L.A. back then instead of C.C.N.Y., he might have found what he needed so much earlier, a psychic distance from them merged into the physical distance.

Yet for her the three thousand miles of continent was also a barrier, and when, during the winter, Ken suddenly suggested that she take a few days' holiday in March, while he was out on his annual business trip, and meet him in Los Angeles so that they might have a few visits with Jeff, she had accepted with alacrity.

The visit was a success, for Jeff as well as for them. They took him to dinner each evening at good restaurants, they saw the small four-family house "on the wrong side of Sunset" where he had a sunny studio flat and porch, they let him drive their rented car whenever he was through for the day. Only once was the visit marred. It was on the last day, and she never told Ken about it.

It had been the only time she was alone with Jeff; so often in the past the setting for flare-ups had been some situation where she and Jeff were alone. This time they had driven with Ken out to Malibu, where one of his firm's authors lived, and after introductions and some polite nothings, she and Jeff had gone down to the wide beach to wait for Ken to rejoin them.

It was late in the March afternoon; the sunlight seemed amber over the crashing waves of the Pacific, the hills behind them were dry and buff-colored, the wind high and free. They both sat watching the climbing, curling and crashing of the waves and she said idly, "It's like watching a fire in the fireplace. You can't take your eyes off it."

"Sounds cozy. The one thing this ocean *ain't* is cozy."

"Anything but, I can see that. Does it ever get calm?"

"Occasionally. I like it this way, though. It makes you feel good, slamming around in it."

"You feel good in general, out here. I can tell."

"Yeah, it's okay."

"That means you're happy. I'm glad."

"Happy enough." He threw a handful of sand with sudden vigor.

"Apart from medical school, I meant. I hope so much that—"

"Christ," he exploded. "Digging. Still at it? Still digging?"

"I wasn't digging. I just hoped you—"

"You never see it as digging, never did, never will. But damn it, that's just what it is, just what it always was, and I still can't stand it."

He leaped to his feet then and tore down the beach, striding off with the fine effortless ease of youth. For a moment she thought only of the sand. She had felt the drag of the sand today, and it was the first time she had ever been conscious of it on any beach, had found herself tiring a little from their walking about in it, looking for a proper place to settle down. All she could think of now was how easily Jeff strode through it, as if it had no substance. Then it hit her; the old familiar clutch at her throat, the anger at his roughness, the debasing feeling that it was all her fault, then the defense, that she had merely been talking as anybody would talk. He could hurt, with apparent impunity, he could let you have it and let you stay with it. He would forget it before the day was out. She would not.

But by the time they had reached New York again, she had reached the point she had come to know so well, the "absorb-it point," as she had once dubbed it. The only thing to do with the pain life dishes out is absorb it. You may not forget it; you may only partially forgive it. But you could ultimately absorb it, accommodate it, merge it with other emotions.

Even the primary pain about Jeff was no longer the unique single pain it had been at the start. In the seven years that had passed, that primary pain had merged with other emotions, had thinned down, had taken on new facets from what she had read, from what Mark Waldo had told her, from her own "consciousness raising" about an injustice she had never really considered before, from her own anger at employers, at hospitals, at government agencies. They are wrong, she would think, not pausing to define the "they." It was the same *they* who were so often wrong about people outside other prescribed patterns, people with black skins, people with Puerto Rican names, girls, women, foreigners, Catholics in some communities, Protestants in others, Jews everywhere, though anti-Semitism had become fairly unfashionable by now except among the true-blue bigots.

And yet the very people who would dislike snide remarks about Jews or blacks or Puerto Ricans, the very people who held themselves superior to all bigotry, so often were perfectly easy with jokes about queers and fruit and gays. The last time they had been at Don and Jenny's, they had actually had an ugly showdown, started by Ken when Don started a story "about these two fags on motorcycles, and a cop waved them down for speeding—"

"Cut the story," Ken had said brusquely.

"What the—?" Don had looked at his father in amazement. It actually was amazement: they were there because of Don's birthday; he was thirty-three and here was his father ordering him to shut up in the middle of a sentence.

"You have the hide of an elephant," Ken had said. "To tell stories about fags when—"

"I forgot. I just plain forgot." Don suddenly wilted. Nate and Margie looked at each other. Ken walked away, went to the window, stared down at the street. It was Margie who changed the subject, something about Lynnie's school, and the moment was over.

Still, after all this time, Tessa thought, looking at her older son. If it were anything else, Don would never be so insensitive, he would never forget. Long ago she had thought, If only it were about something else, something not connected with sex, not tangled with the idea of sexual aberration. Obviously Don still wished that it were something else, wished it so much that he denied it by forgetting.

Damn sex anyway, she thought. Sex was one of the great instincts, yes, but it was one of many. At times it seemed to be the only one, the most powerful one, shoving aside all other drives, all other values. When you were young, it *was* all-powerful, the master; nature had artfully arranged that hierarchy of power, and only as the race itself was assured its renewal with the passing of years, only then did the drive slacken and the appetite grow more manageable and become once more one drive among many drives.

But people everywhere, when they considered sex patterns not their own—to such people, sex was all. A lifetime's training came leaping forward to make judgments, to avert the eye, perhaps to pry—

She still went hot with dismay whenever she remembered the second Christmas that Jeff had spent in California, again finding himself too pressed with work to manage the trip home. Once again she had allowed enough time for the three-hour difference, had waited indeed until afternoon in New York, remembering his ability to sleep till noon on holidays. Her call went through in seconds.

"And Merry Christmas to you," a male voice greeted her before she could speak. A male voice that was not Jeff's.

"Merry Christmas," she answered. "Is Jeff there?"

"Yes, he is. Just a minute."

She heard his call, "Hey, Jeff, it's for you," heard Jeff reply, "Be right there, Roy," and she was left waiting. In the background was music, familiar music. It took a moment to place it; it was not the inevitable "Silent Night" or "White Christmas" of the public airwaves on Christmas morning, but—why yes, it was Beethoven's Sixth, the Pastoral. Jeff himself had never been particularly fond of music; this had been chosen by somebody else. A record chosen and put on a stereo turntable, placed there earlier by this unknown Roy who had answered the phone. Probably the owner of the stereo and the record. Beethoven on Christmas morning. A tranquil scene.

It had never happened before that she had been answered by anybody but Jeff himself. In his one-room place in New York, he had never had a phone of his own. His cab driving didn't permit such luxuries, he had said, especially since there was a pay phone in the lower hall. To call him there meant that he would be summoned by the janitor or his wife; she remembered the raucous shout up the stairwell, "Phone, Jeff," and the muttered complaints about students who took their own sweet time about getting down the stairs.

That there might have been, even then, another reason for the lack of a telephone in his own room had never occurred to her. Now, listening to the Beethoven, she thought, But it would never have mattered if somebody else had picked up the phone; I haven't thought all these years that he never had a roomie.

The word "roomie" now was suddenly farcical. The voice that had summoned Jeff was not the voice of a schoolboy roomie but that of a man. The man who had put the record on the turntable, Roy, the man with whom Jeff lived.

The once frequent vision was suddenly there again, the two young bodies entwined, the vision that had sprung at her with such ferocity that very first night so long ago, that vision she had, a hundred times since, banished, only to have it leap out at her on unpredictable occasions, as savage as ever.

And here it was again, this time against the soaring sweetness of music she loved, and for that reason perhaps more intolerable than ever. Long after that Christmas call to Jeff had ended, the torment remained until she had begun to wonder at the torment itself, to ask herself why it should be so biting this time, so tenacious. Something eluded her, she had felt, something more than the recurring image, something to do with *her*, not with Jeff. She had to find out what it was, had to track it down, as if it were an enemy existing somewhere, able to attack at will and herself helpless against it.

She had failed. For the rest of that day and night she had found nothing to account for this extraordinary sensation that there was something new this time, something within *her* that added itself to the horror of that flashing vision, that gave it extra substance, an added dimension that had never been there before.

And then, in her tossing sleep, as she turned restlessly under her sliding blankets, then out of nowhere came the words "Peeping Tom." Came with an impact that shook her, came with a familiarity she did not pause to question, with a rightness unarguable. It meant something special right now, something that was hers, that had been hers for a long time but that now had taken on an extra substance.

Moments later she had remembered back to that night years before when she had been admitting that she was repelled by "specificity" in writing of sex, heterosexual or homosexual, when she had gone to the bookcase to find *Anna Karenina* in some need to prove to herself that one could write of love and passion without acting the Peeping Tom as so many modern authors were doing, making Peeping Toms of their readers as well. She had copied out a whole paragraph of the Tolstoy, had read and reread it and taken it to the office, had used it several times since, in discussions with young authors about today's "clinical obsessions with erotic specifics."

That had been at the beginning of her own self-education about homosexuals, when she was finding out about Sir John Wolfenden and his now famous phrase, "between consenting adults in private," and she had begun her first faltering steps toward wider knowledge and toward erecting a platform she herself could stand on. Privacy was one of the foundations.

Privacy. She had always respected other people's rights of privacy about everything, their mail, their phones, their thoughts, certainly their sex. But this flashing vision of Jeff and another boy . . . it had been boy then, and across the years it had changed to another young man—

She drew back in disavowal. It was impossible. It was something else. But an inexorable voice seemed to ask her: Did you ever have any flashing vision of Margie and Nate in the intimacy of sex? Of Don and Jenny in the intimacy of sex? Of your brother Will and his wife Amy? Of anybody in the whole world?

The question struck like a rod of steel, pinning her, transfixing her so that she could not move to some other subject. Never, never with anyone else in the world. Apart from a few half-loving, half-bawdy remarks to Ken on the first evening after Don's wedding or Margie's, apart from that filmy powdery awareness that they were making love, she had never visualized, never really considered the details of what they did, what they said, how they sought, touched, embraced, reached . . .

Then why the exception with Jeff? Why this flashing vision of him in his hours of sex? It was as if she permitted herself a spying that would be unthinkable, had always been unthinkable, not only with the other children, but, come to think of it, with herself and Ken. She never thought back to their own sexuality in the first insistent years, never dwelt on precise images of Ken in the act of penetrating—even now she shied away from it.

To have sex, to live sex, to luxuriate in sex, yes, yes, in your own acts of sex. But to evision somebody else in the act of having sex, there was something prurient in it, a Peeping Tom-ish vicarious nastiness.

Then what was this recurrent vision of the two young male bodies? Why the exception, as if she had an inherent right to make an exception? It was a monstrous mistake, a self-delusion that "this is different," generated perhaps by the world's old self-delusion that it had some vested rights in the sex behavior of others. If ever there was a sexual aberration, here it was, her own. If ever there was an obsession with specifics, here it was, her own once more.

She leaped back from the idea, but it pursued her. It is so, it is so, face it, accept it. You never saw it before, but now you do see it and you can finish with it. It *is* a question of privacy, Jeff's as much as anybody else's. It is a matter of good taste, of a decent decorum, *your* taste, your decorum. Remember it, and you need never see that vision again.

A fine elation seized her. Here too was a threshold and she had just crossed it.

*   *   *

The first time they did send airplane fare for a visit home was not until Christmas of 1968. It had been a year of fearful violence, topping nearly a decade of mounting violence, a boiling up within the nation, an eruption of activism, of confrontation, of militancy. "Hell No, I Won't Go" was heard from one end of the land to the other from students denouncing the war in Vietnam, cities flamed from Newark to Watts, the nonviolence of the civil rights movement was constantly clawed apart by people crying "Black Power" and separatism, this very year had seen two assassinations, one of Martin Luther King, the other of Bobby Kennedy, that sent shock waves through the memories of everyone who had watched through the horror-stricken days in November five years earlier when another Kennedy had been shot down. . . .

It was Ken who was the first to remark, during Jeff's two weeks at home—not literally at home, for he had elected to stay with Margie and Nate, and had prepared them for this beforehand— Ken who had said, "It all has slid right off his back, this whole year. Have you noticed?"

"He identifies with young people. All young people do."

"Don't trust anybody over thirty. Yes, I know. But it's more than that, Tessa. He doesn't give a damn, except about medicine, except about his own troubles. He lives off there in that sunny cocoon of Southern California, basking in the sun, and he's peeled off the whole damn world."

"Ken, I don't really think that's it—he never did get worked up over politics, any kind of politics."

Ken ignored the point, though he nodded at the words. "He's peeled off all his family too; even while we were out there, he never fixed it so we'd meet one of his neighbors, one of his friends."

"He's always been an intensely private person."

"It's something beyond that. I just got this image of his peeling himself free, like somebody on a beach, stripping down for sunbathing or a swim, and it rings truer to me than any other way of looking at it."

"Maybe he has to. To survive."

This time Ken fell silent. He looked tired, saddened, and Tessa knew that this sight of Jeff in his old surroundings had reawakened in Ken some of his old misery about his son, misery that Ken had done so much to throw off, to disown, but whose vestigial traces could still freshen with a vigor which he himself detested.

Jeff had changed in the nearly two and a half years since he had left for the West. He was in his middle twenties and looked indefinably older, but externally he had changed as well. It was in part what Margie called "the California look," the permanent deepening of his tan, as if it were laid down to the bone, the thorough bleaching of his light hair, his eyebrows nearly vanished against the brown forehead. He looked different in other ways, as all young people were looking different, and in that he was a conformist, Tessa reflected, but only to herself, as Nate was, as Don was, as all the "nonconforming young" actually were. He wore his hair longer, touching the collar of his shirt in back, his earlobes on the sides, with sideburns loose and full along his jaws. It was becoming, casual and at the same time rather courtly, as if he were a man of an earlier century as well as of his own.

He seemed pleased to be "home again," though when he used the phrase himself a note of protest arose within Tessa's mind, a note she did not utter. Even to Ken she refused to say that she was hurt at his decision to stay with Margie and Nate on this first visit home, that it had come at her as a small insult. Jeff hadn't recognized it as such, most probably because he had never considered it as it might seem to anybody but himself. To consider one's parents? Square, man, square.

That hated concept, "parentship." Here again, she thought, was a new test they had to face, a test neither Don nor Margie had ever made them face. With each of them, the time had come so naturally to let go, to evolve into the new relationship presented by a new family forming, outside of the old family, though with luck and affection, linked to it. Linked in a lesser degree as with Don, or a greater degree as with Margie. But strongly linked still.

Where there was no new family, there was an imprecision about the cutoff date for legitimate parentship, but the estate of parenthood could not be ended by fiat, even of a grown son; to be a parent, to feel what a parent feels was a natural force too, like the sex drive and so many other instinctual forces. It was the tightness of the bonds that could be regulated by good sense, by a proper understanding of the need for independence. But on the parents' side, at least when there was love, the connective tissue would always hold.

Well, she thought, say nothing, show nothing, value this period of calmness. It's a surface calmness maybe, distance-induced, distance-protected, underwritten by separation; don't take chances with it. That idea about asking the Wisters over for dinner, asking Sue as well—don't do it. It might work out in some unexpected way you would regret and feel responsible for. That idea of asking Pete Hill and his wife for drinks—wrong too. If Jeff wants to see them, he will see them himself. That idea of asking Jeff over to Quales and Park to see her new office, symbol of her latest promotion, again, no. Some unsuspected raw place might be touched in him by this overt sign of her continuing success.

Once she had thought, Life is a round. Now she found herself thinking, Love is a round, not romantic love alone, not sexual love, but family love, compassionate love, insight, empathy. Whatever was the essence behind those words was what she meant, those fashionable words, as overworked now in the late Sixties as "charisma" had been in the Kennedy years, "charisma" and "Camelot." The ability to feel for oneself the needs of another was what she meant, to wince with the twinge another felt, to feel elated and proud over another's achievement, victory small or great.

Perhaps Jeff could and did feel this kind of love for others, for those others in his own life. She had hoped often enough that he could and did, hoped it for his sake, for his own fullness. But she had come to feel the conviction that there was little of this compassion or affection in him when it came to his private stance toward his father or toward her.

The calmness and goodwill and merry laughter of this visit home—all under the roof of Margie and Nate—all of it was welcome indeed. But there was a heaviness in it too. This too she refused to say to Ken, and then thought, It's so easy to go from being excluded to excluding. Late that same night she opened her mind to him without constraint, turning to him in her own seeking after fullness.

And this time it was Ken who finally pointed out to her that perhaps there was a necessity even Jeff could not name. "Maybe he has to, Tessa. To survive."

* * *

The night before he was to fly back to California, Jeff seemed reluctant to go off to bed. Even when Margie finally said, "You two can sit here, but I'm beat, so good night," he merely waved her a gesture of farewell and said to Nate, "How's for one more beer?"

"Sure, I'll grab me one more Bourbon."

They drank in silence. In the fireplace two nearly burnt-out logs collapsed, flinging bright sparks upward in a fan of light. Jeff thought, It's like watching the waves curl and roll over, and wondered why the image seemed familiar and right. Aloud he said, "Margie showed me the series you wrote about the two-week shutdown at Columbia. The pieces really were swell."

"It was the assignment that was swell. You get hold of something you can get your teeth into, you come up with a series the boss gives you by-lines on."

"Yeah, well. But you wrote the pants off it. There have been student uprisings other places, and I never read much below the headlines."

"This was full of dynamite, start to finish."

"Okay, go be modest." He looked again at the fireplace, concentrating on it. The embers were blue-purple now, the crackling muted. "Nate, do you still play around with that old notion you used to have, you know, a big piece about gay people?"

"When something happens and I have five minutes to think with."

"What about your managing editor's reaction? Any more amenable than he used to be?"

"He hasn't changed too much," Nate said. "But then I haven't either."

"If you ever do write anything big, a series like this Columbia stuff or anything, you won't let any of it be the kind of liberal crap that does get printed—that's for sure."

"Crap like what?"

"The usual bighearted tolerance stuff. 'Look how broad-minded I am.'"

Nate glanced at him with heightened attention. "What's eating you, Jeff?"

"Or the other kind of crap about how talented all gays are, look at all the gay playwrights and the gay novelists and artists. Not to speak of the famous old Greek fags like Plato and Leonardo and dear old Michelangelo."

Nate said caustically, "You mean, like what great athletes all blacks are."

"Right."

"Hell, I know some blacks that can't hit a ball and some that can. And I know some gay people that are full of talent and some that haven't a bean's worth."

"Good. I hope you get that across when you get writing that series on gays, that and lots more."

"You sound as if you're sure I won't."

"Nothing like that, no. It's just that there's never yet been anything written by a straight guy that said the right things. I've read them all."

"Let me in on it, Jeff, go ahead. What's wrong with what they write? I've read them all too, or a lot of them, anyway."

Jeff looked unwilling to go on. He turned his can of beer in his fingers, studying the label. He looked at the fire; it was more somber than before, its life sinking.

"What are the wrong things?" Nate said again.

"Look, man, those guys that get the crap in, they're not gay. They're straight, and anything they hear about the gay world, they hear through the static of their own straightness. Anything they see, they see through the filter of their straightness. That's why it's all phony, or all distorted."

"And you think I'll have the same static and the same filter."

"Christ, no." There was silence. Nate waited, and finally Jeff said, "There's something gets in the way, if you *try* to talk to anybody straight. That's why gay people never even try. You have to be gay to *get* it."

For the first time, Nate felt his gorge rise at something Jeff had said. He stood up suddenly, moved closer to the chair Jeff sat in and looked down at him.

"Listen, man, don't dump on me," he said. "Don't you give me *that* crap either. That's like telling me I can't read a book by Eldridge Cleaver or Malcolm X, or write a review of it, or *feel* it. That's racist crap, and this that you're dishing out is sexist crap."

"Damn it, it's not. Every goddamn straight that says anything or writes anything or even thinks anything about being gay, is sure as hell hanging on to his straight identity while he does it."

"Should he give up his straight identity, for God's sake? Do I ask any gay to give up his gay identity?"

"*You* may not."

"What the hell is this attack on straights because they can't molt their straightness, like birds molting their feathers, before they're considered fit to write something?"

Suddenly Jeff laughed. "That's funny, 'molting their feathers.'" Nate did not laugh with him and he grew serious again, even ill at ease. "It's not funny and I know it. Nobody wants you to molt anything. There's a friend of mine out in L.A. who belongs to a new group, not sub rosa the way the old groups were—"

"Don't tell me about him if you're listening for my static."

"Come on, Nate."

"Sure, 'come on, Nate.' You've got to clear out some static yourself, mister. This is a two-way street, everything's a two-way street when it comes to hang-ups and shoveling guilt onto people."

"I know that."

"Don't load it off on somebody who happens to be straight, don't prejudge him as a phony liberal with built-in stereotypes."

"Good God, man, I don't."

"Don't be so sure you don't. You know goddamn well what I feel about people who prejudge anybody who happens to be gay."

Now it was Jeff who felt his gorge rise. This was the first fight he had ever had with Nate; he hated it. But Nate was talking the way the old man talked, the way his mother used to talk, and still would talk, if he didn't head her off each time she started one of her heart-to-hearts.

"Christ, even if I did prejudge you," he shouted at Nate, "you wouldn't lose your job tomorrow, your mother's goddamn heart wouldn't break, you wouldn't be kept off a hospital staff."

Nate fell back a step. His face changed. He looked across the room, past Jeff's chair. All he said was "Right. None of that would happen."

Jeff gulped; he heard the dry noise it made, felt the twist of pain in his gullet. "It's rotten," he said, "us having a row."

"It's not a row. Not what you could officially call 'a row.'"

"Good." He breathed in hard, the deep inhalation at the end of a struggle. Unbelievably it had happened; unbelievably it was already over. Why the hell couldn't he manage his rotten temper as well with his father or mother? If they only knew how he hated it *after*; if they only realized it was the same sort of writhing in his guts he used to have way back there at Placquette. He could never admit that either, not to the old man, not to his mother. They probably thought he never gave it another thought, after he had blown his top. There had to be some way to let them know, but he had never found it.

"You were starting to tell about a new group out in L.A.," Nate said at last, in his ordinary voice.

"This friend of mine is tied in with them," Jeff said. "It is one of the new kind, not the old-line kind, the Mattachine and Daughters of Bilitis, not like that, the ones that go back to the Forties or Fifties. This is just the last year or so I'm talking about."

"And—?"

"Their bag is a whole other attitude, about being gay and saying so. 'Coming out' is the idea, and the hell with it."

"It's happening here too. I guess in most big cities."

"What do you think of it?"

"What do you?"

"I used to have daydreams about me telling the whole damn world all about the way I was—boy, it was a great daydream." Jeff looked doubtful. "It depends on how you earn your living."

"It does that, I guess."

"This friend of mine writes comedy for TV. Big dough. If they canned him, he'd write comedy for films, or Broadway, or a novel."

"It's different for doctors. Sure it is."

"And lawyers and ministers and anybody in politics and anybody in ninety million other jobs."

Now Nate looked doubtful. "But there *are* these new groups just the same, springing up all over the place. The whole country is in some sort of sweat—the blacks, the women, now gay people starting fights for their own rights, civil rights, equal rights, whatever you want to call it—"

They stared at each other, each caught by the other's intensity. Then Nate went on, "You know another group you'll be hearing more and more from? Another dissident group that's growing?"

"What sort of group?"

"Analysts, psychiatrists, not the usual run, but people who think you can be gay and okay at the same time—no need of therapy."

"What is this group? Where do they practice? What's their name?"

"Not an organized group with a name and address, nothing that tidy, not so far anyhow. But psychiatrists here and there, objecting to the stereotypes." He went on to tell him about Halston Richards, Judd Marmor—

"Marmor?" Jeff interrupted. "He's out in California."

"Sure he is. What I can't figure is why you've never mentioned his name or what he stands for."

"I don't know what he stands for."

"Don't you ever *talk* about this to anybody out there? You halfway through medical school?"

"Damn right I don't." Pugnacity sounded again but he controlled it. "Remember that TV show about the playwright with the limp wrists, when I said you could call the other writer a coward if you wanted to."

"I'm not calling anybody a coward now," Nate said.

"You don't say anything because you can't. You've been conditioned for a lifetime not to give yourself away. You don't start little conversations about what Dr. Marmor 'stands for,' not with your professors, not your faculty advisers, not with anybody. You shut up and think of your M.D."

Nate felt holier-than-thou, yet he had begun something that had to be ended.

"How do you know all this anyway?" Jeff asked a moment later. "It looks as if you've been digging pretty deep in research already, no matter what the managing editor says."

"Not doing it myself so much. I have a pretty fine researcher—that's where most of this new stuff comes from."

"A researcher on the paper?"

"Not on the paper. It's somebody you know." He looked carefully at Jeff, as if weighing for one last time the wisdom of going on. Then he said, "It's Tessa."

"Tessa?"

"Your mother." Before Jeff could speak he went on quickly. "Look, it's your own business, not talking things out with her, or with Ken either. Maybe in your place I'd shut up myself. I can't say. Margie can't say—we've talked about this a lot, and we agree, everybody's got to play it his own way."

"I've just said—"

"Sure. But there's one thing *you* ought to know, that Tessa's been making a kind of study, a big rounded study of what is known and what is not known, what experts agree on, what other experts don't agree on—which just about covers the waterfront. She's been at it for years now, going at it with the same kind of excitement you feel for your med courses."

"She never told me."

"If she started, you'd shut her off. Even if she mentions some piece in the paper, you shut her right off. Margie asked her once, that's how we know. But she kept on with this crazy research project, and she's been learning from it and changing with it, sure that all sorts of people will start changing too." He turned away from Jeff's tense listening. "I told you all this because she never will. If she did you'd think she was butting in on something wasn't any of her business. The point is, I guess, it's everybody's business."

Jeff shifted his gaze back to the fireplace. Deep in the cooling ashes there was a fine faint tinge of color. It seemed to fade and glow, rise and fall. He thought of the bouncing point of light on an oscilloscope.

CHAPTER FOURTEEN

Tonight was the eve of Ken's final spring trip for his firm, "my terminal trip," he had called it with a grim humor. Next year in March there would be no traveling around the country to jobbers and leading bookstores. By then he would be sixty-five and retired from the publishing house he had helped so long ago to create and which for thirty-five years he had helped to run.

"But you don't have to quit, Ken," his partner, Ted Brannick, had said. "Officially, sure, but you can keep on in a consulting setup as long as you like."

"The boss privilege," Ken had replied, and turned it down. But he felt it deeply, the approaching retirement, felt it as a lowering curtain to his life, and none of the usual hearty remarks by his colleagues about how splendid it would be to be free of office hours, free of sales meetings and rising paper prices and rising competition, none of it struck below the outer skin of his mind. Not one of the people offering these comforting sentences would welcome retirement and the age of sixty-five that made it mandatory.

Tessa understood his refusal of the boss privilege, and also his scorn of the banal cheer. Sixty-five. A Senior Citizen. That infuriating nice-nellyism, that demeaning substitute for the once honorable word "old." Was anybody in the full tide of life dubbed a Junior Citizen? There was a proliferation of repellent words about age that Tessa found insulting on Ken's behalf, wincing internally whenever she read or heard them. The Golden Years,

Leisure Village, Retirement Plaza, Senior Spa. But villain of them all was Senior Citizen.

The word was "old." In ten years it would become her word and she would use it. "Now that I am old," she would say, not "Now that I'm getting older," as so many people did, as if to hold at arm's length for indefinable extra time the truth and simplicity of that small word "old." To his credit, Ken made it even simpler. "I'm sixty-four," he had said the other night. "Next year I retire."

So tomorrow he was starting on his last swing around the country for Brannick and Lynn. Again he had suggested that she meet him in Los Angeles, but this time she had declined, offering no polite excuses, saying openly, "It's too soon, I still feel sensitive about it." It had been more meaningful than she had guessed at Christmas, Jeff's choice of Margie and Nate's as the place to come home to. At the time she had managed it all rather well, she liked to think, with aplomb, with equanimity, but in fact it had left, if not a wound, then a kind of dark stain on her mood, still there. That time he had told them he wanted to study medicine, she had thought, He's letting us help him again, he's accepting us as his family again. But it had proved to be merely a brief intermission in a continuing action, named perhaps Separateness. Not merely Maturity, not Adulthood, but Separateness, another estate altogether. By the start of his sophomore year, Jeff had indeed found out all about student loans, bank loans, government loans, and though he had permitted his parents to co-sign some notes with him, he had made it clear that he never would call upon them for more than this perfunctory show of solidarity.

There was again something to admire in his independence, his decision to make it on his own, and this was warming. Nate had told her of his final session with Jeff, and she was touched that Nate had felt some inner impulse to tell him about "his researcher."

"It hit him like a ton of bricks," Nate had said.

She was glad Jeff knew, glad that Nate had been the conduit for the news of Dr. Richards. Strangely, there had been none of that sense of evaporation when she had told Nate and Margie about Halston Richards, and this she had ascribed to the fact that she had rushed at Ken straight from Mark's office, while she herself felt stunned. In any case, now Jeff too would have this seed of a new viewpoint germinating in his mind, and perhaps he too would find its roots taking solid hold.

Tonight was also the eve of a trip abroad for Margie and Nate, their first vacation ever without the children, a celebration trip for Margie, who was returning in April to the commercial world, instead of remaining exclusively in "the much tougher job of mother, wife and housekeeper." It had taken her all of half an hour to get back the job she had left eight years before, when Lynnie was just about a month from being born.

"And at thirty a week more pay," Margie crowed. "Despite me being as rusty as an old nail. Bless this shortage of women willing to take secretarial jobs, and bless Mrs. Cole for being willing to hire me back on."

"Will you mind working for a woman?" Ken asked, with a sly wink at Tessa.

"Daddy, you needn't try on the male chauvinist act. You can't begin to manage it."

"Oh, I don't know," Tessa said. "There's never been a woman partner at Brannick and Lynn, has there?"

"But we're way ahead of Q. and P.," Ken said, "for all your big new plaid office, and four of our top editors are women and have been for years. How many at your place?"

"Don't rub that in." She grinned at him and then at Margie and Nate. Her large new office at Quales and Park was a pleasant externalizing of her expanding position, and Tessa fully acknowledged her pleasure in her latest promotion, though in this her eighteenth year at Q. and P., she was privately rather mordant about it. Now she said ruefully, "I told you, I'm the company woman, just as Linc Noble is the company black."

"Token Tessa," Ken said and laughed.

"You can laugh, Daddy," Margie said. "You know damn well that if Mother was a man, she'd have had the big office five years ago."

"Plus a few thousand bucks more per year," Nate said.

"I know something else," Ken answered. "From now on, it will be another rung of the executive ladder every few months, until she's the first woman vice-president they've ever had."

"Wouldn't that be dandy?" Margie asked her mother.

"Everybody's consciousness sure is being raised," Nate said. "You've got to hand it to the women this time round."

"But without the first time round," Ken said, "they'd still be yelling, 'Votes for Women.'"

He looked animated and it surprised Nate. Good for him, Nate thought, here's one place where the poor guy is really making it. Of late he had begun to feel warmer toward Ken, prodded in part by Jeff's scorn for the "look how broad-minded I am" people.

Nate understood the scorn; hadn't he felt the same when people were broad-minded and tolerant about his being Jewish? And yet he felt now, more and more, that Ken had come a long way from where he had been; you had to give him some kind of good marks for the distance he had made himself travel, not only demerits because it wasn't as far as he might have traveled. Maybe Ken could never stretch it anything beyond this—it still was a whale of a distance up from that hidebound little pit he had been in way back there when Jeff had first told them. Someday, Nate thought, I'll try to make old Jeff see that.

A boisterous laugh from Margie brought him back to the general conversation. "It's such a great satire, and such a great title," she was saying. "I didn't think she had any humor at all. You'd never think it, not from *Hurricane*."

"What great title?" Nate asked. "Who didn't have any humor?"

"Helena Ludwig," Tessa answered, a note of pride sounding. "She never used to show much humor, but she's been letting it out of hiding, since she did join them."

"These galleys I've been reading," Margie said to him. "It's her new novel, about two girls who are into the feminist movement in a big way, both very bright, one a real sex object, the other definitely not. And Helena Ludwig gets them both perfectly, and the whole scene today, and the title of her book is *A Certain Envy*."

For a moment Nate said nothing whatever. Margie was looking at him so expectantly that it suddenly struck. "Of course," he said. "Good ole penis envy." He laughed. "I gather she doesn't buy the idea."

"She runs it into the ground. The whole book does."

"Challenging Freud?" Ken asked dryly. "Blasphemy."

"Half a century's gone by," Tessa said. "If Freud were alive, he'd be checking over his early theories himself."

"But, Mother, honestly," Margie said. "No woman I've ever known agrees with this penis-envy bit. After all, Freud himself had parents and an environment shaping him too! That whole male-dominated era, that's what he had, genius though he was."

"*A Certain Envy* is one hell of a title," Nate said. "He'd have liked it himself."

At this point the telephone rang and Tessa answered it. "Yes, she is," she said. "Anything wrong, Marta?"

Margie was already out of her chair. Marta was a stout, good-natured old woman who was now part of the Jacobs family, hired some two months earlier when Margie began to lay the ground-work for going back to work. Marta was sixty-eight, acted years younger, and could not live on her small social security checks or find a job any longer as a factory worker. She knew nothing about bringing up children but she had the great faculty of enjoying them, of ignoring them unless there was some pressing reason not to, and of remaining equable at all times. Nate's mother was mov-ing into the house during the European trip, and Tessa was to take over from Mrs. Jacobs each weekend from Friday evening through Sunday. It had seemed an excellent arrangement to both grandmothers, to the children, to Margie and Nate, and most es-pecially to Marta.

"So somebody is here always, somebody that knows more," Marta had said, closing the matter.

Tessa relinquished the phone to Margie before she had assimi-lated Marta's reply to her question. "Yes, wrong," Marta had said, "but all right."

"What temperature?" Margie asked almost at once. "Oh, that's high. We'll be right there. Just tell her we're on our way."

"Lynnie's a hundred and two," she said, turning to them from the phone. "Wouldn't you know!"

"You're a pretty good prophet," Nate said, moving toward his coat. To Tessa he said, "She's been saying one of the kids would come down with something just before we took off."

"You won't have to delay your trip?" Ken asked.

"Not if it's a cold," Margie said. "But if it's measles or anything." She looked at Nate. "You've got to go anyway." To her parents she said, "He has appointments with some newspaper people in London."

"Nuts," Nate said. "I'm a liberated father. We both stay or we both go."

"It might be nothing but *Angst*," Tessa said. "Before, you always took them with you."

"We'll call you when we know."

But the next morning, though it wasn't measles, only an earache, they had already canceled their flight. "We're not worriers," Margie said. "But a hundred and two. You know how it is."

"I do know. That first drink in the plane wouldn't be any fun if you were up there thinking thermometers. I'm so sorry."

"Children! Why do we all fall for them?"

Two days ticked by and then Lynnie's temperature plummeted down to normal. That same evening Margie and Nate caught a night flight, their zest and eagerness restored. It starts on the first day of baby's life, Tessa thought, and it grows each month, each year. Your own life is integrated with that child's life and stays integrated year upon year. You can be the most freedom-giving mother or father, but you cannot be happy if your child is sad, you cannot feel hale and well if your child is sick, you cannot go off on vacations if your child is strapped down by fever.

And was this the dreaded "parentship"? *Angst* indeed. It had become almost imperative these days for parents to know *Angst* if they loved their children and showed that love, mistrusting it as a forbidden delight, condemning it, automatically tagging it "possessiveness."

Modern attitudes, though, so often carried within them strains of an outmoded Puritanism or Victorianism, any of the repressive isms that held it unseemly to be forthcoming and open about love. Parental love, filial love, sexual love—there were so many delimiting restrictions about all of them. Puritan or Victorian children were not to be expansive, either, in their love for their parents; respect and decorum were what they were expected to reveal, not plain unabashed love. And in odd subliminal ways, the same thing was true of the young-old relationship in families today. There was something groovy in being offhand, even rude, to your parents.

But then, thanks be, there were the exceptions. Like Margie. Maybe daughters were always more loving . . . Nonsense, that was to classify Margie in the "dutiful daughter" role, the female role. It was because Margie was Margie, a warm loving human, married to a warm loving human like Nate. They reinforced each other, they interacted upon each other and upon those they loved and those who loved them.

Almost as if to bear witness, an elongated air letter came from London by the end of that same week. Margie had dashed it off in a large tumbling calligraphy, as if pride had unsteadied her hand and made her slightly incoherent. "Our very first night here, this British editor of a magazine, *Orbit*, latched on to Nate, and so he's going to write a big takeout, an assignment for real, about homosexuals in the States, as they call us over here." To which Nate had scrawled a sassy postscript: "So gird up yer learns, Researcher, I'm to have all the space we need. Love, N."

A leap of pleasure told her how much she had wanted this project of Nate's to turn someday from dream to reality, and how remote such a possibility had seemed. Even today, in 1969, if you looked up the listing "Homosexuality" in the index of *The New York Times*, you found nothing but the admonition "See Sex," and when you turned to the proper page, you found a juxtaposition of listings about prostitutes, child molesters, homosexuals, deviants, sex offenses and the like, which in itself revealed all too much of the still-prevailing slant of society in general and the editors of the *Times* in particular. Yet it was true that there were many more listings than there had been a few years back, sign enough that the subject of homosexuality had been emerging as a matter of public interest, and particularly so when the listings included reviews of plays dealing with homosexual men or women, films portraying them, either well or foolishly, understandingly or doltishly, but portraying, not pretending they did not exist.

That evening Tessa began to look over her own "research." Ken would be telephoning her later, probably from Will and Amy's house in Phoenix, if she had his calendar straight. It was a surprise, actually, to see how much material she had amassed since she had first made that embarrassed request for a volume of *Hansard* over at the British Information Service. By now she had two big boxes of clippings and photostats of articles she had read but could not clip; she also had a stack of medical and psychiatric journals, and several textbooks recently published. All of these she had tabbed in her own offhand way that would have made a trained researcher blush, but clear enough to her, the tabs or strips of paper sticking up from book and magazine alike, standing erect like a small forest of bookmarks.

And quite apart from all of this was one special cardboard box bearing a label as yellow as sunshine, which said simply, CHANGE. In this was a collection of what she privately thought of as "the Halston Richards view," although only two of the papers and speeches were actually by Dr. Richards himself. One was a lecture given this past January to a symposium of psychiatrists; the other was a blurred carbon of the original typescript of another lecture still to be given in public by him, later to be published, the carbon sent along to her by Mark Waldo with a penciled note, "the whole A.P.A. is aware that a revolution is in the making."

She paused over Mark's note. Once she would not have known that the letters stood for American Psychiatric Association, once she had never heard of Halston Richards, nor dreamed that he represented one of an entire new wing, as it were, of the profession and the changing estimates of many within it toward the entire subject of the homosexual in the modern world. Apart from the two lectures by Dr. Richards, this box held other speeches, other lectures, other papers, none of them known yet to the general public, but all the most recent work of others "in the Richards' wing," many of them collected by her own efforts from analysts or psychiatrists to whom she had written on her own private stationery, never explaining her interest, always starting her letter by saying, "I am eager to have a copy of the lecture you gave at—"

During the next three evenings, she reread nearly everything in her collection, reliving the long process of learning she had almost unwittingly arranged for herself for so long a period, not then foreseeing the scope and intensity her own study would achieve, haphazard and intermittent as it had been, taking its vigor perhaps from its very haphazardness, a melting pot of opinions and convictions, some old and stately and authoritarian, others young and exploratory and willing to look anew.

Each time she ended for the night, usually after Ken had called, she found herself exhilarated and somehow more in command of her own ideas, as if she had been through a refresher course in a subject that only gained in import from being brought to the front of her best attention once again. She would close that special box with its yellow label, stare at the word CHANGE and wonder at its power to move her.

* * *

Ken knew from the start of his trip that something was a little different, but he attributed this to his own awareness, which he did not share with the people he saw, that the familiar "See you next year" was now merely an empty slogan. The sense that something was a bit different rather puzzled him, though, because it persisted despite his eminently reasonable explanation of it, until one night he admitted that it was depressing him. He felt low, and he kept on feeling low. He had no cold, no discomfort, nothing that could be called malaise or illness, and certainly he had no fever. When he called Tessa in the evening from a hotel room or from the house of some friend or colleague who had invited him to stay the night, he always said, "Everything's fine," but he also said, "I'm a bit tired," not realizing how often he did say it. One night he varied this, to say, "I seem to get lots more tired in cars and planes than I used to, but I suppose by now I should expect that."

"I don't know," Tessa said. "Maybe you ought to see a doctor about it."

"I don't think it's anything to see doctors about. Getting old is a damn hard job, that's the size of it."

"It might be wise to get a check, though. Blood pressure and pulse and all. I wish you would, Ken."

"You're remembering the stroke, Tessa, but ten years have gone by. How many times has Mark said not to sit around worrying about another one?"

"I'm not, but it's important—to me, anyway. I sort of love you."

He said, "And I sort of love you. Okay, I'll ask about a doctor tomorrow and report back."

And when he did report back, there was nothing but good news to give her. Pulse normal, blood pressure within the normal range, electrocardiogram fine. The doctor had called Mark in New York, comparing data, or readings, or whatever they called their findings, and Mark had confirmed him in his okay.

" 'Don't push yourself on this trip' is what they both told me,"

Ken told Tessa. "I wasn't pushing anyway. I guess you just feel your spine and legs more when you're pushing sixty-five."

He sounded relieved and her mood lightened correspondingly, but two days later when he called again, he inadvertently reverted to that telltale little phrase, "Fine, just a bit tired." He was in Los Angeles, to be there for two days, and the next day he was to have dinner with Jeff. The next morning a faint apprehension began rising in her about the hours they would be together, like an uneasy yeast, but she schooled herself free of foreboding and realized that there was in her now a fatalism she could reach for when she needed it, a fatalism which said, "If it goes wrong, it goes wrong; Ken has done everything he could to accept everything as it is, and Jeff has to accept *that* about Ken."

But on his next telephone call, Ken sounded calm, even cheerful, when he talked of seeing Jeff. "He's fine, working harder than ever, full of talk about clinical clerkships at various hospitals, I think that's his schedule for next year . . . sort of rotating through U.C.L.A. Hospital and affiliated hospitals, like Wadsworth Veterans, Harbor-General and Cedars-Sinai—if I'm remembering right."

"You certainly sound right."

"My God, the energy they have. With all that, he's driving a cab one night a week—medics seem to put in twenty-two hours per day and sleep two."

"Don't you try it on for size, now."

"Telling about it exhausts me."

Only after his return home did he talk more fully about his evening with Jeff. "I met a friend of his," he said, not looking at her. "Also in medical school, a senior. Jeff was crossing the campus when I drove up and this Stuart Gerson was with him. But instead of Jeff waving him off when he spotted me, he said, 'Come on, meet my father,' and you could have knocked me over with a feather. You know how he's always arranged to keep all his friends offstage."

"Stuart who?"

"Gerson. Fine-looking young man."

"Fine-looking how?"

"Nice-looking, intelligent face. About Jeff's age, I'd guess, maybe a year older." She seemed to be waiting for more, and he felt that he was careless not to have more to offer. "He's a native westerner, and he's never been east of Lake Tahoe."

A silence fell. She could not bring herself to ask the question. The asking, just the asking, was a remnant of the old compulsive need to know, as if it were an innate right to know. Yet if it had been Margie on the campus of some graduate school, a Margie not yet married to Nate, a Margie saying, "Come on, meet my father," to some young man she had been walking with, would she not have asked Ken perfectly naturally, "Do you think they're in love?"

Aloud she said, "Do you think they room together, this Stuart and Jeff?"

"I've no idea. How would I?"

"It was sort of an automatic remark, skip it."

"I wondered about that too. We only shook hands and a minute later he left, and Jeff said nothing about him. I was glad he didn't. I would have been uncomfortable."

Ken looked away from her. His face took on the higher color that always signaled her to change the subject, but when he spoke again, there was a note in his voice she had never heard before, a note that was somehow tranquil, though it also made her think of defeat and a covering sadness.

"But on the plane coming home," Ken went on, "I thought of this Stuart Gerson and Jeff again, and somehow I hoped they meant a lot to each other."

"Oh, Ken, I know that feeling. I've had it too."

"I got thinking, what it would be like, to get old, if you hadn't ever had somebody you'd shared your life with. I suddenly got thinking that about Jeff. I never did before."

"I'm glad you did, Ken. I'm so glad you did."

* * *

She had relayed the news of Nate's sudden British assignment to Ken and they both waited for Margie and Nate's return and their first chance to drop by for a drink to hear all about it.

Nate needed little prompting. The editor of *Orbit* was a man named Ian Harton and the magazine was "new and small and liberal and good." They had met at a "sort of mobbed doubled-up party," Margie said, "the one we missed because we had to put off our trip for two days, on account of Lynnie, and the one that was on the 'shedule' for that day, so we had two hosts and two hostesses, and nobody even tried to find out whom we knew and whom we didn't."

But Ian Harton didn't seem to mind the confusion, Nate went on, guessing that they had "cottoned to each other." Harton said that some people labeled *Orbit* a New Magazine of the New Left, while others insisted that it was a Young Magazine of the Old Left, but he himself rejected all classifications as glib and inaccurate. He looked far too boyish to be editor of anything but a university paper, but he struck Nate as being entirely in control of *Orbit*'s policies and entirely autonomous about making firm commitments for articles, even those still unwritten.

"He asked me if I had anything he might see," Nate said, "or if I had anything in mind, that might make a transatlantic piece, and I said I didn't. Then I had this big impulse, and told him I'd had a yen for a long time to do a real big takeout on a subject my own paper grudges giving real space to, and his ears went up like a scottie's.

" 'What subject is that?'

" 'Being gay. The whole thing of being homosexual today, getting analyzed, getting jobs, getting busted from the Army, or in bars.'

" 'God knows that's transatlantic enough,' Harton said. 'It's an assignment, if you'll take it on. We don't pay American prices, though.'

" 'How much space will you allow me? The real hang-up on my paper has always been space.'

" 'This much,' Harton answered." Nate showed the tip of his index finger and of his thumb squeezed close together, less than a quarter inch apart, relishing Tessa's disdain. "But then when he saw the rotten look I gave him, he added, 'Or this much,' and flung his arms wide, as far as they'd go, a yard of air between his hands. I gather they're pretty freewheeling about matters of length on *Orbit*. Then Harton said, 'If it's good, it runs long, longer, longest. Maybe two parts, maybe three.' "

"Oh, Nate," Tessa said, "how wonderful. You must be proud of yourself."

"You're damn right I am," he said. "But yikes, the work. It's going to take some doing. Will you give me whatever you've got?"

"When do we start?"

*   *   *

I hoped they meant a lot to each other. Later, much later, it was these words of Ken's that Tessa remembered most vividly whenever she thought of him and herself and Jeff, that special triumvirate as a special grouping in her memory, distinct from all the other groupings that were also forever there in the past, waiting to be picked up and looked at once more, like particular group photographs lifted out of a continuing album recording the years flowing backward.

I hoped they meant a lot to each other. Actually she had again been thinking of it, she no longer remembered why, on that night in the middle of June when Ken had stumbled on his way to bed and she had cried out in sudden alarm, "What's wrong, Ken?"

"Nothing, except I'm so tired." His voice faded on the last word. He was leaning against the jamb of the door to his bedroom, slumping a little, as if his spine were refusing to hold him erect, and she caught at him, her arm suddenly steel-strong as she slipped it around his back below his shoulders, holding him up from that sagging, sliding motion. "I'll call Mark," she said. "Let's get you in bed and I'll get Mark."

"Yes, let's." It was a whispered sibilance, and her supporting arm felt a tremor waver through his body as he stepped across the space between the door and his bed. He let himself down upon it, his hand going toward the knot of his tie but slipping downward ineffectively to lie helplessly beside him, the fingers dangling, curled, over the edge of the bed. He said something she could not quite hear, something, she thought, about his mother. She loosened the tie for him, undid the top button of his shirt, dialed Mark's number and said to the answering service, "This may be heart, so if you can't reach Dr. Waldo right away, please send an ambulance."

The moment she hung up she thought, I never gave my name and phone number or address, and asked Ken whether she had. He seemed not to hear; he made no answer. She dialed once more and found to her relief that she had begun the first call with her name, address and phone number, had said that the patient was her husband, not herself, and that the answering service knew, despite her calmness, that this was an emergency. Three minutes later the service called once more to say they had been able to reach Dr. Waldo and that he was already on his way.

Only then did she realize that what Ken had mumbled about his mother was "My mother was eighty-five." Old Mrs. Lynn had died four years before, the week after her eighty-fifth birthday, and several times since then Ken had remarked that he came from a long-lived family, that his mother had lived until eighty-five.

*   *   *

It was a thrombosis, Mark Waldo later explained, within the brain. It was a swift death, direct and kindly, if any dying could be called kindly. He died in the hospital at three in the morning, in the intensive-care unit, with Tessa and Mark beside him to the end. In the briefest possible time thereafter, following the directions he had set forth in his will some twenty years before, she had signed the necessary documents and left his dead body there, "for Science," and then, in silence, followed Mark to his car and in silence let him drive her home. He went upstairs with her, waited while she called Margie and then Don, and agreed that since Jeff was probably in the middle of exam week, she would put off calling him until the morning. Only when Margie and Nate arrived did Mark Waldo leave. His final words were "Remember, Tessa, he couldn't have known any pain."

Don decided that they must tell Jeff at once, exams or no, but it was Margie who called him, Don shoving the phone at her as if it were hers by natural right, this difficult task of announcing the first death in their family.

"It's pretty bad news, Jeff," she began. "It's about Dad."

"What happened to him?"

"He had a thrombosis, a massive one, in the brain."

"Then he's dead."

"It was very fast. No pain, Dr. Waldo says. He went into coma very quickly."

"When did all this happen?"

"Tonight, around bedtime, I'm not sure. Mama just came back from the hospital and called us."

"Is she all right?"

"Well, sort of. Stunned and—but she's all right. Can you get here, Jeff? We'll pay back your fare."

"Sure, yes I can. Right away."

"Your exams—"

"They're over with. The last one was Monday. I'm hacking a cab again, but I can cut out anytime. I could get there sometime this afternoon or tonight."

"I'm glad. It's awful to think of Dad—" Her voice roughened. "Here, Nate wants to say something."

Nate took the telephone from her and turned his back to the room, lowering his voice, talking tightly into the mouthpiece so that his words would not carry outward in any spray of sound.

"Jeff, may I put in a word here?"

"Go ahead, sure."

"This time, I hope you decide to stay right here with her, not at our house." There was a brief pause. He added, "You always have our place, but this time I—we're over at your mother's now, all of us, and I think your Uncle Will and Aunt Amy will probably be here in a day or so, but of course in a few days—"

"Yes, sure, I'll be there. Tell Mama—can I talk to her?"

"Just a second." He raised his voice. "Tessa, it's Jeff." As she took the telephone, he added, "Margie told him."

"Hello, Jeff," she said quietly. "So you know." She was not crying; she had cried there in the hospital and again when she had called Margie and had to find the words in which to say it, but not since.

"Hi, Mama," Jeff said. "It's hard to believe."

"I still can't, I think."

"I'm getting the first plane I can. I'll get home this afternoon sometime."

"That's fine, Jeff. I'm glad."

"I thought you might like me right there, for maybe a couple of weeks?"

"Oh, I would. That's really good."

"I'm sort of rocked—I don't know what to say."

"You don't have to say anything."

"He looked fine when he was out here."

"When he got home, too. But he was always weary, so he went in early for his annual checkup with Dr. Waldo, and everything checked out the way it should. That was only two months ago, back in April."

"I can't seem to take it in." He hesitated. "I could stay a while, if you want. Like two weeks or so."

"I do want. Thanks, Jeff."

"See you tonight then." But he did not say goodbye and she waited. Then his voice came again. "Mama? I know it must be awful."

"Yes, Jeffie." Her voice broke and she whispered, "See you tonight then."

* * *

There was no preparing for the death of a person you loved, Tessa thought often during the days and nights that followed. No arranging of mind or spirit was adequate, no foreviewing of what it might be like was near an approximation. She had always known that Ken would probably die before she did—his ten-year lead toward that finality was not to be gainsaid. Yet now she was in no way free of astonishment, in no degree able to accept this sense of his *nowhereness*. Perhaps those who did believe in heaven or hell were spared this one particular emptiness, which she could think of only as a spatial emptiness. Perhaps those who had funeral plots in cemeteries and vaults and mausoleums were also spared. They could visualize either a destination, like that famous bourne, or at least a resting place, with destination or resting place the available focus for thought or memory.

When there was only this sudden void that she thought of as nowhereness, it was harder to accept or manage the concept. There was no Ken. At the end of the week there were to be simple memorial services, arranged for by Ted Brannick, insisted on by all members of the firm, but finality had already fixed its icy seal upon her, and the memorial service would be a formality to be gone through for the needs of those Ken had worked with for decades.

Margie, Nate, Jeff, as well as Will and Amy, all felt as she did. Nate's parents, of course, did not, and that was to be expected. But Don as well as Jenny and their children went into orthodox mourning in the sense of prayers and church attendance, and this surprising new turn in Don told her once again how one's children could develop in unexpected new directions as they reached deeper and deeper into lives of their own shaping. In a way, Don's new "churchiness," as Margie called it, added another element to her sense of loss and disorientation: there were many surrogates for nowhereness.

Perhaps it was in part this that made Jeff's continuing quiet presence in the house, even after the others were all gone again, so important to her. She wondered repeatedly whether she might tell him what his father had said after having seen him with Stuart Gerson, yet she kept shying away from doing it. She thought it Jeff's due, thought it was something he might like to know and to have, an antidote to what there had been between him and his father, a keepsake as it were, a small legacy.

But even when she firmly decided that it would have to wait for some future day, she knew that having her troubled son there during a time of her own sorrow gave her a comfort she had not known with him for all the years since Placquette. His presence there for all meals, his considerateness in general, his totally unprecedented volubility about his work, all gave her an unexpected sense of support and understanding. Gone was the impersonal tone of the college thesis in what he said about his medical studies. He made everything intensely personal, as if she were a fellow student, sharing in his third-year work, so advanced now and so wide-ranging, going from obstetrics to ophthalmology, from neurology to hematology, going from classrooms and labs into hospital rooms and operating rooms. He made her see the hierarchies already existing and those ahead, from student to intern to first-year residency to second-year residency, and then on into general practice or specialization.

All of it fascinated her, all of it combined to make his stay a memorable experience. Toward the end of his two weeks, something akin to guilt invaded her. It was almost as if she were happy.

CHAPTER FIFTEEN

"It seems to be working out as a trio of pieces," Nate said to Jeff, glancing over at his typewriter, where a half-written page curved back from the platen of his machine. It was part of his second article for *Orbit*, nearly ready to be airmailed to London. Ian Harton had liked the first one so much, it appeared, that though he was temperamentally unable to be lavish with praise, he had conveyed it clearly enough in terms that Nate found far more stimulating. "It sounds to me," he had written Nate, "like the opening shot in a series, which I gather is just what you had in mind. So I'll hold this one and then run in sequence in three consecutive issues, perhaps four, however it works out. Not to rush you but when you can guess at probable dates for completing the others, please say."

"If you'd like to read the first piece," Margie said to her brother, "Nate has a carbon."

"I'd better wait till it's in print," Jeff said. "If there's something in it that hits me the wrong way"—he looked uncomfortable— "well, I wouldn't want to sound off, as if I were trying on a bit of censorship."

It was a hot Friday night, the end of his second week at home, and he was beginning to feel impatient to get off to his own world again. Not that there had been any tight moments, not even with his mother when they were alone. Right after a death, all patterns altered. Certainly she had not once come close to her old trick of assuming that somehow or other, *this* time if she said something intrusive, it would not be intrusive, or if she asked something intrusive, it would not be what in his earlier days he used to call "digging."

Earlier this evening they had all been together for dinner, with the two kids noisy and happy as if Grandpa Ken had never been, and after dinner, in the oncoming letdown that seemed to lie in wait for mourning people as they began to think of going home, Margie came up with the inspired idea of taking Lynnie and Jeffie to their first night movie, a Disney oldie running in a small theater on Broadway near them. The kids went wild at the idea of going to a movie when it was *dark* outside, and even though Grandma Tessa pleaded fatigue, they both ganged up with such fervent insistence that they *all* had to go, even Marta, that everybody did go. It was only when the movie had ended that Tessa announced she was taking a cab alone, urging Jeff to go along to Nate and Margie's for a final nightcap before flying West tomorrow.

The final nightcap had turned into two final nightcaps. They talked of the two weeks just past, and they agreed that Tessa had been great since Ken's death. This second week, she had gone back to work, leaving each morning for the office as if it were newly essential to her, returning each evening with the familiar oblong boxes bearing manuscript, making it seem to Jeff, who made it a point always to be there at about five in the afternoon, that nothing more than an interlude had taken place, an unhappy interlude, yes, some sort of normal interruption in life's routine, but one that would be accommodated before too long. He never told Margie and Nate that twice he had waked in the middle of the night with the certainty that he had heard her crying; there was always the chance that he had dreamed it. Once he even wondered whether he had dreamed that he himself was the one crying. That rather interested him. For the first time in a long while he wondered what Dr. Dudley or Dr. Isaacs would make of it if he were still spilling his guts out about dreams.

Impossible, he decided, impossible even in a dream, that he would be crying about his father's death. He had for too long been alienated from the poor guy, maybe forgiving him, maybe even accepting all the semantic explanations his father had later dredged up. But under all the forgiving, there still remained his own knowledge that to his father he had spelled tragedy. People who looked at you and saw you as *their* tragedy could never see why they became inevitably *your* tragedy.

"So I'm holding it open," Nate was saying, "until I do get down there. The second piece."

"Down where, Nate? Sorry, I missed that."

"Down to one of the gay bars in the Village. Not that I expect anything much different from the one I took in uptown, but I don't want to fake it, either."

"Any special bar?"

"There's one near Sheridan Square, named Stonewall Jackson or something. Do you know that one?"

"No, but then, bars haven't ever been my bag."

"They raided this one a few nights ago, over their liquor license. I thought maybe I could get one of the owners to open up about the cops hassling them, that sort of thing."

"Liquor license!" Jeff jeered. "Wouldn't you think they'd come up with something more original for a change?"

"Why waste gray matter?" Margie said. "When it serves them so handily."

"Was the raid in the papers?" Jeff asked. "I didn't see a thing about it."

"Nor did I," Nate said. "I got it from a friend of mine."

"How'd he know?"

"He was there when the cops showed."

"He was, hey?" Jeff looked at him, amused. "Some of your best friends are fags?"

"And some of my worst enemies." Nate glanced at his watch.

"Look, Jeff," Margie said sharply. "I wish you'd cut out the word 'fag.' When somebody else says it, it's hateful, so what makes it okay for you to?"

"Sort of an *in* privilege," Jeff said casually. "Shop talk."

"Well, I hate it," Margie shot back. "I hate it when a black calls himself a 'nigger' as a joke and thinks it's okay for him to say it but not for anybody white. Or when a Jew says 'kike' or 'Hebe' sort of as if they were *in* words too."

"Actually, I agree with you," Jeff said amicably. "It's like trying to defang the snake by using the venom first, before he can spit it into you."

Nate glanced at his watch again. "Say, Jeff, about this bar. How's for going down there for a drink?"

"If you want to." Jeff didn't move.

"It's one A.M.," Margie said.

"I might get me a new lead for that." Nate waved at his typewriter. "Or a better windup. It needs one zinger to make it right. I can always tell if it's not right."

Jeff still did not move. Here it was again. The key point, but even a Nate missed it. Every time you showed at a gay bar or a gay beach or a gay hangout of any sort, you risked being seen by somebody who then had you tagged. If you were in a job you had to hang on to, if you were on the verge of a medical degree—God, why didn't straights ever understand that you couldn't go looking for trouble? They thought gays were so damn promiscuous, probably thought every gay in the world was a nightly cruiser, but if they ever saw it as it was, they'd know that gays had to keep to a life style of solitude, except when the rare exception came along, somebody who knew about solitude too.

Nate had gone over to his desk, rummaged about there, and now was fastening a blue plastic shield to his shirt pocket. "Come on," Nate said, his voice a bit slurred, "I'm *Press*, see, and you're a cub reporter on assignment with me, maybe a stringer."

"If Jeff doesn't feel like it," Margie said.

Jeff jumped to his feet. "Sure, I feel like it," he said with too much vigor.

"You're both nuts," Margie said. "This hour of the night." As they left, she slid the bolt in the safety lock and heard a taxi roar away.

As their cab approached Sheridan Square, Nate and Jeff both leaned forward in a sudden excitement. Something was wrong. In the street outside the bar, a crowd was shoving and jostling, mostly a young crowd, mostly male, a shouting jeering crowd, perhaps two hundred people in all, spilling over from the square into Christopher Street. As Nate paid off the driver, his professional eye registered the fact that the name of the bar was the Stonewall Inn, that its front was red brick, that its windows were boarded up as if in a state of siege, and that a sign outside its entrance proclaimed, "Private Club. For Members Only."

The crowd, at first glance, was a typical Greenwich Village

crowd on a hot summer night, in jeans or chinos, in sport shirts, no ties, the usual long hair, beards, sideburns, the whole gamut. Another glance showed some men in women's clothes, others in leather, some wearing medallions on chains on bared chests, all looking like any unruly, excited crowd in a big city in the last year of the Sixties, the Seething Sixties.

"What the hell's going on?" Nate asked somebody near him, but at that moment the door of the bar opened and two men shoved a struggling youth out of the place, while the crowd outside roared louder than before.

"The pigs, the goddamn plainclothes pigs," a voice next to Nate and Jeff shouted. "And the two dames in there—plainclothes pigs too." A beer can whizzed through the air, landing against the closing door of the Stonewall Inn. This was followed by a bottle, then by stones, sticks, coins.

"Watch the glass, Nate," Jeff shouted, and as if they were yoked, they simultaneously pushed forward, a team attacking an unyielding mass.

"How long since this started?" Nate asked the person nearest him.

"An hour, hour and a half. They figured we'd slink off, but we're fighting the bastards." A ring of pride sounded.

"You sure are," Nate shouted back.

Just then, off in the distance, sirens began to whine, screaming closer with every second, and lights of approaching police cars sent rotating beams through the night. Both whine and light acted as signals for an even more frenzied energy in the heaving mass of people.

For a moment Nate paused and looked around, seeing, noting, wanting to remember. The crowd had thickened and he guessed that the newer arrivals were largely weekend tourists from other Village bars and cafés, come to see the excitement, hoping for rough stuff, even hoping for the bloody violence their television screens taught them to expect.

Suddenly an arc of light swept across Jeff's face and he heard one of the approaching patrol cars screech to a halt somewhere beside him. Blue uniforms poured into view, the first he had seen. He said, "Nate, the cops—look there."

In the same instant he thought, My God, I could be pulled in, I could be jailed. My degree, my M.D. . . .

Unwanted, detested in the very forming, the thought struck like a fist: Get out of this, there's only a year to go, you can't kill the whole thing now, you goddamn well can't fuck up all of it now.

"Nate," he said. "I'm getting out. I can't risk . . ." At that moment, something lurched into him from behind and he turned toward it; it was a man, a young man falling, falling backward and away from a nightstick whistling down toward his head, missing his skull, landing on his shoulder, while the policeman wielding it shouted, "You goddamn faggot, you're under arrest."

Instinctively Jeff buttressed the falling body with his own. Again the nightstick plunged through the air, this time horizontally, in the extra room made by the crowd backing off from the flailing weapon. This time, like a sword of wood plunged at the young man's stomach, the blunt end landed and the young man doubled over, a grunt of rage and pain torn from him. Jeff's right arm shot out; he straight-armed the attacking cop.

"Beating up faggots," he roared at him. "I'm a faggot too, so come on."

The cop swung toward him in surprise and fury. Again Jeff's arm shot forward, but this time his stance was better and his whole shoulder and back went into the thrust. The impact was solid. For a crazy moment he remembered football and Placquette. A roar of elation swept through him, a wildness in it, as if he in his own body were that whole stadium up there shouting out in a frenzy of victory.

"*Press*, Officer," Nate's voice suddenly sounded behind him, naming his newspaper, Nate's voice with a new note in it, a note he had never heard. Authority. That was it. Nate, with the sound of authority. "Here's my press badge—this guy's with me, a cub reporter, we're on assignment. Do you want to make a statement?"

The officer glared at the blue plastic Nate was extending toward him, but at that instant a new roar came from the crowd, and a sound of splintering wood. A yell of delight arose and a shout, "They tore it out of the ground." Ahead of them two men were battering at the door of the Stonewall Inn, their rammer nothing other than an uprooted parking meter.

"Come on, kid," Nate said to Jeff, still in the voice of command. "We're for the precinct now, for some quotes." He shoved Jeff ahead of him, past the cop, who seemed transfixed by that rhythmic battering thrust of the parking meter.

"Some quotes, you bet," Jeff said, heaving his way through in unison with Nate. He knew that the precinct and the quotes were pure improvisation, that Nate had no intention of leaving. With a stab of exultation he knew that neither had he.

*   *   *

They had stayed down there until it was over. A paddy wagon arrived soon after the prowl cars, people were yanked and pulled and shoved in, some thirteen arrested. Nate had finally reached one of the Stonewall's owners by phone; it was a smashed-up mess inside, the jukebox smashed, the phone booths wrecked, the cigarette machines, the mirrors, half the plumbing. "Like the atom bomb hit us."

Now it was nearly daylight and Jeff was at home, but he could not sleep. He could not read, he could not calm down. Nate was going to write his piece, but there was no such help for Jeff. He could not yet believe it.

To fight back, he thought, to fight the cops back. To fight the world back. To forget all the reasons and stand there and fight. That fantasy of some sort of new free life, free of the old nightmares of being discovered, betrayed by a Hank, being branded. Those increasing reports of people fed up with hiding, people who had come out of the closet, who said *yes, we are*.

Tonight he had said it with them. Tonight at a place he had never heard of, tonight gay people had stood their ground when the cops came, hadn't gotten the hell out in the fear of a police blotter, but had made a stand and attacked their attackers.

I'm a faggot too, so come on. It rang out in his mind again and again, a shout, a roar of assertion. Never before, not even once in his life had he flung it at the air, at authority and power. Tonight he had. It was that crowd that had done it for him, that had caught him up in their collective will, that had showed the way before he joined them. They had not accepted the age-old stage direction for frightened people, *Exeunt Omnes*, and made for the nearest exit, had not thought of jobs and careers and their secret. They had stood in the open and fought back.

And by that fluke of timing he had fought too. He would never forget it. He might never repeat it, might never know it again, but for now it was his.

He flung himself upright and got out of bed. It was dawn, summer dawn. He went to the telephone. In California it was four in the morning. He would call—

There was nobody to call. This was one of the arid stretches, where there was nobody of any importance. Since Roy, Roy with his Beethoven and Bach, Roy with his political meetings and picket lines, since Roy there had been nobody lasting, which meant about a year of living alone. He had never been one of the people who easily found a man he could love; sex was another matter. If he were straight, he'd be one of the men who didn't easily find a woman he could love. Nate didn't; he'd bet on it. Nate might have sex if he were off on an out-of-town assignment, but Nate wouldn't confuse that with the amalgam of nuances and importances that earned the name love. If Nate were gay, Nate would be like him.

The thought had never crossed his mind: if Nate were gay. He accepted Nate as he was, loved him as he was, just as he accepted Margie as she was and loved her as she was. They were great people, and that was the whole of it. What they did about sex never entered into it for him, and what he did never entered into it for them.

Maybe there were more Nates and Margies in the world, out there waiting to be recognized. Waiting for him to find them, to approach them. If it were the other way around, if it were they who tried to approach him, it was only fair to admit he would automatically put them down as more of the "look how broadminded I am" bunch. So it was he who would have to take the initiative, he who would have to search. Never had that thought crossed his mind either.

But there was something else, something even bigger. He had to find it. It was a night for seeing things in a new focus, but it eluded him. Suddenly he knew. What he really had to search for was not more Nates and Margies, but more gay people like the ones down there tonight, gays who would fight back, gays who knew in their own guts that nobody could do it for them, that they would have to do it for themselves.

Do what? He didn't know exactly. But he did know that whatever it was, he and all the others like him, all the men and all the women like him, the gay people, the gay world, they would finally have to fight it out for themselves. It was theirs to do and only they could do it. They and he with them.

Far down on the street below him in the sleeping city, the peculiar yelping sound of an ambulance siren rose and fell, increasing in urgency as it drew nearer, then diminishing as it sped off. He squeezed his eyes shut as if he could close out sound as well as sight, but in his mind the towering white walls of a modern hospital seemed to rear up, its windows glistening row on row in the early sunlight.

An anguish overwhelmed him. I forgot, he thought, I forgot. There would be no internship, no residency, nothing. Out of the past a familiar blackness seemed to rush at him. The high elation of the night collapsed. He went quietly to his room, stripped, and fell into the dark sleep of despair.

* * *

The morning mail still brought Tessa notes of condolence and this Saturday's was no exception. She paused over the modern-looking "butcher paper" envelope with its unfamiliar handwriting, and then saw the name and address printed vertically along one end of the brownish vellum. It was from Sue Wister.

> Dear Mrs. Lynn,
>   I just got back from a vacation in Rome and my mother told me the terrible news about Mr. Lynn. It's been a long time, of course, since I last saw you, and I can't find the right way to tell you how awful it is, but please accept this brief note as an expression of my deepest sympathy to you and your family.
>
> > Sincerely,
> > Sue

Tessa set it beside her on the breakfast table, uncertain yet how it made her feel. She glanced toward Jeff's room; there still was no sound of him. He had probably stayed up until all hours last night with Nate and Margie, would sleep until the last moment and then have a mad scramble to pack and catch his plane. But one never needed to worry about the logistics of his comings and goings; he never missed trains, buses or planes, and always remembered to set his own alarm clock.

Today when he left, she would, for the first time since Ken's death, know the actuality of being entirely alone, not as somebody waiting for a husband's return from an appointment or a trip, but alone, as a widow is alone. She had thought about it a good deal in the past fortnight, had thought of the millions of other women who were widows and alone, felt herself ready for what the actuality might prove to be and yet also faintly aware that one could never rely on that sense of being ready. Days ago, Ken's clothes had been packed and sent off to a charity; she had wanted, rather insistently, to get that task behind her, had needed to strip away physical reminders, unimportant in themselves but possessed of a power to evoke sudden memory and pain.

She looked at Sue's letter and read it once more. It was a little self-conscious, but it touched her. She and Ken had kept on seeing the Wisters from time to time, but only now did she realize that Sue never happened to be there for dinner, the way she used to be. She could not have married in the two or three years since the last time they had met; the conventional Wisters would have sent out proper wedding announcements. Perhaps she was no longer living with them, despite the address on the envelope; perhaps she was living with some man without being married, as was increasingly the fashion these days, not only for movie stars, hippies and other overachievers or underachievers, but equally for the nice girl next door. She hoped so. She would like Sue to be happy.

The telephone rang; it was Nate. Was Jeff up? Not yet. Should she have him call back when he was?

"Please. We went on a sort of pub crawl last night and I—well, get him to call me, will you? I'm at the paper."

"He'll be up soon. His plane is at three."

"Get him to fit in a fast call. Thanks."

A plane at three. And then there wouldn't be another plane for a whole year. Not even then, for the morning after the Class of 1970 received their degrees next June, Jeff would be reporting in at some hospital in L.A. as a brand-new intern.

When he appeared it was nearly one. She gave him the message and he made for the telephone while she went out to the kitchen for the percolator and fresh toast. When she came out he was standing by the table, eying Sue's letter.

"She just heard about Dad," Tessa said. "Read it, if you want."

He picked it up, read it and put it down. His depression deepened. His call to Nate had added to it. Nate had worked on the story until nearly six, using no names of course, but making it clear that he had been right there at the Stonewall and seen it for himself. The paper was cutting it to the bone, as he had expected, but the *Orbit* piece would be even more clearly an eyewitness account, and when Tessa came to read it, she would probably guess that they had gone down there together. Nate couldn't decide whether Jeff would like him to conceal that part of it from her. He had asked Margie what she thought, and Margie hadn't been very helpful.

"I don't feel very helpful either," Jeff answered. "I just got up and haven't talked about anything yet."

"I did tell Tessa we'd gone on a sort of pub crawl. I guess I want her to know you were in on it."

"But it all seems different today, kind of a one-shot deal."

"That means you'd rather have me shut up."

"Could you just forget it, about me being there?"

"Sure thing. I probably should have figured it this way anyhow."

He had managed a wisecrack as they hung up, but that hadn't fooled Nate any. Now he stared at Sue's letter to his mother, and that didn't fool him either. He had heard that she was living with somebody named Tim Yates, but the address was still the same pale brick house in the Seventies.

Sue was one of the people he should have thought of when he was thinking of all the Nates and Margies out there. He never thought of Sue any more except in passing, had never even wondered before whether that night of catastrophe for him had been a night of catastrophe for her as well.

Maybe one of the symptoms of maturity was that when you looked back to whatever you had done in your teens or early twenties, you could see that it was cowardly or a hang-up or just plain insecure. A few years from now, when he was past thirty and in practice, would he look back and decide that everything he was doing now was cowardly or a hang-up or insecure? Would he remember his elation of last night and be embarrassed that for a while he had promoted it to mean something more than the euphoria of a street fight? It was a bleak thought. He glanced at his watch.

"I know you have to pack," his mother said. "It was good to have you here, Jeff. It helped a lot. *You* helped a lot."

"If anything can help." He looked uncomfortable. "Will it be all right now?"

"I'll keep busy. Scott Prentice just finished his new book, and there'll be a good deal of hard work on that. I can't think what it would be like if I was just 'empty' every day."

"Rotten. And it's good about Margie working again."

"She's still on Ted Brannick's mind."

"Will he offer it to her again?"

"In a year or so, I should think. By then, she might feel she's proved herself enough in an outside job, and take it. It would be good to have a Lynn over there again. They're not changing the name of the firm, so it's like a vacuum wanting to be filled."

"She'd be Jacobs, not Lynn."

"She said she'd be hyphenated. Margie Lynn-Jacobs."

"You'd be rival publishers if she went."

"Dad and I were too."

"That seemed to work."

"Most of the time." She looked pensive, thinking of the schism between herself and Ken about the firms they worked for, about their quarrels over "standards" and aims, about their decision not to quarrel, not to have at each other year after year. She gazed at Jeff, wanting to say that, but it would be trite. Banality did not inhere in the concept that you could love another human being despite deep differences in point of view, in criteria for life or work —yet to phrase the concept was to demean it.

"I'd better get my stuff together," Jeff said, gulping down the rest of his coffee.

"I'll take you to the airport. The car's downstairs. You drive, of course."

He had a prevision of them in the car, stuck in traffic, Saturday-afternoon summer traffic, both trying to make conversation, getting tense and finally having one of those damn unexpected outbursts they had managed to steer clear of these past two weeks.

Right now he couldn't chance it, not in the middle of this nose dive from last night's high.

"Thanks about the car," he said. "But if it's okay—it's funny, but suddenly I feel so damn low about things, I guess I'd better make it out there on my own." He looked at her, knowing she thought he meant his father's death, willing to have her think it. For a moment they remained wordless. Then he turned away and left her sitting there.

CHAPTER SIXTEEN

It was nothing but a prescription blank with the usual Rx, but it might have been an illuminated scroll for the sweep of delight it sent through her. The familiar handwriting below the printed heading was not for a drug, not for dosage, not for medicine at all. It said, "How does this grab you? Love, J." And centered across the top, amid a cluster of telephone numbers and office hours and the street address of a medical group, was a line she had never before seen.

Jeffery S. Lynn, M.D.

It had looked very different on his diploma. There his full name was spelled out, Jeffery Sachs Lynn, proper to a formal document which he would frame and hang in his own office someday. It had been spelled out too on the small certificate, the one she had watched him receive in that special June ceremony held outdoors on a hill under the trees of the campus, together with the hundred or so young men and the two dozen young women, his classmates, who also that day were taking the Hippocratic Oath by which they would all live out their lives. To her that small rolled document, tied with its narrow ribbon, meant more than the diploma that would be bestowed a week later to all the many thousands of 1970 graduates of all the schools of the university, a ceremony Jeff had blithely said he wouldn't bother to attend, and which of course she wouldn't attend either.

But this prescription blank which she had never visualized be-

fore was somehow different in essence from either of the two
formal documents. It was so familiar, so homely, so similar to hundreds of others she had seen throughout her life, and yet it was
unique, because the name at the top was not Mark Waldo, M.D.,
not James Dudley, M.D., not David Isaacs, M.D., but Jeffery S.
Lynn, M.D.

He was already interning at the hospital he had most hoped to
be appointed to, but beyond that he was also "moonlighting," as
several other young doctors were doing, by being on call during
off evenings and on weekends at the offices of medical groups in
Los Angeles or Beverly Hills or Santa Monica. This small sheet
in her hand bore the address of one such group, but to her it was
a tangible evidence of his entry into actual practice, a symbol of
his ability, of his fitness to order the needed antibiotic or antidote
or analgesic, the drops or capsules or powders of healing.

Jeff the patient now Jeff the healer, Jeff the troubled now Dr.
Lynn to whom the troubled would turn, from whom they would
take strength. There's an inversion for you, she thought, and her
heart shook.

She had flown out the night before the ceremony, and to her
astonishment had found Will and Amy as well as Jeff waiting for
her at the airport. Will and Amy had not told her in advance that
they were going out too. They never once put into words their
true reason for being there, that that June was the first anniversary,
almost to the day, of Ken's death and that they thought it would
be painful for her to be there alone. Her mind had drifted, almost
lazily, to that terrible time when she had gone without Ken to
another graduation day of Jeff's, but there was an unreality in the
memory, a disbelief that it could have been so impossible then for
Ken to face his own son.

Nine years ago that had been, only nine, and yet a century of
change seemed to have flowed by since then. You could no longer
think of it merely as change, not for the past year certainly, not
since the Stonewall Riots of the June before. Now the word that
came to you was not "change" but "revolution," now there was
a whole new language to say what the revolution encompassed,
what it was about. Gay Liberation, Gay Civil Rights, Gay Acti-
vists. The Gay Movement.

Recently Nate had told her that the Stonewall Riots were being

called "the Boston Tea Party of the Gay Movement." He liked the
label, he said, and thought it would stand the test of time and
repetition. She liked it too, felt again the surge of participation
she had first felt when she had discovered that Nate had actually
been there himself, seeking a new ending or perhaps a new lead
for one of his *Orbit* pieces, which he was then working on. Stonewall Riots, he had said. Plural. For there had been three of them,
on three successive nights, a Friday, a Saturday, a Sunday.

About Nate's participation she had known nothing until he let
her read his rewritten piece, a week or ten days after it had happened. She had already seen and clipped out for her file a couple
of short reports of it, coming on them deep in the interior recesses
of the *Times*, but even though one of them told of four policemen
being hurt and two hundred young men arrested in the raid, it
was so brief and colorless an account that she had not even remembered the name of the place.

She could still feel the electric jolt that hit her when she had
come to a line in Nate's piece, "As my taxi reached Sheridan
Square, I knew this was no routine raid of a gay bar."

"*Your* taxi?" she had asked.

"I was right there. I sure lucked into something."

"When was this, Nate? Which of the three nights?"

"Friday. After Jeff and I split, I got fretting about my piece,
wanting a better lead or news peg, thinking about a tip somebody
on the paper had given me. And then around one A.M., I grabbed
me a cab and went downtown."

All his pieces seemed superb to her—there had been four in all
—but that second one had held a special impact, that feel of participation, as though Nate were speaking aloud to her, with his
own turn of phrase, his own excitement sounding. In the inter-
vening year she had read that one piece several times and she was
still affected by it. Nate had made of it a ligature between what
had gone before and what was surely about to begin, what had
already begun, that sudden outburst in the streets, of defiance and
forthrightness to replace the silence and shame of decades, perhaps of centuries. His later pieces followed through on that widening movement, told of gay marches in major cities, gay protests
to city councils, to colleges, to churches, to annual meetings of

psychiatrists, an increasing surge of self-identification and revolt against discrimination, not only in New York but in the Middle West, out on the Coast, in the South.

She had waited a while before she asked whether he had sent his pieces to Jeff. Of course, but not until each was in print. Jeff himself had specified that he did not want to see them in typescript, lest he say something that might look like an effort to influence or even censor.

"He's a hell of a guy, that one," Nate had said by way of summary, and she had not pressed for more.

Perhaps she had finally adapted to that condition of life, that there were gaps she could never hope to fill, chasms she could never bridge. Her longing that Ken were still alive to see this new onslaught on the tight-closed laws and the tight-closed minds, this she did not speak of even to Margie and Nate, beyond a phrase in passing that was like a headline in a newspaper, summarizing, leaving the fullness of the matter down below.

She also kept to herself her ambivalence about the phrase "Gay Is Proud." She did not really like it, any more than she would have liked a phrase that proclaimed, "Straight Is Proud." She had, however, long understood deeply that the private phrases of the oppressed, "Black Is Beautiful," were more than simple antonyms for the phrases the oppressors might have used, "Black Is Ugly," and that there was, within those private phrases, not a counter-superiority, not a counter-hate, but only a corrective new strength, an antidote to an old and buried pain. A racist inferiority, a sexist inferiority, a sexual inferiority—there were threads stitching them all together, ligaments, sinews, veins carrying the lifeblood of assertion, of new evaluation, arteries carrying the same throb of one great pulse.

Arteries. She looked down at the prescription slip she was still holding in her hand. What did Jeff feel about gay liberation? Did it make him feel any easier, just knowing it was out there, a new current, generating new attitudes, new strength? Did he ever see any of the TV programs where gay people began to appear under their own names, right on the screens of the nation, usually on the late talk shows, the few where the audience was assumed to have some education, some interest in subjects other than the ceaseless ego talk of movie stars and comics and "personalities"? Long ago these better programs had included people who talked of what it meant to be black, to be women, people who opposed the draft and the war in Vietnam.

And now there were homosexuals, men and women, young for the most part, unabashed, free of apology, another minority at last ready to fight persecution and demand their rights.

"Guilt?" one young woman asked the world at large on one such program. "That was society's old trick, to make us feel guilt, so guilty that we hid in that old closet, which is where society still wants us to stay, because it's not just a private closet but a big political closet, away from political action. If you're hiding in dat ole debbil closet, you ain't about to zap City Hall about ending discrimination against gay people in jobs or housing or anything else."

She was a marine biologist, she said, and might lose her job for appearing on this show, giving her right name, saying she was gay and quite content to be gay, but she had tried the other kind of thing long enough, shrinking her life away in that closet, and now at last she was out for good and feeling a whole person again.

Tessa wanted to write her a word of praise, but even more she wanted to call the TV station, ask whether the show would run in Los Angeles and then flag Jeff to be sure and watch it.

As always she did not call the station, did not tell Jeff about it, did not even write the marine biologist. One of the side effects, she thought, is the sort of shy paralysis you yourself feel, about showing too clearly how much you care, how much you applaud, how much you love.

But maybe even that will change. Once she had thought only, If Jeff could change. Now she saw that it was she who had had to change, she and Ken and the world who had changed.

* * *

Another year passed and then another. Jeff had finished his interning and was in his second year of residency, as always doing well, as always working indefatigably. And then one winter morning early in 1973, Tessa stooped to the scatter of mail at her front door and found a letter from him that once again, as the next seconds of her life ticked off, was to alter it forever.

Dear Mama,

You probably know as much as I do about the gay movement, or maybe more, you being you, and I think I should
tell you now that about two months ago I became part of it.

Not in any big dramatic way—you know I've never been a
political beast, marching on picket lines or parades, and I
can't become a gay activist now. But I *have* come out, and
once you are out, you are out forever.

I told my chief at the hospital back in December, Dr.
Syms, and he gazed at me a while and then said, "So?" He's
a tremendous guy. I also told some other doctors and all my
friends. It is a risk for anybody in medicine and could lead
to disaster, but it is a risk for anybody in anything, and I finally got to the point where it had to be this. It's been growing in me for I don't know how long, and especially a night
just after Dad died—a night I asked Nate to leave me out of
when he wrote about it. Ask him—tell him I said yes.

Well, that's it. I guess it's never easy to talk to parents
about this sort of thing, but I hope you approve and I have
a hunch you will.

Love,
Jeff

She read it twice and thought, The courage, the young courage.
Long ago she had thought of his young courage, but that was for
a letter that was a cry for help when he was seventeen; now he was
nearly thirty and she was filled with that same admiration once
more, but now for a man's statement of a position he had come
to through years of an agonizing development.

No more evasions for him, she thought, no more hiding, no
more fear. Nobody can threaten him, nobody blackmail him. He
is free. I have never loved him so much.

She reached for the telephone to call him, but her hand stopped.
Once before she had stopped lest she be overheard by some idle
boy at the school switchboard. Now there would be no such risk;
she would call him at home and it would be either he who answered or the new voice she had first heard a few months ago,
after so long a time of hearing no voice but Jeff's.

She thought of writing, but abandoned the idea as too slow. It
was then that she thought, Actually I'm not as surprised as you'd
expect me to be. I think I have been getting ready for this for a

long time, I must have been, without letting myself think of it. And Jeff must have been getting ready for it too for a long time, maybe long before Dad died, maybe as far back as when he quit analysis and all that dogged attempt to "get cured."

She began to print out a telegram, remembering that other wire to Placquette when she had tested each word for possible significance to a hostile eye. She could still recall that wire in its entirety, and in a spin of emotion, began to write it once again. But then she struck it out, displeased. This was no time for artifice.

I AM PROUDER OF YOU THAN EVER STOP I LOVE YOU AND ALWAYS WILL STOP THANKS STOP MAMA

She stared at the word THANKS. There was an enigmatic quality in it now that she had not felt as she wrote it. Thanks for what? For doing this that you have done? For telling me? For voluntarily sharing this with me when you have always made it so clear that you would permit no communication between us in this area of your life? Or am I thanking you for being what you are?

She made a gesture of dismissal, as if she could send away her own confusions, then she phoned the wire unchanged to Western Union, saying, "Fast rate, please, it's important." It was only six in the morning out there; she had forgotten that when she considered telephoning him; now she hoped he would receive it before he left for the hospital. Then again he might not see it today at all, since he was finishing out his residency; in either case an imperative within her demanded that it be dispatched without delay.

Ask Nate, he had said. A night just after Dad died—a night I asked him to leave me out of when he wrote about it.

An exploding star seemed to go off in her mind, a shower of sparks, a celebration. The Stonewall—he had been there with Nate. He had seen it. They had got there after it started but he had seen it while it was happening. The Boston Tea Party of the Gay Movement—he had played a part in it, whatever part, he had been right there.

And ever since it had played a part in his own life. It had triggered some new force for him, or activated some dormant one, building it, strengthening it until, months later, three years later, it had become powerful enough to let him do this.

It was a risk, as he had said, that could end in disaster. The words chilled her. He could be thrown out of medicine. No, not out of medicine. He could be thrown off the hospital staff, but never out of medicine. There would always be the sick, and they would always need doctors. There could be disaster too for the other gays who had created the movement before him. There were the old cruelties still, in a large part of society, and there would be for years to come. But when you lived in a hostile environment, you could knuckle under to it or refuse finally to yield any more. It was what you did with your life that made it.

Ask Nate—tell him I said yes. Again her hand moved toward the phone, and again it stopped. She could not talk now even to Nate or Margie. Her voice would quaver; she would feel that swoop of embarrassment when she lost control. Instead she went to the bookcase where the four issues of *Orbit* lay flat, atop some large art portfolios, and drew out the second piece in the series. Standing there, oblivious of the time, forgetting to call the office and tell Gail she would be arriving late, she reread the entire article. But this time when she read, "As my taxi reached Sheridan Square, I knew this was no routine raid of a gay bar"—this time she visualized not Nate alone in that taxi, straining forward, wondering what all the shouting and upheaval was, but also Jeff beside him, Jeff getting out of the cab, Jeff hearing the police sirens keening, Jeff pushing forward into that crowd.

Then she came to Nate's words about a tall young man near him suddenly straight-arming an abusive policeman, suddenly hurtling into the scythe-like sweep of his nightstick—

It might have been Jeff, she thought. It must have been Jeff. I know it. I should have known it long ago—there was something vague, something she could not quite remember, that had seemed odd at the time. That pub crawl, that was it. Nate had said something about some pub crawl and then seemed to take it back, with some sort of white lie as if he were covering up a slip he had made.

Suddenly she sat down at the table and poured another cup of coffee. She felt limp and yet her body seemed to vibrate with a fine young lightness, as though she could play ten sets of tennis or swim three miles. She tried to visualize Jeff hurling himself at that cop and his nightstick, *felt* the impact, knew it was what had actually taken place. She tried to visualize him telling Dr. Syms at the hospital. Dr. Syms was, she gathered, the idol of all the younger doctors on the staff, a man of fifty whose wife was a doctor too and whose two sons were already in medical school. Dr. Syms could have meant disaster in that very moment, but Jeff had gone ahead. And so far at least no disaster.

It would be a day-to-day wondering for a while, but Jeff was ready to undertake it and so too would she have to be. He would not be sending her daily bulletins, not be making verbose reports. She might never hear one more word about Dr. Syms, she might have to live with that day-to-day tension for a long time, but compared to what had once been and had now ended, it seemed like an easy assignment.

Again she thought of calling Margie and Nate, and for the first time added, And Don. Immediately she thought, No, not Don. Don will resist the news, not welcome it. He no longer "forgot" and told jokes in her presence, but he saw only the extremists in the gay movement, the ones he called "the show-offs and freaks and TV grabbers." Once or twice she had pointed out that every new movement had its extremists, but in the main she stayed aloof from the entire subject whenever she saw Don.

Now the battle lines will be clearer, she thought, not only in this family, but all over. The good old barricades, she said in a half whisper, and smiled.

Then she felt ready to call Margie and did. Margie was now a junior editor at Brannick and Lynn, in the Juvenile Department, experimenting with a new approach to children's books, free of the old predestined sex roles for little boys and little girls. She was devoted to her new job, full of wisecracks about the prehistoric clichés that crept into the most liberated stories by the most ardent feminists. "Would-be feminists," Margie called them, a hoot of derision in her voice. As Tessa waited for her call to go through, she heard the small merry hoot again and a fond approval arose in her.

"So this *Girl on the Moon*," Margie had said, "is all about the little six-year-old girl being the first one out of the lunar module, but then later it's the little girl astronaut who prepares the gucky dehydrated food for the little six-year-old boy astronaut."

When she came on the line Tessa made her voice sound casual.

"Can you and Nate come for dinner one of these nights? It's rather special."

"Good special or bad special? You sound happy."

"Am I always that transparent?"

"Only when it's something about the family."

"This is about Jeff."

"And you like it. That's great. Let's see—not tonight, Nate's on assignment tonight. And tomorrow's out too. What about Saturday?"

They decided on time and Tessa began to search in her mind, as she hung up, for a substitute arrangement for this evening. She who spent so many evenings alone, peacefully and willingly alone, did not feel that she could manage it alone tonight. There was Helena Ludwig—they had become good friends by now, no longer restricted to the author-editor relationship, but friends. And there were the Prentices; she had become friends with Scott and Elena too, and they were both closer to her in age, so that she had the comfortable feeling that came from being with contemporaries.

My own contemporaries. It's really Ken I want, she thought, and for the first time she looked at Jeff's letter through the blur and sting of tears. Ken would see this now as she saw it—by now he would have completed his own process of growth and acceptance. Not tolerance but acceptance; the idea of tolerance was insulting, like the body's tolerance of minute doses of arsenic. In any case, tolerance was too easy an aim; the indifferent could achieve tolerance by not caring one way or the other.

But to accept other humans fully for the humans they happened to be, just as they happened to be, in all their manifold needs and desires and practices, to accept them as one accepts one's own self —that was a goal worth reaching, and by now Ken would have reached it fully.

It was then that she thought of Mark Waldo. Mark, of course, Mark. Let this not be one of the nights, she thought in sudden entreaty, when he's off on some emergency, nor one of the rarer nights when he and his wife Nell are at the theater or having people in. Mark's been in on every major step all the way; he will know how enormous this one really is. She pulled the telephone toward her and dialed.

* * *

For a while they talked as if they were indeed in the same family. On the phone she had told him it was "something good about Jeff," but nothing more, and it was past eleven in the evening before Mark could finish his rounds and get up to the old apartment. She did not mind the lateness, and as she watched him read the letter, she knew that he did not mind either.

"I don't think I could ever have predicted it," he said at last. "It's so impossible in medicine."

"As impossible as it used to be?"

"Officially yes. Of course there are homosexual doctors on every hospital staff—the usual Kinsey ten percent—but they still live their lives out hiding it."

"Maybe the young ones are starting to change all that now."

"I *have* heard," he said, as if he doubted his own words, "of two young interns right here in New York getting set to do the same thing."

"There must be a few everywhere." She straightened her back, lifted her head, not knowing she was doing either. "There must be, Mark. Sort of spontaneous combustion."

"Among other ideas whose time has come?" He drew out a filing card from his pocket, scrawled over with notes, and for a moment kept her waiting while he consulted it. "I made a couple of calls today after you said this was about Jeff."

"To Dr. Richards?"

He nodded. "There's to be a closed meeting up at Columbia's Psychiatric Institute this week—you'll keep this off the record, won't you, until the papers print it?"

"Of course."

"It's a special committee of the A.P.A., the Nomenclature Committee. They propose to eliminate homosexuality as a diagnostic category—knock it right out of the official *Manual of Mental Disorders*." He was reading from his card, not looking to see her reaction.

"Oh, Mark."

"They are drawing up a statement of their proposal, to present it officially, later on, to the whole A.P.A. membership."

"I don't think I understand what it means—knocking it out of the official manual."

"It won't be classified as a mental disorder needing treatment any more." He consulted his card once more. "There are twenty thousand members of the A.P.A."

"And a majority will vote in favor?"

"Richards says yes. He says Marmor says yes, and that their whole wing in the profession says yes. The opposition will be ferocious—there are plenty of analysts in the old-line, stand-pat group—but Richards says it will pass."

"What makes him so sure?"

"This general shift in psychiatry has been building for a long time, remember." Without transition he added, "Dr. Marmor, by the way, is now vice-president of the A.P.A. and also president-elect of the Group for the Advancement of Psychiatry. That's quite impressive to me."

"Oh, Mark, it *will* pass. Dudley will vote against it, and Isaacs, and all the others who talk about twenty-five percent cures, but it will pass sooner or later."

"So it seems."

"It all seems to be happening at once." She repeated, "At once," mocking herself. "Oh, Mark, how long it's been."

* * *

Nate said, "I felt in my bones that he'd come around to it sooner or later, but I thought he'd wait until his residency was over and he was set up in his own office."

"I don't know what I thought exactly," Margie said. "A girl at the office started telling everybody she was lesbian and I had a terrible fight with her."

"For heaven's sake, why?" demanded Tessa.

"I called her on the word 'lesbian.' I said it's a sex-role word and she got sore." Margie looked irritated. "If anybody called her an editress, she'd yell, but she hangs on to that sexist label just the same. Did a male gay ever call himself a non-lesbian gay?"

Tessa looked mollified. "I never thought about that, but I think you have a point."

"Sex labels always bug me," Margie said. "They're demeaning, that's what. My Gawd, if we don't want to be stipulated 'Miss' or 'Mrs.' what makes 'lesbian' okay?" She suddenly laughed. "But

I'm sorry I got so worked up about it. As for old Jeff and his letter, let's call him."

"You do, if you want to," Tessa said. "I wired him yesterday, and that's it for a while. I'm not going to let myself carry on about it."

"You're right," said Margie. "He's such a half-wit."

They all laughed and Tessa thought, I wish he could be here for just ten minutes and see for himself. She told them she had guessed from Jeff's letter about the Stonewall, and Nate told the entire story once more, putting Jeff into it for the first time, she seeing it with a new vision, hearing it direct from him. Then they talked of Mark Waldo's news; the *Times* had already reported the nomenclature meeting, but now, as if in a reversal of roles, they seemed to find a new meaning in it, hearing it directly from her.

"That annual session of the A.P.A. will be in Honolulu in May," Nate said. "I wish I could get my paper to let me cover it."

"Please, me too," Margie said. "Let's go anyway."

They launched into a great discussion of the idea, and Tessa sat back listening, saying little. For the rest of the evening she seemed almost passive, somehow feeling none of the old compulsive need to talk to their sympathy, to reach for their closeness. And later, after they were gone, the quiet within her persisted, an ease, an absence of listening for the telephone, a knowledge that it would ring in due time.

It was not until the next night that Jeff called to thank her for her wire. She knew he could hear the faint tremor in her voice, knew he would diagnose it correctly and that there was no need for her to say she was happy. He talked as he always talked, about his work, about his belief that his permanent appointment to the staff would come through on schedule.

"As a matter of fact," he said, "just this morning, Dr. Syms rather made a point of telling me so."

"Good. Jeff, I just feel good about everything."

"Yeah, me too."

* * *

The idea came to her one day in early spring, when the morning was so inviting she decided to walk to her office through Central Park. The blossoming shrubs and trees all about her filled the air with a composite scent of earth and bark and bud and leaf, and there was a sparkle in the air, a tonic briskness in the capricious wind that lifted her spirit as if it were a light and palpable thing.

She felt alive, with her old aliveness. It takes a long time, she thought. She wondered what Jeff thought of the proposed change in nomenclature, wondered whether it seemed important to him as it did to her, indeed whether he even knew about it in full detail. At last these parlous matters were receiving the same fullness of reporting from the good old *Times* as other news did, but that was not necessarily true in the papers out on the Coast. She did not know either, of course, what he felt as he read and heard and saw more and more about this great new force of rebellious young men and women of the gay movement, this army appearing in the light of day, an army growing all the time, recruited, God knew how and God knew by whom, from the secret places that had been their West Points and St. Cyrs and Sandhursts.

"You probably know as much as I do about the gay movement," he had written, "or maybe more, you being you, and . . . about two months ago I became part of it." He was not a political beast and never had been, but he was part of it. In his own way he was *of* it. And it was now *of* him, of his substance, of his destiny from now onward.

Illogically the idea came at her then, rushing at her, through no train of thought that she could trace. She would ask for an appointment with Halston Richards, now, before he left for that May meeting in Honolulu, would drive up to Poughkeepsie to see him as she had once driven up to see James Dudley, but this time for her own purposes, on her own behalf, to try to persuade him to write not another paper for a medical journal, not another speech for a psychiatric symposium, but a book for her to publish, a book for the layman, for the boys and girls stricken in their first discovery that they were gay, for the men and women who had tried analysis and were still gay, and a book too she had seen no authority do at all, a book also for the parents of the gay people, for the mothers and the fathers, for all the Tessas and all the Kens everywhere—

The idea sang in her heart like a bright light; she felt uplifted and lissome and young. A light can't sing, idiot, she thought sternly, and laughed aloud. Ever the editor! Each year had made her more of an editor, but this was not being an editor, thinking of a book like this one she wanted from Halston Richards—this was being one of the rebels too, one of the ones fighting back, young, creative, whatever her biological age. She laughed again and then saw with astonishment that she was already at Fifty-ninth Street, the southernmost limit of the park. She had raced along, she was out of breath, her face was warm with exertion and excitement.

It was good to be alive. She would have to talk this over first with Tom Quales and Jim Park, but now she could. *Once you're out, you're out forever.* She was out too.

CHAPTER SEVENTEEN

It was mid-December when she phoned Jeff about Christmas. Again she was answered by the voice that was not his.

"Dr. Gerson speaking," it said crisply.

"Is Jeff there? It's his mother, in New York."

"No, but he should be home by nine. Shall I have him call back then?"

"Would you? Thanks a lot."

She hung up, conscious of the thudding of her heart. Dr. Gerson. Stuart Gerson, the young man Ken had liked the look of. A fine young man, he had said, maybe a little older than Jeff. And then those words. She could hear them again, as if Ken were right there, but in a moment she turned away from them. That undisclosed legacy would probably remain forever undisclosed.

She had called Jeff only twice in the past six months, and once or twice he had called her. She wrote him brief notes, always bearing news, a vacation for her with Will and Amy in Rome, a new author or troublesome manuscript, anecdotes of Lynnie and Jeffie, news of Nate and Margie. She felt closer to him than ever and thought of him less, and sometimes thought, The gay movement has made me over, too. She found herself, somewhat to her own astonishment, never worrying about what might lie ahead in Jeff's career. If disaster were still to strike, he would weather it in his own way, and make something of it.

She was contented, often lonely, often wishing for Ken or somebody to replace Ken, but she knew that she would not easily again be able to make a major new relationship. But her life was full, her mind active and yet lazily at ease. If only, she thought at times, if only there had been some short cut. These thirteen years. If only they could have been condensed.

Now there will not have to be thirteen endless years for other mothers and fathers, she thought, unless they seek them out in the old rigid pattern, clinging to them, needing them. Now there need not be that initial shock and grief, those years of trying everything, of hoping and failing, of that fiercely burning self-blame, of "getting over it." She remembered that first night so long ago, that blind seeking of hers for Absalom, my son, my son, and abhorred the memory. Then she marveled at the distance they had all traversed since then, Jeff, Margie, Nate, Will and Amy, herself. And beyond them an enlarging part of the world, certainly the youth of the world, the suppler younger minds in the universities and the professions . . .

Just this week in Washington, the results of that Honolulu meeting were formalized. The Board of Trustees of the A.P.A. had voted—unanimously voted—to abolish homosexuality from the category of mental disorders. The *Times*, in its page-one story, quietly remarked that it was "altering a position it had held for almost a century," but there was nothing quiet in Tessa's mind as she read the words. This was only one victory, yes; it did not mean an overnight end to scorn and discrimination against gay people, there would still be much to endure as they fought on, much to struggle for. But what a victory it was.

The membership at large would be voting now, and they would vote in favor. "Probably three to one in favor." Dr. Richards had said so, said it to her himself, and so she knew it as an "insider" knows things, with a small riffle of pride in being, now, an insider in a new sense. She had spent half of a long evening with Halston Richards, and she had made a clear strong case, she had felt, for the book she hoped to persuade him to write, the book Quales and Park hoped to persuade him to undertake. There had been time needed, an exchange of letters, but finally a rough outline, mainly chapter headings, that Dr. Richards had sent to her of "this book I seem to be starting to write."

It was well past midnight when Jeff called back. "Are you asleep or wide-awake and reading?"

"Wide-awake and making lists of Christmas gifts."

"Oh *that.*"

"I suppose there's no such thing as Christmas off for Dr. Lynn? That's what I called you about."

"As a matter of fact, this year there is. Probably three days of it—that weekend is our free one by rotation."

"Would you consider a trip home?"

"I actually have been considering—hold on a minute."

She heard him speaking over a loosely covered mouthpiece; he was making no great effort to conceal what he was saying. When he returned to her, he said, "Sorry, that was a consultation about plans."

"Jeff," she heard herself saying, "if you'd like to invite Stuart Gerson—"

"Stuart Gerson? How'd you know his first name?"

"Dad met him, that last trip of his out there."

"Dad? He couldn't have. I didn't meet him myself until I started interning at the hospital." He laughed.

"You must have. You introduced him to Dad. He liked him."

"Well, what do you know?" He laughed again, and then said, "Why, sure, come to think of it, I guess we were heading toward Sunset when I spotted Dad's car parked there."

"Not that it matters."

"It does, sort of. We really met at the hospital—he was already there when I started." There was a brief pause. "We've been living together this past year."

"Yes." She considered for a moment also. "He's never been east of Lake Tahoe, and it might be—"

"He hasn't for a fact. Now how the hell do you know *that?*"

She laughed, this time without constraint. "You must have been more chatty with Dad than you seem to think. He knew it and told me, it's as simple as that. You know me and my memory."

"That's right, about his never being East. He's an Oregonian."

"If you would like," she said slowly, "to invite him here for the holidays, he couldn't be more welcome."

"Well, that's an idea."

"I would like it very much."

"Let me call you back on it? In a day or so?"

"I hope it will be yes."

* * *

The days and nights crept by and then it was the Friday evening of the Christmas weekend. For once the time differential between the two coasts loomed large to her, for though they were leaving California in their afternoon, they would not be taking off, in her reality, until about eight at night, landing here after one in the morning and not reaching the apartment until two. The sensible thing would be to go to bed and to sleep, and greet them in the morning, but nothing seemed more impossible. Before the evening was half over, she began glancing at her watch at ten-minute intervals, not in impatience but in a kind of expectation, a sense of readiness within her, a waiting that was pleasant, as waiting rarely manages to be.

At last the bell rang and she went swiftly to the hall and reached for the doorknob. Her hand trembled slightly then, and she held the solid brass as if it were the round head of a cane which would support and not betray her. Then she opened the door.

They stood there, two young men in the dim light of the hallway, two young intelligent faces, two good faces, Jeff a little muted as he said, "Hi, Mama, this is Stuart."

"Hi, Jeff, hello, Stuart, come in." She put both her hands out toward them, one on Jeff's arm, the other on Stuart's. They are here, she thought, at last they are here. It's been so long but they are here.

They came in past her, stowing their suitcases in a corner of the hall, and for a moment she did not turn toward them. The image of the two faces arose again, the two young faces, sensitive, strong, facing her with candor, together. Her beloved son and the man he loved.

Consenting adults, she thought, and a fullness rushed to her heart. To consent, to assent, to be in harmony, to give your blessing. I give my blessing, all my blessings. Then I am a consenting adult too.